C000010635

CONTRACT

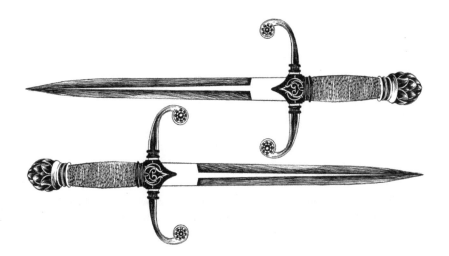

BOUND

ELLE MAE

This is a work of fiction. Names, characters, places, and incidents either are the product of the author's imagination or are used fictitiously. Any resemblance to actual persons, living or dead, events, or locales is entirely coincidental.

The Price of Silence

Copyright © 2022 by Elle Mae

All rights reserved. No part of this book may be reproduced or used in any manner without written permission of the copyright owner except for the use of quotations in a book review. For more information, address: contact@ellemaebooks.com

Cover design by SeventhStar Art
https://www.seventhstarart.com/
Edits by Corbeaux Editing
https://www.corbeauxeditorialservices.com/

www.ellemaebooks.com

NOTE

This is a work of fiction. Names, characters, business, events and incidents are the products of the author's imagination. Any resemblance to actual persons, living or dead, or actual events is purely coincidental.

Before moving forward, please note that the themes in this book can be dark and trigger some people. The themes can include but are not limited to; sexual assault mention, death, gore, parental abuse, nonconsensual biting, off and slight on page SA, trafficking mention, dubious consent, blood play, biting, self harm, torture, violence.

If you need help, please reach out to the resources below.

National Suicide Prevention Lifeline
1-800-273-8255
https://suicidepreventionlifeline.org/

National Domestic Violence Hotline
1-800-799-7233
https://www.thehotline.org/

Also by Elle Mae

Stand Alone:

Contract Bound: A Lesbian Vampire Romance

Other World Series:

An Imposter in Warriors Clothing

A Coward In A Kings Crown

Winterfell Academy Series:

The Price of Silence: Winterfell Academy Book 1

The Price of Silence: Winterfell Academy Book 2

The Price of Silence: Winterfell Academy Book 3

The Price of Silence: Winterfell Academy Book 4

The Price Of Silence: Winterfell Academy Book 5

Short and Smutty:

The Sweetest Sacrifice: An Erotic Demon Romance

Eden Rose (Contemporary):

The Ties That Bind Us

Don't Stop Me

To those who loved the first version enough to read the second.

CONTRACT

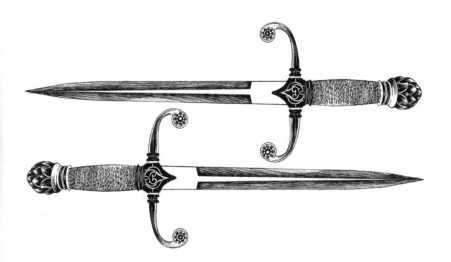

BOUND

CLAN WATCH LIST

PRIVILEGED AND CONFIDENTIAL.
PROPERTY OF THE ORDER. DO NOT
DISTRIBUTE.

Montres clan
Location: WA
Status: Active

Carpe Noctem
Location: WA
Status: Active

Blood Fall Clan
Location: NYC
Sun Clan Location: WA
Status: Active

Kazimir clan
Location: WA
Status: Active

Volkmar clan
Location: CA
Status: Active

Bextiyar Clan
Location: NYC
Status: Unknown

Waita Clan
Location: OR

Status: Active

Yahya Clan
Location: NYC
Status: Unknown

Makariou Clan
Location: FL

These clans have been flagged by The Order and will be monitored until deemed safe or the clan is exterminated, whether that is by our own Hunters or rival clans. Any Hunter that comes into contact with these clans must notify your direct captain *immediately* and take the necessary safety precautions as outlined in **section 72** of the **Vampire Hunter Guidebook.**

Hunter Rankings

PRIVILEGED AND CONFIDENTIAL.
PROPERTY OF THE ORDER. DO NOT
DISTRIBUTE.

7850762

Missions: 4

Kills: 7

1749627

Missions: 4

Kills: 7

5744826

Missions: 4

Kills: 7

8620628

Missions: 3

Kills: 5

2201934

Missions: 3

Kills: 5

9009715

Missions: 3

Kills: 5

9761566

Missions: 3

Kills: 5

1488899

Missions: 5

Kills: 3

5067924

Missions: 5

Kills: 3

3468430

Missions: 5

Kills: 3

3468430

Missions: 5

Kills: 3

8205006

Missions: 7

Kills: 1

3854905

Missions: 7

Kills: 1

3981785

Missions: 7

Kills: 1

Note: the above numbers do not take into account human deaths

For more on rankings please look to **Vampire Hunter Guidebook section 32**

PROLOGUE

SILVIA

G od really fucked up when he made vampires.
Humanity had already been hanging on by a thread before their existence and after. . . well, let's just say the human population declined quickly.

At first, they came to us wanting peace, stating that they had been hiding in the shadows for far too long. They wanted to work on a way to coexist beside humans and witches to suit our needs, and theirs.

But what they didn't tell us was that, right after they came out, there would be nothing keeping those bloodthirsty animals from murdering anyone and everyone they pleased.

It didn't matter the age, sex, or race, we were all a part of the feeding frenzy, and if you were unlucky enough to be caught outside at night, then you were a goner.

Humanity had taken precautions since then.

Creating the Order, putting in place regulations and blood donation systems, and even allowing vampires to have their own blood slaves, as long as it was consensual. . . but that still didn't stop the mayhem.

1

I wasn't alive back then. Neither were my parents or their parents. . . but I felt as though I was witnessing the same chaos firsthand.

All the years since the Order had begun and forced the vampires into their place, crumbled right in front of my eyes.

I knew it was only a matter of time before I would see the vampires' *true* colors, but even after learning about them for most of my life, I couldn't imagine. . . *this*.

My mind was empty as I stood outside my family's home.

Sirens were blaring in my ear, but the rest of the air around me was a deafening silence. There was not a stir in the neighborhood. No cries or screams like my family deserved.

It was just me and my silence as I watched the Order violate them in ways the vampires wouldn't even dare.

No one dared speak as they filed into my house, their booted feet trampling all over the lawn in a way that would have made my dad furious.

There were people on all sides of me, mostly hunters coming to see the latest victims they had failed to protect, and this time it was three of their own. *A disgrace.* The Order, which was known as the single most powerful force in this world against those bloodsuckers, still couldn't figure out how to protect their own?

I pulled my gaze away from my house as they brought out the body parts. The vampires who had attacked my family had brutalized their bodies and torn every limb from them. It wasn't in line with a vampire's normal feeding habits. This was. . . cruel. You could feel the hatred in the air. They didn't leave any surface clean, all of it was splattered with the blood from my father, mother, and sister.

It was a crime that stunned even the most tenured Order members.

I recognized a few of them as people who worked closely

alongside my parents. Came to family functions, invited us over for dinner. I hoped to find solace in them, but as each one of them looked at me, I only saw one look in their eyes.

Pity.

I looked over the rest of the small cul-de-sac and noted a few of the blinds moving as people peered out into the street to see what was going on, but they didn't dare step outside.

It would be suicidal, after all. Blood attracted those monsters, and if you were not a hunter trained to kill, you would be as good as the dead bodies in my house.

But I didn't hide like them, I couldn't. What else could I hide from? My worst nightmare had already come true. My mother, father, and sister all lay dead in our home even after they had taken the precautions to protect themselves.

They were hunters for God's sake. . . and they were killed in their home?

It was ironic. They went on missions all the time to bring down bloodthirsty vampires, yet the *one* time they were home together. . . they get torn limb from limb.

No matter how much society had changed to accommodate vampires, we would never be able to live peacefully. They took and took and *took* until there was no blood left.

Hate unfurled inside me and lit my veins on fire. I had always had a distaste for those monsters, but now I wanted to wipe them off the face of this planet. I wanted to single-handedly ensure that I would never see a glint of red eyes *ever* again.

I hate those disgusting *fucking* vampires almost as much as I hate myself for letting this happen. If I had just been here, with them. . . maybe I could have helped them. Saved them from their deaths. . . or at least I could have gone with them. But now I was alone.

I forced my gaze back to the house, my bloodied fingernails gripping into the threadbare sweater I was wearing.

I needed to see this. I needed to see what the remains of my family looked like as they were brought out. I needed this memory to be singed into my mind for however long I may live after this. It was the least I could do. If I couldn't get revenge on those vampires then I would at least ensure that I was punished thoroughly enough.

The Order's hunters marched out in their signature all-black uniforms, the newer recruits obviously affected by what they saw. The reactions varied from disgust to openly crying over the bodies. Though it all felt muted compared to what I was feeling, almost *performative*.

I expected more anger, especially since they had worked so closely together, but each Order member seemed to accept the fact that this was a sad normal for us humans. Even as I forced myself to look at the Order members as they exited, I couldn't step any closer to them. Seeing my family members' thoroughly destroyed and bloody bodies just once was already more than I could handle.

I wasn't as close to them in recent years as I had been before. I had grown up, moved away, and tried my hand at various careers while lecturing them about the dangers of their own. And for people who found pride in what they did, my distaste for their jobs put a large wedge between us. They tried to support me in all that I did, my sister especially, but there wasn't a light in their eyes when I talked about my interests.

To them, the Order was life. The Order was where they met each other, where they accumulated those mountains of debt, where they fought for their fellow humans. *Hell,* we were practically raised there.

So for one of their daughters to openly go against the Order and all it stood for. . . that hurt.

But that doesn't mean I was unaffected by this. If anything it made it worse, because now I had no chance to take back what I had said and done to create that wedge, and now I was the only person alive to blame.

I was stuck between violently throwing up and ice-cold panic. Throwing up because of the smell and gruesomeness, and panic because I had no idea what I was going to do. My fingernails, if they had not been so bloodied, would have been gnawed clean off with my current state.

I tried to steel my face, even as the emotions violently swirled around inside me.

I wanted to *scream*. I wanted to cry. I wanted to take the vampires who did this and tear them limb from limb, just like they had done to my family. . . But that wouldn't bring them back.

Nothing would.

A small group of Order members left the house with bags that were now filled to the brim. I made a noise of disgust when I realized they were holding my family in trash bags. I watched them come back and forth, changing out tools and getting more evidence bags. Some of them arrived with extra bags to pick up the excess limbs.

In their carelessness, the Order members left a trail of blood that led from the house and across the yellowing grass of the front yard. Dad wouldn't have let his lawn get this yellow, and that fact weighed on my conscience even heavier. Their bodies had been in this house for a long time. Long enough that they had rotten food in the fridge and the grass had yellowed.

Their bodies were left there, decaying, while I had the audacity to live my life. Blissfully unaware that their corpses were rotting on the floor of my childhood home, their silent screams heard by none.

There was no one there for them.

Not me. Not their neighbors. *And most certainly not the Order.*

My stomach clenched painfully. There was nothing left to throw up even if I wanted to. As soon as I was assaulted with the smell of rotting flesh, I lost my lunch. When I saw their bodies for the first time, I lost it again.

The bagging and evidence collection took hours. As I watched the process, and ignored everyone that tried to talk to me, a numbness swept over me. It started in my toes and made its way slowly up my body. When it reached my head I could finally stare at the bodies without wanting to puke. But the numbness was far from pleasant. I felt lost.

There was no reason for this chaos. Missing limbs and wasted blood were not how those monsters usually worked. They *wanted* as much blood as possible, so why would they tear them apart and paint the walls with the thing they yearned for the most?

"You should stay with the Order until the house is cleaned, Ms. Reiss," Captain Moore said, placing a hand on my shoulder. I shrugged it off.

Captain Moore, the Order's current head and the person who had roped my entire family into working as vampire hunters. Growing up, I had seen him at all our family gatherings. He was an old, lonely man who I had always loved as a child, but when I grew up, I realized that he was only there to make sure he had his claws deep into my family.

I didn't need his mock pity. I had seen it many times before and knew he was only playing the part the Order carefully crafted for him. I bet it was a trick to get people comfortable enough to sell their soul to him.

"And add more to the debt my parents owe you?" I glared at him.

Captain Moore was a tall, muscular man who was now

graying due to his old age. He was the type of guy who didn't take failures lightly and no doubt was willing to go to extremes to get what he wanted. His dark eyes and wrinkled face once comforted me, but now they only chilled me as I saw how callous he really was.

"We don't have to talk about the debt now," he said, hushing me. "Just for the night. We can plan for the future tomorrow."

I spared a glance at the semicovered dead body that was being walked out of the house by four Order members. It was my sister, Jane. She was the only one who still had an arm attached, and it now hung out of the black body bag. Her snow-white skin was a stark contrast to the blood that was caked on it.

She was still wearing the braided bracelet that I had given her on her fifteenth birthday. It was all I could afford at the time, but nonetheless she accepted it as if it was the most valuable thing on this planet and continued to wear it after all these years.

I felt a stab of pain through my chest, chasing the numbness away for just long enough that tears were able to sting my eyes.

I didn't want to leave this place, because then I would be leaving them for real this time. There would be no going back, and I doubted that I could live in this house ever again. But what would I do?

I barely had money and I knew that, when I was rested enough, Captain Moore would talk to me about repayment of my family debt to the Order.

It left only one other thing that I could do.

I sent my sister a silent goodbye in my head and begged for her forgiveness. She would not be happy when she realized what I was about to do. She was the one who supported me leaving behind the Order. She was the one who hoped for a life away from the blood and death that the Order brought. . . She would be disappointed.

I'm sorry.

I gave Captain Moore a hard look before nodding. He stepped back and waved me over to one of the Order's black sedans. I took a deep breath before I took the first step forward. The next step was easier, though pain shot through my legs as I felt the stiff muscles.

With each step my resolve hardened. I was going to kill as many of those creatures as I could.

CHAPTER I

SILVIA

Vampires, while sometimes terrifying, were mostly just predictable idiots who liked to get high off the blood of unwilling women. They liked to parade around like they owned the various parts of this city, but they were just one wrong move away from drawing the Order's attention to them,

I can't wait to slice this one's throat, I thought as I brought the whiskey up to my lips.

I normally wouldn't have drunk on a mission, but this one was tough. Not only was he one of the worst vampires that I had seen, but I was also nervous about how risky this was.

I looked around at the dingy basement we were in and spotted our informant. A vampire already had her pushed up against the wall and his teeth buried into the crook of her neck. Her eyes were wide yet hazed over, the telltale sign that the vampire venom was affecting her. My heart ached for her, but I didn't let it deter me. I had a job to do.

The basement had been made into a makeshift club for this

single group of vampires, complete with an open bar, pool table, and couches for when a vampire was feeling frisky.

There was a hallway toward the back of the bar, one that I knew led to the rooms. . . But vampire didn't need sleep, so those were left for *other* activities.

The room was packed with far more humans than vampires. There were only five while the humans seemed to crowd the space, turning the once-chilly concrete space into a suffocating cement hotbox. Some of the humans were in ratted clothing, some with none on at all, and they were all littered with bites.

I don't know how the humans got into this situation. I knew it was common to get kidnapped, but by the smiles and laughter of some, I couldn't help but think that they volunteered for this.

A bead of sweat fell from my neck and my breathing quickened when my target locked eyes with me.

The men around the pool table at the far edge of the basement laughed suddenly. It was almost comical how relaxed they were, so unsuspecting that there was a rat in their midst. They were too focused on collecting as many humans as possible, thinking they were untouchable.

And after all, who would suspect a dressed-up blood bag? Vampires loved to play with their food, and this was just another way they did it. An underground party filled with food for them. They had their pick of all the most gorgeous women they could find. All of them ready for their fangs.

I leaned against the bar and took another sip, tearing my eyes away from the table. I had a cue to wait for and needed to act as uninterested as possible.

It was getting harder for the vampires to get blood sources. Many people volunteered for this type of work, but it was nothing compared to how many vampires were roaming this country.

The Order was born out of pure necessity. The police force proved insufficient to protect against vampires and so they were left for human-on-human crime. It was better this way, because it allowed the Order to oversee all blood contracts and hold each of the clans responsible when they breached the terms, whatever they may be. But the most dangerous were not clan affiliated but those who had a passion for hiding in the dark.

And that was where I came in.

The stuffy higher-ups talked boring legal contracts while my team and I could be the cleanup. And while I loved seeing the life slipping from the vampires' eyes as their own disgustingly dark blood fell to the ground, they were *fucking* hard to kill.

They could easily walk in the sun, and stakes would do nothing if you didn't hit an artery. They could only be killed if you got close enough to slit their throat before they slit yours. The only difference was the blood helped power their hearing and speed, so you'd better move quick, or you would be dinner.

Elixirs had been provided to the Order through close collaboration with witches to help close the gap between vampires and humans, but it was not like many vampires would stand there while you poured it into their mouth, making them *almost* useless. Though I had a few ideas on how to make it work.

"It's time, Silv." Cain's voice echoed through my ear. It was barely above a whisper.

We had to be careful in case the vampire senses were able to pick up the frequency, but with the loud music and people talking, I doubted they could hear anything.

Finally, I thought with a grumble.

My eyes narrowed at the one at the head of the table, the leader of this pitiful gang, Dimitri. His small gang had been breaking the law for far too long. Instead of dining on the blood donations and criminals he was allotted, he decided to start hoarding humans. He would be the first to die. The rest would follow not too long after.

He was as handsome as all vampires were. They had a sort of ethereal look to them that made them stand out. He had wavy black hair, a strong jaw, and hooded eyes. The only thing that gave any indication of his life of crime was the deep-set scar running diagonally across his face.

His eyes drifted across the room and stopped when they met mine. No one else was daring to look, save the few slaves who actually enjoyed the vampires' favor.

I had dressed well for the occasion; I knew what he liked. I was in a small silky black slip and my long hair was up to show him my neck. I angled it as if taunting him to take a drink and watched as his body stiffened.

Getting him alone was the first task, and judging by the way his eyes trailed my body, it wouldn't be hard.

I gave him a smirk and then turned around to get another drink from the bartender. I pitied the shell of a human he was. He must have been here longer than the rest. While he was not as frail as the others, or covered in bite marks, his eyes had no light. He had seen some things, that much I knew because my eyes looked like that once.

I smiled at him and waved my empty glass. He didn't return the smile but gripped my glass nonetheless. He quickly refilled my drink and then froze when he looked behind me.

I didn't need to look back to know that my target was right behind me.

A large cold hand made its way up my back slowly, drifting a bit too close to my ass for comfort. It took all I had not to shiver in disgust at the movement. I grabbed my drink from the bartender with a forced smile and steeled myself.

"I haven't seen you here before." Dimitri's deep voice came from behind me. "Who invited you?"

I tried to keep the small smile on my face and turned around to meet him, with my drink in hand. He was as tall as the file had said, but seeing it up close made my heart rate pick up. This one was a risky mission given how many vampires were in here. If I could not get him secluded, I may die.

I gestured to the women who had brought me here, who was still getting mauled by her vampire of the night.

"I haven't had the honor of being invited until now." I made a show of trailing my eyes down his front. "And I guess you could say I was. . . curious."

"And is your curiosity satisfied?" he asked and shortened the distance between us so he was almost pressed up against me. I got a whiff of his scent and couldn't help the shudder when I realized it was blood. He had fed not long before this, and here he was trying to get some more.

I locked eyes with him, his turning slightly red. A vampire's tell, though if one could handle emotions well you wouldn't see the change.

Disgusting creatures.

I closed the rest of the space between us and stood on my toes in order to reach his ear. "Not yet." I let my free hand rest on his arm. "But I am sure you could help with that."

Dimitri let out a small chuckle while his arm circled my waist, then dipped his head so he could also whisper in my ear. Luckily it was the one without the transmitter. "I could do more than help with that." He bit the shell of my ear, earning a hiss from my lips. "But your skin is so clean. This must be your first time with one of our kind."

He pulled away slightly to meet my eyes, testing me.

"Maybe not. . . but I guess you can be the judge of that when you remove my dress." I let my hand trail down his front.

He turned slightly to look at his gang still at the table. "Don't disturb me."

He spoke as if he was talking to me, but I knew his voice was loud enough for the other vampires to hear. I could hear some comments thrown at him, but he paid them no mind.

Dimitri took a step back, then motioned me to follow him into the back of the place, where the rooms were. If the map served me right, his room was toward the back and the biggest one they had. After I was done with him, I would be able to escape from there before the place was set to blow.

Given the signal earlier, I was sure that I had less than twenty minutes to decommission this dude and leave. It was almost too short of a time, but that was probably why Captain Moore rated this job so highly and gave it to my team. Because he knew we would get it done.

His hand gripped mine and he sent me a devilish smile as the room came into view.

"You nervous?" he asked, his sharp canines poking out from his lips.

"A bit," I said in a low voice. "But I have a feeling you'll take care of me."

His chest puffed with the praise, and he pulled me forward, his pace quickening.

As suspected, he brought me to the back room. It was just as the map provided; I felt a twinge of guilt knowing the informant would be caught in the blast but reminded myself that this was the price of working with the Order.

We needed to bring down these vampires one way or another, and there was no way for us to get all the humans out without risking the rest of the vampires fleeing.

As soon as he opened the door, he pulled me in with a hard

yank and slammed the door behind us. He did not lead me to the bed, instead I was slammed against the wall so hard my head ached and my ears rang.

His lips met mine, and he began devouring me. I met his kiss with the same eagerness and wrapped my arms around his neck to pull him closer.

His hand wrapped around my neck, too tightly for comfort, but I continued to play along and yanked at his hair harshly. I felt him groan against me, his hand loosened around my neck and was replaced with his mouth. Panic shot through me when I felt his fangs brush against my throat.

So far, the information was correct, I hoped his favorite bite spots were too.

I let out a small moan and arched into him, pushing his head down, trying to lead him to where I needed him. His lips curled against my throat and his large hand slipped the straps of my dress off. Shimmying it off, I left myself exposed in only a thong. He looked down at my bare chest, his eyes hungrily taking in my form.

When his eyes met mine, they were fully red.

"I heard you have a very sensitive place you like to bite," I said, panting, and bit my lip. I arched my bare breasts up to him, inviting him to have a taste.

The bastard smiled at me.

"Is that why you came? It seems like you are new to this," he mused, letting his fingers trail over my exposed breast. The actions caused goosebumps to rise across my skin. And my nipples hardened of their own accord.

"I want my first bite to be memorable," I responded and let out a breathy moan as his fingers twisted my nipple.

Chuckling, he trailed kisses down my chest until he got close to my nipple. His lips finally enclosed around one of my nipples and I moaned, gripping his hair roughly.

I hope the elixir is as good as the witches promised.

He sucked lightly, at first showing no effects, and my heart pounded in my chest as his hand played at the straps of my thong. If this didn't work and he actually bit me. . . I would be totally fucked. Vampire venom had a funny way of making humans weak, wanton messes, and I couldn't exactly kill someone in that state. Slowly, I watched his eyes start to close. His stance wavered slightly, and the grip he had on me began to loosen.

I smiled and pushed his weakened body off me. His eyes widened, but he could not find his balance and fell into a heap on the ground. The elixir should decommission him for the time being and allow me to escape.

"You bitch," he gargled as foam started coming out of his mouth.

Maybe the witches are on to something.

I smiled, fixed my dress, then locked his door and searched for the window.

"It is done," I said into my earpiece.

"Get out," Cain said, his voice filling my ear once more.

It was not long before Dimitri stilled on the ground after a short and utterly useless fight. The amount of elixir wouldn't be enough to kill him, but the blast would be.

The only escape route was the window, and while I had seen it in the blueprints, I didn't realize how hard it would be to escape from there. It was much smaller than the picture showed, and it was at such a high angle that it wouldn't be accessible to my short form, even in heels. The room was almost bare, the only things in here besides myself and the half-dead vampire were a dirty bed, a flimsy desk against the wall, and a shattered chair nestled into a corner. I cursed under my breath and made quick work dragging the desk across the room. The screeches of the metal dragging across the concrete were louder than the music outside, and I prayed that the other vampires wouldn't hear it.

I was panting by the time I lifted myself onto the table and stood, reaching for the window. I pushed it open with just the tips of my fingers, cold air hitting my heated skin like a freight train. A flash of hope fluttered in my chest but was quickly diminished when I realized the window was still too *fucking* high.

"God damn it," I grumbled and tried to reach outside the window, my hands coming in contact with rough asphalt. I clawed at it, panic igniting my entire being knowing the destruction of this building was mere minutes away.

A cold hand grabbed my ankle and forcefully pulled me back in. I hit my chin against the windowsill, pain exploded in my head. I was flung to the floor and the wind was knocked out of me.

I am going to fucking die here.

I let out a groan as pain racked my body. Dimitri's legs straddled my hips as his forearm pushed down, crushing my throat.

"You really think that would have kept me down for long?" he asked and trailed his tongue across my cheek.

I bared my teeth at him, and he gave me a smile in return.

"Scum," I spat at him.

His eyes flashed dangerously. "Scum? You won't be saying that for long." He chuckled and his other hand pulled at my dress again.

Fucking disgusting bloodsuckers.

I didn't even have my weapons with me and was left with only the elixir I had slathered over my entire body. His tongue trailed down my neck, right where the elixir should be, but he showed no signs of stopping.

"You smell so good," he whispered and leaned back, his

blood-red eyes burrowing into me. His arm was still blocking air from entering my lungs and even as I clawed at his arms, he didn't budge. His eyes roamed my body and I felt a shiver of disgust shoot through me.

This is a really horrible way to die. After all my time in the Order. All my missions. . . this is how I'll go out?

As my vision blurred, I couldn't help the images of my family's mangled bodies flashing through my mind. I would end up just like them. Torn apart by a vampire. Maybe that was our destiny, a curse that had been embedded in our bloodline.

I felt my consciousness slip. Dimitri's face disappeared for a second before I heard his chuckle fill the room. Just as he leaned down to sink his fangs into me, an arrow lodged itself through his skull, effectively splattering me with vampire blood.

It took me a moment to realize what had happened. Even As Dimitri's body fell onto me, I lay limp on the cold ground gasping for air. It burned as it filled my lungs, and when I realized Dimitri was now dead on top of me, I scrambled to get his body off me.

When I finally got his heavy corpse off me, I turned to the open window to see my teammate Cain waiting for me with an outstretched hand and a bow with a nocked arrow at his side. His brown eyes were filled with a worry that I had rarely seen before, and his normally combed-back brown hair was in a mess around his head. His breathing was heavy, and a light sheen of sweat covered his face like he had just sprinted here.

Thank God.

I ran to him and let him help me through the window, the asphalt tearing at my exposed skin. We didn't speak as we jogged toward the van waiting for us around the corner. Jade, our other teammate, was there waiting in the driver's seat with a worried expression. Her large brown doe eyes were brimming with tears, and her plump pink lips were pulled into a pout. She gripped the steering wheel so hard that I was sure it would snap clean off in her hands.

I nodded toward her and climbed into the back of the van while Cain loped around to sit in the passenger seat.

"Go," he commanded and, with a shaky hand, Jade high-tailed it out of there.

It was less than five minutes later when we heard the explosion. I peered out the window to see a black cloud of smoke filling the sky, and it was not long after that I heard sirens. They would be too late though, everyone in there had to have been dead by now. We made sure of it.

"Are you okay?" Cain turned around and asked. He unzipped his gray jacket, exposing the all-black Order uniform underneath.

"I am fine," I lied. In truth, I was shaken and my throat would most likely be bruised. Pain still pulsed through my body, and I was shivering from the cold Seattle air. But besides that, no life-threatening injuries.

"I can't believe the captain gave you such a stupid mission," Jade hissed, her eyes still on the road. She pushed her dark purple hair out of her eyes, causing the car to swerve.

I gritted my teeth and held on tight to the back of Cain's seat, hoping that for once Jade would be careful while driving. We couldn't afford to end up in *another* accident.

"Someone had to do it," Cain said, running a hand through his messy brown hair. "He likes the redheads."

"It's true." When I spoke my voice was grainy and my throat felt like it was on fire. It was the only time that I had felt truly cursed to be a redhead. . . but we all knew that wasn't why the captain had chosen *me* for this job.

"Still, there were five of them in there and you couldn't have any weapons. We were lucky that the information was true. What if he bit her instead of licked?" Jade asked, her voice rising an octave.

"Then I would have lost some blood," I explained. "Not the first time."

Another lie. I have never been bitten before.

"But—"

"We all needed the money," Cain said, cutting off Jade. "It should last us for the next month."

We sat in silence for the rest of the ride to the base.

I was lucky to find this group while still in the Academy. We were anything but close, however, they knew the pains of being a part of the Order. The money was good and just enough for us to live decent lives. . . but the price was high and there was not a mission that I had been on that hadn't cost at least one human life.

They kept us in debt so that we would be forever tied to them and have to do their bidding. Everything from the food, to the clothes, to the rooms we rented from them was tacked on to our debt. Not to mention the academy that you had to go through in order to become a certified hunter was more expensive than anyone could afford . But, for people like me, it wasn't much of an option. I had no prospects for the outside world, and that was how they reeled you in, with promises of stability and money, while slowly keeping you bound to them forever.

The Order was an eighty-eight-floor building with black glass that towered over the others in the area. Per our training, it was said that the Order had started out as a three-story building in the early twentieth century, but as the years went by and the threat of the vampires rose, they continued to build on top of it. Inside we had all of our dorms, various training rooms, the Academy, and many of the high-ranking officials lived in the top floors, through no hunters were allowed higher than the thirtieth floor.

Security here was tight, and no one was allowed within thirty yards of this place if they did not have the proper identification. The Order had tabs on all hunters and vampires in the area, so as soon as one of the hunters spied a license plate they would report it to the home office for clearance. The Order was surrounded on all sides with hundreds of fresh-faced academy students primed with their newest order-appointed weapons and they watched us as we drove past.

For many, it was their first mission and that caused them to become quite trigger happy at times. I had heard horror stories of them jumping the gun and firing at a high-ranking official's car on multiple occasions.

No one could blame them though, it was a part of the rush that came with joining the Order. Suddenly you went from a struggling human to one who was now in charge of making sure that the harmony between vampires and humans was protected. It was *your* job now to make sure humans, like us, had a place in this world.

But it wouldn't stay like that for long. If you were good through the Academy you probably would have escaped punishment and not had to witness some of the horrible things the Order does to hunters who disobey the rules, but once you got your first *real* mission. . . it became real obvious what the Order valued.

And it was not the lives of humans.

After we returned the van to the underground parking lot and handed over our keys to the attendant, we went straight for the debrief. Cain and Jade followed me silently into the elevator. I pushed the button for the thirteenth floor and leaned against the cool metal wall of the elevator as my strength left me.

I was exhausted from almost dying at the hands of that bastard, and his blood had begun to dry on me, but I couldn't afford to take any detour. I would have liked to change out of the torn dress and clean up my face at least, but protocols are protocols. Even Cain obeyed this one and that was saying something.

He loved to push the Order's limits. You could do that when you were a witch. Both him and Jade had been poached by the Order, and while Jade was a witch who was better off than I assumed Cain to be, they were both highly valued here at the Order.

After all, they were the only thing helping to close the gap between us and the vampires. Humans paled in comparison.

The door opened with a ding that caused me to jump and I pushed past Jade and Cain, ignoring their stares. Our footsteps echoed across the linoleum ground as we walked down the hall. The main interior was a stark white, except for the black doorways, and made the hunters in their all-black uniforms stand out like a beacon. Many of them stared and whispered as we passed, but no one dared to stop us. They knew what would happen if they tried and possibly compromised the integrity of out mission, and they would not risk any punishment from the Enforcers.

Jade was the one to knock on the captain's door when we arrived. The dark door with *Captain Moore* engraved on a silver plaque on the wall seemed to radiate an aura that made my skin crawl. Her small hand shook as she brought it down three times, then she pulled it back like it had burned her. The captain scared everyone, but Jade was especially shy, she would not even dare to look him in the eyes.

"Come in," the captain's voice called from inside.

When we opened the door, we were met with not just the captain sitting at his desk but also a man dressed in a suit sitting with his ankles crossed in the chairs that were reserved for clients. His light hair was slicked back and glasses covered his vibrant blue eyes.

My eyes narrowed when his gaze met mine. He was a vampire. While his eyes were not red at the moment, all vampires seemed to share the same elegant features, as if they were all from the same fucked-up family.

Wouldn't be surprised if they were all inbred, I growled internally, not liking that I had to share a space with him.

I let the sneer show on my face, not afraid of what the captain or this stranger would do. Everyone knew of my hatred for their kind, I never tried to hide it, and it was why I was so good at my job.

Jade moved to hide behind me. Her hands gripped the back of my dress and I could feel her shaking. She didn't usually scare much when it came to vampires, but then again, she was scared of everything.

"It's done," Cain reported.

My eyes did not leave the vampire's and his did not leave mine. He was sizing me up as much as I was him. He should have smelled the blood of his kind that was splattered all over my body, and for once I was glad that I had to come to the captain before washing. At least now this vampire would know he shouldn't fuck with me or my teammates.

"Good." The captain put an envelope on the desk. Our payment.

I went up to receive it, only tearing my eyes away from the vampire's to meet the captain's. Standing, he was over six feet tall. His dark hair had started graying and his face had begun to sag slightly. He was rumored to once have been the best hunter in the Order, though I had never seen it in person.

"The elixir sucked," I hissed and forcefully grabbed the envelope off the table. His eyes narrowed and his lips pursed together in a hard line. "I could have been bitten."

"But you were not." He dismissed me, then sat back in his chair. "And besides, that's why you have a team, is it not?"

I crushed the envelope in my hand. I would love to smash his head against the desk, yet I knew that if I did, not only would I get a beating by the most ruthless sector of Hunters around, but they would no doubt add my hospital fees to my debt. That is... if they even bothered to send me to the hospital at all. They may just throw me in the Dark Room and have me ride out my days in pain.

The Enforcers, or the sector of Hunters who had been tasked with keeping Order members in line, were some of the worst humans out there. They made the vampires outside these walls look like children. They didn't care if you would permanently scar, or if you were close to death, they had a job and it was to punish you. And like all other hunters, they were *great* at their job.

I huffed and turned to leave the room but paused to glare at the vampire once more. I didn't want him thinking I was weak or that he had won this battle.

He only smirked in response.

Cain and Jade followed me out and I could feel the smaller girl's sigh as we left the tense office. I didn't wait until we got up to the dorms, but paused right outside the door and ripped open the envelope.

They were good partners, and that was more than I could have asked for. Even if I was the one that led the missions and put my life on the line, I divided our shares equally, though I knew other teams did not.

"We should take another next week," Cain said after placing the money in his jacket pocket.

24

"You shouldn't push Silv so hard," Jade chastised and punched his side. Cain merely shook her off.

"I could always be the main if you let me," Cain offered.

"No," Jade and I said in unison.

The last time Cain was the main and I was backup, he had almost blown the whole mission. He had a tendency to get lost in the mission and was interested more in his own fun rather than the successful completion of the mission.

"Next week sounds fine," I said and made my way back toward the elevator, pushing the button for the sixth floor. My feet were aching and I couldn't wait to slip into my pajamas and curl up in my tiny bed, just to probably sleep the rest of the day away.

"We should get a place together," Jade said and pushed the button for the seventh floor.

The elevator doors opened with a loud ding and I was relieved to see no one was in there. It would be awkward having to stand next to them while the dark vampire blood still coated my skin.

It was starting to flake.

"Then we would have to pay more," I said as we all piled into the elevator.

"The rooms aren't that bad," Cain said, while leaning against the wall.

I wished I could be as unbothered as him. I fucking hated the dorms.

"I just thought it would be nice to have a place together. . . away from the Order," Jade whispered, looking at her feet.

I placed my hand on her head and ruffled her messy purple hair. "It would, but that wouldn't stop the fact that we will probably be here until we are even older than the captain."

The doors opened and both Cain and I stepped out onto our floor. We waved to Jade as the elevators closed and then turned to the hall. Just like the rest of the Order, the walls and floor were a stark white while the doors were pitch black. The only things that differentiated them were the shiny silver numbers right in the center of them.

It was easy to get lost in the Order, but after the first year people got used to it. I stopped at door 648 and Cain stopped at the one across from me.

"Don't bother me unless you need something," I said before Cain put his palm flat against the door. There was a beep and then the click of the lock could be heard faintly . It was one of the most high-tech things the Order had, though it only served as a reminder of how tightly they controlled us.

He paused and sent me a smirk, telling me he wouldn't listen to jack shit.

"We will see," he responded and left me in the hall.

I smiled slightly and placed my hand flat on the door. It unlocked with ease and I pushed it open, ready to end the day. I was lucky and unlucky to be living so close to Cain. He had little concept of privacy and tended to wait outside my door, while yelling my name, hoping to get me to open it for him so he could raid my fridge and lounge on my bed. Him and Jade were the closest things I had to friends in this godforsaken place.

My room was as standard as they came here. It was a small studio with a small shower, small kitchen, and an even smaller bed. It was graciously provided by the Order at just a slightly cheaper rate than a normal apartment in Seattle would be. They gave us a place to live after graduating, but still made sure to squeeze out any additional money they could and tacked it on to our debt at the end of the year.

I wasted no time kicking off my clothes and running into the shower. I spent time vigorously scrubbing my skin until it was red and raw before finally feeling clean enough to change into my only non-Order clothes. I changed into a band T-shirt and sweats and caught my reflection in the mirror as I towel dried my hair.

The fucker had choked me so hard that the whites around my eyes had turned bloodshot, causing my silver irises to look even more haunting than usual. The place where his arm had crushed my throat was already starting to turn a spicily deep purple. I cursed and rummaged through my drawers to find the healing ointment Jade made me, only to find the container empty.

"Are you serious?" I growled and threw the small container to the ground, a burst of anger simmering under my skin.

I braced myself against the counter as the images of all those humans today in the basement filled my mind. Our informant's unfocused eyes hit me the hardest and my stomach flipped.

"Fuck all of them," I growled.

CHAPTER 2

KEIR

It had taken mere weeks for the last hunter to be kicked off the compound by my angry father and a disappointed Gil.

This one was a bit harder to shake off than the last, but she fell for the same thing, just as the others had. I just needed to up my game a bit. She had been hesitant at first, someone who was fully devoted to the Order... but they all caved in the end.

All the humans in the Order had proven to be a disappointment. The Order praised their hunters in public and tried to say that they hand selected the best of the best to work for them, but all I had seen was disappoint.

These humans would fall easily into temptation, didn't matter if it was booze, money, or sex... They just couldn't seem to help themselves when I handed it to them on a silver platter and assured them that no one would find out. I would promise them that they could trust me, that they could relax around me... then I would turn around and feed it to the Order.

They even acted surprised when Father called them out on

it. Their shock and anger toward me were so comical that it was worth the anger of my father. Though the grin in my father's eyes as he berated the hunters didn't get past me. He hated them as much as I did and enjoyed when he could make them squirm.

It would take some time for Gil to go back to the Order on my father's command and demand a new hunter, so I took my time getting ready tonight.

I never put on anything fancy, I wouldn't need to. Even if it was unspoken, the places I frequented knew that I was heir to my father's clan. The biggest and most influential vampire clan in the country. We had thousands of businesses and millions of employees all funneling into our clan bank, many of which funded the areas I frequented.

To them, I was their most important clientele, and they wouldn't dare kick me out over something as silly as dress code. Hell, I could even kill a human on their grounds and probably be let off without even a slap on the wrist. I wouldn't be surprised if it was *them* who apologized for their horrible service.

After fussing with my cropped black hair and pulling on a leather jacket, I left the compound feeling lighter than I had in weeks. Maybe it was the rush of escaping Father's anger, or maybe it was finally getting this hunter off my back, but regardless, I reveled in the feeling of freedom.

I had lost count of how many Order members they sent to the compound, but each time they sent another one, proclaiming it was their best, and I watched with amusement as they cracked all the same. Humans were *so* predictable, and they seemed to really hate being disobeyed. Some of them were easy to sway. One dirty look and an innuendo and you could smell their arousal in the air, those were the fun ones.

The last girl was by far my favorite. She was easy to crack, hypersexual, and let me drink from her anytime I wanted. I almost played with the thought of obeying her just to keep her around for a good fuck.

Almost.

The club that I frequented was twenty minutes away from the compound and was surrounded by seedier vampire bars that probably had their fair share of criminals in them. I had to park my bike around the corner and weave through multiple alleyways before I came to a stop at the bright neon lights that indicated the entrance. I could smell the faint perfume the owners sprayed in the vents even from outside, along with the smell of fresh blood that made my mouth water.

Ducking into the entrance, I noted that my favorite club was bustling as usual. I nodded to the bouncer as I descended the stairs that led to the rest of the club. Couples who were lingering on the stairs stirred and looked at me as I walked past. I inhaled deeply as I passed, enjoying the scent of blood and sex that filled the area.

Some of the braver human girls gave me a sultry look as I passed, but I ignored all of them as I went straight to the bartender, who smiled as I came up.

"It's been a minute," he commented and started to prepare my glass of blood without me having to ask.

Jack was one of the only men that worked in this lesbian bar, and he had never given me trouble, for that he had landed on my good side. His black hair was slicked back showing his tanned skin and his brown eyes twinkled with delight, as if he was actually happy to see me. Though I knew it wasn't *me* he was excited to see but the idea of what I had, the power and the money.

"A week?" I asked remembering that I did drag the hunter here, though she was too shy to actually come into a place full of lesbians, claiming that she was not out of the closet yet.

"Well," he said with a sigh and pushed my drink toward me. "You were here on every one of my shifts before, so I've been guessing that this is an everyday thing for you."

I gripped the blood in my hands and raised my brow at him.

"I should be offended by your insinuation," I teased.

Jack sent me a smile before being called by a woman farther down on the bar. He gave me a look and I knew he was asking to be dismissed. He wasn't in my clan, but his actions caused a burst of satisfaction to rise through me.

I waved him off and turned to scan the dimly lit bar. It was a small place, but it was clean and comfortable. The strobe lights ahead flickered in time with the loud music, but the sound wasn't overwhelming. They had a mix of vampire and human customers, so they made sure to lower the music for sensitive ears.

I looked over the few couches that were littered near the far edge of the club and caught sight of two women in a heavy make out session. One was straddling the other, and I saw a hand slip underneath her dress, which earned an audible moan from the girl.

I smiled and shifted my gaze to the rest of the club. Women were grinding on each other, vampires were drinking from their humans in the corner, and I could hear more moaning sounds coming from all around me. I felt excitement bubble up inside me.

This was what I looked forward to when going out. The euphoric sensation of losing yourself in sex and blood, all while listening to the comforting bass of the music that blasted in the small place. Humans and vampires alike were coming here and giving in to their every want and desire.

Hell, I even smelled a witch here once or twice.

No one cared where you came from, or what responsibilities you had outside these doors. All they cared about was whatever was *right here* in front of them, and I longed to be able to turn off my brain the same way they did and just enjoy myself.

My head was filled with heavy thoughts of the outside world and I took a sip of my blood, hoping to wash away some of the worry and stress that followed them. I moaned as the sweetness of it coated my tongue and warmed my insides. My head spun and I greedily ate up all the warmth and tingles it sent through me as it worked through my body. It hadn't been long since I last drank, but it was so satisfying either way.

Even with the blood making my body and mind feel more relaxed, the thoughts refused to stay away. I didn't know what my life would look like after the transfer of power. People had been congratulating me for years after it became public that our new contract with the Order would only allow clan heads to stay in power for so long. My father was one of the longest-standing clan leaders, ruling over everyone with an iron fist and zero remorse, and to be honest even though he was a piece of shit. . . he did a good job at running everything.

I on the other hand. . . didn't want to think about having to run things myself.

I wasn't cut out for this life, I never was. I knew, as soon as saw what my father did to my mother, that I would never *ever* want to be like him. And that meant that I would try to get out of ruling any way that I could.

I had tried, for years actually. . . but with the transfer only a few months away, I knew I had no choice.

My eyes shifted over to a human woman who had been eyeing me for a while now. I felt her, and saw her, but had chosen to ignore her until I was somewhat satiated. She was petite human woman and had a body that caused my stomach to tighten. When she realized I was staring back, a small sultry smile spread across her face and she began walking over toward me, her hips swaying seductively. Her V-neck top was purposely too tight against her breasts and caused them to pop out of her shirt. I lazily took in her short skirt and licked my lips when I thought of how easily I could push it up to her hips.

As she got closer, I could smell the arousal coming off her in waves, and I prayed that she wasn't wearing anything underneath. She didn't stop in front of me like I expected, instead she took it one step further and pushed her body flush with mine. Her big brown eyes looked up at me and her hand trailed to my arm and then teased at the hem of my shirt.

I have always liked a forward women, I thought as I watched her, not willing to say anything first.

"I've see you here before," she purred, her hand slipping into my shirt. Her hand was warm against my stomach and it caused me to suck in a deep breath.

I gripped her chin and leaned down to brush my lips across hers. The blood just under her skin was taunting me and was so potent I could almost taste it on my tongue.

"So you know how this works then, hm?"

I should have known that my freedom, and the lack of Father's anger, was too good to be true.

Father had always had a short fuse when it came to me and I thought maybe for once, because he was due for the transfer of power, he would leave me alone. But of course I was wrong.

As soon as I walked in the door I felt that something was off. The normally warm and welcoming manor stilled and a cold, tense silence filled the rooms. No servants or blood bags lingered as if also afraid of what was hiding in the shadows.

But the person who was in charge of this sudden change

would never demean himself by *hiding*. My father was ruthless, unfeeling, and sometime crazed. . . but he wasn't a coward.

He didn't even have to summon me, after years of being with him my body knew instinctively to seek him out.

I took my time walking up the multiple flights of stairs and down the winding hallways of the manor. I could smell his scent tangled with the blood of his newest victim and hear the sounds of her small whimpers.

When I reached the large double doors to the feeding room, I paused, trying to steel myself. I loved fresh blood as much as the next vampire, but Father and I differed on one thing:

I *could* not—and *would* not—torture the humans who offered me blood.

Father had come from a time when everything was won through bloodthirsty battle and had no regard for human life. It was how our clan stayed at the top even after all these years, because Father refused to work with anyone he deemed unworthy. And if there was ever the slightest hint of someone disrespecting my father. . . he had no problem tearing their head off in front of everyone.

I pushed into the feeding room and was met with the image of my father sitting on a chair, his newest victim on her knees in between his legs, her head angled up and to the side, giving my father access to her long, pale throat.

The feeding room was a large space filled with comfortable chairs, a few small tables, and a washing station in the corner, in case things got a bit *too* messy. Though Father didn't care about mess, if anything he purposely spilled blood in front of other vampires just to show that we could afford more, even from a live source.

His red eyes were watching me and they narrowed as I stood there waiting for him to finish playing with his food. His dark hair was shrouded by shadows and instead of turning on the chandelier lighting above, he chose to light the candles in each of the corners.

"Barely one day without a hunter and you have disgraced us yet again," he said into the neck of his latest victims. The girl remained still and did not move even as Father's tongue dragged across her neck.

"Just out for a drink," I told him, trying not to look at the girl in his arms. She was a young one this time, seemed barely over sixteen. Her limbs were thin, and her face had lost its flush. "She seems young for a feeder."

"She's perfectly of age, aren't you darling?" he cooed into her neck. She shuddered in his arms and tried to verbalize her answer, but it came out jumbled and unrecognizable even with my advanced hearing.

Her plain white dress was stained with her own blood, and I wondered when was the last time Father had provided the feeders with new clothes.

I made a mental note to ask Gil to check on them.

"Did you need something, *Father*?" I spat the word at him, trying to fit as much hatred into my words as possible.

It wasn't just that the man in front of me was the worst vampire alive, but I *hated* when he did this. He knew I had a soft spot for the human feeders and used every chance he got to show me he was still in charge and could do *whatever* he wanted. And he would.

And I knew that right now, this was my punishment.

I couldn't believe I was *stupid* enough to take his bait.

"Don't think that you can act like this for long. I won't let you destroy all the work that went into this kingdom," he said and snapped the feeder's neck. Her lifeless body fell to the floor with a thump. "There will be more consequences than just a hunter assigned to you if you continue down this path."

I shuddered. His threat was clear and expected.

The door to my right opened, and as if on cue, another human worker came in and headed straight for the body. They didn't so much as blink as they lifted her lifeless corpse and carried her back the way they came. I couldn't stop my gaze from falling to her shocked, frozen face that would remain with her for the rest of eternity.

Moments like this fueled me to take over the clan and make it a respectable place no matter how much I didn't want to. I wanted to change something, *build* a clan that made Mother proud. A clan that didn't run on fear and death. I wanted to take my father's throne violently from under him and force him to watch as I tore down everything that he had ever fought for.

I worked hard to contain the fire that was raging inside of me, knowing that if I showed even a smidge I would make this situation worse. If he knew I was affected by anything that he did, he would make my life a living hell.

I assumed it was to get back at me for taking over his throne, even if I didn't have a choice in the matter. He and I both knew that I didn't want it, but he still insisted that I act like the heir I was supposed to be.

If only his dick worked better. Maybe then I would have a chance to live the life I want to, I thought wryly.

"So just a warning," I said and swallowed the knot in my throat. "Understood, Father."

I turned and walked out of the room before he could stop me. I would probably pay for that display of disrespect, but I couldn't stand staying in that room with him for even a moment longer. I felt like I was going to explode and all the happy feelings that swirled around inside me disappeared in the night air.

He was the disgrace.

CHAPTER 3

SILVIA

S weat was dripping down my back and my heart pounding in my chest as I jabbed at the black punching bag. Each time my fist connected with the leather, the faces of those vampires in Dimitri's basement played over and over again in my mind.

Their smirking faces entered my mind and their laughs rang in my ears even over the heavy rock music that blasted through my Order-approved headphones. I blamed them for it all. They were the reason we had to blow up that building. They were the reason that I was forced to take that mission. They were the reason our informant—

Stop, I hissed at myself and sent another punch toward the bag.

The other hunters refused to visit the academy training grounds after they graduated, but for me it was the only place I could find my peace, especially after a mission like the one yesterday. It also helped with the dreams.

Every time I woke up in a panic with a scream lodged in my throat, I would sneak down here in the early hours of the morning and work out among the new recruits. Many of them already knew my name and nodded at me as I passed, though I didn't make it a habit to talk to them. I wasn't here to make friends, and with the number of hunters who had gone missing or died in the line of duty. . . it wasn't worth the heartache.

I paused in my attack to catch my breath as my chest began to burn. I could feel the sheen of sweat that dripped over my body, and my eyes drifted to the now almost-full training room. No one was paying attention to me, but I suddenly felt all too seen in my sports bra and leggings.

The bruise on my neck ached and I walked over to the benches where my towel and my water bottle waited for me. I paused in my strides as I saw Jade and Cain patiently waiting for me on the bench.

Exactly how long have I been here for?

Jade's short purple hair was pulled back in French braids and she wore a baggy sweatshirt that overtook her entire form. There was a latte in her hand, and when I noted it, she smiled and lifted it for me to take.

"I got us coffee," Jade said.

I first grabbed my water bottle as I came to a stop near her and gulped down as much as I could. Both her and Cain watched me as I did. When I looked back down at them, I noted their eyes drifting to the bruise on my neck.

If I had known that they would find me here today, I would have been more careful with my time. I felt uncomfortable under their stares and wished to just sink back into my hiding place and ignore everyone around me.

I grabbed the coffee and gave her a grateful smile.

"Thanks once again, Jade. But you should save your money," I said half-heartedly.

Even as I resisted, I would never say no to her coffees. We

both knew that. Coffee was the one guilty pleasure I allowed myself, even under the crushing debt of the Order.

"I know. . . I always feel like you deserve a little extra for all you do," she said and grabbed the coffee placed between her and Cain. It was the sugary frozen one that she loved so much, and while I couldn't stand it, I wouldn't chide her on what she chose to treat herself with. We all had our vices.

"It's nothing. I would be dead without you two," I said, then sipped. I sighed as the bitter coffee hit my tongue.

"That looks bad," Cain said, finally mentioning the obvious bruise on my neck. I wanted to throttle him for bringing it up, knowing that Jade was already a ball of anxiety and guilt because of it.

"Don't worry about it," I said and quickly searched for something to change the subject. "Are we still the top?"

Jade nodded though the guilty expression didn't leave her face and made her looked like a kicked puppy.

"Jess's squad is close though," she murmured. "I don't know how they did it but they got three vampires in one go."

I cursed under my breath.

Rankings were everything in the Order. Depending on how risky and impactful the work, you would move up and down in the ranks. The higher you were the riskier the missions and the bigger the payout. If you were at the bottom. . . you would never be able to pay off your debt.

That was why I was lucky to get two very accommodating witches on my team. We chose each other out of need and a disdain for the others. None of us had many friends even after the years of Academy, so we melded perfectly together. Though, compared to most other squads we were one person short, but that didn't seem to hinder us much.

Even though I was the lead, I wouldn't be able to do what I did without them. The explosion and backup all came from them. If there was ever a time like at Dimitri's where I found myself cornered, one of them would always be there to pick up the pieces.

Some squads didn't even get witches as many of the witch families were well-off through decades of monetizing and profiting from their magic. It could be potions, elixirs, barriers, but whatever it was many didn't need to turn to the Order to make a living.

Which always left questions revolving around Jade and Cain's desire to be here... but I wouldn't push much, they liked their privacy as much as I liked mine.

"I could help," Cain volunteered after a moment of silence. I wanted to groan aloud but I swallowed it.

"Me too!" Jade piped in.

"Don't use your magic on me," I hissed. Jade's face fell slightly. Cain just shrugged. "Save it for when you need it."

"But a small healing charm doesn't cost much magic," Jade insisted and pouted at me. I gritted my teeth against the want to give in.

"Maybe she likes the pain," Cain deadpanned.

"Yep, that's it," I said in a dry tone. I waited for Jade to respond, but when I looked at her, her eyes were locked onto a figure behind me.

I hesitantly turned my head, expecting a student, but I was surprised when I came face-to-face with the captain's emotionless mask.

I turned back to Jade and Cain giving them a look as I reached down and wrapped the towel around my still-sweaty neck. A headache started to bloom at my temples as I turned to face him again.

"How may I help you, Captain?" I asked, filling my voice with a sweet tone.

"First it would be great if you stopped using the academy

training ground and just used the gym," he grumbled, his dark eyes narrowing.

I shrugged and took another sip of my coffee, refusing to respond. I would use this place as long as I was here and if he didn't call the Enforcers on my ass, then it meant it wasn't breaking any rules.

"Second, I have something to discuss with you." His voice held no emotion, so it was hard to tell if he was mad but regardless my curiosity was piqued.

"Do I have time to change?" I asked.

"No," the captain replied. "But you have to put a shirt on."

I rolled my eyes.

"Do you see an extra one lying around?" I asked and waved my arm to the bench where Jade and Cain sat.

"Take my jacket!" Jade said in a hurried tone. I turned to watch her pulling her hoodie off, a fitted tank top underneath.

As she stood to hand me the hoodie I couldn't help but notice the way Cain's eyes lingered on her. When his gaze shifted back to me it was as if the small moment never happened at all. His face so calm and collected even after being caught.

If this was what they wanted, I wouldn't stop them. The Order didn't have any clauses in our contracts about dating other hunters. It was only when we were contracted out to others that the "no dating and sexual contact" clause came into place.

"Thank you," I said and handed her the coffee so I could put the hoodie on. I grabbed the coffee once I was done and sent her a smile before turning back to the captain.

"Lead the way," I said and sent my teammates a goodbye as he led me out of the Academy and back up to his office.

"I hope this isn't about my debt," I teased. His eyes didn't drift toward me, he just kept them steady in front of him.

"Everything you do here is about your debt."

I rolled my eyes at him. He may have been scary to others, but to me he was just another old man who got on my nerves. He played the good little hunter, and the higher-ups liked him so much that they decided to just hand him this place on a silver platter. He was already in his position when my parents started their work at the Order, and that was saying a lot.

With all the high-risk missions you had to take during your time here, the average hunter only lasted a few years after their graduation from the Academy and never ended up paying back their debt.

But that was not a statistic they tell you when trying to recruit you.

Since he had picked me up from outside my parents' house after they were murdered, his appearance hadn't changed much despite the few wrinkles and gray hairs that popped up. I fully took responsibility for those wrinkles. After my first few months, I snuck back up to his office and demanded he answer questions about my parents and their work here at the Order, but he never did.

He refused to mention anything worth noting and kept our relationship strictly professional. Treating me as if I were any other hunter instead of the one that he had countless Christmas dinners with. Maybe he felt bad about forcing his friends' daughter into a lifetime of debt and despair and that was why he refused to treat me like he once had. I eyed him and noted the deadpan face he gave me when his eyes met mine.

Not likely.

We ended up walking the rest of the way to his office in silence, and I couldn't help the thoughts that flew around my head.

Did the vampire from our last mission get away?

Did we take it too far?

Am I being kicked out?

Is something going to happen to Jade and Cain for helping me?

The storm of questions only paused when he opened the dark door to his office and inside sat the perfectly poised vampire we had seen yesterday. I had a sinking suspicion that I would be very unhappy with what was about to happen.

I had never once had to meet with a vampire in the captain's office. Correction, I had never met with a vampire besides ones that I was going to kill. So, seeing him here in this office, and in such a close space, put me on edge.

I stayed standing as the captain made his way to his desk. He motioned for me to sit next to the vampire, but I refused. The space was too close, and I was unarmed. I didn't care if we were surrounded by hunters, I wouldn't chance it.

"This is Gillard," the captain said, gesturing to the vampire.

I slid my gaze to his. The vampire's cold blue eyes met mine. They were calculating and took in every part of me as if trying to find my weakness. I knew just by his look that he was dangerous, and he wouldn't be sitting so comfortably in that chair if he was not a high-ranking member of a nearby clan.

Another red flag.

"It's an honor to meet you, Silvia."

His voice was elegant, indicating that he must be an older vampire. Judging by his accent he was not from the Americas, though most of his kind had migrated at some point so I was not surprised.

"I have heard everything about you and your missions," he said, his voice full of distaste at every word.

The sentiment is returned, I thought as his expression turned into one of disgust.

"My missions. Killing your kind, you mean," I corrected.

His eyebrow raised slightly. "And witches and your fellow humans, if I am not mistaken."

My jaw locked and anger flamed within me when he mentioned humans. I would not lie and say that I never did. Just last night I exploded a whole building full of them.

But that didn't mean I took pleasure in their killings, unlike his kind. I would gladly kill his kind over and over again until they disappeared from the face of this planet.

"Gillard hails from Carpe Noctem, the clan under Raphael," the captain said after a moment of uncomfortable silence.

I know that fucking clan.

My eyes widened and instinctively I brushed the bare spot on my thigh where my dagger would have normally been. I felt bare, vulnerable in front of a creature such as himself.

The familiar fire started to build up in the pit of my stomach. I gritted my teeth and met his eyes again. There were thirty clans in the Seattle area and hundreds across the country, how the fuck did I end up in a room with this one?

This bastard.

Raphael's clan had been around for far too long, holding too much power.

All the other clans looked up to them and they were essentially the clan of vampires that held the rest of the world's vampires by the throat with an iron fist.

Even as a child in school, I had learned about his clan. Many clans come and go throughout the centuries either disbanding or being consumed by another. . . but they stayed at the front.

The bastard that ran the clan stayed hidden in the shadows with his offspring, only coming out when absolutely necessary. He was called a king by the other vampires and his family were treated as if some type of royalty, but it was all complete and utter bullshit. There was no such thing as royalty in their world. It was all just a barbaric practice to keep other vampires in line.

"I also know of your history with my clan," Raphael's underling said.

"History is a weird way to say your clan insignia was drawn on my walls in my parents' blood," I said, with venom laced in my voice. I would rather sit in a locked room with no weapons blindfolded with whatever was left of Dimitri's clan than sit here with these monsters.

"Gillard is here to work with us, Silvia. Show some respect," the captain chided.

I closed the distance between me and the desk before slamming my hand down on the wooden surface. The sound reverberated through the small office, but he didn't even flinch. His dark eyes held my gaze and his actions only made me angrier.

Does he not get it?

They know what this clan did to my parents, his friends, yet he doesn't fucking care?

"With you," I hissed at him. "I will never work with him."

"You will, and you *must*." His tone was as sharp as a knife and his eyes dared me to fight back. It was like I could literally see him holding my debt overhead with a fishing rod. It was dangerously close to being dropped right on me. He was threatening to drown me with it.

"Miss Silvia, I promise you that the family had nothing to do with their deaths," the bastard said.

I grabbed the letter opener on the side of the captain's desk and pointed it at the vampire's throat. He didn't even react, so I pushed the sharp edge into his throat, watched the skin indent. He just continued to stare at me.

The family, ran in my head over and over again. Working with a clan as big as Raphael's could mean anything. They had hundreds of sectors all with various responsibilities. . . but the *family* was the core of everything. They were Raphael and his offspring and no one else.

Why would the family need the Order's help?

"The *family*?" I questioned, my voice sounding weaker than I wanted. "You are doing dealings with the royal family?"

The last question I spat toward the captain but kept my eyes on the vampire in front of me.

"Remove your weapon. I can promise you that this is a job you will want to take," the captain said.

I faltered slightly at his tone. It had softened and reminded me of the day he picked me up outside my family's house. I paused, and after another look at the vampire, I threw the letter opener back onto his desk. If he really came from the royal family then the job must be big and would hopefully make a dent in my debt.

"How much?" I questioned, relaxing slightly as I stepped back from the vampire. He relaxed slightly too, as if he was actually worried I would do something.

Good.

"Your entire debt," the vampire answered instead of the captain.

My heart stopped. "Why would the royal family drop that much money on me?" I asked, unable to believe a word this bastard said.

"Because I told them you are the only one that can complete this mission," the captain jumped in.

I eyed the captain suspiciously. There were many other skilled hunters, even if they were not in the top ranks.

"We have actually been through many hunters for this role," the vampire continued.

I raised an eyebrow at him. "So, a suicide mission," I concluded.

The vampire had the audacity to laugh. "Not at all." He

waved his hand, trying to dismiss the seemingly absurd idea. "We need you to protect the heir."

"The prince?"

It was normal for powerful clans to have an heir. The strongest out of their offspring to continue on with the clan, before the new agreement with the Order there was no need for heirs, but now they needed one for the transfer of power.

Normally I wouldn't have batted an eyelash at the mention of an heir. . . but the *prince* had sort of a reputation among humans. People would say that the prince alone could bring down all the clans in the surrounding area with ease and that he took after his father's brutality. I had heard a lot about him through the grapevine, but like everyone else, had never seen him in person.

"Why would he need protection from a human?" I asked. "Don't you have, like, thousands of bloodsuckers at your disposal?"

His lips twitched at the nickname.

"I would say it's more like *babysitting* with a small amount of protection. Just in case anyone would like to use one of those fancy new vampire-fighting devices your kind has so generously made."

A smile pulled at my lips.

The device he was talking about was such a crude design, really. Vampires were apparently *very* sensitive to sound, so if you took a speaker and made a few tweaks. . . a vampire could be brought to their knees if played at the right frequency.

It was normally used by the rebellion, a group of humans who hated our work with vampires, though I would be lying if I said that I hadn't previously begged the captain for us to make our own to use on our missions.

"Wouldn't a witch be better?" I felt the headache creep up at full force. This was too good to be true.

Not only did they just want me to *babysit* but they would also pay off my entire debt?

I wanted to believe it *so badly*. Even just the thought of finally being debt free made my heart soar, but how could it be true?

"The family doesn't trust them," he responded.

"But they trust a human who loves to kill their kind," I said quickly, pointing out their obvious flaw.

He only smiled at my words.

"We need you because you hate them, Silvia," the captain said, rubbing his forehead. "The reason the other hunters didn't work is the heir. . . has a way with them. The heir wants this job as much as you do, so they will do anything to make hunters quit."

I shifted on the balls of my feet taking this all in.

"How long?" I asked.

The captain paused.

"Just for a few months," the vampire said.

"Months?" I gasped. "What about Jade and Cain, Captain Moore? They can't go on missions alone." There was a reason I was the one to head our missions, and without me I just knew that they would get hurt.

"They will be taken care of while you are gone," the vampire said again. "We have thought this through already. There really is nothing you can point out that will hinder you from taking this job."

I sighed and stared down at my feet, not wanting to meet anyone's eyes. As much as I hated Raphael's clan, this was my ticket out of this hellhole. Or at least out of the debt it caused.

And the others would be taken care of.

It had been a rough couple of months with the Order, more and more hunters were joining, and it was a struggle every week to keep up our rank. So, this may have been one of the few chances I had left to put a dent in my debt.

Or take it out completely, if they are to be believed.

I turned to the captain one more time, taking in his expression,

I had yet to fail a mission the entire time I was here, and each new mission was harder than the last. I thought of it as him trying to test my skill, possibly to compare me to my parents, to see if being a proficient hunter was in my genes.

Could this be another one of those tests?

My parents wouldn't have even hesitated. As soon as the vampire walked into the room they would have said yes to this mission and that would be the end of it. Even if it was a risk to their lives, they didn't care. . . not even when they had children at home depending on them.

I let my eyes trail the vampire next to me. This just *had* to be another one of his tests. Out of all the hunters in the Order, he chose the one that disobeyed him the most, even after all the fights and disrespect I threw at him. I wasn't someone who was easy to control, easy to brainwash, which made it all the more suspicious that it was *me* he had chosen for this job. He should have chosen someone he could mold into the perfect hunter, someone who would take his word as gold. . . He practically handed me my freedom on a silver platter.

"I will take it," I said after a pause.

Neither the vampire nor the captain spoke for a full minute afterward, both of them watched me, probably waiting for me to take back my words. . . but I couldn't. I *needed* this more than I cared to admit.

"Great," the vampire said, clapping once, and then stood. His sudden movement jarred me and forced me to take a step back. My hand reached for my dagger once more, but I frowned when I remembered it was gone. "You will start tomorrow and will live with the family while you complete your work."

I nodded hesitantly. "Will I be allowed my weapons?"

"Yes. The captain insisted on that before you joined us," he said then cocked his head before continuing. "After all you would be useless to us if you didn't have anything to protect the heir with, hm?"

Anger bubbled through me and I almost regretted my choice to work with them. As Gillard walked out of the office, I kept my eyes trained on his back.

"See you tomorrow, Miss Silvia. We will be working closely together from now on," he said before walking out the door. When he turned I caught the hint of a smirk on his face.

I marched out right after him ignoring the captain's yells.

Fuck the Order.

CHAPTER 4
SILVIA

I didn't have much time to bid the others goodbye. Just like the vampire had said, as soon as the day broke an academy student stood knocking on my door and with shaky words asked me to report to my latest post.

I groaned and began cursing the vampires through my entire shower and as I dressed in the all-black uniform the Order required us to wear. It was a thick black turtleneck with tight-fitting pants that molded to the skin, aiding us in any battle we might encounter.

"Silvia, please," the academy student moaned from the other side of the door. "If I don't get back in time I'll miss morning rounds and Cap—"

"I'm coming!" I growled and reached for the weapons I had discarded on the table after my last encounter.

The Order provided two, anything else we could buy out of the store located on the ground floor, but no one spent money on them. . . and I quite liked my old academy blades. I grabbed my dagger, a calm washing over me as the familiar weight was strapped to my thigh. Next I wrapped a harness around my waist which would carry my sword. I pulled it until it was snug, not wanting to chance any vampire grabbing at me.

Not that it would be any use, I thought smugly. Each of them was coated with vampire poison, so just one stab would have them burning from the inside out.

I grabbed the duffel bag full of all the elixirs and changes of clothes that I could get on such a short notice and darted toward the door.

The fresh-faced academy student jumped when I swung the door open and bolted out of my room. I quickly walked down the hall with him on my heels yelling for me to slow down.

"I thought you were late, Hunter," I said and sent a sly smirk back at him as I called the elevator.

His tawny skin was slightly flushed under the fluorescents, and he gave me a sheepish look. I had seen this hunter maybe only once or twice in the academy training grounds but had never really talked to him.

He seems nice, I noted as he stood up straight, though his eyes flitted from mine as if he was nervous. *That makes two of us.*

When the elevator rang out it took all I had not to jump. My nerves crept up steadily last night and I couldn't sleep. Every sound set me off and I found myself tossing and turning until early morning. It was hard to imagine how I would even sleep in a place crawling with vampires, as soon as I let my guard down. . . I was likely to become food.

But it's worth it, I thought and steeled myself as I stepped into the metal box. *After this I can leave the Order for good.*

The hunter bid me goodbye and we parted ways when the elevator reached the ground floor. The vampire from the other day was waiting for me. He was standing next to a limo and looking up at the building, the sun shining on his face. It caused me to trip over my own two feet. His eyes drifted toward mine as I righted myself.

He looked so human in that moment as he basked in the sun. It was easy to forget how effortlessly they could blend in with us.

He knocked on the door and less than a second later a vampire appeared at my side, the speed of him throwing me off. I did jump this time and glared at him as he took the duffel bag from my hand. He gave me a smile and began to load my bag into the car.

"You shouldn't sneer at them like that. They didn't kill your family," Gillard chastised, as I walked toward him. I ignored him and opened the back door, climbing in only for him to climb right in with me.

"Doesn't mean you guys don't kill for your food," I growled and tried to put more distance between us.

It's a huge limo and he has to sit right next to me?

"All those working for us have never murdered a human in their life. That is our standard for employment," he explained.

I rolled my eyes. "That's a pretty low standard."

"You know, vampires are not like what you believe we are," he said, his eyes narrowing when they lingered on my sword. "I hope that during your stay you can realize that."

I wondered if he could smell just how many of his kind's disgusting blood was on my sword? I was tempted to ask him, but that would mean talking to him more

"Never," I muttered and crossed my arms over my chest.

Gillard didn't speak for the rest of the long ride to their compound. Luckily, the family lived away from the rest of their clan and sat snug in the middle of a forest outside of Seattle. It was hard to believe that anyone was able to live this far out, but I reminded myself that I would most likely be the only human in the compound.

I never understood the need for vampire clans to build huge compounds like they do. It was like the knowledge of someone belonging to their clan wasn't enough, they needed to show everyone just how obnoxious they were.

When I was in school, I was actually excited to learn about how the clans worked and how many there were. . . but I didn't know then what I knew now. I didn't see the way the vampires cornered weak women in alleys, I didn't see how they attacked people in broad daylight when their hunger became too much. . . and I didn't see my family's torn limbs.

The trees became thicker as we drove through the single road up to the compound. If I squinted hard enough, I was able to see forest animals roaming in between the trees, but they scurried away as the limo passed by. If this were another situation, I would have been ecstatic to be this far out into the forest. It felt comforting and safe.

But now, I couldn't shake the nerves. All I could think about was how far away I was from backup if I ever needed it.

I rubbed my neck absentmindedly; the bruise was even darker this morning and it ached. But the pain centered me and chased the nerves away. It reminded me to be vigilant and made sure my anxiety didn't get the best of me.

"Looks painful," Gillard commented. He watched me intently and it caused me to squirm under the intensity of it.

I flashed him a look and readjusted my turtleneck, making sure I could conceal as much skin as possible. Having your neck exposed was just begging them to take a bite. I kept my hair up for fighting, but I made sure that my neck was always covered no matter what.

The compound gates entered into view, and I was taken aback by how beautifully intricate they were. They were made out of iron, but the iron was twisted in a way that made it resemble flowers. They opened slowly and revealed rows and rows of multi-story houses.

Probably filled with their offspring.

I eyed a house as we passed. It was bigger than even the one my parents had when I was growing up.

"Servant quarters," Gillard commented.

My eyes widened. Servants got their own mansions?

What the hell?

As we passed them, the houses became bigger. The outsides had fountains and trimmed hedges in the shapes of exotic animals.

"For their offspring I'm guessing," I said under my breath.

"Extended members of the *royal family*," he corrected.

It was another few minutes until we reached where the immediate members resided. It was bigger than any mansion I'd seen before. It could probably stack up against the White House for sheer size alone, but instead of a white exterior, it was made with brick, which gave it an old-English vibe. There was an enormous pool in the center and an intricate stone carving of some type of goddess was erected in the middle with water flowing out from all sides of her.

"This is not the style of Washington State," I muttered bitterly.

It is fucking beautiful.

Gillard chuckled.

"We've been around for a long time, something your kind surely knows," he said, his words fanning my annoyance. "It's a style we gravitate toward."

It was so out of place in the forest, because while it looked light and clean, the shadows from the trees around it darkened the entire area, and paired with the constant overcast sky. . . it was creepy.

We parked right in front of the entrance, a grand staircase

led us up to the double doors that reached at least eight feet tall. The assistant grabbed my luggage and Gillard waved his hand out, inviting me into this hellhole.

The first thing I noticed was how many workers here were human. I gritted my teeth at the sight of a young maid waiting for us as the doors opened. Her neck was clean, however, I had no doubt there were bites hiding somewhere underneath her clothing.

"Welcome home, Master Gillard." She smiled and bowed at him. Her eyes drifted to me.

"This is Miss Silvia," he introduced. She gave me a polite smile and followed us as Gillard led me farther into the house where even more human servants stopped in their tracks and greeted us as we passed.

I tried not to get distracted by the inside, yet it was something else. From the old-time paintings on the walls to the extravagant floor that seemed to be mixed with gold, hell even the ceiling looked like it had been carved and angelic faces stared down at us as we walked.

"Impressive right? Maybe not what you had imagined?" Gillard said, bringing me out of my own thoughts.

"It doesn't matter," I snapped.

He shook his head, then led me down some winding corridors and a few staircases. I memorized the layout as I followed him, noting potential escape routes. It was big, but I had prepared for this a hundred times over.

It's like any other mission, I told myself though I felt a sheen of sweat on my skin.

Gillard stopped in front of one of the doors and opened it.

"This is where you will stay," he said and gave me a small smile before letting himself into the room.

He went inside and had the assistants place my stuff near

the dresser. He dismissed the others, and it allowed me a second to drool at the room in front of me.

It was big. Much bigger than anything I had ever lived in, and built for a princess. The four-poster bed itself was double the size I currently had and had the fluffiest-looking comforter on it. There was a dresser to my left and a desk to my right. Near the large windows on either side of my bed there was also a love seat with a small pillow.

There was a door near the left-hand side which I assumed was the bathroom, but I was almost scared to check it out. If *this* was the size of the room. . . I couldn't wrap my mind around what the bathroom could look like.

"This will do," I said after I swallowed the knot in my throat. Gillard let out a snort that startled me.

"Time to meet the heir," he said and turned to leave the room. I had to jog to keep up to him, though it was short-lived as he stopped one door down from my own. He paused and knocked on the door three times, I peered over and saw his lips moving, but no sound came out. A moment later he pushed opened the door and waved me in.

"We put your rooms close together in case anything happens," he explained. He stared down at me through his glasses, and he had a hardness to his tone that I did not like.

I rolled my eyes and stepped into the room. Unlike my room, this one seemed to be used as an office. There was a large dark wood desk at the back of the room, a large bookcase covering the wall behind it. In front of me were two deep-red couches and a table between them. Looking around, my eyes caught sight of some booze and a closed door. I assumed one went to a bedroom, but almost scoffed aloud when I realized how absurd it was for a vampire to own a bed.

Those monsters don't sleep.

Gillard sat on one of the couches and motioned for me to

do the same, but I refused and leaned against a nearby wall. He glared at me and motioned for me to come again, but when I refused he leaned back and sank into the couch with a sigh.

Not a moment later a figure entered from one of the doors. Their whole aura filled the room and I felt the hairs on the back of my neck rise. My body tensed and the blood rushed to my ears.

I was scared.

Even after all of the missions I had gone through during my time at the Order, I had not had a reaction like this to a vampire before. My body was telling me to run, to give up the prize money and run back to the Order where it would be safe.

Their inky black hair that was neatly slicked back, with only a few strands falling onto their face. The buttoned-up shirt they wore had the top buttons undone, showing off a bit of their collarbone and some of their chest. Their skin was free of blemishes or scars and was a rich color that was complemented by their light shirt. Dark-brown dress pants hung loosely from their hips with only a leather belt to hold them up.

When the vampire's eyes met mine, a chill went up my spine and the voice that was telling me to run got louder. Their eyes were bright red and if I had to bet, they had just finished feeding. I gritted my teeth and my hand found the hilt of my sword. I didn't know what I would do, or the plan from here on out. . . but I knew I couldn't just stand here.

"It would be a pity for you to kill the one you were supposed to protect," they said. Their voice was deep, silky, and only added to the tension that was swirling through this room.

For a moment I thought this was the prince. . . but I was mistaken, she was a hundred percent a girl.

She had the same bone structure as normal vampires, with

high cheekbones and strikingly beautiful features, but never had those same features made me feel so attacked and unsafe as they did now.

"Where is the prince?" I asked Gillard, my tone filled with anger.

He smiled but did not respond.

The girl also smiled, showing a bit of her fangs. She rubbed her chin in mock contemplation. "A prince? I didn't know humans were still so dumb," she said and stalked over to me.

She towered over my frame and even as I stood up straight it was almost laughable, our size difference. I looked up into her eyes, a heat flaring throughout my body. On one hand, my mind told me that this would be the easiest and most surefire way to avenge my parents. All I had to do was stab her and the reign of this clan would be over.

But my debt and the ice-cold fear she injected into my veins stopped me.

"If you know what's good for you, you will step back," I warned.

Her smile widened and she placed a hand on the wall behind me, trapping me in. I inhaled her scent, it was a deep floral that itched my nose. Normally I would have liked this type of smell. It reminded me of the garden my mother had in the back of our house, but even that thought brought me back to the present. Reminding me that the person in front of me had a hand in my parents' deaths.

I reached for my dagger.

"You signed a contract, Silvia," Gillard said.

I know, I wanted to scream. *Damn it all.*

"I wonder." She leaned her face down to the crook of my neck. "Would you give your blood as easily as the others did?"

Disgust filled me and my stomach lurched.

"This is a warning," I snapped, it took everything I had in me to plant myself against this wall as she leaned closer.

She pulled back to look in my eyes, then her gaze traveled the length of my face and down to my throat, her tongue swiped across her bottom lip before she leaned back in. Her hot breath fanned across the small sliver of neck that I had exposed.

"Or what? You'll kill me? Or even better, quit?" she asked with an amused tone.

The heir will try to push you, the captain had warned. *They want you to give up. They want you to leave, but if you do, your debt will only increase.*

A flick of her hot tongue as she dragged it along the side of my neck was the last straw. I raised my leg up and kicked her hard in the stomach. She hissed and backed away, freeing me from my place against the wall. I sent her a glare.

Vampires may be strong, but we spent a shit ton of time training in the Order to become just strong enough to stand a chance against them. It was a small chance, but where it didn't work, my dagger came in handy.

"I have a job to do here. Not even you will interfere with it," I growled

She paused, still clutching her stomach. "Insolence," the heir muttered. Her eyes met mine slowly. The red had faded slightly, showing the brown that was underneath.

"I do not know why you have chosen to push away so many other hunters, but you should know that I am not like them. There are no tactics that will make me leave," I spat at her. "You are all scum to me, so there is not a trick that I will fall for that you have up your sleeve."

There was a silence that fell over us, the only thing breaking it was my own erratic heartbeat as I stared both Gillard and the heir down. I would not let her push me around like the others, I had more dignity than that, so if she wanted a plaything they picked the wrong hunter.

"Told you," Gillard said, breaking the silence. A small smile had made its way to his face, and for the first time, I saw a small sparkle fill his eyes.

The heir let out a growl that reverberated around the room, but this time her actions didn't scare me. . . they enraged me. Her eyes stayed planted on mine and somehow I knew, just like myself, that she was holding herself back from attacking me.

Come on, my mind pleaded. *Fight me.*

I wanted so badly for her to come at me so I would have a chance to bury my knife in her chest.

"Anyone can be broken," she muttered and left the room, going out to the hallway we just came from. I stood and looked at the now-empty space. The aura that surrounded her lingered and the hair on the back of my neck still hadn't relaxed.

"That went well," Gillard said, as his lips twisted into an even bigger smile.

CHAPTER 5
SILVIA

After I bid goodbye to Gillard and settled into the night, I lay in my bed unable to even close my eyes. I was wrapped up in the obscenely warm comforter, and the bed was so soft I felt like I was lying on a cloud, but that didn't stop the anxiety that rose in my chest.

I couldn't shake the feeling of the aura that the heir exuded. It was heavy and scared the living hell out of me. She was powerful and knowing that all of my fellow hunters had failed this mission only added to my fears. I was sure that as soon as I closed my eyes her fangs would be sinking into my throat.

She was dangerous, I mean all vampires were. . . but her. . .

I kept my sword close and my dagger even closer, one propped against the night table and the other under my pillow with my fingers gripped around it at all times. There were noises all around me, and even though they were nothing to be alarmed by, my heart pounded in my chest and my grip on my dagger tightened.

Finally, after listening to the howling of the wind through the trees that surrounded the compound, I found myself drifting off to a dreamless sleep. I was exhausted from barely sleeping the night before, and no matter how hard my heart pumped in my chest, my mind was shutting down.

I did not know how long I had been asleep for, but it couldn't have been long because right as I heard the blood-curdling scream that echoed through the silent night, I catapulted myself out of the bed with my dagger by my side. When the next one sounded, I grabbed my sword and ran out the door, making my way to the heir's room.

I didn't know where it was coming from, but I knew that first I had to secure the vampire I was sworn to protect. I pushed open the door to her office and let out a sigh of relief when I found it empty. The room was dark, so I scanned it three times before I took a step back, ready to retreat back to my room.

But then there was another, and it came right from the closed door on the far side of the room. Cursing, I rushed toward the door and pushed it open.

Inside was a dimly lit room that resembled my own with a four-poster bed right in the middle. . . but that was where my gaze stopped. I froze and opened my mouth to speak, but nothing came out.

The bed was not empty and now I saw all too clearly what vampires needed a bedroom for. In front of me, there were two people on the bed, both naked, their sweaty skin glistening in the dim light. One of them was the heir and the other a human she currently had her fangs buried in. Blood escaped from the heir's mouth and spilled down the human girl's front. I couldn't tear my eyes away as the beads of blood ran down her body.

The human was blindfolded and on her knees, facing me to give me a clear view of her curvy body. The heir was behind her, drinking from her neck with one hand on the girl's throat, tilting her head to the side. Their bodies were flush together and the screams were now just soft moans coming out of the human's mouth. The heir's blood-red eyes met mine and she detached herself from the human's neck, giving me a smirk.

That action was what stirred my movements.

I took a step backward, trying to process the scene. The girl ground against the heir and my eyes traveled down, only now noticing the heir's fingers buried in her. She began pumping in and out of the human, the sound of the human's wetness filling the room. The blood that fell from the wound on her neck met the heir's hand and it spread across the girl's skin.

The heir's eyes never left mine, she was challenging me to look away... but I couldn't.

I felt my face flush and heat coiled in my belly. The control she exuded caused my throat to tighten and my mouth to water. Her arms were so tightly wrapped around the human, not enough to hurt her but enough so that she would stay propped up against her. The girl did not dare move, even as the heir's fingers pounded into her. The heir gripped at the girl's throat tighter and dragged a long moan out of her mouth.

I felt a sick desire spark through me. I craved that type of touch. The controlled, experienced kind. The one that caused you to melt into them as they brought you to oblivion and back. I imagined the way fingers like hers would feel as they fucked me, imagined how she could choke the life out of me and—

The girl let out another scream as she began to come all over the heir's hand.

Oh my God. I turned around and ran back into my room. I didn't stop until I had thrown myself back into the bed and covered myself with the comforter, trying to erase the last few moments from my mind.

I knew there were humans that gave themselves willingly to vampires, but this was something else entirely. The way *my* body reacted was something else entirely. I was no stranger to the things that they did. . . but I hadn't been able to be with someone like that since the academy.

That's what it must be, I thought as I gripped the comforter tighter to me. *It's just because I've been busy. After this is over, I will start my life for real, I can settle down, meet a nice girl, buy a—*

The screams continued and I let out a loud groan.

I was *not* going to be getting any sleep tonight.

Gillard was the person who interrupted my sleep just a few hours later. I tried not to throw a fit as I got ready, but the screams from the night before still played in my mind. I had even dreamed about it. A disgustingly sexual dream that had no business being in my mind, with a vampire no less.

Gillard was supposed to give me a tour of the rest of the mansion today, which I would need if I was to do my job properly. Though, as I lay awake last night I was really starting to wonder if I needed this job any longer.

When I finally got myself together and splashed cold water on my face, I opened the door to meet Gillard. I was disappointed to see that the heir was with him as well. She stood tall next to him and was dressed in similar clothes as she was the day before. She looked down at me with knowing smile. I sneered in response.

"I hope you enjoyed the show last night," she said.

Gillard's eyes widened and he glared at her.

"You did not, Keir," Gillard moaned, his tone exasperated. I almost felt for him. If *that* was what I had to deal with on the first night. . . what had he had to go through?

So that's her name, I thought as I looked her over.

She held up her hands when he glared further at her. "It's not my fault she came in, bursting through the door at three in the morning."

Anger boiled in me. *My fault?* I pulled my sword from it's sheath and held it close to her neck in warning.

"You knew what you were doing," I hissed. "I am here to protect you if I hear *that* of course I will check on you."

She simply stepped away from my sword and shrugged as if I could not have just ended her existence.

"Forget it." Gillard sighed and ran a hand through the top of his hair. It was in a loose ponytail and his actions caused the front strands to fall into his face. "We have a tour today, let's not waste time. I assume the human needs to eat something."

"Yes, humans do need to eat," I grumbled. I hardly ate anything the day before, too busy trying to get used to living in this house with a load of monsters.

"I heard you like coffee as well. We have our own café on the compound. I could take you?" Gillard offered.

"You shouldn't be nice to someone who called you scum, Gil," Keir said, sending me her own glare.

"It will do," I answered.

Gillard sent me a small smile and gestured for us to follow him.

I almost moaned as I took a sip from the latte Gillard got for me. This had to be the best one I'd tasted in my life. I admit that I'd tended to gravitate toward cheaper coffee, so many of the ones I tried were subpar. . . but this was *delicious*. I grabbed the chocolate croissant that he brought as well and took another bite.

Fucking delicious.

I would savor every single moment of this breakfast, even with the two vampires sitting across from me. I would take advantage of the luxuries this compound and clan had to offer because God knows when the next time I'd be able to afford one of these would be.

The café was outside the main house in an open garden. It was nothing more than a small kiosk with tables and chairs surrounding it, but it was the fanciest coffee place I had seen, even despite its size.

The air was fresh and the sun had peeked out, warming my skin. I inhaled the scent of the coffee mixed with the scent of the roses that grew on the sides of the garden. If you ignored everyone here, this place could quite literally be perfect.

"Aren't the humans here only servants? Isn't giving them their own coffee shop a bit much?" I asked Gillard, not that I was complaining.

"We have humans and half humans here," Gillard answered. "Not all of them are servants. Raphael's extended family is quite large."

I chewed on my croissant thoughtfully. I hadn't learned much about vampires breeding humans before. . . The thought didn't sit right with me.

"Half humans?" I asked, swallowing a sliver of fear at the idea of being surrounded by the royal family, even in human form.

"Yes. As you saw last night, we like to fuck our humans here," Keir answered with a smirk. Her expression told me she was waiting for the fight that was about to come.

"Keir," Gillard warned.

"Disgusting," I said and discarded my croissant, my stomach turning sour all of a sudden.

"They come willingly," she teased and leaned across the table, her face getting dangerously close to my own. "And seeing by your reaction last night, maybe you will too."

"You wish." I glared at her.

I would rather die than get in bed with a vampire.

"That seemed like your wish, not mine," she said. "I do not need an inexperienced hunter in my bed to satisfy me."

I bristled at her comment. I was not as inexperienced as she may have thought, but I don't know why I felt such a push to tell her I wasn't.

"That's none of your business," I said, trying to sip my latte in peace. I felt Gillard's eyes on me and it caused me to flush.

"Ohh? You have me curious now. . . Which little hunter's bed have you been in?" she asked and leaned back in her chair, finally giving me enough space to breath. "Any of the ones I've seen?"

Gillard gave out a long sigh.

"Michael? James? Chris? Justin? Nick?" She paused between each name, but I gave no reaction. "Hm, a girl then? Cristy? Brittany? Rose?"

When I didn't answer she let out a sigh and looked up to the sky, as if really trying to think of all the hunters she had ever come across. I was getting tired of her games and a headache was already starting form.

"How about Jane?"

I froze slightly at the name. She knew Jane. How did she know Jane?

Jane was a hunter, a *good* one. . . but I didn't think a job like this was common. Did the heir always have hunters at her side?

"Don't," Gillard warned.

"So little Jane, huh?" Keir placed her head in her hand and watched my reaction closely. "Did you know I took her vampire virginity? She was much more complacent than you. It only took a small amount of probing, and before long, she was begging for me."

I gripped the latte cup a little too tightly and the rest of it spilled out onto the table.

"When was the last time you were with her, huh? The last time I saw her was over four years ago, she was every vampire's wet dream. Long neck, sweet blood, she would practically melt when you buried your fangs in her. How is she doing now? Maybe you can give me her number?"

I jumped from my seat and launched myself across the table, tackling the offending vampire to the ground. I didn't care about the table clanging behind us or the gasps from the people around us. All I saw was red and I wanted, now more than ever, to cut Keir's throat open.

She smiled under me, enjoying the reaction.

I gripped my dagger and held it close to her throat, not enough to break the skin but enough so that she could feel the cool metal and know that I was not joking.

"I am going to fucking kill you if you mention her name one more time," I spit out.

"What did she do? Scream my name when you fucked her?" Keir egged me on with a laugh in her voice.

I pricked her skin, my hand was shaking from anger.

"She was her sister," Gillard said and tried to pull me off Keir. "Did you not read the file I sent you? She died shortly after she left."

"Don't you fucking touch me," I hissed and held on to her.

Keir's eyes widened and her smirk dropped. "She died? I didn't know."

I let out a humorless laugh that hurt as my insides twisted.

"She died because of your *fucking* people. They didn't stop there, though. They tore my family apart *one by one* and let them bleed out on the floor, gasping for breath." I hissed every word, wishing that each could be a stab to her chest.

It took all my strength to pull myself off her.

Maybe the debt is not worth this.

Hunter Rules

rule 3 sec 1

All Hunter's must complete
Academy Training. If a Hunter
leaves the Academy before
graduating they will be
obligated to pay back all the
debt accrued during that time.
If the Hunter would like to
return to the Academy they
must start from year one
regardless of how far they got
the first time.

CHAPTER 6
SILVIA

K eir was strangely quiet the rest of the day as Gillard showed us through the compound. We didn't run into any of the other royal family, but I was not complaining. As long as I had a silent heir by my side, and I didn't have to interact with any other vampires besides her and Gillard, I was fine.

"What will the heir even do all day?" I asked Gillard, fully ignoring Keir.

We were walking back to our rooms. The sun had set over an hour ago, and the lack of sleep was pulling me down with the sun. I don't know if Gillard noticed, but I was excited to get into bed and didn't mind the early time.

"Anything she pleases really, but the longer she stays away from her office the bigger the pile of documents she needs to sign gets." He sent a glare to Keir. "There are also a few events she needs to attend in the next few weeks, you will need to attend those as well. After that, you are free to do whatever."

I nodded and searched the empty hallway. The large floor-to-ceiling windows let the moonlight shine in, and normally I would be worried about them and the possible risk they could cause to the heir, but everything today had been quiet enough that I no longer thought it was a concern.

"This place seems relatively safe," I noted and turned back to Gillard. "I am not sure why you did not just ask for my services as needed for the events."

While there were vampires crawling across the whole compound, I had not seen anyone treat Keir with anything other than respect.

"She also tends to sneak out at night when the rest of the manor is otherwise asleep," Gillard said with a grimace.

"She's an adult," I fought. I wanted the money. . . but it just was weird. She was a grown vampire and probably three times my age.

"Doesn't mean she's responsible," Gillard mumbled and shot a glare toward Keir.

"Vampires don't sleep. Why can't you just watch her?" I asked, cocking my head.

"He's half," Keir interjected for the first time all afternoon. "He needs sleep and it's not like anyone can stop me. I mostly need someone by my side while I go out."

Looking at Gillard, I would not have been able to tell that he was half, but then again, I had never seen a half vampire before. I continued to ignore Keir.

"You still live as long as them?" I asked.

"Unfortunately." He sighed. "My mother was human. Vampire pregnancy was hard on her and she died shortly after my birth." I shifted uncomfortably at the news.

"My. . . condolences," I whispered, my eyes drifting to the dark forest outside. I knew what it was like to lose a parent. Vampire or not, it must have hurt.

"Thank you. It may have been better that way. My previous clan was. . . less than agreeable," he said after a moment.

"I guess I will have to change my own sleeping schedule then," I said, trying to change the subject, and turned toward my room. "I'll sleep now, please wake me before you leave."

The last part was directed toward Keir, but I didn't look at her as I slipped back into my room.

The heir did not wake me up before she left, but I expected as much. She may have admitted she needed someone to go out with her, but I had already learned enough about her to know her word was shit.

I awoke after only a few hours of sleep, got dressed and sat in the room's only chair. . . and waited. I looked out over the grounds through the large windows, trying to see if I could spot anyone. The grounds were quiet.

When I heard the telltale sound of the door of the room next to me opening, I ran to open my own door. As I threw it open, I caught her just as she turned to close the door.

"I told you to wake me," I growled.

She shrugged and her eyes met mine, and if her smirk was any indication of her thoughts, she had to have known I was awake and had been waiting for the perfect moment. Her now bright-red eyes did not get past me, and I bet if I got closer I could see the blood still staining her fangs.

"I thought you would have given up by now," she said with a cool tone and walked toward me. I tried not to stiffen as she passed and instead focused on her clothing.

I had no idea what the heir liked to spend her time doing. . . but it couldn't have been good.

Instead of her more formal attire, she was in a band T-shirt, ripped jeans, and Doc Marten's. Something similar to what I would have chosen for myself. . . and it was strangely human. Her scent invaded my senses and instead of the sweet scent she was wearing the other day, a spicy, deep one swirled around me.

I cleared my throat and turned to follow her before it was too late.

"Where do you go this late at night?" I asked, trying to keep pace as she strode through the still house. Even though vampires don't sleep, the house was quiet and the only signs of life were our footsteps that echoed through the halls.

"Many places," she said. "None of which you would like."

She led me down the grand staircase and back behind the main entrance. With one more staircase, I came face-to-face with a garage that spanned the entire length of the house with a ramp to the far side that allowed cars in and out. There were enough cars in here for the vampires to act as their own dealership.

I almost groaned when I saw her beeline toward an all-black motorcycle.

"Pick something else," I ordered.

She stopped in her tracks and glared at me before looking back toward her bike. From my position I couldn't see much of her face, but I saw enough to know her full lips had turned into a frown.

"But the ladies like my bike," she said in a tone that resembled a pout.

"I need to keep my sword with me. Pick something else," I ordered and crossed my arms over my chest.

To my surprise, she actually listened to me.

She sighed and looked around, trying to pick out the next

suitable thing. A smile flashed across her face as she eyed a shiny red Porsche and swiftly crossed the lot to it.

I rolled my eyes. It was better than the bike at least. However, the inside still smelled new, and it sent a flare of jealousy through me. I told myself that I would never be jealous of a vampire, but here I am.

It's all the money, I reminded myself. *It's nothing to do with them.*

She settled herself in the car and ran her ringed hands over the steering wheel, marveling at the feel. As she reached over the dashboard her eyes sparkled, almost as if she was just as amazed as I was.

"This isn't yours, is it?" I asked, narrowing my eyes at her.

"Nope." She gave me a crazed smile and floored it out of the garage.

Driving with Keir had to be the scariest experience of my life. She had no care for the rules of the road or the people on it. A drive that should have lasted forty minutes lasted twenty, and by the time we made it to our destination, I was about to hurl.

As soon as she parked, I pushed the door open, collapsed onto the ground, and began heaving. The world tilted and it felt like my mind was still back at the compound, trying to catch up to us.

"Don't be such a baby," she chided and grabbed the back of my shirt, forcing me into a standing position. Keir was much taller than me, so it was easy for her to lift me high enough that my feet didn't even touch the ground. I tried to swipe at her and force her to put me down, but she didn't until she had dragged me all the way across the parking lot and to the entrance of a shady, worn-down building.

"Don't touch me," I hissed and fixed my shirt as I followed

her into the building. As soon as we stepped in I was assaulted with music and flashing lights. The smell of alcohol and something musky filled the room, and the damp heat of the place made my Hunter uniform stick uncomfortably to my skin.

She brought me into a *fucking* bar. Out of all places she could decide to sneak out to. . . she went to a bar?

This was a vampire whose family *literally* ran everything around here. They could buy anything, go anywhere. . . and she choose a run-down bar?

"You sneaked out to go to a bar?" I asked, glaring at her. "Are you that stupid?"

"I like being around people," she said, shrugging as if the answer was as simple as that.

"Food you mean," I corrected, but she only smiled.

The bouncer waited for us, his eyes narrowing on my weapons. Behind him was a staircase that I assumed led to the rest of the bar. His black T-shirt fit snugly across his chest, and he had dark tattoos marring his face.

"A hunter?" he asked while stepping aside for Keir.

She sent him a small smile and me a look that only fueled my anger.

"Obviously," I sneered and pushed past him to follow Keir inside before the bouncer could ask me to remove my weapons.

"Can you even drink?" I asked and ran down the stairs to keep up with her. Some stray girls stood on the stairs and watched us with interest as we passed.

When my sword smacked one of them in the leg I threw an apology over my shoulder but pushed forward until I almost ran into her back at the end of the stairs. Peering from behind her, I saw a crowd in front of us and started to panic at the idea of her being so close to the people in here.

Food or not, there could be an enemy hidden here.

"Here I can," she said and pushed through the crowd. With a curse I followed her. It was hard to keep up with her with all the sweaty bodies grinding against me and pushing me back the way I came, but she was tall enough I couldn't miss her.

As I pushed through girl after girl, my face began to heat as I realized she took me to a lesbian bar. Not only that, it was painfully obvious that I was the only hunter here, and as I pushed people out of the way they sent odd looks toward me, especially the vampires who were mixed into the crowd. I had unhooked my sword, as it hit one too many people, and brought it up to my chest. When I finally made it to the bar, I let out a sigh. There was enough space for me to breathe and stretch out my limbs without running into bodies.

"What is the point of coming here?" I asked her. She didn't answer me right away as she was turned toward the bartender, talking to him in a low voice with a smile.

When he finally turned and begun making whatever she ordered, she turned to look at me, her once-bright eyes fading back to their normal brown. She leaned back against the bar and looked me up and down as if critiquing me.

"Is this your first time to a lesbian bar?" she teased.

No, I wanted to say. . . but I kept my mouth shut.

When the bartender placed two metal cups on the counter she didn't hesitate to hand me one. I took mine but watched as she turned to grab hers and take a deep sip of it. When she finished, her eyes had turned back to the bright red they had been.

I felt bile rise in my throat and looked down at my drink.

"Yours is Jack and Coke," she explained. "And I don't think I need to tell you what mine is."

No, she didn't. The bright-red blood still lingered on her

pearly whites. I *really* needed this drink after the last few days... but the captain's voice in my head discouraged me.

"I am here for work," I said and placed it back on the counter.

"Come on," she whined. "Live a little. Don't worry. . . I won't snitch."

I rolled my eyes and shifted, eyeing the bottom of the steps. It seemed like a good enough place to be for the night. She reached out like she was going to grab me, but I slapped her hand away before she got too close.

"I will be watching from near the exit if you need me," I said and turned. Even with the music blaring and the voices surrounding us, I heard her scoff as I left.

I pushed back through the people and stood on the stairs, leaning against the wall. The cool air from the door at the top washed against my heated skin, and I felt a weight lift off me. Even in the Order, it had been a while since I had been around so many people, and a small amount of anxiety ran through my veins as I watched everyone.

Keir was easy to spot from this area, and it didn't take her long to start wandering from the bar. A bitterness rose in me as I watched girls flock to her immediately. She had a pull on the humans and smiled down at them before grabbing one and pulling them to her side.

I trained for this job for years and accumulated God only knows how much debt, and the biggest job of my career was babysitting a grown ass vampire *child*. I had to admit that I thought someone rumored with her power would have been more impressive. . . but besides that first-time meeting, I had yet to feel that dangerous aura that poured out of her again.

Now she just looked like a normal vampire who was intent on sampling the beautiful girls around her and not like the heir to a throne.

The vampire child had already found her victim for the night after the first group of girls left her side. This time it was a short blonde girl with a red minidress that hugged her figure. She leaned against the wall next to Keir and played with the hem of Keir's shirt. Without warning Keir pushed the small girl against the dirty wall and leaned forward. In their position Keir towered over her, but I had a clear view of how starstruck the girl looked. Acid heated in my stomach at the sight.

Keir smirked and placed her long fingers on the girl's chin, forcing her to bare her neck. I froze as her lips came into contact with the girl's skin, but she didn't bite yet. Instead, that bastard's eyes flitted to mine. She was testing me.

Would she really drink here? In front of all these people?

"Silv?"

A familiar voice tore me away from the heir. I looked down and saw a familiar figure walking closer to me. A person that I hadn't seen for over four years and had cut off contact with completely.

Nat, my ex-girlfriend. It wasn't unusual for us to go out to lesbian bars when we were together, but seeing her here after so long stirred me. I had left her behind, along with the rest of my life, after my parents had died.

"Nat? It's been so. . ." My words trailed off as I took in how much she had changed.

Her brown hair was still cropped short, and her face was still filled with freckles, but her eyes were no longer the vibrant green they once were. They were red.

Her features that I had loved waking up to so much on Sunday mornings were now sharpened and higher, just like every other vampire. She looked beautiful, breathtaking. . . but it hurt to realize what had happened. She had no doubt changed into one of those monsters, but I couldn't under-stand how or why. Nat never worked in a dangerous job and never strayed too far from human areas. There shouldn't have been a chance for this to happen. . . unless she went willingly?

Through all our time together she had never said anything that would push me to believe she would ever want to become a vampire.

"Silv, I heard about your family. I am so sorry. I tried to find you, but you weren't at your address." She tried to step closer to me but stepped back when I placed the sword between us. She looked down, hurt filling her face.

"Don't," I commanded, my mouth feeling dry.

"What are you doing?" she asked, her voice low.

"What am I doing? What happened to you?" I demanded.

Her eyebrows pulled together slightly, and her lips formed a pout.

"What do you mean?" she asked, her tone filled with hurt.

"Your *eyes*," I hissed, unable to force the word *vampire* out of my mouth.

"I was in an accident," she explained. "A vampire saved me."

"I wouldn't call this saved," I spat and looked her up and down.

She may have looked the same, but I couldn't trust her. . . not like this. This wasn't right.

"We used to be so close, don't treat me like this," she pleaded, covering the hand on my sword with hers. The smoothness of it felt the same as before. As human as before.

"You should leave," I said, trying to look for Keir. Said vampire child was now making her way toward us with an unreadable expression, her new blonde friend under her arm.

"No, we should talk," she noted, her voice rising. "I haven't been able to find you—"

"Oh? Did the little hunter find someone she likes?" Keir

teased, pulling up behind Nat. Nat's eyes widened in recognition and she bowed slightly.

I rolled my eyes. *Of course, Nat would know this idiot.*

"Don't you think for one second you are bringing her back to the compound," I snapped at her.

"I would never. We're going to fuck in the car." The girl next to her giggled. I blanched at her words.

"You've been to the compound?" Nat asked disbelievingly.

"Unfortunately, yes," I grumbled.

"She's there for an *extended stay*," Keir said, her eyes twinkling.

"Wait, you're living with her?" Nat's eyes passed between us like she was trying to make sense of whatever was between us.

"Actually, she lives—"

I cut Keir off with a dagger to the throat.

"You really must not care for your life," I spat

Nat reached out to touch my shoulder lightly, Keir caught the action her eyes narrowing. I shrugged Nat's hand off and scowled.

"Fine, we can stay here for now," Keir said and sent a glance toward Nat.

"We leave in another hour," I ordered.

It was Keir's turn to roll her eyes. She waved a hand at me and turned back into the bar with the girl at her side.

"Silv," Nat started, but I put the dagger back in its holster and glared at her.

"I don't associate with your kind anymore. Please leave."

My chest tightened when her face dropped, but I reminded myself that she was not the girl I once knew.

"You seem to associate yourself with the heir," she said.

"Don't mention her status here," I said quickly, my eyes darting around to see if anyone heard her. "I am not here by choice, and I hate associating with her as much as any other vampire. Leave so I can do my job."

After that she left without another word. I watched her form as she disappeared back into the crowd.

Was it really an accident? Would she have died without changing?

We had been close and a part of me wanted to see if she was still the same girl I had been with long ago. . . but I couldn't bring myself to go after her.

I shook the thoughts out of my head and focused on the mission at hand.

An hour was far too long. I was way too generous. Many people had come and gone, but Keir stayed with the same girl. They were huddled near the corner and in a heavy make out session each time my eyes flitted back to them.

At the hour mark I had to push through the crowd and interrupt them.

"We have to leave," I snapped.

Keir's back was to me, and she didn't so much as flinch when I called out to her. She was still groping the girl against the wall, her hand gripped her bare thigh as she pulled it around her waist. The dress was rolled up almost around her hips, and she was practically flashing her bare pussy to the world.

Getting annoyed, I stabbed Keir with the hilt of my sword. That seemed to get her attention because in an instant her head snapped around, her eyes wild and red. She let out a growl that rumbled deep in her chest, and I felt like I had literally just poked a bear.

I caught sight of the girl's bloodstained face from underneath her and my heart skipped a beat.

"Leave her be," I ordered.

"You can't order me to do anything," Keir responded, licking the blood around her mouth.

"I can if it endangers your life. You have been here too long, with too many people coming and going. We need to *leave*," I growled.

She bared her teeth at me and the girl underneath her let out a strangled moan. My blood turned to ice and I jolted into action. I roughly pushed the vampire away and took the girl's face in my hands. Her eyes were glossed over and she could barely hold herself up.

"Don't go," she moaned, trying to grab on to my shirt. I sighed and cleaned her face with the sleeve of my shirt, carefully cradling the girl's limp neck.

"I can't fucking believe you," I muttered and turned to face Keir, but she was nowhere to be seen.

I cursed. I couldn't just leave this girl here, she could barely stand on her own two feet. I fixed her dress before I pulled her arm over my shoulders. Her head flopped around, and she tried to speak, but I couldn't decipher her words.

Holding her close, I brought her to the seating area.

"Who are you here with?" I tried to ask, but my words had no effect on her.

I waved away the random girls that loitered by the couches and carefully laid her down, being mindful of her head. I tried to sit her up but she kept falling, so I had no choice but to sit by her. She sagged against me, muttering something, but again I couldn't hear it clearly.

I was going to fucking kill that vampire when I saw her next. This was exactly why their kind deserved to perish. Leaving a helpless girl like this, in a bar no less. She would be better dead. If I wasn't here, I wondered what her fate would have been.

Just then a bottle of orange juice and crackers filled my

vision. I looked up to see Keir staring back down at me, her mouth still stained with blood. I glared and took the juice forcefully from her, then sat the girl back up and forced her to drink.

It was another twenty minutes before she was awake enough to eat, however she was at least much more alert now.

"I apologize for getting carried away," Keir said to the girl.

The girl shot her a smiled and a bright blush crept up her neck and face.

"Don't be, I enjoyed it," she replied.

Keir chuckled and sent her a look that made me shiver.

Disgusting.

"Where are your friends?" I asked her. She looked at me as if I was the bad guy. "Don't look at me like that. If I didn't step in you would be dead."

"No she wouldn't—"

"Shut up," I hissed at Keir. "Where are your friends?" I demanded from the girl once more.

She pointed to two girls huddled near the other side of the bar. They were gossiping and staring at us, but seemed to be sober enough to stay out of trouble for the rest of the night.

"Go to them *now*," I demanded.

Her eyes widened at my tone, but she obeyed nonetheless, but not before sending a small wave to the heir. I glared as Keir winked at her.

"We are leaving."

She tried to object but I prodded her with my sword until she started moving back through the crowded bar. It was not long before we were in the car and speeding toward the compound.

This time I welcomed her speed as the day's exhaustion was wearing on me. I couldn't wait to curl up in the ultra-expensive comforter and sleep like the dead.

"If you just allowed me to bring her back to the compound this wouldn't have happened," she said, her voice hard and her eyes focused on the road.

My anger flared at her words.

"Don't you blame your mistakes on me. I don't think you realize the situation you are in," I growled.

Her hands gripped tightly on the steering wheel and her eyes seemed too dark in the night light.

"Don't scold me like a child," she spat.

"Then don't act like one," I retorted, my hand lingered on my dagger.

That seemed to hit too close to home and she pushed her foot down on the gas. She refused to talk to me after that and only focused on the dark road, her anger filling the car and threatening to choke me.

Even as we parked and entered the quiet house, she didn't once turn back toward me. I was fine with it, I could barely keep my eyes open at this point.

When we finally made it up to our rooms, I was overcome with joy at the thought of the bed waiting for me. I paused when my hand settled on the cool metal doorknob and looked over to Keir. If there was one last thing I needed to do, it was make sure she stayed in her *damn* room. She paused and in the blink of an eye I was pushed against the wall.

My head hit the hard surface, pain shooting through me, and white spots filled my vision. I glared at Keir through the pain, more awake than I had been the last few hours. She gripped the sides of my neck, fingers digging into me and blocking the air from entering my lungs. She bared her blood-stained teeth at me.

"You ruined my plans for tonight." Her face was so close to mine that I could smell the metallic scent of blood mixed with her fading cologne.

"You really are a child if this is how you act when you can't get what you want," I gasped out.

She was not totally crushing my windpipe, but the grip she had on me was locked tight and enough to cause me to gasp for air. I tried to push her off and kick her, but she stayed still.

"Did you really think you had a chance against me?" she spat. "You are a *weak* human. Every time you pushed me, I have *allowed* it. *I* have the control here. Don't think because Father paid you that I give a *shit* about what you say."

I struggled against her grip as she squeezed harder.

"Let go," I choked out.

"How does it feel to know your life is in my hands?" She leaned in closer and inhaled my scent deeply. "How would you feel if I took a drink?"

"Don't you dare, you filth," I spat.

"Ohh, testy," she teased and released her grip, only to grasp both of my hands and place them above my head. "I think—*no* —I know you will enjoy it when I finally sink my fangs into you. I know deep inside this act or whatever is just a farce, and once you feel what I can do to you, you'll be begging for more."

She was mere inches from me and I could feel the heat of her body seep into mine.

"If you think this will make me quit, you are wrong," I said, trying to keep my voice firm, but inside I was wavering. The aura from before was back and it was stifling.

"Who said I wanted you to quit?" Her eyes flashed dangerously. "Now that I know your *preference*, I am more excited to keep you around. All the other hunters they sent me were straight. Straight people are no fun after a while."

She held my hands with only one of hers and started to feel down my side slowly.

"I would never fuck trash like you," I spat at her. "Let me go before I hurt you."

She threw her head back and laughed like she had just heard the funniest joke on the planet. That was all the signal I needed.

I hit the heel of my boot against the wall and smiled when I felt the knife free itself from my sole. I went to kick her, but found the spot in front of me empty and my hands free. I turned to see her leaning against her door with an amused smile on her face.

"Let's do this again sometime, Little Hunter."

CHAPTER 7
SILVIA

It had taken a little over a week for the heir to finally realize that I would not get fed up with her actions and leave. Every night we would go to the same club and I would watch as she buried her fangs in another human. Sometimes she would surprise me, trying to find a new way to push me and get me to quit.

Sometimes she would hook up with them right next to me.

Or hold eye contact as she pushed the girl against the wall and fingered her.

Sometimes it wouldn't even be at the club. During the day she had resorted to trying to touch me, but after my dagger came close to slicing her fingers she had stopped that.

She had also taken to stealing my clothes from me as I showered. Leaving me to have to burst into her room with only a towel, but I refused to be humiliated by her. If this was how she would act, I would try and find ways to mitigate it so that she would get bored.

After the first time she stole my clothes, Gillard had to step in and force her to give them back. By the time she tried it again, I had already hidden some extras around the room.

The most annoying, though, was when she would interrupt my sleep. She had found out very quickly that without a lot of sleep, I was miserable and less likely to yell at her. So on the off chance that we came home early from the bar, there would still somehow always be something that woke me up.

One night it was her music blasting through the walls.

The other was more women in her bed.

The last was her knocking on my door only to have disappeared when I opened it.

It was childish, all of it. It became very clear that Keir was intent on getting me so irritated that I would have no choice but to leave, but compared to the years of hell I had to suffer at the Academy. . . this was nothing.

The Academy was cruel, especially when the Enforcers were involved. I had learned to live in a constant state of discomfort. I could be tired, that was fine. I could be so annoyed that even someone breathing would set me alight, I would live. But what I couldn't stand was the idea of letting this chance slip by me.

So every game, every night at the club, I endured.

Things changed on the eleventh day.

That was when for the first time, Keir listened to me. I had told her that we needed to leave in twenty minutes as I was almost dead on my feet, and sure enough, she left on time with me.

Then she stopped interrupting my sleep. One night I woke up so paranoid that I burst into her room, Order gear already hastily pulled on. I had for sure thought that she had left me, but she was sitting there at her desk looking at papers.

The change was great but also suspicious.

There was no reason for the heir to suddenly start acting

this way if she didn't have something up her sleeve. She had gone through how many hunters? And suddenly she didn't want to play anymore?

Bullshit.

"How did you do it?" Gillard asked, also noticing the change one morning outside the same coffee shop he treated me to every day.

This place may have sucked, but I would be damned if I gave up free coffee, even if it meant sitting so close to the vampires every morning, and right now I needed to inject this coffee straight into my veins in order to keep me functioning. I still couldn't get used to Keir not sneaking out, so I had stayed up all night last night, trying to listen and catch her in the act. . . but she never left.

"She has to be faking it," I said and watched as Keir brought over an iced latte for me.

She had never once brought my coffee over for me. It was always Gillard and Keir would use that time to mess with me while he was gone. She would ask how I slept or if I liked the show last night, but not today. I eyed her suspiciously.

"I am not," she said, her brown eyes locking on to mine. I looked down at the latte in her hand. "A peace offering."

I raised an eyebrow and Gillard choked on his coffee. He had to beat his chest to clear his throat. At least I was not alone in my shock.

"What do you want?" I asked, suspicion gnawing at me. I refused to take the coffee until I knew her reasoning, and I wouldn't put it past her to poison me.

"I realized I was being immature," she said, her voice lacking all its usual teasing. "Starting today, I will stop going out at night."

"Don't lie," Gillard snapped, his eyes narrowing at her. Obviously he had also tired of her shit.

Keir let out a huff and glared at him.

"I'm not," she insisted and shifted on her feet. "Her dedication surprised me. And she is so tired she can barely keep her eyes open."

She wasn't wrong. . . The late nights tired me immensely, and with the constant outings and having to join them in the morning for whatever Keir needed to do that day. . . I wasn't holding up well even after she had stopped sneaking out. I had hoped it wasn't too obvious, but of course the vampires could see through it.

"So what will you do instead?" I asked, still not believing her one bit.

Finally I took the coffee from her and took a sip. Bitterness spread across my tongue and my body immediately relaxed in the chair as the caffeine flooded my system.

God this is delicious.

"I am behind on paperwork," she said. "I will do that first and then prepare for the upcoming gathering."

"A gathering?" I asked and looked toward Gillard.

He let out a heavy sigh. "I knew it wasn't for nothing." I shot him a look. "It's when the leaders of the clans get together and they discuss important laws. It's just a game of social chess."

Great, I thought bitterly.

A bunch of high-ranking vampires, known for having human playthings, all in one place. If I wasn't loyal to the Order, I would think it was a perfect place to end them all.

"And I will need your assistance there," Keir said, finishing for him.

"What can I do?" I scoffed.

The vampires were more than capable of protecting themselves.

"Well, you can't go as a hunter. That would kill our reputation for working with your organization, but that would be the best place for an attack. So, we should be prepared." She paused and grabbed my hand, forcing me to come closer. "So, you will go as my date."

I ripped my hand away from hers, disgust filling me.

"Like hell I will," I growled. "I will not demean myself as such."

"That's actually not a bad idea," Gillard said in a soft tone.

"You can't be serious," I whined.

"Very," Keir said, satisfaction filling her tone. I turned and glared at her, but she met me with an irritating smirk. "And that's what we will be doing in our free time. You will be learning how to be presentable to other vampires."

"I don't give a fuck about that scum," I blurted out. Keir's eyes narrowed and she opened her mouth to say something, but Gillard answered first.

"But your employer does," he interrupted, his voice lowering. "And this is exactly what we hired you for."

He hadn't used that tone since we first met, and I knew he wasn't messing around. I swallowed the knot in my throat.

"Fine."

Keir gave me a sinister smile.

"Don't you fucking touch me," I snapped as Keir tried to reach out to me for the millionth time that day.

She ran her hand through her hair and let out an exasperated sigh. For the first time it was like our roles were reversed, and I was the one pushing her buttons. But I couldn't even enjoy it because I was constantly trying to shake off her touch.

It didn't take long for Keir and Gillard to start putting together their plan for how to make me a presentable date to the rest of the vampires. It was only mere hours until they dragged me across the house to some dusty and obviously unused ballroom. I shouldn't have been surprised at the scale of the place. . . but this clan seemed to put all the rumors about them to shame. They were much more than just the *royal family.*

The ballroom was empty save for the chairs and tables that were stacked near the back of the room, and our voices and the squeaks of my boots echoed around us. The floor was a white granite that was mixed with gold and shimmered under the five crystal chandlers that hung from the mural-painted ceiling. Both sides of the room had multiple floor-to-ceiling windows, letting the entire world know what a traitor I was.

It was downright embarrassing.

"But you have to learn," Gillard insisted. He crossed his arms and sent me a stern look. Dark purple bruised under his eyes, and his skin seemed paler than usual.

Gillard was almost always with us, except for when he was sleeping. . . but looking at him now I couldn't help but think that he got just as much sleep as I had the past few days.

"Then send a human if you want me to learn so bad," I said and crossed my hands across my chest.

Keir let out a small sigh and I turned to glare at her.

"You will have to touch me at the ball, you might as well get over it now," Keir said and circled her arms around me, forcing me against her body. She gripped one of my hands and placed it on her shoulder. I reluctantly held my other hand out for her to take. She wasted no time winding her fingers through mine.

I gritted my teeth against the instincts that told me to jerk back. One of her hands lingered on my waist and slid around to rest on the small of my back.

"See? Not bad. And I didn't even have to play the debt card that time," she joked.

"Shouldn't you be dancing with a man?" I jabbed at her as the hand on my lower back pushed me closer to her. Our chests were almost flush, and I was eye level with the bare skin of her collarbones.

A shiver of disgust ran through me, and I averted my gaze to the shoulder that my hand was clasped on.

"They know my sexual preference, and even if they didn't, I have nothing to hide," she said.

I could feel her eyes burning holes into the side of my face, so I took just a moment to look up, only to see her gaze fall to my lips. Her eyes flashed just the slightest red and the side of her lips twitched with amusement.

I rolled my eyes at her before planting them back on my own hand, feeling uncomfortable at the constant staring.

"Okay, now step back," Gillard commanded and both Keir and I followed suit. "To the side."

Keir and I had different definition of sides because she went right and I went left, causing me to stumble over her feet. Her grip on my waist tightened and stopped my descent to the marble floor below us.

"This is useless," I grumbled feeling my cheeks flush.

Keir helped me back into position, this time pulling me even closer so our entire bodies were flush.

"Just let me lead," she said in a low whisper that was far too close to my ear.

"Fuck off," I growled under my breath.

"Again," Gillard commanded.

Gillard continued to walk us through the steps while Keir and I silently danced in the empty ballroom. After a while I stopped stepping on Keir's toes, but only after I finally just allowed her to pull me around like a rag doll. She didn't even listen to Gillard's commands and was always a few steps ahead of him.

Her fingers were still threaded through mine and her other hand sat against my lower back, far too close to my ass, which made my mind wander far too often during the last few dances. It is not that there was anything wrong with her hands, and *that* was why they were distracting me. . . it was because they felt different than I expected.

They felt *human*.

They were soft as they threaded through mine and with each shift of her hand on my back, and the way her thumb rubbed mindless circles on my skin, there was a burst of heat that ran through me.

Now I couldn't even be disgusted by her touch. . . because there was nothing *wrong* with her touch. . . it was *me* who I was disgusted with.

"You have to look at her," Gillard ordered from his seat.

I was about to groan out a complaint, but I swallowed my pride and lifted my gaze to hers. My pulse stuttered when I realized she was already staring at me. The black hair that was usually so neatly combed back fell lightly into her face, breaking the perfectly crafted royal facade she put on. Her lips were tilted, but this time into a small smile instead of a smirk.

And her eyes were pure brown.

"Don't look so confused," Keir drawled. "It's not like this is the first time you have seen me."

I averted my gaze as a heat crept up my neck. I was staring too long.

"It's not the first but I wish it was the last," I said under my breath.

A growl sprang forth from her chest, and I flinched at the suddenness of it.

"Look at me," she commanded.

I looked back up at her and tried to keep her gaze as long as possible, like Gillard had asked. Without her eyes giving away her vampire status. . . she looked almost human. So much so that I began to relax against her as she pulled me through move after move.

My feet were sore, and my legs began to ache, but I didn't dare utter a complaint. Instead, I just followed Keir's lead and tried to keep eye contact with her, just like a loving date should.

"Is my touch as disgusting as you thought it would be?" she asked.

My mind was pushed into frenzied thoughts, panicking as I realized she read me *far* too well. Not even Cain and Jade could pull thoughts from me so clearly as that. I didn't *want* them to, I didn't want *anyone* to.

Before I could respond she crushed me against her. Her shirt was still unbuttoned and had spread open, showing a lot more of her chest as we danced. I felt the heat of her skin against my cheek and it startled me. This was intimate, much more intimate than we would ever need to be. Until now she had taken precautions to only touch my skin where needed, but this became too much. The hand that was on my waist started roaming slightly downward.

"Well?" she coaxed, her voice low in my ear.

"Spin her," Gillard commanded, breaking the tension that had surrounded us.

Keir chuckled softly and did as she was told. I followed her spin but was caught off guard when she snapped me back to her, far harder than a human would, and dipped me. Her hand slowly made its way up my stomach, then over my breasts and finally gripped my neck and forced my chin up to expose my neck. I felt her bury her head in my neck and inhale deeply.

Against my better wishes, I felt another shiver pass down

my body. This one was definitely not from disgust. When her lips brushed across my neck, the flimsy turtleneck material was no match for the heat radiating out of her.

"Enough," I snapped.

She slowly let me up but kept her face only a few inches from mine. The playfulness in her eyes told me she was enjoying this far too much. I narrowed my eyes.

"Don't look so scary," she teased. "It's unbecoming of a lady."

"Good thing I am not one," I said and put some distance between her and me. "I will be checking in at the base tomorrow."

Keir frowned and crossed her arms over her chest. The image of the overgrown vampire child flashed through my mind, and I tried to keep down the smile that was forcing itself to my face.

She doesn't want anyone else taking her toy.

"Can't you just call them?" Keir asked.

I raised my eyebrow at her. "Afraid I'll quit?" I challenged with a small smirk.

Her brows furrowed at my words and her eyes searched mine.

"I will have someone give you a ride," Gillard said, interrupting the silence between us.

I was about to say thank you, however, I caught myself before and turned to leave the room.

"Don't take too long!" Keir called after me.

CHAPTER 8
SILVIA

"Silv, you're alive!" Jade practically screamed as I entered the base.

Her erratic footsteps echoed off the walls and that, combined with a flash of purple hair, was the only warning I had before she crashed into me. I wrapped my arms around her and looked over her head to see Cain slowly walking up to us. He was in his Hunter uniform and gave me a small wave.

"It's only been a few weeks," I reminded her and held her at arms length.

Jade was also wearing her Hunter uniform, which raised some red flags in my mind. I looked down and noticed that thankfully no weapons were strapped to her, but I didn't feel good about this.

"I know, but I was so worried," she said, her eyes started to tear and her voice held a slight tremble to it.

"Are you getting taken care of?" I asked Cain.

He shrugged and buried his hands in his pockets. His expression was blank and his gaze held mine, he gave absolutely nothing away.

"It's not much, but better than having to go on actual missions for money. We will be fine until you get back," he said after I held his gaze for a moment longer than normal.

"Then why are you both in uniform?" I asked and looked down at Jade. When she looked down I squeezed her shoulder lightly.

"It's nothing really," she replied, her voice trailing toward the end.

I looked back to Cain, but this time his eyes were locked onto Jade.

"Come," I said and turned Jade around to face the empty hallway. "I need to debrief and head straight back."

The walk to the captain's office was a short one, but I slowed my pace as Jade began to ramble on about the happenings since I had been gone.

"The academy students have been asking where you've gone to," she said with a light laugh. "Cain told them to stop bothering us one day, but they refused until they had some idea of what you were doing."

A small smile spread across my face. My chest warmed at the thought of being missed by them. I may hate the Order, but the people who enrolled here were just like me and all came from various tough situations. The Order was the last resort of many when the world had chewed them up and spit them out. . . They all but crawled to the Order for saving.

I could understand that.

These were people who just wanted to *live*. They just wanted the same luxuries as everyone else in the world, and many people didn't even know just how shitty the Order was until they were already bound by their contracts.

"I don't even talk to the students," I said, the smile still on my face.

"Apparently they watch you," Cain said.

Immediately my face flushed and my smile dropped. I came in the morning and pounded into whatever available punching bag they had and left a sweaty, god-awful mess.

"No-o," Jade stuttered. "He means they watch to learn. Learn from your form."

I nodded but stayed quiet. This is the second time someone has read me so easily in the last few days, and I was worried it was becoming a pattern.

"Are they making you work?" I asked as the captain's office came into view.

Jade and Cain both paused by my side. I stopped as well and turned to look back at them. Cain was giving Jade a cold look while she was fidgeting.

"We've been working on this new project since you have been gone," Jade blurted and her words started to rush out like she had been trying too hard to hold them in.. "You would not believe how ingenious it is. It is going to change how we fight vampires forever. Like you cannot—"

"You can't talk about it, Jade," Cain commented.

I frowned and walked forward to loop my arm through Jade's and pull her down the hallway.

"Why not?" I asked. "We're a team, you can tell me anything."

"I can't, Silv." Jade pouted and tried to removed her arm from mine but I held tight. "It's top secret! Captain made us swear!"

"Speaking of *top secret*," Cain nudged my side. "How's the royal family treating you?"

I gritted my teeth at the reminder of Keir. I was not excited about the upcoming event, and I really was starting to regret taking such a stupid job.

"Fine," I said. "Nothing exciting."

Not wanting to talk about this anymore, and realizing that

I had delayed my debriefing enough, I gave Jade a small hug and waved my goodbye. Just as my hand touched the cool metal knob Jade's voice rang out.

"Can we visit you?" she asked.

I paused.

"No," I said. "They do not trust witches apparently."

When I looked back at Jade her face had already fallen, though Cain's showed no sign that he was offended by that comment.

"I'll visit soon," I promised.

Jade nodded and without another word I entered the office.

Luckily there was no random vampire in the room, and I was met with just the captain sitting at his dark wood desk as he stared at the computer in front of him. He gave no indication that he heard me come in, so I waited by the door and watched him.

His hair had been graying for years, but today it seemed extra prominent. His lips were pursed into a scowl, and his eyes were narrowed as if wishing death on the contraption in front of him.

I had only been gone for a few weeks, but it felt like much longer as I took in details of the man that I hadn't noticed before.

"Sit," he commanded, his eyes still not leaving the screen.

With a sigh I walked forward and sat on one of the chairs in front of him, the leather squeaking against the fabric of my pants as I sank into it. I reached for the pens on his desk, just to find something to mess with until he gave me any attention.

When he still didn't talk to me after a few minutes, I trailed my fingers along the edge of the desk and my hand grasped the metal picture frame. Even though it was facing him, the image of the old graduating class had been burned into my mind since the first time I saw it on his desk. But it wasn't just any class.

It was my parents'.

"How is the job? Any mistreatment of humans?" he inquired.

The captain was a sentimental man even if he didn't say it, but like him I wasn't much of a feelings person.

"No sign, yet," I said, pulling my hand back from the frame and crossing my arms over my chest. "There is an event coming up apparently that the heir needs protection for. Besides that, it really is just like babysitting."

He rubbed his chin and let out a humming noise. For a minute I played with the idea of telling the captain that the heir was a girl and not a guy like I originally thought, but I decided it wasn't worth the trouble to explain.

"The royal family has only just recently begun working with us in this capacity. And on top of that they have been paying more than any of our other clients," he mused.

I shifted in my seat. They had been through hunter after hunter, and each had failed spectacularly. If they had to pay my debt on top of whatever the Order charged for fees. . . they were willing to pay a lot of money for such a mediocre job.

"Because the transfer of power?" I offered.

"Only time will tell," he said with a sigh, "If you really do accomplish this, it will be nothing short of amazing. There have been far too many hunters that have failed. It is giving the Order a bad look."

I didn't know if I should be happy about the compliment or panicked about the additional weight he just dumped on my shoulders. There was still a long time to go, and given how she'd been acting, I was scared that this was just the calm before the storm.

"That's kind of you. . . *sir*. I should get back, though."

He nodded and waved me off. I stood and turned back to the door, grateful that this was such an easy debriefing.

"Don't hesitate to get in touch with me if anything seems fishy," the captain called out.

A coldness ran through me and I turned back to look at the captain. When his eyes met mine I couldn't help but shudder at the intensity.

"Does something seem weird to you?" I asked.

The captain sat back and thrummed his fingers at the edge of the desk.

"It's just a lot of money for babysitting," he said. "And not a job I would have normally given to someone of your level."

I swallowed thickly and nodded.

"If I see anything I will contact you," I said and rushed out of the office.

I didn't run into Jade and Cain on the way out, and for that, I was grateful.

The talk with the captain hadn't left my mind the entire way to the compound. Luckily, I had come alone, so I had time to think over his warning and the oddities that surrounded the royal family.

They were known to be the most powerful, most blood-thirsty clan that had forced all the others into submission. . . and yet their heir was a full-on child and they lived in harmony with the humans. Whenever I had a free second I would peer around corners and sneak into rooms to try and find any evidence that the family was mistreating humans. . . but I found nothing.

Even the waitstaff and maids that they employed seemed to be happy under their care.

I had no doubt that they had fresh blood bags somewhere, royalty like them wouldn't demean themselves by drinking from anything but the source. But laws that protected the contracts between vampire and a consensual giver were complicated and would be much harder to use if I wanted to bring them down.

As I stepped through the compound's double doors, a vampire maid was already waiting for me. Her blonde hair was pulled into a perfect bun that sat on top of her head, and she wore the blouse and long skirt combo that the other maids in this house wore.

"Is there something you need?" I asked.

Her eyes shifted to the stairs and her hands gripped the fabric of her skirt.

"I am here to take you to the young mistress," she said and averted her gaze.

I shifted on my feet, my hand automatically landing on the dagger that was strapped to my thigh. She caught the movement and took a step back, her eyes shifting to mine once more.

Is she. . . scared?

"Is she not in her office?" I asked.

"No, miss," she answered.

The grip she had on her skirt turned her knuckles white.

I nodded and motioned for her to take me there. With jerky movements she walked in front of me and took me through a corridor that I had only seen when Gillard first gave me a tour of this manor. He didn't go into much detail on what or who resided in this area, but I had a feeling it wasn't good.

While the decoration and style of the house did not change, the entire aura of the house shifted, and the temperature dropped a few degrees. Each step echoed through the hallways and as we got closer, her pace sped up.

She abruptly turned when we reached an unassuming door and motioned for me to open it. I stared at her for a hard moment and saw a drop of sweat fall from her temple.

Clenching my jaw, I turned and without hesitation pushed the door open. There were three figures standing in the middle of the dimly lit room, but that was all I got before loud slaps echoed in the small space.

I watched in mute shock as the vampire who I was charged to protect and watch over until they accepted their position as head of this clan was slapped across the face not one, not two, but *three* times. Each slap reverberated in the room, progressively getting louder, the man in front of Keir undoubtedly using his vampire speed to deliver the blows.

The man's hand gripped at her collar and lifted her so her feet were barely touching the ground. She didn't struggle or stiffen as he delivered the blows, her body hung slack and her head turned away from the door. Her dark hair had fallen over her face, and for a moment, I thought the man had actually killed her.

The man had long dark hair that was pulled into a loose ponytail that rested at the nape of his neck. His wild red eyes snapped over to me and his lips turned into a snarl before he blinked once, then twice, and straightened himself. He wore a navy jacket over a button-up shirt and slacks, the same type of curated clothing that I noted as common among those with royal blood. Vampires didn't age so he looked only a bit older than Keir. . . but something about his aura made me think he was much older than he looked.

Gillard shot a panicked look toward me, but I ignored him and focused solely on the man who was harming my current contract.

Inside I was screaming for her to fight back. To show the man the same person she showed me when she threw me against the wall that night in anger. I wanted her to snap out of whatever trance he had her in and demolish him. . . but she didn't.

"I seemed to have missed something while I was gone," I commented coolly, one hand fell to my dagger while the other grasped at the hilt of my sword.

Each move was watched by the man and a smile spread across his face. Carefully he put Keir back down and stalked toward me. I stood straight and held his gaze as he approached.

"My apologies that you had to see that." He bowed slightly and gripped the hand that was against my dagger as if he wanted to kiss it. I yanked my hand out of his grip before he could think to do anything with it.

He smiled at my actions as if it amused him.

"I was just teaching my *daughter* a lesson," he said in a low tone.

His daughter.

My eyes narrowed at him and I gritted my teeth as I bowed in front of him. It made my blood boil to have to show any submission to their kind, but he was no one to mess with. He could snap my neck in an instant, and if he treated his daughter with such violence. . . I didn't have to guess what he did to humans. He dismissed my bow.

This was the man who had a choke hold on the entire vampire race. They feared him and did his bidding regardless of what it was. If he was unhappy, so was everyone else. If he asked you to kill for him, you would. He had everything and anything at his fingertips, which included me at this very moment.

The rumor was that he had become tired of ruling after all these years, but I could see right through that facade. He was weakening. You could tell by his hollowed eyes and thin skin.

It was also obvious in the way he tried to overpower her. If he had any real power, he wouldn't need to go to such lengths to force her into submission.

A coward if I've ever seen one.

"May I ask what lesson she needed to be taught?" I looked toward Gillard, and he was shaking his head at me. Keir still didn't meet my eyes.

"You should already know very well," he said and stalked back toward Keir. "She has been sneaking out again."

Even though he had already slapped her, he was poised to do more damage. It was in his stance. In the way he walked. He had a mind full of awful things, and I knew if I hesitated too long I would see them unfold right before my eyes.

"Where did you hear that from?" I interjected.

He stopped in his tracks but did not turn to look at me.

"I have eyes everywhere," he said, watching Keir closely.

"She has been behaving," I said and tried not to shrink when his gaze snapped to mine. "I've been keeping an eye on her, and she hasn't been sneaking out. I even switched my sleep schedule to make sure she didn't."

"So, my eyes have been lying?" he asked. His tone was disbelieving, as if no one would dare lie on her behalf.

Looking at Keir now, I still wasn't sure why the words even came out of my mouth.

"I would say they are mistaken, not lying," I replied.

"I thought you said she was the one, yet here she is fighting for her," he spat at Gillard. His rage was palpable and swirled around us erratically, creating a thick tension.

"She is, sir," he said, his voice shaky.

"If it's about my hate for your kind," I trailed and gripped the hilt of my sword. "Then that's not a lie. Every minute I'm here I rethink if paying my debt is worth the hell that I put myself through, having to see your kind every waking minute of the day. I just want to make sure everyone's facts are straight, but if you don't believe me then hit her some more. I have been dying to do it myself."

Keir's eyes met mine, her expression unreadable.

Raphael let out a booming laugh that caused me to nearly jump out of my skin. The once-angry aura disappeared, and we were left with a different version of the clan leader. He clapped a hand on Keir's shoulder and made his way to the door where I was standing.

"Maybe you were the correct choice," he said in a low voice. "If you would like to deliver the next punishment, I would gladly give it to you."

His words twisted my stomach.

"If I'm here, that won't be necessary," I said in a tense tone.

Both Keir and Gillard watched the two of us. Raphael let out a hum and, without any other words, left the room. I could hear the maid that brought me in here scurry after him, her heels clicking across the floor.

We all stood still without talking. I understood what needed to happen, and I waited for their signal that Raphael was out of hearing range.

The signal I was given was being slammed against the wall by Keir. The wind was knocked out of me and my vision went blurry. The only thing that I could hear over my own pounding heart was her snarls. Her face was mere inches away from mine and her fangs were on display. Her eyes were as crazed as her father's were.

"Do you understand what you have just done?" she snarled. The hand that had felt so human once was now wrapped around my neck.

"Saved you from a beating apparently," I pushed out through my gasps of air.

Gillard pulled Keir off me and I had to reach out to the wall to keep myself from falling over. After a few deep breaths Gillard finally decided to speak.

"Lying to him was stupid," he said, agreeing with Keir.

"It wasn't a lie," I said, trying to calm my heart.

Keir stood a few feet away from me, still breathing heavily. Her cheek was still red and there were distinct finger marks from her father's hand.

"It doesn't count as sneaking if I let her go," I said. "I knew where she was going and who went with her. No sneaking involved. I was in full control of the situation"

"Why did you interfere?" Gillard asked softly.

The softness and change in his demeanor made me want to tell him that the real vampires who were scum were people like Raphael, but I clamped down on that feeling and locked it deep inside.

"It doesn't matter," I responded and left the room without another word.

The next time I saw Keir, she refused to look at me. I followed her around all day, but she did not look at me or talk to me. It was not until late that night when she was shuffling through paperwork and I was reading a book that she make any conversation.

"I didn't have sex with your sister," she whispered.

I paused, afraid she misspoke.

"I said that to get on your nerves," she admitted. "I actually just met her in passing, I didn't know what became of her."

I took a deep breath. I hadn't put much thought into if it actually happened or not, but somehow still felt glad that it wasn't true.

"I'm sorry," Keir said after a pause.

I watched her carefully, her brown eyes met mine and my heart skipped a beat once more.

"I didn't know your kind was capable of feeling sorry," I said and went back to my book, uncomfortable with the feeling her words brought.

"If you weren't so disgusted with my kind, I could show you how sorry I am." Her voice did not have a teasing edge. It was dead serious and made my heart skip another beat. The hair on the back of my neck stood up and a flush traveled over my skin. My mind immediately went back to the night that I saw her on the bed with another women. The way she brought that woman to orgasm again and again caused my own core to ache with need.

"No need," I responded thickly.

She chuckled.

I tried to focus on the book in front of me, but ended up rereading the same paragraph multiple times. The tension in this room had changed and my uniform began sticking to me uncomfortably.

What is happening to me?

I let out a sigh and leaned back on the couch, trying to regain myself.

"We are not as bad as you may think," Keir said after another short pause, then added, "My father may be, and the people who killed your family, of course. But we are not. *Most* are not." She paused one more time. "*I* am not."

"I'll believe it when I see it," I muttered turning back to my book.

"You know," she trailed, I could hear the smile in her tone. "Your indifference kind of turns me on."

Heat flashed through me so strongly that I had trouble keeping a straight face. I turned to her with a glare.

"You're disgusting, you know that?" I asked.

She leaned forward and propped her chin on her hand, her eyes twinkling in the dim overhead light.

"Your wet cunt tells me that's a lie," she purred.

Jesus fucking—

I instinctively clenched my thighs together. I gripped the book hard enough that the sound of the straining pages filled the silent air.

If there wasn't tension between us before, now there definitely was.

The air was thick and was as hot as my face as it flushed. I tried to swallow, to reel myself in, but what was happening between us was overwhelming.

"I almost thought you had a heart," I said in a shaky voice. "Turns out you are just as disgusting as you have always been."

She smirked before looking back toward her papers.

"It's cute," she said in an amused tone. "When the color of your face matches your hair."

Letting out a noise of disgust, I threw the book down to the ground and practically sprinted out of the room. Keir's chuckle followed closely behind me only to be cut off as I slammed her door.

CHAPTER 9

KEIR

H er actions infuriated me. Started a fire so deep and so potent that I truly believed it would burn me from the inside out. She was such a stupid, reckless hunter that I wondered how she even became such a high rank.

She had to have been lucky through her last few years at the Order. . . or maybe she was paired with people with much more sense than her, because who the *fuck* would look my father in the eyes and lie so blatantly. He wanted her to see. He wanted me to be humiliated in front of her, but instead of taking the bait she turned around and surprised us all.

She should have told the truth, I thought as I stared at the smooth wood of the desk in front of me. *Why didn't she?*

After her actions, I couldn't help but feel even worse about what I had said regarding Jane. I didn't understand why her actions made me feel so strongly. One moment I was ready to tear her limb from limb and the next I wanted to *beg her* to believe me. I didn't understand why I wanted her to believe me so much. I didn't know why that every time her eyes softened, a rush went through me.

It is about sex, I tried to remind myself. *That's what I am after.*

But the more I saw her unusual reactions, the more unsure I became.

It was fear, I realized. When I saw her stand up to Father. . . a new type of fear filled me. If I was being logical, I should have pushed her to disobey Father even more and gotten her fired or worse. It would be the easiest way out of this contract and the best way to secure my freedom. But when I saw her icy blue eyes harden and her hand grip her sword, I was overcome with emotion. I thought for sure she would just watch, but she even interfered on my behalf.

She was ready to fight a battle no one even dared to start. . . not even me.

No one had ever stopped him before. Even when I was just a child and was beaten and starved by him, no one would step in. They would let the small, sad child cry herself to sleep every night, even when those cries had turned into screams.

But Silvia. . . the person who hated our kind with such a fiery passion, was the only one to stop his assault. A few slaps were nothing compared to what he had done before, but the humiliation of it was far more potent. When she spoke out, all the fear and anger hardened and felt like a weight in my stomach. When his red eyes met with her unwavering stare, I thought for sure that I could see the thoughts in his head.

Hunter or not, he would make her scream for him. Make her regret her actions, no matter the cost. He was the only one in this family who still loved to use and abuse humans. He would show her no mercy and wouldn't stop until she paid him back in full for what she had done.

As soon as he left, the fear that filled me turned into anger.

I was ready to give her the beating myself. Teach her that my kind wasn't to be taken lightly and if she ever did that again. . . she wouldn't come out of it alive.

Even after she had left for the night, the events played in my mind on repeat. My fear and anger mixed and made a volatile combo.

How dare she put herself in harm's way like that?

How dare she endanger her life like that?

Does she know that my father would love to keep her as his pet?

But then she met me with more lies. We knew she was lying, that much was too obvious to deny. . . but why?

Why did she endanger herself like that? Did she really have no self-preservation tactics?

The apology from me came naturally. I was sorry and did feel bad, after she had stood up to Father for me, that I had thrown her dead family in her face like that. It wasn't right, even if I wanted to get a rise out of her.

I could hear Silvia's light breathing in the other room and let out a sigh. She had stayed awake for a long time tonight, tossing and turning, but finally she was asleep.

"Gillard," I called and in less than a minute Gillard was walking into my room with a strained smile on his face.

"I like to sleep early as well," he said in a joking tone. "Maybe I should move my room farther away just so I can catch some sleep."

I rolled my eyes at him. He may have told Silvia that he needed sleep, but he never told her how much. He could sustain himself with about four hours and be a functioning vampire the next day, but it helped that Silvia could cover those four hours for him while she "babysat" me.

"Get me all the files you have on her family's murder," I said.

His eyes widened and he paused. I could feel his brain trying to work at a thousand miles a minute.

"Are you sure you should be getting involved to this extent?" he asked.

"I owe her for what she did with Father," I explained.

Gillard hung his head low. I knew why. He had never once dared to openly go against Father. He was afraid, but so was I. The only one who seemed not to be was Silvia, and I desperately hoped she would not live to regret it.

He nodded and left back the way he came. I sat back in my chair and peered at the dark ground outside, waiting for him to come back. It was less than ten minutes before he came back into my room with the file in hand.

"I have seen most of it before," he explained, crossing the room, and dropped the file on my desk. "But have at it."

I looked over them with Gillard watching over my shoulder. He pointed out some of the more gruesome details that stood out to him. . . like the arms of the parents being torn off, presumably when they were still alive. It was hard to hold back my disgust after looking at the pictures. The murders were brutal. No vampire would dare to leave a mess like this for a feeding.

No, there had to be much more than this. When feeding, adult vampires were usually very neat and even in the ones that ended in murder, there was always another reason for that. A lot of those cases were sexual in nature, but this was nothing of the sort.

This was hatred.

"Silvia found the bodies," Gillard whispered and handed me a picture of a younger, bloodstained Silvia. Her blue eyes that were normally filled with a spark of defiance were dead, and her red hair was a mess around her head.

"It wasn't a feeding," I concluded. I couldn't look away from Silvia's face as she stared at me through the picture.

I knew she was in the room next to me and perfectly fine, but I couldn't shake the sadness that radiated from this picture. This was a person who had just lost everything and was in pain.

"No. . . my guess is revenge. Everyone in her family was a hunter," he said and reached over me to turn the page to see the family's history. "Great ones at that. Over three hundred missions between them. The Order gave them a Medal of Honor when they died."

I scoffed at the actions of the Order. They were the reason they died in the first place. If they had not built a reputation for themselves, they may have still been alive today.

"Yet they gave Silvia her family's debt," I mused and pulled the picture of Silvia back out and placed it on my desk. I ran my finger over Silvia's bloodstained cheek, and an obscene picture of her covered in her own blood and writhing under me flashed across my mind.

"Probably to keep her with them," he mused. "They were reluctant to hand her over if we paid for her full debt. Rumor has it she has yet to fail a mission."

Until this one, a voice whispered in the back of my head. Though, I wasn't so sure of my plans anymore.

"How did you get them to agree?" I peered at him, and he met me with a smile.

"I told him if we did not get the best, we would cut ties with the Order for good." He paused. "Not like we would ever get out of *that* contract."

I let out a laugh at his coyness. "You devil."

CHAPTER 10
SILVIA

O n the day of the event, I was awoken by Keir storming into my room with boxes in her arms. I jumped up and flung myself toward the knife that was resting on my nightstand. She rolled her eyes at me and shut the door with her foot before she crossed the room and sat directly on my bed.

I pointed the knife at her and pushed myself far up the bed, as far away from her as I could get.

"Oh stop," she said. "It's not like that flimsy thing could do anything."

I scowled at her.

"Want to test that theory?" I growled and flung the covers out of the way to stand at the side of the bed. She watched me closely as I did, her eyes drifting down my form.

Angered by her lack of respect and violation of my space, I placed the dagger under her chin just so she could feel how real my threat was.

"Just the other day you were willing to lay your life down for me," she said and licked her lips. "What happened?"

Her red and swollen cheek flashed across my mind and slowly I withdrew the dagger.

"Don't get cocky," I warned.

She leaned back and brought a hand to the boxes that were on her lap.

"I hope you are ready for today," she said in a low tone. "It is important for me. For the future of our clan."

I swallowed thickly. This was the first time I had ever seen Keir this serious, and for someone like her who seemed to love to party more than she liked to work, I never expected this from her.

But then again, I didn't know her that well. All I knew were the rumors of her family's brutality and the little bit of her life that I had seen the past few weeks. But even then, I knew this was her plea to me.

"I am ready," I said and put the dagger back on the nightstand. With my free hands I reached out to grab the boxes in her hand, but the smirk spreading across her face stopped me.

"Maybe I should wake you up more often," she said, her voice dropping an octave. "That is some nice sleepwear you have there."

The flimsy thing in question was a light blue night slip that barely covered anything and was something I totally forgot I was wearing until this moment. I had been too distracted by her storming into my room, so I hadn't even tried to cover myself.

I ignored the urge I had to cover up and reached toward the boxes again. I refused to let her know that she had any sort of impact on me. Opening the boxes, I was met with a beautiful gown that made my heart skip a beat. As I pulled out the dress, marveling at the soft fabric, I felt her hand gently curl around a lock of my hair. I froze and cringed internally at my reaction.

She lightly brushed my hair off my shoulder, making me shiver at the contact.

"Don't touch me," I muttered.

"We have to act the part, remember?" she teased and yanked my hand, making me drop the dress.

She used the chance to push the boxes to the floor and pull me between her legs. I tried to pull back, but her hands moved to my hips, and with a strength like hers, I was planted to the space. The thin fabric of the slip did nothing to protect against the heat of her skin, and I couldn't help but shiver at the contact.

"In public. This is private," I reminded her, avoiding her gaze like the plague.

One of her hands brushed the outside of my thigh softly, making another round of shivers go through me.

"It's okay," she whispered. "It's just us."

Her hand slipped under the hem of the slip, and heat pooled in my stomach as she lightly massaged my thighs. My breath caught and I glared down at her, but her gaze was elsewhere.

I gripped her shoulders tightly.

"Stop," I commanded.

"But they are so perfect," she whined and leaned closer to my breasts.

The shivers had caused my nipples to harden, and they now stood out clear as day against the fabric. She saw them too and her mouth was heading right for them. The heat inside me intensified and in that moment I could think of nothing more then her mouth on me.

I should stop her.

I could stop her; she wasn't holding me very tightly. But a part of me didn't want to. A part of me had been waiting for this. Whether it was her or another woman, I longed to be touched after so long of not.

She took one nipple into her mouth through the slip and gave it a soft bite. I had to close my eyes to re-center myself, and by now my nails were digging into her shoulders. My breath hitched as she bit down, harder this time, and I could feel my now-wet panties sticking to me.

"I don't want to be touched by your kind," I complained, yet I didn't push her away.

She noticed as well and softly sucked on my nipple. Her hands trailed farther up and under my slip, playing with the lace underwear I had on. As she tugged on them, I felt myself lose all sense of self, all I could focus on was the way she was making my body feel. She bit my nipple once more and this time I couldn't stifle the moan. She paused and I could feel her eyes, but I couldn't look at her.

"It seems like your mouth tells lies," she said, her words muffled by my nipple. She moved her hands from under my slip and onto my shoulders, slipping off the nightgown, exposing my breasts to her. The familiar sensation was what called me back to reality.

The image of Dimitri pulling off my dress in the same manner filled my head. I snapped out of whatever trance her lips had put me under and pushed her away for real this time. She let me and said nothing as I tried to regain myself.

I put my slip back on and took a calming breath, glaring at her. My skin was flushed, and the room felt far too small for both of us to occupy this space.

What came over me?

I was acting like some type of animal, letting her paw at me like that. Had this place really messed with my head that much?

"Don't do that again," I warned, though we both knew it was an empty threat.

She watched me, then leaned back on the bed. Her head tilted and clear amusement played on her face. Her shirt was spread open, due to my pulling at it as her mouth was on me, and now showed a dangerous amount of bare chest.

I swallowed the knot in my throat.

"You don't hate us as much as you say you do." Her fangs showed as she flashed me a smile.

It would be a lie if I didn't admit how attractive Keir was. Her sharp jaw, straight nose, and hooded expression could make anyone's knees weak. She topped that off with the sinful outfits she wore, which nearly gave me a heart attack.

"I would rather die than let you touch me like that again," I hissed and began to pick up what I was going to wear.

"We will have to see, won't we?" she asked and stood.

She stepped toward me and I had to step back to take in her expression.

"Don't do that again," I repeated, more to myself than her at this point. "I have a job to do."

She hummed but said nothing before she turned to leave the room.

"Three hours," she called just as she opened the door. When she turned to me she licked her lips before shutting the door behind her.

Bastard.

I took my time getting ready. I made sure to shower using all of the fragrant soaps they provided and put extra time into taming the red mess that was on my head. Normally, I wouldn't have cared much, but the way her voice sounded when she told me how important this was stirred something in me.

Stepping out into the hallway, I wasn't surprised to see Gillard and Keir already waiting for me. Keir was dressed in a way that made my mouth dry. She wore the same white open-necked shirt, showing off the long golden chain necklace she wore. The pants hugged her figure and rings decorated each of her fingers. Her hair was slicked back, and for the first time, dark charcoal lined her eyes. I shook off all the naughty thoughts in my head and held it high.

I was more than this, and I was determined to prove it.

The gown from the box was a deep-blue silk with a hem that stopped right at my ankles. It was held on with flimsy straps that left the majority of my back exposed, which also meant that I couldn't wear a bra. Luckily there was a white shawl that wrapped around my shoulders. It was all paired with small gold heels that would be god-awful to dance in.

Gillard was also dressed up slightly but did not look as different as Keir did. His hair was neatly pulled back and his skin was refreshed. He was not decked with jewelry and makeup, but he looked good nonetheless.

"You look nice," he commented.

"So do both of you." I quickly froze when I realized what I'd said. "For scum, that is."

My face felt hot as a laugh escaped from Keir. Gillard's eyes twinkled, and I thought maybe for a moment he would join in too, but he remained silent.

Keir grabbed my arm and laced it through hers. The action bringing flashbacks of earlier through my mind.

"Time to pretend," she whispered in my ear.

I cleared my throat and gave her a smile. Her eyes widened and she straightened her posture. A light blush coated her cheeks before she cleared her throat as well.

"Let's go," she said and pulled me down the hallway.

Surprisingly she took me right to where we had practiced a few days before, and the space had been transformed. The dusty ballroom was no more and now in front of us was a lively party that packed the area. There were tables strewn throughout, but most people were up dancing and chatting.

It was hell on earth for me when I realized just *how many* vampires had come. They littered the place and many had brought their slaves as dates. There were bites marring the humans' skin and it was almost as if their bites were intentionally shown. The humans wore dresses similar to mine, but they had no shawls, and the violence committed against them was on display for all to see.

As long as the human consented to giving up their blood, the law allowed it. . . but I wondered how many of them lost their reasoning after the first bite. Vampire venom had many properties, healing being one of the better ones while the lust-filled haze you got after the bite ranked lower on the list. Humans have been shown to get easily addicted to the feeling and many times the Order has had to intervene to save them from themselves.

It was why I refused to let a vampire bite me.

"Let's dance," Keir whispered in my ear.

I gulped, a sudden nervousness running through me as I realized all eyes would be on me. I took a deep breath and nodded, letting her guide me to the dance floor. Gillard left us with a nod and went to go mingle with the vampires.

I followed Keir's steps like we had practiced, making sure to hold on to her gaze, no matter how uncomfortable it may have been. I forced a smile on my face, and in return she gave me a devious smirk.

"Don't get any ideas," I warned.

"It's not me who has any ideas, I assure you." She chuckled

and squeezed my waist. "Just remember how willing you were to have my mouth on you."

The issue wasn't her words, but that they were correct. Anger boiled under my skin and I opened my mouth to deliver a snarky comment, but she interrupted me.

"Remember our deal," she whispered.

"Yes, I remember," I said under my breath, keeping the fake smile on my face. "I can't wait until you try that again and see what happens to your throat."

"Maybe we can ditch this early and you can show me," she said with a suggestive tone.

Before I could speak again, we were interrupted by Gillard.

"It's my turn to dance with Miss Silvia," he said with a smile.

Keir frowned but passed me to him. She lingered for a moment before dismissing herself and disappearing into the crowd.

"I hope she has not bothered you too much," he said.

My fake smile faltered when I remembered what transpired this morning. Not only that, but I was so close to all these vampires and was even dancing with a few.

"No, I am still good to finish this mission," I assured him.

"Good, I do believe you are the only. . . person able to put up with her," he said, then lowered his voice. "And one of the only ones not to fall for her acts."

My blood froze at the underlying meaning of his words. How much did he know?

"Yes, I could see how her acts could be convincing," I muttered.

It was not long after our conversation that he allowed me to take a break from dancing. By that time my feet were aching in the heels, and I had lost count of how many times I had stepped on Gillard's toes. Dancing was the least of my worries though. As I rested on one of the seats near the edge of the ballroom, I surveyed the crowd. There were so many influential vampires here, it was the perfect opportunity to take them all out.

The world would change overnight. Clans would lose leaders and the contracts that the Order had signed with them to keep the peace would be null and void. As much as I wanted to see them all burn in hell. . . the killing of all of them would cause more harm than good.

And I would be forced to pay back my debt.

Just then, in the corner of my eye, I saw a figure sneak out of the ballroom and into a dark corridor. There were only a few exits, and many of the people who have come and gone had been servants of this compound. . . but this person looked to be in a rush. Suspicion weighed heavily in my gut and I looked to see where my current prison guards were. Both Keir and Gillard were in deep conversations with other vampires and paying no mind to me. I used this chance to sneak away and follow the person.

The corridor was darkened, but it was light enough to see a woman at the end. She was dressed in a floor-length gown and she was covered in bite marks, much worse than a lot of the others I had seen dancing with their vampires. I walked toward her quickly, my heels clacking against the marble and alerting her to my presence.

I released a sigh when I realized she was just more food for them and not a part of the rebellion. Her eyes widened when she saw me. Fear was evident on her face, and it caused my chest to tighten.

"Ma'am, are you okay?" I asked.

Her eyes shifted behind me and that was when I saw the device in her hand. Blood rushed through my ears and the sounds of the party behind us fell into nothing.

Everything happened so fast, yet at the same time my body felt heavy, as if weighed down by an unforeseen forced that caused my movements to slow.

Her crazed expression turned into a smile. She pressed the button on the device, and the hallway filled with the loudest, most ear-piercing noise imaginable. I pushed my aching legs forward and tackled her to the ground. I took both of her wrists in hand and tried to get her to let go of the device.

With the noise, the vampires should all be forced to their knees, their overly sensitive ears popping from the sound. They wouldn't even hear the enemies coming and it would be the perfect time to kill any one of the clan heads.

Or Keir.

I punched her in the face and gripped for the dagger strapped to my thigh. I pushed it against her throat hard enough that a sliver of blood fell from her neck. She froze and I grabbed the device, pushing the single button on it and finally, the screeching stopped.

"Are you a part of the rebellion?" I questioned.

Her eyes widened and then narrowed at me.

"Why are you protecting those *monsters*?" she growled.

"I am just doing my job," I replied, though my voice had lost it strength.

Why am I doing this?

Not a moment later, we were surrounded by vampires. I didn't even hear them come up, but I felt the rush of wind that followed their movements. Without a second through, I slowly lifted up the device for one of them to grab without looking away from the girl I was currently straddling.

"You are a blood traitor," she spat.

I was pulled off her by familiar hands gripping my bare shoulders. The shawl had fallen off at some point and now, with all the eyes on me, I felt more exposed than ever. Gillard stood next to us and shifted so that he was covering me from view.

I did not push Keir's hands off me, instead I leaned into her touch like a good, scared date would do. Raphael's red gaze met mine before he signaled for some vampires, and they descended on her without any need for direction. She screamed as two vampires pulled her off the ground, each of them with an arm in hers. She kicked wildly as they restrained her, but it was no use.

"Bring her to the jail until the Order can get here." His eyes passed over me once more and sent me a nod.

"Fucking traitor!" she screamed, as she was dragged down the hallway.

I stood still while the other vampires around us left. Her words swirled around my head, each time cutting open a part of me.

I am a traitor.

I had killed hundreds of other humans and vampires alike, but never had their words stuck with me as much as hers did. The way the tears and anger mixed as she screamed at me created a coldness in my chest that was hard to shake.

Keir's hands squeezed my shoulder, pulling me out of my destructive thoughts. I blinked a few times and pushed her away from me.

I turned and met her eyes and she flinched as if I had hurt her.

The corridor was empty now and it left just me, Keir, and Gillard to deal with the remnants of my actions. It was the emptiness of the area that finally gave me the space I needed to speak.

"Don't you *ever* touch me again," I whispered and stalked away without another word.

I could not sleep that night. Not with the look on her face playing on repeat in my mind. She was right. I was a human working for the worst of the vampires out there, helping them continue the pained cycle that turned her. . . *like that* and stole my family from me.

I had been here in the monster den and somehow forgotten how these were the people who had stolen my family from me. These were the people who had ripped my sister's future away from her and left me bloodied and alone in this world.

And it was *I* who had allowed it to happen. I let them pamper me and get close enough for them to touch me in ways I would never have dreamed of before.

I am a disgrace, and I didn't even see it until now.

True to Raphael's words, they called the Order and the captain strolled in no more than twenty minutes later with two other hunters in tow. When it was safe, he pulled me aside and said that Raphael sang praises for me. I plastered a fake smile on my face and thanked him, but my stomach twisted at the thought of what I had done. I didn't *want* the praise. I wanted them to hate me as much as I hated them.

And I couldn't help but wonder if she would even live through the night. Raphael was not known to be lenient, so if the Order hadn't shown up as soon as they did. . . what would have happened?

A soft knock sounded at my door. I ignored it and pulled the comforter tighter against me.

"I know you're awake," Keir said, her voice muffled by the door.

She paused, waiting for my response, but I didn't say anything. I wanted to scream at her and tell her to get the fuck away from me. . . but the energy to do so left me.

"Do you want to go get drunk?" she said after a moment.

I don't think I had ever gotten up faster in my life.

I didn't complain as Keir found another shiny ride for the night, or as she dragged me to the bar she was so fond of. I sat down on the dirty, sticky barstools and patiently waited for my alcohol. Within a few minutes, I had downed three shots of vodka and was ready for more. Keir did not drink this time. Instead, she just watched me as I continued to order drink after drink.

"You should go find a human to fuck," she suggested. "You know, to get you out of this slump you're in."

Blood traitor.

I shook my head and signaled for another shot.

"I don't get why you are so upset," she continued.

I threw back another shot, not even wincing as it burned my throat.

"I am not," I lied and slammed the glass down on the bar. A few of the patrons stirred and looked over to us, but I ignored them. I signaled for another shot and the bartender looked to Keir, who nodded, before he decided to serve me.

"You were just doing your job," she said, annoyance evident in her tone.

"I don't need *you* to comfort me," I muttered and threw back another shot.

"Which is why I said you should find a *human*," she shot back. I glared at her, but quickly looked away when I met the intensity of her stare.

"It doesn't feel right after what I did," I said and took another shot. This time I didn't need to signal the bartender for another.

I shouldn't be with a human because I stood against everything humans fought for. I cozied up to the vampires for money and turned against my own when they got in trouble.

"Slow down," she chided and stopped me from taking another shot by putting her hand on mine. I jerked away, almost spilling the alcohol.

Grumbling under my breath, I tried to look for a spill but didn't find one. She tried to reach over again and take the shot. This time it did spill as her skin brushed across mine.

"So, I see a vampire is a no-go," she said with a forced smile. "Otherwise, I would suggest your ever-loving ex."

Keir motioned toward the entrance, and when I turned to look, I saw Nat descending the stairs. As soon as her eyes met mine, the smile I was so familiar with spread across her face, and she pushed through the crowd.

I turned back to my glass to see it had magically been refilled for me.

"Silv, it's nice to see you," Nat said from my side. I refused to look at her, my eyes zeroed in on the shot in front of me.

"She had a bad day," Keir interjected. I glared at her but she ignored me. "I told her to fuck it out with a human, but she refused."

"Stop fucking talking," I ordered, and I took the shot.

"I don't get the big deal," Keir continued. "Who cares what others call you?"

"What did they say?" Nat inquired. I felt her hand on my back, but I didn't push it away.

I liked the way it warmed my body, and the familiarity of it caused my tense muscles to relax. I wished to go back to the days where I could wake up in her apartment and sleep until noon. Wished to go back to before the event. Wished to go back before my parents' death.

"Blood traitor." The words out of Keir's mouth ignited another wave of self-loathing through me. I was too aware of how close Nat was, and my body wanted so badly to lean into her.

She is a vampire, I reminded myself.

But does it even matter if you are a traitor? a small voice whispered in the back of my head. *Why not go out with a bang?*

"Silv. . ." Nat trailed off.

I felt tears prick at my eyes, frustration getting the best of me.

"I ruined a plan that I would have been overjoyed to see go through," I said and Keir stiffened next to me. "Vampires are filthy creatures that only know how to kill, and I decided to save every last one of the important ones for money."

Nat removed her hand from my back and stepped away from me.

Good, I thought. *It's better this way.*

"Sorry, Nat," I whispered and pushed myself off my chair.

I took one last shot and slowly pushed myself through the crowd, not caring if Keir followed or not. Walking up the stairs was a struggle, but when I finally made it to the top, I let out a sigh of relief. The small, enclosed bar did nothing but make the feelings bottled up inside me worse. As soon as the cool air hit me, I felt the alcohol go straight to my head. I wobbled on my feet but felt arms circle around me.

"For what it's worth, I am grateful for what you did," Keir whispered.

It's not worth much, I wanted to say, but shut my mouth.

I let her guide me back to the car and did not speak to her for the rest of the ride. She had to help me up to our rooms, stopping every few minutes when my head got too dizzy.

She brought me into my room and went straight to my bed.

"You should change," she suggested and sat me down on the soft surface.

I was becoming more sober by the minute, and I hated every thought that rushed through my head. Not only was I all too aware of how shitty a person I was, but I was also all too aware of how Keir's mouth on me had felt. It was different than what I had felt with Nat, this was stronger, and I felt as though I may combust if she didn't touch me again.

She came over with the slip I had worn the previous night. Without even a pause, I started to undress. She did not stop me, instead, she knelt and helped me untie my shoes and take them off. I lay back, then slipped my leggings over my butt. She pulled them off. I didn't meet her eyes as she did so.

"I hate you," I said.

"Sit up," she commanded. I listened to her and looked up at her. Through the darkness of the room, I could barely make out her facial features, but her bright-red eyes cut through everything.

"I hate you," I said louder, needing some type of reaction from her.

"Arms up." I obeyed again. She slipped the dress over my head.

"I hate you."

"Get under the covers."

I did not obey her this time. Instead, I stood up and took her hands in mine before I turned us around and pushed her onto the bed. She sat down on the edge, her hands gripping her thighs and her red eyes locked on me.

I climbed on her lap and got a better look at her expression. Her eyebrows were pushed together, and her lips were pouted. I ran my hands up her shoulders and circled my arms around her neck.

My heart was pounding but my mind was more clear than it had been in days.

"I hate you," I said out loud, though it was more of to remind myself.

"I know," she finally responded.

Her hands slowly made their way up my thighs. The feeling

of fire seeping into my skin returned, and I spread my legs further before tightening my hold on her and pulling her closer. At the moment I didn't care about *what* she was, only the way she made me feel. The way her long, roaming fingers made my breath hitch and heat pool in my belly. I wanted to feel the same way she made me feel this morning and lose myself in her.

I leaned closer to her face, our lips so close to touching. Her lips parted and mine followed suit, her hot breath wafted across my tongue. Her lips were so inviting. The normal smirk was gone now, and I prided myself on being the one to make her lose it. Her tongue swiped over her lips, almost touching mine.

"I hate you," I whispered.

"Prove it," she dared.

My heart skipped a beat. Without wasting a second, my mouth claimed hers. She returned the kiss and easily took the lead, devouring me with no hesitation. Keir kissed with a passion like no other. She wasn't sweet or caring, she took control of my mouth and forced me into submission. Her hand cupped the back of my neck and pulled me closer, making sure there was no room between us. When her teeth pulled at my lips, I let out a small moan.

I gripped her cropped hair, as much as it would let me, and pulled myself closer. Her hands came around to my ass and guided me against her. The friction of her pants and buckle against my already wet core caused my head to swim, and I let out a whimper.

Never once had I felt this way with a human before. Never once had I felt such a strong need to be touched by someone. I *ached* for her to touch me, and I couldn't wait a second longer.

One hand left my ass to twist my nipple. Another moan spilled out of me. She left my mouth and trailed wet, hot kisses against my throat, but she didn't stop there. She slipped off my nightgown and enveloped my nipple with her mouth.

I threw my head back and moaned at the feeling of her hot mouth. My core tightened, and I knew that if her hand traveled she would feel how wet I was. She moved to the other nipple and bit down, just like she had this morning. I moaned even louder and arched into her. Her hand finally moved to cup my wet folds.

I heard her suck in a sharp breath.

"You don't feel like you hate me," she said, teasing my swollen slit with her fingers. She was exactly where I wanted her, but her touch was far too gentle for my liking.

"I hate you so much," I assured her.

This time she slipped her whole hand into my underwear and cupped my pussy, pulling a whine from me. I needed more. I needed her to throw me to the ground and fuck me right here and now, but I refused to be the one to cave.

Her fingers teased my entrance and then made their way back up to my swollen clit. I shuddered and began grinding against her as she rubbed circles on the bundle of nerves. Her mouth found my nipples once more, and I felt myself rising closer and closer to my orgasm. I began to ride her hand, but just as I felt it crest. . . her hand left me.

A ripping sound filled the room and I looked down to see that she was ripping my underwear off. I shot her a glare as she threw my underwear away, but it was short-lived because almost immediately, she plunged two fingers inside me.

"Fuck," I groaned and ground against her fingers.

She pumped in and out of me with ease. I started to match her rhythm, but she gripped my hips, threw me back on the bed, and crawled on top of me. Her fingers were back to relentlessly pounding against my pussy before I could even utter a complaint. Her lips found my neck and she began sucking.

"Tell me again," she ordered, but my mind was too preoccupied with how her fingers moved inside me. I spread my legs further, trying to take her deeper. I felt myself tighten around her fingers, the lost orgasm coming up again fast, but she did not slow. Instead, she pounded into me harder, and her thumb brushed across my clit with each thrust.

"I. . ." I couldn't finish the words as I felt myself thrown violently over the edge. It took me a moment to regain myself especially as she continued to rub my clit as I came down from the orgasm.

Finally, I met her red eyes.

"Hate you," I finished. "I hate you."

She gave me a smile, showing she didn't believe me one bit.

Hunter Rules

rule 5 sec 1

Hunters are indebted to the
Order and until their debt is
fulfilled their <u>body</u> and <u>soul</u>
will belong to The Order to do
with as they wish.

CHAPTER II
SILVIA

I regret everything I did yesterday. From giving the rebel over to engaging in. . . those acts with Keir. I felt disgusting.

How could I let one of their kind touch me like that?

After what happened last night, I had pretended to fall asleep not long after our encounter, and she had ended up leaving. After that, I stayed awake most of the night until my exhaustion overcame me and I was forced to fall asleep. I thought over and over in my head what I would say to her in the morning, and to be honest. . . I was not sure how I would face her or Gillard.

I couldn't believe that I failed my hunter duties so spectacularly after the captain had insisted that I was the only one for the job. Anxiety and panic rose up in me, and I pulled the blankets tighter.

They still smelled like her.

What about my debt?

If Gillard and the captain found out. . . would they take me off this job? Would they make Cain and Jade pay back what they were earning during this time? Thoughts raced through my head at a thousand miles per hour. I royally fucked up and I had no idea what I was going to do about it.

My thoughts were interrupted by a knock on my door.

"Miss Silvia, let's go get us some coffee," Gillard's voice called from the other side.

I got up and opened the door for him, ignoring the painful pounding in my head. He was primed and ready as always, this time in a button-up and jacket. He even had a tie today.

"Come in and wait while I get ready," I said and motioned for him to enter.

"You look like shit," he said, but came in and sat down on one of the chairs anyway.

"You could say that, after yesterday, I needed to drown my sorrows." I searched for my normal clothes and went to the bathroom to freshen up. When I came out Gillard was staring at my bed with his brows furrowed.

"Is there a problem?"

"It smells like Keir," he stated, and his eyes slowly made their way to mine.

"She dropped me off last night while I was drunk."

"You got drunk on duty?"

I shrugged and secured my weapons on my belts. Gillard was in front of me in an instant and placed a firm hand on my shoulder. I refused to look up at him and instead focused on the intricate details of his tie.

"You need to be careful," he whispered. "You are here for a job and nothing else. We have spent a lot of money on you, don't forget that."

"I have not forgotten anything," I insisted, my heart speeding up at the thought of all my efforts here being for naught.

"I will let that slide and keep it from Raphael for now, given your heroic efforts yesterday," he said, his tone low.

I knew a warning when I heard one. I nodded and jumped when his cool fingers pulled up my turtleneck. The feeling of Keir's lips on my neck came to mind, and my face heated when I realized he was helping me cover up the evidence.

"Am I interrupting something?" Keir's voice broke the tension in the room.

I slowly looked over at her, she was leaning against the door in black slacks with a matching black button-up, her eyes watching Gillard and I.

"I was just telling Miss Silvia that we will not accept any more drunken nights on duty," Gillard answered, squeezing my shoulder tight enough to bruise. I gritted my teeth against the pain. "Right, Miss Silvia?"

"Right," I forced out. "I apologize for my weakness last night. Won't happen again."

Gillard finally removed his hand and beckoned for me to follow him. Keir stayed near the door, letting Gillard through, but when I passed she slipped her arm around my shoulders. I froze as she did so.

"You were pretty drunk last night. I wonder how your head feels?" she asked, her teasing voice coming from above me.

I pushed her away with as much strength as I could. Her eyes widened and her mouth opened in shock.

"You would do well to remember not to touch me," I threatened.

She straightened herself and opened her mouth to speak but Gillard interrupted her.

"Coffee, Miss Silvia. Let's go," he called out from the end of the hallway.

I left a confused Keir frozen by the door and joined Gillard .

Keir was silent for the rest of the day, but I did not miss the looks that she gave me. I pretended not to see them. However, I knew that as soon as Gillard left she would jump on the questioning. It took me all day to think of what to say to her when we were finally alone, yet I couldn't think of any good excuses.

I even flirted with the idea of quitting for real, but it only took a second for me decide that that would be the last resort. I also wondered briefly what Raphael would do if he found out. I shivered at the thought.

It only took a few warning looks from Gillard for me to realize that he was too smart for his own good. I regretted letting him into the room this morning. He must have figured it out as soon as he stepped in.

Stupid vampire senses, I thought. *I had gotten too close to him anyway.*

I don't know when I had stopped looking at him like a vampire. He was better than Keir, but it happened far too soon.

It wasn't until later in the evening that Gillard left us alone in Keir's study together with a final warning.

"Remember my words, Miss Silvia," he said, his voice low and his eyes locked on me. I nodded and with that, he left the room.

I focused on my reading, hoping that Keir would stay silent, and she was for about five minutes. But as soon as those five minutes passed, my book was ripped out of my hands and her mouth was on mine. It took me a few seconds to recover, but I filled with panic when I realized what was happening. She let me push her away. When her eyes met mine, they were already a dull red.

"What do you think you are doing?" I snapped at her, ignoring the heat that filled my body.

"Continuation of last night," she said, giving me a smirk. She went in to kiss me again.

"Stop."

She stopped mere centimeters away from my lips.

"What do you mean by 'a continuation of last night'?" I asked.

Her eyes snapped to mine, and she pulled away to search my face. I begged that she would take the lie at face value, but her eyes narrowed.

"So, we want to pretend that nothing happened?" she asked, fisting her hand in my hair and pulling it so my neck was bared to her.

A guttural moan left my mouth and I gripped at her shirt. The pain that spread across my scalp shouldn't have cause heat to pool in my stomach.

"I am not pretending," I moaned.

She leaned down but instead of meeting my lips, her teeth tugged at my ear.

"Don't," I warned.

"You disappoint me," she whispered in my ear. The words settled deep and hurt more than I would have expected from a vampire like her.

"Join the club," I growled.

I still didn't push her away. In my mind, I had already pulled her closer and we were locked in a passionate kiss as we shed our clothes.

"What if I told you we could keep this little relationship to ourselves?" she asked, her breath wafting across my neck and face.

Her mouth trailed down my neck, leaving wet, hot kisses as she went. I tilted my head to give her more access.

"What if I told you that we could pretend that you hate my kind in public"—she paused and let her other hand trail up my thigh and into my shirt—"but in private, you're *mine*."

My heart skipped a beat, and I felt my stomach tighten at her words. I swallowed thickly, trying to regain my thought process, but I was lost in the patterns her tongue drew on my skin.

"Do you do this to all your hunters?" I asked. "Is this the game you play with them?"

"This is no game," she responded, then pulled back so she could meet my eyes once more. "I want to keep this hunter around as long as possible."

"Why?" I gasped, as her long fingers cupped my breast.

"You are more interesting than the rest," she replied.

I would have rolled my eyes if we were in any other situation.

"I am not playing this game with you," I snapped, and with whatever strength I had, I pulled her hand from under my shirt.

She sighed and left me on the couch to go back to her desk.

"My offer will stay open as long as you want it." She started looking over papers once more. "Hand me the book by you, would you?"

I almost didn't understand her. I was too stuck on what had just happened and the feeling that she left raging in my body. I found the book that she mentioned, then jerkily stood up and gave it to her. She grabbed my wrist instead and pulled me in closer.

"Clean yourself up before you see Gil next," she said in a low tone, her eyes turning fully red. "We can smell your arousal."

I felt my cheeks flame and removed my sword from it sheath to point it at her chest. She only gave me a smirk.

"I refuse your deal. Don't bring it up again unless you want this through your throat," I threatened.

"Think about it," she responded, almost daring me to act on my threats.

I pushed the sword against her chest harder and watched

as a drop of blood ran down her chest. I wanted to push it in farther, but I knew if it was too deep she would get hit with the elixir I smeared on the sides and would start burning from the inside out.

I sighed, then turned and left her room, not stopping until I got to my shower and viciously scrubbed the feeling of her lips off my skin

CHAPTER 12
KEIR

I knew it was coming.

Gillard had been glaring at me all day, and I could feel that he was on the edge of exploding. Luckily he hadn't been too hard on Silvia or made it too awkward, because if he did. . . I was sure that I would never get to touch her like I did the other night.

Even just thinking about the way she looked as she spilled those lies from her mouth caused heat to pool in my belly and my fangs to ache. I wished so badly to be able to sink my teeth into her, but even I knew that was crossing a line, so I would just have to settle for tasting her in a different way.

I moved to sit on the edge of my desk as Gillard paced my office. Anxiety was rolling off him in waves, and it was just a matter of time before he let me have it. He had a right to be angry, this was supposed to be our last hunter, and Father had made it clear what he expected from both of us and the Order. Defying him like this was a death wish and put the transfer of power at stake. . . but I couldn't help myself.

Ever since I had seen the way she glared at me, with so

much hate and anger boiling under her skin, I knew I had to have her.

"If we want to fuck you shouldn't stand in the way," I said, glaring at him. "I have everything under control."

I listened to Silvia tossing in her bed, making sure to keep my voice low enough so she wouldn't wake. The last thing I needed was for her to walk in on us having this conversation, because even if we stopped talking, she would feel the tension between us and I didn't want to deal with her questions. I wanted this to be easy between us. I wanted her and she wanted me, that was all it should be.

"It's not safe for her or you." He huffed and removed his glasses so he could run his hands across his face. "Raphael would not be happy to find out you are fucking our last hunter."

Father wouldn't be happy even if I retreated to this office for the rest of my existence. There was no pleasing him, not since he realized that I would be taking over for him whether he liked it or not. He hated me growing up, made me miserable, but it had been nothing compared to how he had been the last few years.

The only reason I wasn't dead in a ditch right now was because he had no other offspring to take over. If he did, he would have no doubt chosen someone much more presentable and gullible than me. But he was stuck with me, and the only way for him to keep some sort of power was to exhibit some type of control over me. . . And for him that was in terms of the hunters he brought on and the power moves he played.

"Then help me cover it up!" I snapped.

I was growing more frustrated by the minute. Silvia had *finally* let me touch her, and I understood what I had been missing out on this entire time that she was near me. The taste of her on my tongue, and the smell of her blood rushing through her face as she flushed under my attention, was something I would not soon forget. Even now my mouth watered thinking about how eager and wet she was for me.

She was fire and passion wrapped into one volatile package. She had no problem disobeying me or Father, and I doubt there was anyone on this planet that could make her bend to them. *That* was the type of person that made my heart pound and my blood heat. Human or not, she was the perfect match.

And I was not willing to let this go just yet, no matter what Father or Gillard said.

"Find another person to fuck, Keir," Gillard ordered. "You know what Raphael will do to you when he finds out. You could *literally* have any other person you wanted! Don't you realize how dangerous this is? His fuse is shorter than ever and you are not making this any better."

"He won't find out," I grumbled, but even I didn't believe myself.

He had eyes everywhere and I knew they were probably watching and waiting for us to fuck up. He loved to give out punishments left and right and had no remorse for the poor fool who had to bear them. To fail the single most important task he had given me, right before the transfer of power. . . It would royally piss him off.

"You have less than two months until your transfer of power, Keir," he said, thinking the same thing I was. "Just do it peacefully. All he asked was to keep up appearances and act like the royalty you are. Please, Keir. I don't want to see you hurt."

I paused, guilt flooding my system. Gil had always been looking out for me, even when I pushed him away and continued to disobey my father. He was the closest thing I had to any real type of family in this place, and I knew he came from a good place. They way his voice cracked toward the end as he pleaded for me caused my chest to tighten and my throat to constrict. I didn't want to burden him.

"What if I like this one?" I ventured. Gillard's eyes snapped up to meet mine. I did not back down, I wanted to show him how serious I was. I knew inside he liked her too. Never before had he treated a hunter with such kindness, offering them coffee and explaining the rules of our world to them. Usually, he would brush them off and tell them to do their own research. . . but this one was different for him too.

"Don't play that game," he growled.

I knew that I was wearing his patience thin. He'd been with me for years and I had only seen him this angry a handful of times.

"You can leave. I won't sneak into her bedroom tonight," I said with a sigh and waved him off. I stood up straight and was prepared to go back to the mountain of paperwork that I had been neglecting the past few weeks, but I paused when Gillard didn't move from his spot. Looking over to him, I saw that his gaze was locked onto the floor and a frown marred his face.

"Do her words ever hurt you?" he whispered.

A smile made its way toward my lips and suddenly the man standing in front of me wasn't the hundred-something-year-old vampire, but a kicked puppy that was pouting in the corner after a scolding.

"That's quiet a change of topic," I said in a light tone. Gillard put on the front that he needed to while working with my clan, but I knew from firsthand experience that inside he was nothing more than a child that longed for love and affection. His previous clan were downright monsters and having to grow up around that was not easy. Coming here quite literally saved his life. Though it had taken a while to get him used to how things work here, he slowly came around. So, I could understand where he was coming from.

"I was just thinking about it," he muttered, still not looking at me.

"She has to get a better insult than *scum* to hurt my feelings," I said truthfully. "But sometimes she can get pretty close to something that hurts." The way she called me a *child,* for one, did cause an ache in my chest, but I was angrier at her insolence than anything else.

"Do they hurt you?" I asked.

His eyes remained glued to the floor as he took in my words.

"Sometimes," he admitted, then shifted on his feet. A heavy air hung around us, suffocating me. I didn't remember the last time we had a conversation like this. "I don't want to be a monster."

Like your father. The unspoken words hung in the air around, and I had no comfort that I could bring him in the moment. . . Because I also didn't want to become the monster my father had.

I didn't want people to fear me. I wanted them to respect me.

I didn't want to see people treating humans like trash and killing them for shock value.

I wanted to be better for this clan, and better for the world.

"You're not," I said sincerely. "You will never be."

He gave me a small, forced smile before nodding and turning to leave the room. With him gone, I was left in my own flurry of thoughts and emotions, all of them relating back to Silvia.

I wanted her, so badly. . . but I didn't want Gil to get hurt, and I knew that if there was any ounce of responsibility in me I would need to stop this and focus on bettering myself for the transfer of power.

. . . but even so, I couldn't get her out of my mind.

When morning came, and Silvia and Gillard got up for the day, we all made our way down to the coffee shop that we frequented. Gillard's words still echoed through my head, and I found myself unable to concentrate as I sat between them. The scent of bitter coffee filled the air, but it did nothing to conceal Silvia's scent and I found myself struggling to keep my cool.

I had always been careful about feeding, but since I had stopped going out, my fresh supply had been cut off and I refused to use Father's feeders, so my control had been weakened.

I swallowed thickly, my throat far too dry, and I couldn't help but look toward Silvia's neck. Most of it was covered by her Order uniform, but the part that wasn't called to me. I imagined leaning closer to her, pulling down the offensive fabric, and sinking my teeth right into that pale neck of hers. She would hate it, hate me afterward, but I could make it enjoyable for her. That much I could promise.

"We will have another event," Gillard said, breaking me out of my trance. Only then did I realize that my eyes had been locked on Silvia for far too long.

"Same as last?" she asked and shifted in her chair. I averted my gaze, not wanting to make her too uncomfortable.

Gil nodded and sent me a warning look before responding.

"We will be hosted by the Kazimir clan," he said.

I couldn't help the groan that came out of my mouth when I heard that bastard's name. They were the clan I hated the most, and it had nothing to do with their affiliations or how they conducted themselves, but all in how moronic the heir was.

"I didn't know your kind disliked each other," Silvia said. There was a lightness to her tone that made my stomach flip.

She was teasing me and I *fucking* loved it. I ran my tongue across my aching fangs, trying to center myself before speaking.

Gillard wore an obvious look of amusement as he watched me struggle. He may have been pissed about me crossing the line, but he loved to see me reap the consequences of my own actions.

"His son is worse than me," I explained, my tongue felt thick in my mouth, and it was difficult to force the words out. "And he always fights me over women."

No matter the event, if one of us brought someone there was always some type of confrontation. It started when we were much younger as a joke, but he got burned one too many times and now sees it as a real competition.

"You dislike him because he steals your women?" Silvia asked with a scoff.

"The other way around," Gillard said with a slight chuckle. "Keir likes to see how many of his girlfriends she can seduce."

A smile made its way to my face. I was actually pretty good at it.

"Does your kind have nothing better to do than to have sex and fight?" she asked.

I just shrugged at her. We had long lives and far too much time on our hands. If we had nothing else to fill it with we would surely go insane. Humans were different though; half of their life was spent sleeping, while the other half was spent working to death so they could have a somewhat decent life outside of working hours. They didn't have time to mess around like we did, so I didn't expect her to understand.

"Disgusting," she whispered under her breath.

Do her words ever hurt you? played in my mind as I watched Gillard's face tighten.

"That's more on brand with how you should be acting. I

thought it was suspicious that you were being so nice to us," he said. "Was it what happened with her father?"

Fury and humiliation ignited my blood. His jab was not just to her, I knew this was his punishment to me as well. Reminding me of my place here.

"Gil," I warned.

I could feel Silvia's eyes on me, but I didn't meet them, I couldn't. I hated that Father showed that to her. I hated that I still *let* him have this control over me. It was embarrassing, and yet there was nothing I could do about it.

"I may have just gotten too comfortable," Silvia explained quickly. I turned to her and watched as she played with the almost-empty latte in her hands. "And I forgot myself. Forgot what your kind has done to me."

"But it wasn't us," I insisted. None of my clan's members would have done something so crass, so horrible. We were honorable even if the head of our clan was not, that much I was sure of.

"It was your people," she accused, her tone was clipped and told me that no matter how hard I tried, I would not win this argument.

I didn't know how Gillard did it, but that devil really just created a bigger divide between us than ever before. Silvia's eyes had a fire in them once more, and she stared at me with the hatred and defiance that caused my entire body to vibrate with excitement and need.

I need to feed, and soon, I thought and shot Gillard a look. He seemed to understand my struggles and jumped in before I could make a fool of myself.

"It's better this way," Gillard said, his eyes shifting from me to her.

"So, can I bring my weapons this time?" she asked, changing the subject.

"No, you must play the same role," Gillard insisted.

Which meant that I would have to stand close to her, with the scent of her blood invading my senses, her neck on display for all to see. It would be pure torture.

"But they should know after the last event," she muttered.

I wish they did, but Father was too much of a control freak to even let this one thing slip. He was too worried about reputation to let the others know what she was really here for.

"They do not," Gillard said and got up to throw his coffee away in a nearby trash can.

"Father covered the tracks," I muttered.

"Right. Okay," Silvia said with a tense nod. A sweet scent filled the air and I almost moaned aloud as the scent reached me. Little Silvia was thinking of the night we shared after the party.

I sent her a smirk, unable to help myself.

"I hope you can play the part again," I said and reached over to tug on the end of her ponytail. "Try not to fall in love with me."

She smacked my hand away, but I didn't miss the flush of red that creeped up her neck. With a smile, I got up and turned so that she wouldn't see me pressing the back of my hand to my mouth. My fangs were aching as her smell blossomed, and I knew that if I didn't get this solved before the next event, I would be fucking screwed.

CHAPTER 13
SILVIA

Before I knew it, it was time to check in at the Order again.

It was perfect timing because in just another few days we would be going to the event hosted by another clan. An important one by the looks of it, but it felt wrong. It would be a great place for another attack, but the way Keir and Gillard talked about the heir raised more red flags. I didn't want to go into it unprepared.

The Order was strangely quiet as I walked the halls, with only a few hunters out and about. An air had fallen over the entire building and even the newest academy students seemed to be busy with something. A part of me worried that more hunters had gone missing, but they couldn't have taken the entire building, could they?

I was tempted to let Jade and Cain know I stopped by, but I didn't really feel like talking to them at the moment. The situation with Keir and my obvious lack of critical-thinking skills made me want to hide. I was worried that, as soon as they saw me, they would see right through me. . . and I *needed* to make sure that I got this debt paid for.

Their questions would only create a bigger problem for me.

When I arrived at the captain's office, I went in without knocking and stopped in my tracks when I realized he wasn't alone. This time he had another vampire sitting right across from him who eyed me as I stepped through the threshold. He looked fairly young, with dark-brown hair that was tied at the nape of his neck, a strong jaw and narrow features. He looked a lot like a younger version of Raphael, and the comparison caused the unease to rise in me. I noted his eyes were a bright red, indicating that he had probably just had his fill of human blood. . . or for some reason he was *really* excited to see the captain.

I ground my teeth and looked toward the captain, who didn't even acknowledge me.

"Well, it seems like your next appointment is here," the young vampire said and stood. He fixed his coat and straightened his wrinkled slacks. Just like the other vampires, his aura and clothing screamed that he was much older and more important than his looks indicated. My guess was that he may be like a Gillard in another clan.

"Yes," the captain said, annoyance obvious in his tone. "We can discuss more thoroughly during your next appointment, Vance."

The captain gestured for me to come closer. I obeyed but did not take my eyes off the vampire in the room with us. The air around him didn't seem right. It was sticky and almost as dark feeling as Raphael's.

Whoever he was. . . there was something wrong with him.

As I came closer, his eyes narrowed slightly, then he inclined his head and inhaled deeply. His lips twitched and his eyes locked onto me. There was something behind them I didn't like, something animalistic. He walked closer to me and I stiffened, putting my hand on my dagger as a warning. I felt far too much like the prey in this situation.

He didn't speak, only clapped his hand on my shoulder, not once but twice. If the captain's eyes were not burning holes in mine, I would have sliced his hand off. He hesitated for only a second longer his eyes burrowing into mine.

He looked like he was going to say something but instead he just let out a small chuckled and walked toward the door.

"See you next time," he said and shut the door behind him with a soft click.

"Go on," the captain prompted as the door shut, but I stood frozen.

Would that vampire try and listen in?

I wouldn't put it past him, or any vampire for that matter. This place was a gold mine of information. If I were in his position I would probably try to get as much as I could from this single meeting.

Though from the way the captain spoke to him, it seemed like he would be back in no time.

Who is he really?

I did not speak for a moment, intent on waiting long enough that no one would be able to hear our conversation. The captain sighed in frustration and rubbed a hand over his face. He looked tired, much like he had in the last meeting. I wanted to ask about it. Breach the gap that had shown up after my parents had died. . . but I couldn't.

He wasn't the same man I grew up around and I had to remind myself of that.

"Don't tell me you messed up," he groaned.

"I did not," I lied. "Just don't want any prying ears."

The captain took my explanation and sat back in his chair with a loud sigh. I walked over to the window and watched as the man from earlier left the building. I could have sworn he glanced back up to this window, but from this angle I was unsure. As he got into his limo and drove off, the weight that had been resting on my chest lifted, and suddenly I could breathe again.

"Nothing of note since I last saw you," I said in a low tone, searching the perimeter. The view from this window gave me the perfect view of the surrounding streets and buildings. "There will be another event, hosted by the Kazimir clan, which I will need to attend."

"What a coincidence," the captain said with an amused tone that I hadn't heard from him before. "That was their heir."

So *that* was the man Keir seemed so intent on annoying. I walked back around his desk and sat down on the chair in front of him.

The news worried me more than it consoled me. If *that* was the man that Keir wanted to go up against, my money was on him. Keir may have been a bloodthirsty vampire... but I could tell the Kazimir clan's heir was dangerous.

It was in the way he held himself.

The way his eyes traveled my body in equal parts want and disgust.

He seemed to hate humans just as much as I hated vampires, and a vampire's hate for a human was far more deadly than the opposite. They *literally* slit our throats for fun.

"Of course it was," I grumbled and crossed my arms over my chest. "Apparently, the heirs do not like each other."

"Not our problem," the captain grumbled. "Just do your job and get out."

His dismissal angered me. I *knew* it wasn't my job, but didn't he see how weird everything had been up until now?

"But is there anything I should *know*?" I pried and leaned forward. "Something seems off about him, *dangerous.*"

The captain leaned farther back in his chair and turned so that he was facing the window.

"They haven't broken any laws or contracts," he explained. "They are actually one of the better clans we have to deal with. The heir can be. . . somewhat entitled, but I don't see any other issues with their clan."

I nodded and tried to take the words at face value, but I still had an uncomfortable feeling in my stomach, and it had never led me wrong before. I had been on countless missions and had seen every type of vampire imaginable, my gut knew when something was up.

The captain cleared his throat.

"They have asked for some hunters at the same event," he said. "Theirs will be standing guard outside, but I assume we can use you as ears inside."

I didn't want to do this again, but I might as well suck it up because it didn't seem like I would be getting out of this any time soon. If the captain was involved this time, this event must have been even more important than the last.

"Is that why the Order is almost empty?" I asked. "Or have the hunters suddenly gone missing again?"

He turned to lock gazes with me, his jaw was clenched, and his hands balled into fists.

"Watch your tone, Ms. Reiss," he hissed. "The Order does not take kindly to *that* type of talk and we do not need rumors going around that can frighten the hunters."

He meant *he* doesn't like it when his star hunter questions the Order, but how could I not when there were so many things left unanswered?

"You assume correct," I said after a pause. "I will go undercover with Keir and look for any rebel activity."

He nodded and turned back to look at the window.

"Am I. . ." I paused unable to find my words. "Is my team—or myself—in danger, Captain?"

His jaw clenched but his eyes were still locked on the window.

"The hunters are preparing for the Kazimir clan's party," he explained. "They requested a significant amount of heads given the rumors of rebel attacks."

I relaxed in my chair, some of the weight that had been threatening to pull me to the ground lifted.

"There are no more missing hunters?" I asked, just to make sure.

"No."

"Thank you," I whispered and stood. "I will keep you updated."

He waved me off and I left the Order feeling lighter than I had in days.

At least my team was safe.

It was getting dark by the time I headed back, but I knew that Keir would still be in her study, so I headed there before my own room.

I didn't knock and instead just opened the door; I knew she heard me coming up anyway. I had left her earlier while she had been working and she was still in the same seat she had been, but instead of looking at the papers, her head was resting back against her chair, showing off her elongated neck. The chair was leaned back and her eyes stared up at the ceiling. They were glazed over and it looked like she was resting, though I didn't know vampires needed rest. They couldn't sleep, so why would they get tired to begin with?

She was wearing her normal button-up and slacks, but there was something slightly disheveled about her. Her hair was gelled back but some pieces fell into her face, covering her eyes. Her shirt was partially unbuttoned and the collar was slightly lopsided. I didn't ask about her appearance and instead just stood near the entrance.

She lifted her nose in the air and took a deep inhale. Her eyes turned red and her head snapped toward me.

"Who did you see today?" she growled.

"The captain," I responded and lifted my eyebrow at her. *What is her deal?*

"You lie," she growled and pushed off her chair to cross the room in record time. I stood still, rooted to my spot. Fear pricked at my spine, but I tried not to show it. She stopped in front of me and sniffed my right shoulder. "You saw Vance," she concluded.

"He was at the base," I said and tried to step away from her, but she grabbed my arms and forced me to stay.

"Did he see you?" she demanded, gripping me even harder.

I wondered if she knew how hard she was gripping me. Pain blossomed from where she held me and I was sure that I would end up with bruises after this.

"Yes," I whispered. "He was meeting with the captain."

"What is going on here?" Gillard's voice demanded from the open door.

"You heard her. Vance saw her," Keir growled and she pulled at my shirt. "Her cover is blown."

"Stop you will rip it," I hissed.

I grabbed her wrists to stop her from tearing the fabric, but I recoiled as a loud growl ripped through her chest.

"Stop that." Gillard's voice was cold and Keir stopped pulling at my clothes almost immediately. "She is a hunter. It doesn't matter who she smells like. And besides, Vance has nothing to gain from telling anyone."

Keir looked like she wanted to say something, but she unhanded me and put space between us. The change was like whiplash and I would have thought I had hallucinated it all if it wasn't for the pain that now traveled up my arms.

The air was thick and Keir and Gillard were in a heavy stare down. Whatever was going on between them, I really didn't want to be in the middle. I swallowed the knot in my throat and turned back to the door, regretting coming into this office.

"I will retire for the night," I said and left both of them standing in her office.

That night, when I checked myself in the bathroom, I saw three sets of bruises. One on my right shoulder that was now yellowing, where Gillard had squeezed when he found out what we had done that morning after the last event. And two on either side of my arms where Keir had grabbed me not long ago.

I prayed that they cleared up before the event.

CHAPTER 14
SILVIA

The days before the event passed slowly but before I knew it, Keir was once again storming into my room with a handful of boxes.

I groaned and sat up just as she sat down on my bed. I rubbed my eyes and met her already red ones.

"Do you have to do this every time?" I asked.

"This is the only time I am allowed to see you in that skimpy dress of yours," she said. "I wouldn't miss that for anything."

Her tone was playful but her eyes were sharp and watched me like a hawk. She was already dressed, and I couldn't help but marvel at the vampire in front of me. She always cleaned up well, her hair was perfectly gelled back, her neck and hands decked in the shiny gold jewelry, and her clothes fit like they were made for her.

. . . they probably were.

My eyes trailed down the patch of skin that was showing and I felt a low heat rise in my belly. The last time we had been in this situation she had her mouth on me, the same one that was now pulled into a devious smirk. Her tongue swiped across her lips, and I found myself wanting to lean forward and taste her.

"If you wanted to see more, you could've just asked." She chuckled and began pulling at her shirt.

"Stop," I said and rushed to get out of bed.

Her long fingers circled around my wrist and we were suddenly back in the same position we were weeks ago. Me in between her legs, and her staring at me as if she was ready to devour me.

My breath got caught in my throat as her hand made its way up my back and to my neck.

"Your hair looks good down." Her voice was husky as she spoke. Her hand gripped the hair at the base of my neck, forcing me to expose my neck to her. She leaned forward and dragged her wet tongue across my neck.

"Even without using my fangs I can taste how sweet your blood could be," she mumbled against my neck. Her voice sent shivers down my spine. "I want to taste it so bad."

"I am going to kill you one day," I muttered, but could not find the strength to push her away.

Her free hand glided up my thigh and dipped under my nightgown.

"Would you let me taste you?" she asked and nibbled on my neck before sucking the already wet skin. Pleasure shot through me and I had to grip her shoulders to steady myself. "I would treat you so well. You wouldn't even feel anything."

"I wouldn't let any vampire bite me," I growled. "Especially not you."

"Don't lie to yourself," Keir cooed and her hand brushed across the front of my panties. "I can feel how much you want this."

She traveled lower and lower, then abruptly pulled her

hand away before placing it on my back and pulling me closer to her.

The door was pushed open and Gillard stormed in looking angrier than I'd ever seen him. Panic flooded me and I tried to push Keir away, but she held me tightly against her. Her hands pulled on my hair even tighter and she continued to lick the length of my neck. I let out a pained whimper.

"Keir, I swear to God," Gillard called out to her, but she did not stop.

I felt myself start to get uncomfortably hot and I knew that at any moment Gillard and Keir would know how I felt about her actions.

"I'm scenting her," she explained matter-of-factly. She moved to the other side of my neck and did the same thing. "You may be convinced that Vance won't do anything, but I am not. He found someone that smelled like me and went out of his way to mark her. That doesn't sit well with me."

"Stop it and get out," I snapped, almost feeling relieved when I finally felt her tongue leave my neck.

"Outside now," Gillard demanded and almost dragged Keir out once she removed herself from me.

"Don't shower," Keir called back, giving me a shit-eating grin just before my door was slammed shut.

I let out a breath and tried to steady myself. I almost wished Gillard didn't interrupt us, but beat myself up internally as soon as that thought popped into my head. I needed to get myself together. Today was just as important as last time and I needed to show that I could do this.

I decided to ignore what Keir had asked and showered. Not just showered, but vigorously scrubbed my entire body and didn't leave the shower until I was sure that no one would smell her on me.

The dress that Keir had provided was almost a copy paste

of the one previous, but instead this was a dark-green satin dress that had a slit that showed off my leg as I walked. Unfortunately, with the straps being just as thin as last time, the bruises on my shoulders and arms would show. There was another white shawl to cover my shoulders and it would have to do for now.

I took a deep breath to center myself before I finally built up the courage to leave my room. As I walked outside, I was met with a disgruntled Keir and a bare-faced Gillard. I had to do a double take at Gillard, without his glasses he looked like a totally different person. Younger, and seemingly less tired than he had been as of late.

"No glasses works for you," I said to him and he gave me a strained smile.

"I told you not to shower," Keir grumbled and moved toward me, however, Gillard held her back.

"It was good that she did," he said. "If anyone else found out you scented her, there would be too many rumors."

"She's my date," Keir hissed back. "It only makes sense that I would scent her. It's weirder if I don't."

"And if Vance has his way," Gillard continued in a low tone. "A known hunter."

I sighed and waved my hand, dismissing the two. I was already embarrassed enough to begin with that Gillard had walked in on us, I didn't need them to keep bringing this up.

"Let's get this over with," I grumbled and walked down the hallway, not waiting for them to follow me.

An SUV was waiting for us out front with a vampire guard posed as a driver. He gave me a nod as I walked up and I tensely returned it.

Without speaking he opened the back door for me and I climbed into the car. Gillard and Keir were arguing behind me, and I watched as Gillard practically forced Keir into the front.

She grumbled something under her breath, but it was too low for me to hear.

He climbed into the back with me and the guard joined us in the front seat, the car rocking as he fit his giant body into the small space.

"Make sure to address her as 'my lady' when speaking to her," Gillard explained, as we pulled away from the compound. "It was my oversight last time. This time, we are in the company of many others and there will be more prying ears. Call Vance 'my lord' as well."

I nodded, not saying anything. My stomach twisted uncomfortably at the idea of seeing that man again. The captain had assured me his clan checked out, but I knew there was more to him.

We sat the rest of the car ride in a tense silence. There was still an undeniable tension between us after what happened this morning. Even if I had pushed her off, Gillard was smart enough to realize that he had caught us red-handed. I would have to be more careful going forward. I was literally one more mess-up away from being fired.

It took over an hour to get to the venue, and as soon as we rolled up, my jaw dropped at the large manor that spanned what seemed like miles. They were even more conspicuous than Keir's clan. The entire manor was painted white with gold trim and the windows that littered the sides shone brightly in the light. It was blocked off by large golden gates that opened automatically when we passed. In front of the manor was a shimmering pool that had multiple stages reaching almost as tall as the house. The grass on either side seemed to be recently trimmed and not a blade was out of place.

I was pulled back to myself when I saw hundreds of familiar black uniforms guarding the perimeter. There was barely ten feet between each, and all of them were armed and ready to take down any threat that came into their view. Their eyes watched each car as they drove down the winding roads and turned to let out guests right in front of the main staircase that led to an open entrance.

"You didn't tell me your friends would be here," Gillard grumbled next to me.

"You didn't ask," I said simply.

I wiped my sweaty palms on the shawl I was wearing and tried to calm my racing heart. I recognized some of these hunters, they were all from the Academy. The only time I saw them was when I trained in the morning, but I would recognize those faces anywhere.

They have been asking about you. Cain's words flashed through my mind.

Well. . . I guess they would know where I had been.

I wondered briefly what they would think when they saw me on Keir's arm. Would they be embarrassed? Ashamed? Would they laugh at me?

After all, I hated vampires, yet I was dressed up so prettily for them.

When we came to a stop my pulse fluttered and panicked thoughts plagued my mind. Keir and Gillard were the first out, and I watched as Keir took in the sight in front of her. For the first time her straightened posture and slight smirk didn't feel like arrogance. Here it felt like power. This was where she was meant to be, and it was what I needed to climb out of the car after Gillard.

The guard who was driving left the car and appeared by my side, offering a hand out to me. I sent him a forced smile and pushed down the alarm bells in my head as I took his hand and let him help me out of the car.

For looks, I sent him a beaming smile.

"Thank you," I said and turned to Keir and Gillard, but they weren't what caught my eyes. . . it was the eyes behind them. The Order members had already seen me and I saw some eyes lock onto me and others turn to their neighbors, whispering behind their hands.

I hated the way it made my stomach dip.

Keir grabbed my arm and wrapped it around hers, pulling me as close to her as acceptable in this situation. I felt her lean down before I heard her say anything. I kept my eyes glued on the stairs in front of us, refusing to let anyone see how much she bothered me.

"What will your friends think when they see you on my arm?" she whispered in my ear. "Will they be just as disgusted as you, or do you think they will be jealous?"

Gillard covered my other side and I could almost feel the disapproval radiating off him.

"Many do not hate your kind as much as I do," I said in a low tone. "But if they see me here, then they know that they shouldn't fuck around. The ones on the perimeter look like academy students, I have seen them a few times before."

"Let's get inside," Gillard said from my side.

I nodded and moved inside with them both by my side, the stares following us as we walked.

The inside was just as extravagant as the outside. Large crystal chandeliers hung from the ceiling and shined in the light. The wall paper was a mix of golds and whites that complemented the white marble floors. There was a large dance floor surrounded by tables decked in dark-red cloth, and each was already set with glasses for the guests. The only thing that threw off the beauty of the place were the Order members stationed at the exits and near the windows, a stark black contrast to the mostly white building. Light music filled the space but it was slow, probably so it wouldn't hurt the vampires' ears.

As we stepped in, I realized that there was a checkpoint in front of us being run by hunters. They were separating the humans from the vampires, no doubt trying to search for the sound device that had been used at Keir's last event.

He sure is thorough, I thought wryly.

"I'll be quick," I whispered to Keir and without hesitation stepped toward the Order member.

It was a single person who was doing the checking, and behind him stood a few more. Their eyes were trained on me as I stepped forward. His messy, dark auburn hair was combed back, showing off his freckled skin and hazel eyes. With a start, I realized that I knew him more intimately than the other hunters. He'd been in a majority of my classes at the Academy. Though he didn't ever speak much, I remembered how good he was when we had a chance to spar. After that I never forgot about him, he was one of the stronger hunters I had ever had the chance to spar with.

"Silvia," Damon greeted in a curt tone.

"Damon." I nodded at him and stood with my arms and legs open for him to pat me down.

"I assume you have something hidden on you," he said in a low tone and began patting down my right leg. He paused when he found what he was looking for. "I have to take it."

I had had the same weapon since the Academy, so he already knew what he needed to find. I don't know if I should be impressed or annoyed that he remembered.

I gritted my teeth, annoyance getting the better of me. Against Gillard's advice I had brought a weapon. I blame it on the anxiousness that Vance had left me with after he visited the base.

"Go ahead," I said.

His hands dipped under my dress and removed the dagger

strapped to my thigh, quickly, trying to avoid unwanted attention.

"I apologize," he whispered when he patted down my arms once more. He moved the shawl, feeling around the light fabric, as if I could hide something in it. The thought made me want to laugh, but I let him do his job.

"I understand," I said. And I did. I had a stupid job in this Order as well.

He paused when he saw the bruises on my arms, his eyes shifted to mine but when I didn't say anything he moved on.

"People have been asking," he said in a low tone. "I bet most are glad to see you alive and well."

"Let's not talk about that here," I said quickly after catching Gillard's gaze. He and Keir were on the other side waiting for me, both staring at me intently.

"Understood," he said. "Stay safe."

With that he waved me through and without paying any attention to the hunters behind him I walked toward my date for the night.

"The bruises. . ." Gillard trailed off.

"You were both there for them," I stated plainly and rejoined my arm with Keir's. I pulled them farther into the large room, ending the conversation. "What is this place anyway?"

"A special place they use just for parties," Gillard explained. "They live here on occasion, but I have only been here for events. There are hallways near the end of the room that lead to some studies and bedrooms, but this place is mainly just used for guests."

I nodded. It would make sense, the room seemed to span a majority of the house, and instead of being hidden away like it had been in Keir's home, this room seemed to be the sole purpose of the place.

I wanted to ask more about this event, but quickly vampires began to surround us. It took all I had to keep the fake smile plastered on my face. My body stiffened as they began to invade my personal space as they dove to shake hands with Keir. I couldn't keep track of all the faces that came up to us, but there was one thing that stood out to me: many of them had human feeders of their own, but none of them dared to speak to me.

None of the vampires dared to touch me either, they just stood in front of us and rattled off to Keir who politely listened to every single word they said. She was polite with them and when I thought she would give a sarcastic response to their dumb questions, she instead met them with understanding. A totally different person than what I had seen in the last few weeks with her.

Just like when she first stepped out of the car, I came to realize that she really was in her element. She drew vampires in like honey to a bear, and as they rambled off to her, I watched as she catalogued the information and met them with a thoughtful and polished response. I wouldn't lie and say that I knew anything about running a vampire clan, but Keir was obviously much smarter than she let people realize.

But everything changed when Vance pushed through the crowd, and took his turn.

"Keir, nice to see you again," he said to Keir, but his eyes were trained on me. "Who is this lovely human?"

I gritted my teeth. I knew he recognized me by the look in his eyes, but he must be doing this because so many people were around and to save face.

"Silvia, my lord," I said, bowing like I had seen the others do to Keir not too long ago. Instead of bowing back, he took my free hand and brushed his lips lightly across my knuckles. My fake smile faltered.

"A pleasure," he said against my hand, his eyes coming back up to meet mine.

There was something sickly sweet about his tone that made me feel like a film was placed wherever he had touched.

"It is nice to see you as well," Keir said. "Glad to finally show you the woman who has been taking up so much of my time."

Keir's tone was polite, but it was so fake sounding that it was hardly believable.

"Is that so?" he mused, running his fingers through the hair that hung down to his shoulder.

The people who were waiting for the two vampires dispersed as if they knew they may not want to stick around for this conversation.

"Yes, now if you excuse us, I would like to dance with her," Keir said, then dragged me to the dance floor.

She pushed us through the dancing couples and took us as far away from both Vance and Gillard as possible. I was grateful to be given an out, but her hasty getaway panicked me more than it calmed me.

The entire time she was talking to the others, she was surreal and perfectly poised. . . but as soon as Vance came into the picture the facade dropped. It meant she was just as worried about him as I was, and it only solidified my previous thoughts about him.

I did not speak as she turned me to face her, taking one hand in hers, the other resting on my waist. The familiar feeling of heat licking at wherever she touched me came again, and my steps faltered as she pulled me along.

"Remember to look at me," she said pulling me out of my erratic thoughts.

I did as she said and my heart jumped at the face she was giving me. It was dark, and her eyes were turning a dull red.

"You shouldn't have showered my scent off," she said in a dangerous tone that sent shivers up my spine.

"You shouldn't have scented me in the first place," I countered.

"You liked it," she whispered, leaning forward so her lips were at my ear. "My offer still stands you know."

"I don't want it," I lied.

Here, so close to me, she was already making my body react in shameful ways. Keir pulled me even closer and she spun us around. I inhaled the perfume she was wearing and felt heat settle deep within me. It had been a while since we had gotten this close, and my thoughts veered off in a dangerous direction.

"I want it," she whispered. "I've been thinking about the way your face looked when I took you that night."

I gripped her shoulder tightly and felt my stomach clench, remembering the way her skillful fingers filled me. As we spun again, I caught sight of Cain at one of the exits. He was watching me.

"The way you tasted," she continued "The delicious lies you told me as you came on my hand."

Her words stirred something inside me and embarrassment filled me. I knew that if she continued, the vampires would know exactly what was going on with me, and that was the last thing I wanted.

"Stop it," I snapped. "Aren't you afraid that they will smell me?"

"So you admit I turn you on," she teased.

I had never wished for a blade more in my life than in that moment.

"I want them to smell," she admitted. "I want them to know how much my *date* wants me."

I swallowed thickly.

"That would be bad for you," I tried to whisper as low as possible. The other vampires had yet to look over to us, but I knew they could hear if they strained.

"I think it would be really good for me," she said with a small chuckle. "And if my plan works well enough, I can take you into one of the rooms and eat that wet cunt of yours until you forget your own name."

My face flamed and I couldn't help the gasp that escaped me.

"It's my turn," Gillard said from behind me, breaking the tense moment between Keir and I. I had never been more grateful for that vampire than right this moment.

I let out a loud sigh and practically pushed Keir away. I reached out to grab Gillard's hand and didn't look back at Keir.

"Thank you," I whispered and fell into step with him. Even though I still wasn't used to the vampire's touch, Gillard's half-human skin made me feel more at ease than Keir's and I felt myself relax against him.

"No need to thank me. If anything, I am hindering you," he admitted. The cold exterior he held faltered only slightly, and I could see something softer there.

"It's better this way," I said. "And I just. . . need a moment."

His icy eyes searched my face and suddenly his hand gripped me tighter.

"Agreed. . . but I don't think you will get that moment." He paused. "Vance will come over to ask you to dance. Please remember what I said to you."

His voice was low, careful.

A warning.

Gillard was gentle as he moved us around the dance floor. He had lost whatever anger he'd previously had and even gave me a slight smile. If I was being truthful, I would say I liked this side of him and missed when I saw it during our morning coffee runs. But I would never admit that. Not now, not ever. I wasn't capable of *missing* a vampire.

I cursed when I saw Vance making his way toward us just as Gillard had predicted. Not a few minutes later, I felt his presence beside us, and when I looked toward him, the dangerous smile that he had on made the hair on the back of my neck stand up.

"May I have the next dance?" he asked politely.

I pulled myself away with one last glance at Gillard and turned toward Vance. I gave him a smile and put my hand in his, following the protocol Gillard had taught me. He smiled back and pulled me toward him, rougher than he should have with a human. He was much more brutish in his dancing than either Gillard or Keir, but it wasn't hard to follow. His hands were gripping me hard and he spun me a bit too fast, making me realize that he normally didn't deal with humans in this respect.

He leaned down toward my ear. It was an act that reminded me too much of Keir, and I hated that it was him getting this close to me now. I wanted to push him away, but I couldn't risk making a scene with all these vampires around me.

"I didn't know a hunter wormed its way into the royal family," he whispered, his words making my heart pound in my chest.

"What can I say? Keir swept me off my feet," I said, trying so desperately to keep the smile on my face.

I searched around for Keir or Gillard, but I could not see either of them around his form.

"Oh, so you are not hired help?" he asked, squeezing my hip.

I bit the inside of my cheek to ground myself. The film felt like it was traveling across my skin and I had to hold in a shudder.

"I am not," I confirmed. "Just someone involved with Keir who happens to also have a job."

"Are you aware of the relationship between Keir and myself?" he asked, digging for more information. He was moving us across the dance floor and, I assumed, away from where Keir and Gillard were.

Panic shot through me. If I couldn't get to them there was no telling how this conversation could turn.

"Can't say I am," I mumbled and shifted my gaze. I could feel his eyes on me but I refused to look at him.

"She has a game where she likes to take what's mine," he explained. "It has gotten quite annoying."

"So it's about women," I summarized, still trying to look for those stupid vampires.

"Everything is." He let out a small chuckle. "When you live as long as we do, there is rarely anything to look forward to other than blood and getting off."

"That's crude," I said, meeting his eyes. They were dark and there was a bare hint of red seeping into them.

"Even so, Keir should know not to overstep the lines." He inhaled my scent deeply. "Maybe I should return the favor. An eye for an eye. You smell so sweet, I wonder what you taste like?"

"If they left so easily, were they really yours?" I snapped, getting tired of the way his slimy hands traveled along my body. I regretted my words as soon as they left my mouth.

His hand gripped my hip painfully, the pain radiated down my leg.

"And it seems that this is the first time I have been able to get ahold of what is hers," he whispered huskily and inhaled my scent once more.

"I am not *hers*, I am my own, so save your breath," I hissed, not liking where this was going, especially when I didn't have a dagger.

"She didn't scent you, so I assume she mustn't care that much." I almost let out a sigh at his words. "But the way she is glaring daggers at me right now tells me otherwise."

"I am tired of dancing," I said, trying to cut the conversation short.

"Yes, humans do tire easily. I forgot." He sighed and stopped dancing. He walked me to the edge of the dance floor where Keir and Gillard were waiting. Keir's mouth was pulled into a frown and she was glaring openly at Vance.

"Here is your human," Vance said, dismissing me as if he was handing off a toy he was bored with.

I grabbed Keir's outstretched hand with a shaky one of my own.

There were few words exchanged before Vance left, but as soon as he did I was whisked away to a less crowded corner of the room.

"What did he say?" Keir demanded.

"He asked about me being a hunter," I whispered, trying to keep my voice low enough for the vampires not to hear. I relayed the rest of the information and watched as Keir got noticeably angrier.

"I can't believe you just handed her over," Keir whispered angrily to Gillard.

"She's a hunter. She can defend herself. And it's not our job to keep her safe, it's the other way around," he shot back at her.

"I don't have my dagger," I explained. "I am at a disadvantage."

"Humans are what we need to fear here. Not the vampires,"

Gillard growled, also getting angrier as the conversation went on.

I rolled my eyes at them both and left to an empty table near the corner of the room, away from the other vampires. I tried to find Cain again, but I could not see him among the faces. The panic and anxiety that built up in me during that dance still ran through me and my knees felt weak.

Among the glasses of blood that had been placed on the tables were cups of water, no doubt for the feeders, which should have angered me, but I didn't care in this moment. I grabbed the closest water and gulped it down. Vance was a dangerous vampire and I couldn't wait to finally get out of here. I felt the longer I was here the more in danger I was. I prayed that it was obvious that Keir hated me because if not I would be in trouble.

Gillard and Keir stood near me, neither speaking though I could feel the anger rolling off them both. I wanted to snap at them and tell them that this was their fault to begin with, but then a pounding started behind my temple when I thought of fighting them.

"Gil, I will guard her," Keir said. "Go get her a drink to calm her nerves. I can hear her heart across the room."

Gillard narrowed his eyes but did as he was told, leaving us with not so much as a single complaint. She grabbed the chair closest to me and pulled it over so she could sit with me.

"What?" I snapped, not liking the way she looked at me.

"I am disappointed that I can't smell how much you want me anymore," she mock whined.

I rolled my eyes at her. This is what she was on about now?

"I never wanted you," I muttered, wanting to give her a glare but knowing better.

"Give me your hand," she ordered. I paused. "For the pretending, of course."

"Fine."

I gave her my right hand and she turned it over so my pulse was facing her. Her eyes gleamed as she brushed her lips against the inside of my wrist. They stayed there for a second too long and parted her lips, her tongue darting out for a taste. I snapped my hand away from her as my face heated.

"Don't do that when he's watching," I muttered at her, looking around and noticing Vance's stare from across the room.

How long had he been watching? Had he seen that? His smirk told me he saw it, and it also told me that he knew I was lying about not being important to Keir.

"Don't act like you don't like it," she teased, seemingly not caring what Vance thought.

"It doesn't matter what she likes," Gillard interjected, handing me champagne. I took a generous gulp, feeling a different kind of warmth flush through me. I was tempted to down it all and order another one, but I paced myself. There were still too many eyes around us.

"Buzzkill," Keir groaned.

"Between the three of us, at least one of us has to do their job, Keir," he growled.

Unable to handle the anger flowing around us combined with my own racing heart, I quickly excused myself to the bathroom, leaving them alone to fight among themselves. While I was in the large women's bathroom, I splashed water on my face, hoping it would bring me back to reality. I needed to get myself together and reign in whatever part of my brain thought it was okay for me to feel the way I did for Keir.

She's a vampire, for God's sake! I screamed at myself.

I leaned forward, my hands splayed against the cool counter, and tried to recall the anger that made her kind so disgusting to begin with. I forced myself to relive the pain and fear that I felt when I first stepped into my childhood home after years of not being there. I forced myself to remember the way their bodies were torn up and brutalized in ways that were unthinkable.

"Miss?" I jumped at the voice and opened my eyes, only to see a hunter who I didn't recognize appear behind me in the mirror. "The heir was asking for you."

I nodded and followed her out into the hallway, but instead of going back to the ballroom that housed everyone, she headed in the opposite direction.

"The party is the other way," I said, not following her.

She gave me a smile and motioned down the hallway.

"The heir was tired of the party and found a resting room," she explained. "They asked me to bring you there."

I nodded and followed after her. If Keir was done with this party and wanted to leave early, I was more than happy to get away from it. I hated all those eyes on me, and I didn't want to have to deal with Vance anymore than I needed to. He had already proven to me that he was not someone I should mess with, and I was inclined to believe him.

It was short walk to the sitting room, barely three doors down from the bathroom and not much farther from the exit of the party, but far enough that we probably wouldn't run into anyone else for the time being. She held the door open for me and gestured for me to go inside. I gave her a smile and stepped in and the door slammed behind me. It was not a second later that I heard it lock with a loud click.

"That was easier than I thought." Vance appeared in front of me and I scrambled back. He let out a laugh at my actions and took a step forward. I gripped for my dagger instinctively but cursed when remembered it was taken from me.

"What do you want?" I muttered and stepped back again, trying to put space between us, but he only mirrored my steps.

I searched for an exit, but this room had none. Bookshelves covered the wall and there was a desk in the middle of the room, behind that were some windows, but I would never get there with the vampire blocking my path.

"That's not a way to talk to a lord," he chided and backed me up to the wall. I gritted my teeth and tried to push him, but even using all my strength, he barely budged. "Hunters are weak without their weapons."

"Don't touch me," I shouted and smacked his hand as it came toward me.

He only wrapped his fingers around my wrist and twisted it up painfully above my head.

"I usually don't take human lovers," he said. "They are weak."

Without any other option, I slapped him, hard, but it did nothing. His eyes narrowed and he slammed the offending hand against the wall, causing me to cry out in pain.

"You are already testing me," he growled. "I was going to try to be gentle with your pitiful human body, but if you want it rough, I am willing to oblige."

"I am not interested in men," I spat at him.

"Even better," he said with a laugh. "None of mine were interested in women and look how that turned out."

"I am not going to fuck you," I growled.

I connected my knee with his groin and took my chance to kick him off when he crumpled down in pain. I ran toward the door, trying to break the lock, but he caught up to me too fast and slammed my head against the door.

"You fucking bitch," he growled from behind.

I sent my elbow flying back and it hit his face with a satisfying crunch. He howled in pain but did not release his grip. Instead, he slammed my head once again against the door, then pulled my hair back painfully, exposing my throat to him. Without hesitation, he sank his fangs into my neck.

My scream was cut short by his hand covering my mouth.

I never knew what a vampire bite felt like. I had assumed it would be the most painful thing I could experience. And it was. . . at first. The pain felt like my entire neck was on fire and it slowly spread throughout my entire body. If it was just pain, I would endure it. Pain was something I was familiar with and embraced every single day of my life. . . but this was different.

With stunning clarity I realized why the human slaves never left their vampires. Why Keir was so obsessed with using bites with her sexual conquests. Many humans fawned over vampires, because with just this once bite, my entire world changed. I was hit with the realization that I was no different from the other humans I had seen clinging to the vampires' arms.

It started slowly from the wound. Instead of the burning pain I felt, it was chased by the most pleasant warmness. It commanded my muscles to relax and my vision became cloudy. It was like I was dunked into a warm bath and my body slumped against the door, all the fight leaving me.

He removed his hand then, but I couldn't bring myself to scream now. Slowly the warmth made its way across my body, and I felt my stomach tighten. I couldn't even panic at what I was feeling. All I knew was that my core started aching, it needed to be touched, it was begging for some kind of friction. I clamped my thighs together, a low whimper coming out of my mouth. Vance slowly removed his fangs.

"You taste just as sweet as I imagined," he groaned against me and moved to my shoulder before biting down there as well. This time the pain was almost nonexistent and pleasure flared through my entire being.

I wanted more. I needed more than this. My body felt like it was going to explode, every touch was setting me off and I couldn't hold in the tremors that shook my body.

"Please," I begged, though I didn't know what I was begging for anymore. Was it more bites? Did I want him to touch me? I didn't know.

My vision became blurry and I had no choice but to fall against Vance, my legs refused to cooperate.

"That's it baby," he cooed. "Just relax. I got you."

CHAPTER 15

KEIR

I was really starting to hate parties. They were nothing more than a show of wealth, and it's not like we even needed to do that anymore. Everyone knew who had the most power, there was no need to try and prove it. . . though the hundreds of hunters that littered the event were a nice touch.

From the others' perspectives, this could look like another power move. Instead of being controlled by the Order, the Kazimir clan was now controlling them. Vance wasn't the smart one of this family, it was his father. So even though Silvia had said that she'd seen Vance at the Order, I was sure it was his father who had put him up to this.

"Can you at least pretend to be interested in the people here?" Gillard complained under his breath.

I rolled my eyes at him, brought the blood I was holding up to my lips, and took a deep sip. It had been far too long since I fed, and the blood helped to quench the mind-numbing thirst I had been pained with the last few weeks. But it was far from satisfying. It was stale and obviously far older than it should have been.

Or maybe I was just too enamored by the thought of tasting Silvia's blood that I didn't even want to entertain any other source. Speaking of Silvia, it had been a while since she had left.

I sat up and looked around the room, or tried to listen for her, but I was met with nothing. I saw a hunter come up to us from the corner of my vision, but I ignored him, too occupied by looking for Silvia.

"Where is Silv?" he asked as he came to stand near us.

I lifted my brows and took in his form. While he didn't seem to be much, I saw the way his muscles stood out under his uniform as he shifted. There was a bow and arrow strapped to his back and a dagger strapped to his thigh, much like Silvia had. I inhaled deeply and was caught off guard when a woodsy, burning scent filled my senses. He was a fucking witch. I gritted my teeth and stared at him.

We didn't normally associate with witches. We had something of a bad reputation with them in the earlier days of our lives on this earth, and the relationship remained distant throughout the years, neither party really willing to work much with the other since.

But how does he know our little hunter?

"Who are you?" I asked.

"I'm her partner," he growled. I tried to hide the shock on my face. Silvia never told us she worked with witches, nor did I ever smell them on her. "This place is filled with vampires and she has been gone for far too long."

He wasn't wrong, through I was curious now to know how long he had been watching us. Better yet, what did he think of Silvia's work with me?

"She has been gone for a while now," Gillard echoed. He

had lost his angry act, and his eyebrows were now pulled together as he searched the room.

Anger filled me and I stood up, trying to peer over the crowd once more. I was angry at Gillard for acting like he had, at this *witch* for his attitude, and at myself for not noticing that Silvia had been gone that long.

"She said she was going to the bathroom—"

I was cut off by the witch's growl as he stormed toward the adjacent hallway.

As I followed him I realized that Vance was also nowhere to be seen. This time it was ice-cold panic that flooded my veins and pushed me forward. I followed behind him, trying to pick up any sound from Silvia in hopes of finding her whereabouts. As soon as we entered the hallway, I inhaled deeply and was assaulted by the scent of Silvia, but not just any scent. It was her blood and the scent of her arousal. I gritted my teeth against the flash of anger that boiled inside me. My vision turned red and I felt my hair stand on end.

I ran down the hallway faster than I ever had, intent on finding the source. Gillard was behind me in an instant, but I didn't pay attention to him. The smell of her blood was putting me on edge, and not just because I knew Vance was doing the unthinkable to her. . . but because the hunger that was tearing me apart was so intent on tasting that blood. When I found the door to the room she was in, I couldn't stop myself from kicking it open. My kick was so strong the door flew off its hinges and crashed into the darkened room.

Inside I was met with a sight that caused a growl to rip violently from my throat.

Vance was on the couch with Silvia on his lap, his fangs sunk deep into her neck, bite marks littered all around her upper body. Silvia lay limp against him, her eyes closed, and while she was panting, her breaths were short and shallow.

She was struggling to breathe. Vance's red eyes met mine as he disconnected himself from her throat, his teeth stained bright red with her blood. He smirked at me as his hands trailed up the inside of her thigh.

"Keir," Vance chided. "Don't interrupt us, we were just getting to the good part. She was so good for me, begging for me to bite her. I feel sorry you weren't her first."

Silvia would *never* let a vampire bite her, and there was no way she would let him touch her like this.

When his hand dipped under her dress, it was like the chord that had been holding me back snapped and I lunged forward. The world moved in a blur and I couldn't focus on anything other than ripping apart the man in front of me.

I needed to make him pay for touching her. I needed to make him feel the pain he inflicted on her. I wouldn't stop until he lay dying beneath me, begging for me to save his life.

Just before I connected with him, I watched Silvia's body fall to the couch only to be pulled away by a pair of pale hands. As we rolled to the ground, I looked back to see Gillard holding a barely conscious Silvia and relaxed enough to turn to the man under me.

I threw punch after punch at him, my anger rising each time he blocked me. He tried to throw a punch at me as well but I dodged and brought my fist down on his face, hitting his nose with a satisfying crunch. But it wasn't enough.

As he moaned about his nose, I stood and grabbed him by his hand and torn shirt only to use all of my strength to throw him into the wall.

The books fell to the ground with a loud thud and hit him multiple times, but he was already up and running toward me at full speed before even a second passed. This time I was ready for him and met him with open arms. I used his own momentum to swing us so he would crash into the desk behind me. The desk couldn't hold his weight and burst into splinters.

I grabbed one and moved to stand over him.

"You touched what is *mine*," I growled and raised the large wood piece above me. "And I will make you pay for it."

"Keir, no wait!" he yelled and lifted his hand as if that could stop the blow. "She came to me!"

I brought the wood piece down onto his shoulder, his howls of pain sounding like music to my ears.

I reached down and grabbed another one.

"You're a horrible liar," I said and brought the second piece above my head. "She *is mine* and therefore a part of my clan. Do you understand now? You took from my clan, fed from her without permission."

I could hear other voices in the room but none of them broke through the rage-filled haze. I needed to see this fucker in pain, I needed to see him pay for what he did. The little hunter that I had been so intent on annoying and pushing away, the same one I sought out over and over again. . . was *hurt* by him.

"I didn't know it was that serious, Keir." His voice cracked as he spoke. "Please, *please*, Keir. I'm sorry, please no more. I understand. I won't come after her again, I swear."

"Too late," I growled and brought the stake back down, only for it to be stopped by a hand reaching out and grabbing it mere inches away from his heart.

I snapped my head toward the intruder and came face-to-face with my father's red eyes.

"Enough, Keir," he said in a low, threatening tone. "We can settle this amicably."

"Not good enough," I growled and pushed down, the stake digging into Vance's chest.

"Keir, listen to me," he commanded.

"Keir," a weak voice called. It was Silvia. My head snapped up and I peered over my father's form to see Silvia being held up by the witch that had called attention to her disappearance from the start. She reached out to me with a shaking, bloody hand.

I threw the stake to the side and crossed the room to pull Silvia into my arms, ignoring the witch's glares.

"I got you. I'm sorry, I'm sorry," I whispered.

I noticed Vance's father waiting near the entrance of the room, his eyes wide and a scowl marred his face.

"Keir, I—" He started to talk, but I cut him off.

"Your son and I are even," I said. "For now. You better expect me to bring this up later. In our negotiations."

His eyes widened and panic flashed across his face before he nodded and ran to his son.

The negotiations were an important part of any transfer of power. It would be when I met with each of the clan heads and renegotiated our terms with them. It included everything from land, to blood, to business ventures, so the threat was a serious one and he knew better than to fight me.

My father may be in charge now, but his threats meant nothing if I am due to be in charge in a few short months. Which is why I was within my rights to do whatever I wanted, even kill that bastard. . . but it wouldn't help my father's anger. I knew he would be waiting to talk to me about it, or to punish me for my display, but I didn't care.

All I cared about in this moment was the shaking woman that clung to my shirt.

Hunter Rules

rule 1 sec 2

Every Hunter must remember the
following when coming across a
vampire

    a. <u>Never</u> let your guard down
    b. A bare throat is a death
       wish.
    c. Vampires are <u>stronger</u> and
       <u>faster</u> than humans
       therefore Hunters must
       always be at their sharpest
       or risk being bitten.
    d. If you come across a rabid
       vampire do not approach.
       Call the Order for backup.

CHAPTER 16
SILVIA

"We are leaving," Cain insisted as soon as Raphael, Vance, and who I assumed was Vance's father left the room.

Keir ordered them to get out and leave us be while I got ahold of myself. I expected Raphael to yell at her, and me, but he just nodded and lifted Vance up before seeing himself out.

"She's not going anywhere until I heal her wounds," Keir said from above me. Her arms were wrapped around me, and I couldn't stop shaking. The effects of the vampire venom were still wrecking my system, and I didn't dare look at the others, ashamed of what they may see.

Especially Cain. I had no idea when he entered the room, but I hoped to God he didn't see how I reacted to the venom. I don't know how I would be able to live with myself if my own teammate saw that part of me.

"We are going to back to the Order," he insisted. "She is done with this job, you'll have to find someone else."

"No." I choked out and peered over Keir's arms.

Cain was angry and he was gripping his bow in his hands, knuckles turning white by the strength of his grip.

"Silv, it isn't worth this," he argued. "They are incompetent. How did they even allow him to get ahold of you?"

"She was the one who wandered off," Gillard said. His words were like a shot to the heart. I did wander off but. . .

"She didn't bite herself," Cain growled. "Do you even hear yourself? You make me *sick*."

Gillard stepped forward and I saw Cain ready himself, but Keir's growl cut through their spat.

"I am taking her to the adjacent room to heal her wounds and then we will go back to the compound where she will rest," Keir said with conviction, then she paused and looked down at me. Her eyes were still red, but there was a wrinkle between her eyebrows. "Is that okay with you?"

My heart jumped in my chest and I nodded.

"Let me talk to Cain real quick though," I pleaded. As much as I didn't want to face him right now, I had to explain this to him.

Keir nodded and slowly unwrapped her arms from me.

"I'll wait outside the door," she said. "Gillard will get the car. . . but don't take too long, you're bleeding a lot still."

I swallowed thickly and crossed my arms over my chest as they left. The door was ripped off the hinges so I could see Keir's form lingering outside, but she turned to give us some privacy.

"Please don't tell me Jade is here," I begged, shame filling me once more. How many hunters knew what happened here? How many of them heard how I was found? Would they look at me the same?

"She is not," Cain replied softly. He reached out to grab my hand. "I am so sorry I wasn't here sooner."

"It's not your fault. I shouldn't have—"

"Don't you dare finish that sentence," he interjected. "Let me use my magic to heal you. And then we can go back to the Order."

"Not back to the Order," I said. "But you can heal my head, and my wrist as much as you can, the rest will be taken care of by Keir and at the compound."

"Silv—"

"Please," I said, cutting him off. He gave me a pained look before stepping forward and holding his hands over my head. I felt a warm rush of magic engulf me and let out a sigh in relief as the pain slowly started to dissipate.

"It's bad," he murmured. "Fractured in two places."

He shifted closer to me and I could see the small sheen of sweat glistened off his face.

"If it's too much—"

"It's not," he insisted. "Just let me finish and then you can have the doctors at the compound look at it for you."

His voice was strained, so I decided to just sit quietly and let him take care of me for once. Cain had proven to be somewhat irresponsible in missions, but he had never *not* been there for Jade and me. Even when things were tough during our first weeks as hunters, he was always there trying to find ways to make us money. . . even if that meant taking the stupidest jobs. I remembered one time he found a higher Order member who would pay us to unload groceries into his house, but failed to mention his three Great Danes, which scared the life out of Jade.

I couldn't help but chuckle aloud.

"Uh oh," Cain paused and looked down at me. "Did I fuck something up in there?"

I shook my head and smiled at him.

"I was just remembering the early days as hunters," I said.

"And I wanted to thank you for always being there for us. . . for me."

He swallowed and took a step back.

"Any time, Silv," he said. "Your head should be mostly healed for now, but please take it easy." His eyes trailed to my throat. "I think it's time your vampire helped you clean those."

My vampire, it was funny to think about, but I didn't dwell too hard on it.

Keir stepped through the doorway and motioned for me to come out with her.

I walked out with Cain and waved him goodbye. He lingered a bit longer, glaring at Keir.

"Don't let it happen again," he warned.

"I won't," Keir said and pulled me along with her to the room next to us. I turned back to see Cain watching us and he didn't turn even as I was pulled into the room.

The room over was a smaller version of the last, this time with two love seats instead of couches and a smaller desk. The windows were a bit bigger and covered the majority of the back wall. Keir's hand lingered on the small of my back before she pulled me to the soft love seat. I melted against it, still feeling the effects of Vance's venom running through my system.

"I am going to have to stop the bleeding with my venom," she said as she knelt in front of me.

Seeing Keir on her knees before me stirred me. Someone as high-ranking as her in this world shouldn't bring herself down to my level, but here she was doing it anyway.

"I know," I whispered and leaned forward. I winced as I stretched my neck for her, the wound was deep and I could still feel Vance's teeth sinking into my flesh.

Her eyes were already red, but they somehow got even darker as she leaned forward.

"If it's too much, stop me," she said. "Or call for Gil, he's not far."

My heart slowed in my chest and a tingle of excitement ran through me.

"What do you mean, 'If it's too much'?" I asked.

Her eyes shifted to mine, and then back to my neck.

"I have been..." she cleared her throat. "I haven't had fresh blood since I stopped going out, and I am... *very* thirsty."

Her tone was forced and her hand gripped the side of the love seat, the fabric straining against her strength. I swallowed thickly and averted my gaze to the closed door of the room. A warmth started to coil in my belly thinking about what Keir would look like out of control.

I should have been scared. Should have demanded that she take me out of this room and bring me to a real doctor... but I didn't want any of that.

"Go ahead," I said and tilted my chin. "There are five bites, one on either side of my neck, two on my shoulder..."

I trailed, my face heating.

"Where is the other?" she asked, her eyes searching. They stopped at the top of my blood-stained gown. My entire right breast had been covered in blood, so I assumed she didn't see it until now.

"I am going to kill him," she growled. The sound of the chair's fabric ripping filled the air. "Slowly, painfully, and I'll make him beg for your forgiveness just before I take his life."

Oh, God. The words shouldn't have turned me on, but there was an undeniable thrum inside my body.

"I asked for it," I whispered. Her eyes shifted toward mine. "Not the others, just this one... I'm sorry, I wasn't—"

Her hand covered my mouth to stop me from speaking and she shook her head.

"You were overwhelmed by your reaction to the venom, it's

okay," she said. "Please don't say sorry about this. You weren't in your right mind."

I swallowed the knot in my throat and nodded. She leaned forward, her breath fanning the side of my neck.

"I am going to start now, okay?" she asked.

I nodded and strained so she had better access to my throat. She let out a long sigh before I felt the first touch of her tongue against the bite. It was painful, but as she continued to lick the wound clean, I could feel her venom working through me, healing me, and also eliciting the same response it had before.

I leaned into her, feeling the effects of the venom relax my body. Her hand moved from my mouth to pull at my hair, forcing me to tilt my neck even further. She moaned against me before moving to the next bite on my shoulder.

"One down," she said against my skin. "God, you taste so good."

I shuddered as her tongue traced the second one. A low groan made its way out of her mouth and my body heated. I pushed my hand to my mouth and dug the other into the side of the love seat, trying to control my reactions to her cleaning my wounds. The venom had already made its way through me and begun to settle low in my belly. My panties were soaked, but this time I welcomed the reaction. This time I wanted nothing more than for her to tear off my panties and bury her fingers deep inside me.

She pulled back and looked up at me, her expression dark, and I could tell she was struggling just as much as I was. Her hand pulled at my hair and forced me to bare the other side of my neck to her. When she leaned forward this time, instead of licking the wound, she planted a sizzling kiss to it, pulling a strangled moan out of my mouth. She paused before licking the length of my neck.

My hand flew to her shirt and pulled her closer to me. She let out a groan against me and the edge of her fang traced the wound, pulling a shiver out of me. It didn't hurt, it was quite the opposite now.

"How mad would you be if I took a bite?" she asked against me, her lips trailing down my neck and to my chest. She looked up at me as she peeled the bloodied clothing down, baring my blood-stained breast to her. I was panting by now, my nipples erect and just waiting for her mouth.

Instead of answering I arched my back, welcoming her to take the bite she was longing to.

She didn't at first. Instead she ran her tongue across the bite, watching my reaction. My hand flew up to my mouth to keep my whimpers inside me. It was all she needed before she leaned forward, pulled my nipple into her mouth, and sucked on it lightly. Then without warning she opened her mouth wider and bit right over Vance's bite.

I let out a muffled sob as the sharp pain mixed with the pleasure of her venom traveling through my body. She began sucking out my blood, and I arched further, my hand flying to her hair and forcing her closer to me.

She let out a moan and her free hand to traveled up my thigh, only stopping when she reached my lace panties and pulled them off me. Her hand found my wet folds, cupping me before she let her fingers travel to my swollen clit.

"Ah, *fuck*," I groaned as her thumb circled and two fingers pushed themselves into me.

She used her hand to cover my mouth and disconnected herself from me. Her red eyes and bloodstained mouth turned me on further, and I felt myself clamp down on her fingers. She pumped in and out of me, and I spread my legs for her. Her strokes were gentle at first, but as they turned harder I couldn't keep the moans inside me.

"You hate me, remember?" she said in a low tone. "You hate my kind, you wish we were all dead. Remember?"

I nodded furiously and gripped on to her wrist to steady myself as her hand drove into me.

"I hate you," I said against her hand.

"And you are going to remember that out there," she growled. "You will sneer at me, call me names, tell me you hate me. Do you understand?"

"Fuck," I groaned against her hand and threw my head back as I felt my orgasm cresting.

"Say it," she commanded. "Say you understand."

"*Fuck, fuck,* I understand," I groaned against her hand. "Please, *please,* Ke—"

She removed her hand from my mouth to lift my leg and place it on the arm of the chair, baring me to her.

"God look at how wet you are," she breathed as her eyes focused on my exposed pussy. She slowed her pace and used her free hand to spread my folds. "*Beautiful.*"

Her words sent a lightning bolt exploding through me, and even at this slower pace, pleasure shot through me.

"Please," I begged her again. "Harder."

She smirked.

"I think the little hunter is enjoying this a bit too much, hm?" Even though she was teasing me, she obliged.

I couldn't stop the sobs as they fell from my mouth. I was already too far gone. My mind was hazy and my body was overstimulated. Each thrust, each brush against my clit, sent bursts of pleasure through me that were too much for me to handle.

"Now cover your mouth so they don't hear you come on the hands of the person you hate," she growled.

I covered my mouth and was rewarded with her pounding into me at an unimaginable pace. I couldn't even scream as my orgasm racked my body. I went totally limp and tears leaked from my eyes.

Without waiting for me to get over my orgasm, she leaned forward and licked the last wound on my shoulder.

When she pulled her fingers out of me she pulled back and made me watch as she licked my release off them. She stood, both hands placed on either side of me, and stared into my eyes.

"This didn't happen," she said in a low warning tone. "The rest of the party is almost gone, *including* my father who made his retreat after the fight." Her eyes lowered to my mouth and she leaned forward to capture my lips in hers. I could taste myself on her.

"I—"

"Tell me you understand," she growled as she pulled away from me. "This didn't *happen*. We came in here and I cleaned your wounds. You and I both had reactions to the blood, but we did not take it further than that."

"I understand," I echoed.

She nodded.

"Gillard will see us out the side doors to avoid any unwanted attention," she said. "Again tell me how you feel about me."

I swallowed the knot in my throat.

"I hate you," I uttered.

She nodded, though her facial expression remained tense.

"Good," she said. "Now get up. We have to get out of here."

CHAPTER 17

SILVIA

As I stared into the mirror, I couldn't help but feel ashamed of the person I had become.

It had been almost twenty-four hours since the incident at the Kazimir clan's event, and I still didn't know what came over me. I couldn't sleep at all last night, and I couldn't look away from the mess that my body now was.

My red hair was pulled into a messy bun atop my head with a few strands framing my pale face. My eyes looked sunken and the bags under them were darker than I had ever seen before. I stood in my bra and Hunter-approved pants, unable to pull my eyes away from the scars that littered my upper body. Especially the mismatched bite marks that peeked out of my bra, showing that Keir was slightly off when she bit down on me.

"Fuck," I growled under my breath. Each mark would leave a visible reminder to all who saw just how much of a shameful hunter I was. They would remember how Vance took me and forcefully buried his teeth in me. But what they didn't know...

was that I liked it. I liked the way the vampire venom filled me and the way Keir's teeth sank into me.

I loved it even more as she fucked me on the chair in their study while feeding from me.

"Fuck, *fuck*," I growled and tore my gaze from the bites that littered my skin to look at the sink below me.

How will I get out of this now?

"*And you are going to remember that out there,*" she growled. "*You will sneer at me, call me names, tell me you hate me, do you understand?*"

"I understand," I whispered. . . but I couldn't even believe myself.

How did I let this happen? What did Jane and my parents think of me now? Instead of avenging their death, I am fucking the vampire that ran the clan who murdered them. I couldn't tell if it was ironic or just plan wrong on my part.

Even when it was Vance, I fucking *begged* that fucker to bite me. Bile rose up in my throat and I ran to the toilet just in time. After I finished emptying the contents of my almost-empty stomach into the toilet, I washed my face for the third time that day and brushed my teeth so hard my teeth began to ache.

I heard the knock echo through the room and let out a sigh.

"Go away," I muttered.

"I just want to check on you," Keir's voice said, muffled by the door. It was loud enough for me to hear from the bathroom, but I still strained to hear.

She was the last person I wanted to comfort me now. I knew it wasn't all her fault, and I was just as much of a player. . . but I couldn't help but blame her for everything. If I had never come here I would be still slaving away at the Order, never knowing exactly how it felt to be bitten.

It would have been better that way, at least I wouldn't be

so marred now. I could go through life hating them. . . *really* hating them.

"Disgusting," I said to my reflection.

I was disgusting and there was no denying it now.

A knock came at my bathroom door and I averted my gaze from the mirror back to the sink.

"Please, Silvia," she said from the door. Her tone stirred something in me and a wave of guilt washed through me.

"You are the last person I want near me right now," I said truthfully.

Before I heard her enter, I felt her stand behind me, the heat radiating from her, but she didn't touch me.

"They may fade, eventually," she said. "It would have been better if he had healed them but. . ."

"He wanted to mark me," I said and looked up to see her staring back at me in the mirror.

She nodded. I moved my gaze to the one she left on my breast that was peeking out of my bra.

"I did too," she said. "If I am honest."

Heat and anger flared in me. I hated that her words still caused my body to react in such ways.

"Do you regret it?" she asked.

I shifted my gaze to hers, but I couldn't speak.

"Because I don't," she said when she understood I wouldn't continue. "I do regret how it came to happen, but I don't regret you."

I don't regret you. The words circled through my head.

"I wish I never came here," I admitted and watched as her brows furrowed. "The debt is not worth *this*."

"You're angry," she noted.

"You're *fucking* brilliant," I growled.

Her jaw clenched and she stepped back. She was searching

my face for something, though I do not know what else my scowl could tell her that it hadn't already.

"But at me," she said. "Why me and not Vance?"

I closed my eyes and steadied myself against the counter.

"Because I hate you," I answered.

"No," she said and I felt her hands join mine on the counter, her front mere inches from my back and her breath hot on my neck. "You hate me *out there*. Not here."

I grabbed the hilt of my dagger, ready to pull it out and end her life, but she gripped my wrist, stopping my movement.

"But we can play this game if you want," she said in a bitter tone. "Lie to yourself, hate yourself, I don't care. We can't change what happened."

I was ready to fight back, but she stepped back and cleared her throat.

"Gillard is waiting for us," she said. "You'll get your coffee and go back to work like a good little hunter."

I gritted my teeth against the anger that boiled under my skin.

"You are not in charge of me," I growled and glared daggers at her in the mirror.

She sent me a smirk to tell me that she believed the exact opposite of my statement. She turned and left the bathroom without another word.

"Oh yeah," she called from farther in the room. "Don't forget to put on a shirt. Though I wouldn't complain if you decided to walk around naked."

A scream ripped itself from my throat and I grabbed the nearest object, a ceramic soap dispenser, and ran out of the room to throw it at her. She was turned toward the door when I first saw, her but she quickly stepped out of the way, causing the object to break on the door.

She sent me a devilish grin before disappearing out of the room.

"You could have caught it," I grumbled as I stepped out of my room for the first time that day.

I had dressed and brushed my hair out, deciding keeping it down for the day, before having to step around the mess of the soap on the ground. Keir and Gillard were waiting for me outside, Keir with her usual smirk and Gillard with a frown.

"I'll have the maids clean it up later," Gillard said and I noticed that he was missing his glasses again. This time he had large dark circles that bruised his face.

"I didn't know your kind could get dark circles," I said and his lips twitched.

"I am half, remember?" he reminded me. "As much a human as you."

"Or as much a vampire as her," I said and nudged the offending vampire with the hilt of my sword.

Keir sent me a smirk that told me she was proud of her vampire self, and what I said wasn't much of an insult.

"Come on," Keir said and led us down the hallway. "The human and half human need their caffeine."

At this Gillard did let a smile grace his face, but I didn't allow mine to show.

I walked faster to keep up with Keir and him as they both fast walked to the downstairs garden café. There was a comfortable silence around us, and I was grateful that they didn't try to broach the subject, but it was short-lived.

As soon and Gillard and I ordered my coffee and sat down at a nearby table, Keir decided to push her luck.

"Vance—" Keir started but I cut her off.

"What's the plan today?" I asked Gillard, fully intending to ignore Keir. I wasn't ready to talk about this. She had made her intentions clear in the bathroom, and so had I.

"She has a negotiation with a small clan leader today, so you will need to act as a guard," he finished, also intent on leaving her out of the conversation.

"Her clan is the most agreeable to work with," Keir interjected. "She doesn't allow for the mistreatment of humans in her clan."

"What she does with her clan does not concern me," I replied, ending the conversation. Keir sent a glare my way, but I ignored her and focused on devouring my coffee. My stomach was aching and begging for food, but I didn't chance it, knowing that it wouldn't stay down for long.

"We have to leave soon," Gillard said and abruptly stood. "Bring your coffee, I'll explain more on the way."

I nodded and followed suit. Keir was the only one lagging behind, but she easily caught up.

The car ride took forty minutes and during that time Gillard went into depth on how this clan came to be. Apparently they were a smaller clan that migrated over with them, but instead of coming from Europe they came from places all over Asia, China being the main contributor to those migrations.

Just like Keir stated, Gillard assured me they were the best clan they had worked with so far. They didn't cause fights and kept their blood usage to a minimum, mostly relying on donations from the community around them. The idea of donating to the vampire next door wasn't what I would have found appealing, but to each their own I guess.

As the car entered a thicker forest area, the smaller compound came into view. The architecture was traditional Chinese—with vibrant greens and reds painted on the wooden buildings that stood out against the forest—but seemed much more at home in this space than the glaring monstrosity Keir's clan had.

As we stepped out of the car I was hit with a gust of clean air. I inhaled deeply and greedily, unable to remember a time that I had been able to breathe such fresh air.

"It's so clean here," I murmured.

"Higher altitude," Gillard said. "And we are much farther from the city than our compound is."

I nodded and let them lead me into the compound. Vampires greeted us as we passed, not even looking twice at the weapons strapped to my sides. It was odd to see the vampires look at a hunter with such indifference. . . but it wasn't *really* indifference, they just weren't scared or wary of me. They treated me like I belonged here as much as they did.

I could hear the faint sound of running water, and finally as we turned a corner, I saw a wide bridge and under it a pool, filled with brightly colored fish and lily pads floating on the surface. Just beyond it was a makeshift waterfall and the pool itself was surrounded by green plants.

It was peaceful here, more so than any place with vampires that I had been before. Gillard pulled me out of my trance by pulling me across the bridge and to the largest building in the compound. It only spanned two floors, but it took up almost the entire middle of the compound and had a wooden porch that wrapped around its entirety.

"Keir, you made it," a woman said, meeting us as we entered the building. She was dressed in a loose sweater and jeans, surprisingly casual clothes for a negotiation. Her dark hair was tied up in a messy bun on the top of her head, and her reddened eyes watched us closely.

I tried to push down my uneasiness and planted a hand firmly on my sword, watching her carefully as she approached.

I had been caught off guard yesterday and I wouldn't let that happen ever again.

"Of course. I always look forward to our talks." Keir went in for a hug and the other vampire's eyes met mine as she looked over Keir's shoulder. Bitterness bloomed in my stomach at the intimacy of the move.

"And you brought a hunter," she said, removing herself from Keir and walking over to stand in front of me.

"Yes, Father has unfortunately deemed it necessary that I have one at all times." Her words sent a twinge of annoyance through me. It was not like I wanted to be there either.

"My name is Xin," she said, and held her hand out for mine.

"I wouldn't do that. She literally hates every single one of us," Gillard said, but Xin's face did not drop nor did she remove her hand. She continued to hold my gaze, forcing me to be the one to make the decision.

"Maybe it is because of your attitude, Gillard," she remarked and I felt my lips turn up slightly. "I hated our kind when I first turned as well. I can understand the feeling." She leaned to the side and nodded. "I see you are hiding some fresh bites there. It's hard not to hate our kind after an experience like that."

I shifted, but tried not to fix my hair like I wanted to.

"You were not born a vampire, yet you are in a position of power," I remarked, not fully trusting her words.

"Well, they don't trust me for a lot of reasons, but I proved to them that I was capable," she explained. "And don't get it wrong, we are a small clan and barely hold a candle to that sorry sack of an heir."

Keir made a disgruntled noise but didn't say anything else. I slowly took Xin's hand and gave it a quick shake. Hers felt cleaner than the ones that plagued my mind. Both Keir's and Vance's.

"Silvia," I said and tore my hand away almost as fast. Her smile reached her eyes.

"Perfect," she said in a tone more heartfelt than I had felt in a long time. She reminded me of an older, calmer Jade and it made me feel safe.

She guided us down the hall and took great lengths to explain the history of how her clan had migrated so far. I nodded while she spoke, trying to act as nonchalant as possible, but my inner history nerd was screaming. When I was a child I would have eaten this shit up, back when life was simpler and I didn't have to think about my debt or my parents' murder.

"Before the humans knew about us, this compound was much smaller and we would allow them tours," she said with a small laugh. "It was a way to get money, but also to interact with the population. Imagine the surprise of our normal customers when they put the pieces together."

She showed us to a small room, just big enough for the four of us, and gestured for us to go in.

"Did they ever try to come back?" I asked.

I don't know what pushed me to ask, but she didn't act too surprised when I did.

"Many," she said. She sent me a smile and motioned for me to take a seat. I shook my head and stood against the wall. The table's seats were far too close to each other and it's not like I was here for rest anyway.

"Though they did stop bringing us food," she said with a mock wistful tone. "Pity, the dogs quite liked it too."

I gave her a forced smile but did not respond.

"All right, let's get to it," Gillard said, interrupting the conversation. He cleared his throat and fixed his button-up. Today he had forgone the jacket and tie, probably already knowing that Xin would dress as casually as she did.

"You are so impatient, Gillard. That's not going to get you a husband anytime soon," Xin chided.

I had to force my smile down.

"I heard there was a small gang on your territory that was taken out," Keir said, bringing the group back to business.

Another vampire entered the room with a tray that held four cups. She handed mine to me first and then handed some to the others. Theirs were obviously blood, but mine was a fragrant green tea. I eyed it suspiciously, not sure I trusted the drink here yet.

"Yes well, I wouldn't say I am too upset about it," she said. "Though I do wish whoever had killed Dimitri had at least saved the humans in the building as well."

Something tickled the back of my mind as she spoke, I knew that name from somewhere. It was important, but it wouldn't come to mind.

"Were the humans a part of your clan as well?" Keir asked and took a sip of her drink, her brown eyes already red.

"Yes, but many of them were stolen from their positions and were forced to serve." She sighed. "They even took Pen. I had wished she'd gotten out alive, but they damn near blew up the entire block."

My heart started pounding in my chest and I tightened my grip on the cup of tea. I should have known as soon as they mention Dimitri. It was me. I was the one that blew up that building, along with Cain and Jade. And Pen was the informant who I didn't pay any attention to.

This was too much of a coincidence. I couldn't seriously be in the same room as the clan head. . . did she know it was the Order? Know it was me?

I shakily brought the cup to my lips and took a small sip. The hot liquid did nothing to calm my nerves.

I hadn't wanted to kill the humans, but it was the job. . .

They would surely understand that, right? I had already felt like shit about myself after I had let what happened yesterday happen, but this brought on a new wave of shame.

Maybe this was my punishment. Maybe this was why all of the things stacked up the way they did. That bastard of a God was forcing for me to repay my sins. I should be glad that I was finally getting what I deserved, but all I wanted to do was sink into the wall behind me and hide forever.

I focused on controlling my breathing, but they had already paused and looked my way. They could probably hear my heart racing. Gillard's eyes narrowed at me, but Xin looked at me with sad eyes.

She knows, of course she can put two and two together.

"Tell us what you know," Gillard said, almost growling at me.

"I cannot," I forced out. "The Order has strict confidentiality policies."

But even saying that much told them all that they needed to know. They knew I knew something, and that the Order would forbid me from talking about it. What else was there for them to know?

"I never suspected the Order to be so cruel," Xin murmured into her cup.

I had the sudden urge to beg for her forgiveness. She had been so kind to me, so understanding and so unlike any other vampire I had met so far. I didn't want to hurt her. I blamed my already unstable emotions. . . but it was so much more than that. It was *her* I felt bad about hurting.

"Can you at least tell us why?" Keir asked without looking at me.

"If you knew Dimitri you would know why," I said and gripped my sword.

"Did you know Dimitri?" Xin asked. Her lips in a slight frown.

"I met him once," I confirmed. "At his hideout."

My throat ached as I tried to force myself not to let out this flash of emotion she raised in me.

"And Pen?" she asked softly.

My silence was deafening.

"Her too," I choked out, remembering the way her glazed-over eyes watched me from across the room as a vampire bit into her.

"There is no need to bring up the past, but it does disappoint me greatly," she said. "We have fought for years to ensure that the humans are safe and not just because of the Order's rules. We truly wanted the best for them, but now I see we may have to keep them safe from the people who were supposed to protect them."

I don't know why her tone made my heart hurt. I didn't understand fully why I even cared about her words to begin with. I wanted to tell her that everything I did at the Order was because I needed money. Assure her that *I* didn't even want to go through with those missions. I wanted to tell her that I was better than that, better than the same monsters I killed.

But are you? a voice whispered in my head.

I'm not. I realized. *I wasn't better. If anything. . . I was worse.*

"It was you, wasn't it?" Gillard asked. He had to have known with the pounding of my heart meant.

"I was sent to kill Dimitri," I confirmed, not caring about the contract that bound me anymore.

"How did you even get in a place like that?" Xin questioned.

"I acted as a new blood bag," I answered truthfully.

"That must have been hard for you." Her sympathy felt real.

Please don't feel bad for me, I begged internally. *I don't know if I can handle it.*

"It wasn't," I spluttered, trying to find the words. "Pen was. . . she was. . ." I couldn't formulate the words with Xin staring at me with those pity-filled eyes.

"You feel bad all of a sudden?" Gillard asked. His voice had an edge to it.

"Gil," Keir warned.

"No, where does she get off on calling us scum, but it was her all along?" Gillard's fist hit the table. "Did you ever look in the mirror once in your entire pathetic life, Silvia?"

I didn't get angry at his words, since I knew they were justified. I had been thinking the same thing the entire night and well into the morning. I just never knew that someone of his kind would be so affected by the human lives lost.

"They picked me as the last resort for a reason," I told him.

"Because if it was humans that tried to kill us, you wouldn't hesitate to bring them down?" he accused.

Blood traitor.

"No," I answered truthfully. "I wouldn't."

He met me with a shocked silence.

"I think you should wait outside," Xin said to me.

I nodded, then quickly left the room and didn't stop until I was almost out of the building, where I assumed was out of hearing range. I remembered the mission all too clearly now, the way the humans looked at me with pleading, dead eyes. The way Dimitri's hands choked the life out of me. The way the building sounded as it exploded in the distance. Gillard had even commented on my bruises.

No one in the Order had ever questioned me about the fairness of my actions. It was always a job well done and that was the end of it.

213

Did you ever look in the mirror once in your entire pathetic life, Silvia?

I was too distracted to notice the small vampire girl who had moved past me until she was almost out of reach. She was not carrying any trays, and I assumed that this area was off limits to most.

"What are you doing?" I asked and she froze. "Turn around."

She stood still, not listening to my command. I walked over and grabbed her shoulder and turned her to face me. It wasn't the snarl on her face that sent panic rising through me, but the device in her hand.

Without a moment to think about my next move, I sent my fist straight to her face, but she dodged it with ease. I pulled out my dagger and lunged forward, trying to slash at her face. She jumped back and landed in a crouch; her wide panicked eyes met mine and I ran forward, reaching for the device. Before I could stop her, she pressed the button. A shrill sound emanated from the box and she dropped to the ground with it, covering her ears with her hands. I scrambled for it, but when I pushed the button nothing happened, the sound continued.

"How do you turn it off?" I yelled at her, gripping her by the shirt and shaking her harshly.

Her face was pained, yet there was a smile resting on her lips now. I slapped her, and still, she had no response. I gathered the box in my hands, trying to ignore the ear-splitting headache it caused. The box was made of some type of reinforced metal, which was much stronger looking than the one at the last event.

I grabbed ahold of it and tried to break it by slamming it down against the floor, but it stayed strong.

"Come on!" I yelled and hit it on the floor over and over again.

However, there was no change. The ear-splitting headache it caused turned my sight blurry, and I knew that if this was what I was feeling, the vampires in the room I left had to be in agony. I grabbed the vampire by her shirt and dragged her out of the building with the device. It was slow work, but I wouldn't dare leave her in the hallway alone, not when she could easily go back and finish her job while I was distracted.

I placed it on the ground outside and with the hilt of my sword I tried to break it once more, but it barely made a dent. I let out a pained groan as the headache intensified. Spotting the lotus pond not too far away, I prayed that this would work and threw it straight into the water . It landed with a splash and the shrill sound disappeared. I was about to crawl over and end the vampire's life for good, but before I could even blink my vision clear, I found myself surrounded. They were dressed in all black, in similar uniforms to the Order, and had silver masks covering their faces. I couldn't tell whether they were vampire or human, but I knew for sure I had come face-to-face with the rebellion.

I had never expected my life to turn out like this, but here I was at the mercy of the people.

"Blood traitor," the man in front spat out and held a sword much like my own at my neck.

I didn't move nor did I grab for my weapons. I didn't have the energy to do it. I mean surely it wouldn't be hard to end them. . . but was that really what I wanted? I was *so tired.* I had been fighting for years for an organization I hated that protected people I hated. My family was gone, and I had turned into a monster who was no better than the ones the Order sent me after.

Was this really the life I wanted? Even if I paid off my debt. . . what would be left for me? How could I even live in a world without them? Tears welled in my eyes, and I tried to blink them away and stare up into the man's eyes in front of me.

"Do it," I said and threw my head back even farther so he would have a better shot.

He faltered, dropping his sword slightly.

"Do it," I demanded harder this time and pulled down the fabric on my neck, hoping they could see the bite marks.

"We know who you are," a girl from my right said. "And we know the countless human lives you have taken. We know you work for the heir."

"If you know so much then stop talking," I snapped and pushed my neck into the edge of the sword. I felt it slice open my skin and realized it was not too much different than when Vance had used his teeth.

"We have space for you if you are willing to right your wrongdoings," the man in front of me said.

Why is this so hard for them? I growled in my mind.

"I don't want it. Just do what you came here to do," I spat. "It's me, right? Why else would you send a vampire to their own death? You must be mad that I ruined your little plan last time."

It was not a moment later when the vampires came out. I could hear them, but I didn't dare look away from the man in front of me. The others looked up to them, but the one holding the sword did not look away. His brown eyes peered into mine even as the vampires got closer.

"I will kill her," he said.

I rolled my eyes, the rebellion was proving to be more incompetent than I realized.

"They are vampires. You should know they don't care," I said with a sigh. "Just do it already, what are you waiting for? Didn't get far enough your training to cover murder?"

I grabbed the blade and began pushing it farther into my

neck. It sliced through my hand, a burning sensation shot up my neck and into my face. I let out a groan as the flesh of my neck tore.

One of the rebels held up another box with a shaky hand.

"Back away," he said. "Let us escape or we will use this."

The man's eyes didn't leave mine.

"Coward," I whispered and removed my bloody hand from his sword.

He slowly removed the sword from my neck. I felt my skin pull and had to grit my teeth from letting out any noise.

I pushed my hand into my neck, trying to stop the bleeding, but I still felt blood starting to seep out. The humans ran away and the vampires were at my side in an instant. Keir was in front of me and replaced my hand on my neck with hers.

"You have a death wish," she growled at me.

"Never said I didn't," I argued, as the pain traveled up the side of my face. "They wouldn't kill a human. It's not in their rebel handbook."

"But it's in yours," Gillard shot back.

"Everyone is fair game." It felt like a lie coming out of my mouth.

"The wound's bleeding too much. I need to close it," Keir said and I blanched.

"I refuse. Go get a witch if you have any," I snapped. My head began to feel light as dark spots started to crowd my eyes.

"You know that's not what I mean," she whispered. I knew what she meant, but I didn't want to do it again.

"I could do it if you feel uncomfortable," Xin said from behind me.

I cursed. I would rather die than have her lips on my neck again, but I did not trust Xin as much.

"Do what you must," I said to Keir, trying to act as though my vision wasn't getting worse by the second.

She removed our hands and tilted my head to the side to get a better look at the wound. She paused, then ran her tongue across my skin. I bit my tongue as I felt the same heat spread over me as it did yesterday. It was embarrassing, shameful, and overall just disgusting. Tears pricked my eyes, but I did not move as she ran her tongue up and down my wound.

Keir pulled back and told me that she was done, but I was too weak and achy to answer. I heard her talking to me, yet I couldn't understand what she was saying. All I could focus on was how tired I was becoming and how much I wanted to sleep.

I'm so, so tired.

I succumbed to the darkness not a moment later.

CHAPTER 18

KEIR

"It doesn't make sense," Gillard mumbled next to me.

Both of our eyes were on the Silvia's still body before us.

After she fainted I stopped her up and followed Xin to the medical bay. It was only big enough for three beds and a few chairs, but it would do for now. Witches had already heard the commotion and were waiting for us near the bed. They hovered over Silvia, trying to replace the blood she had lost and heal the rest of her injury. Only when they pulled away panting and sweating from magic overuse did they tell us that her injuries from the night with Vance weren't fully healed.

Her wrist was sprained and while most of her head was healed, they stated there was still a part that was fractured. I asked them to see what they could do about the bites on her skin, but they told me it was too late for them to help. The scar tissue had already set and she would be stuck with them for the rest of her life.

"Nothing makes sense," I said and sat back in my chair.

Gillard shifted next to me before he began pacing behind my seat once more. "*Gillard,* please *sit down* for God's sake."

"I can't," he said and wrung out the hem of his shirt. "Why would they send a vampire? How did they even get ahold of one? Why did they slice her neck open like that? The rebellion shouldn't want to hurt humans, even if they wanted to get back at her for what she has done. You heard them too didn't you? It didn't sound like—"

"Gillard," I hissed and sent him a glare. "They tried to recruit her, we all heard it."

It was fuzzy and my head was still pounding by the time I pushed myself out of the meeting room, but I heard it loud and clear. They were not here for me, they were here for Silvia.

But it didn't make sense. . . Why would they recruit her here?

She went alone to the Order quite often, they could have just grabbed her there. Why did they sneak into a compound full of vampires when we weren't even their target to begin with?

"But it didn't *feel* right," he said and then paused to run his hand through his hair, destroying the low ponytail he had put it in this morning.

I had seen Gillard like this a few times before. He had a tendency to freak out, especially if it was just him and me. . . but over Silvia?

"We will ask her when she wakes up," I grumbled and brought my gaze back to her.

Her red hair and black clothing stood out against the all-white hospital bed and sheets. Her skin was pale from the blood loss, but the steady rise and fall of her chest assured me she was still living, even if her body looked more like a corpse than her usual spitfire self.

"Do you think. . ." Gillard trailed off. "Never mind, now I *know* I am crazy."

I let out a loud sigh and pinched the bridge of my nose, the headache from that stupid device coming back full force.

"What is it?" I hissed.

Gillard paused in his steps and came to stand beside me. I looked up to see his gaze trained on Silvia with a frown.

"Do you think it's the same people who killed her parents?" he asked.

A silence cut through us, the only thing filling it was the rhythm of Silvia's heart and her soft intake of breath. I swallowed thickly before answering.

"They would have killed her if that's the case," I said and crossed my arms over my chest. It was a simple enough answer, but even after my rebuttal the heavy aura between us didn't lift.

"Maybe they knew they couldn't," he said. "Maybe they wanted to get her far away from us before doing it."

I sat on the thought and kept my mouth shut. I didn't want to refute his claims, because I agreed it was weird, but I offered no other explanation either.

The racing of her heart told me she was about to wake up.

"Leave us, please," I whispered to Gillard. "Stay near though."

He didn't say anything in response, just turned to leave and, just like I asked, stayed close. Right outside the door actually.

He was worried about her as well. I didn't fault him for it. . . but we were both in too deep now.

As I watched her fall to the ground, blood pouring from her wounds for the second time in less than forty-eight hours, I started to understand that this wasn't a game anymore. I had messed with her far too much, and now that I had developed a soft spot for the little hunter, I couldn't watch as she risked her life over and over again.

And for someone who was as ungrateful as I was. . . because that was what I had been.

I let her run head first into danger, even when I had the ability to keep her from it. Everything that had happened until now could have easily been avoided if I would have just paid better attention to our surroundings. And that didn't even go into the unspeakable things that I did to her after Vance had violated her in such a horrible way.

I heard her crying last night in her bed. She tried to muffle it with her blankets, but I heard. I also heard the muttering under her breath. She was calling herself useless, disgusting. . . Suddenly I didn't want to make her come to me. I didn't want to prove her wrong anymore.

If hating me brought her some consolation, I would gladly become the worst possible version of myself.

But even the thought of that felt like a knife to the chest. I wanted to touch her. I wanted to be near her. I wanted her to *want* me the way I wanted her.

And it wasn't just sexual. . . at least not anymore.

She let out a groan and her eyes fluttered open. The silver-blue orbs snapped to me immediately and she tried to push herself up on shaky arms. I had to grip the uncomfortable plastic arms of the hospital chairs to keep myself from rushing over to help her up.

"You should resign," I said once she had pushed herself into a sitting position. Her long red hair fell around her and covered her face like a curtain.

"Keir," I heard Gillard hiss from the hallway. I ignored him and focused solely on Silvia.

She let out a sigh and tucked her hair behind her ear, giving me a perfect view of the bite mark that peeked just above the collar of her turtleneck.

"I should, shouldn't I?" she said with a light laugh.

I sat back and gritted my teeth. Why wasn't she angry at me? Why wasn't she yelling? It would have made this so much easier.

"We can get someone to fill in for you," I said. "I am sure we can talk to—"

"Did you change your hair?" she asked, cutting me off.

I opened my mouth to reply, but no sound came out and I quickly snapped my mouth shut.

Well, there goes that plan.

"Yes," I answered through gritted teeth. "I did."

Three days ago to be exact, as she slept. She hadn't noticed until now? It wasn't a huge change, just a trim, but for someone as attentive to their surroundings as her I had assumed she noticed, just didn't mention it.

"I am not resigning," she said, her tone wasn't hard, but it had a definite edge to it, telling me this was not up for discussion. "I have a debt to pay."

"I don't *want* you here anymore," I lied, annoyance filling me.

Her lips twitched before a full-blown smirk spread across her face.

"Then you should try harder to get rid of me," she said and with a sigh pushed herself to the back of the bed and leaned against the headboard, her gaze never leaving mine.

"Why did you let them hurt you?" I asked. "Do you really have that much of a death wish?"

She shrugged and her gaze dropped to her hands.

"I wasn't in a good head space," she said in a low voice. "I felt bad for what I have done up until now. With the Order, killing humans left and right—"

"That wasn't—"

"Let me finish," she interrupted, her eyes flashing to mine and narrowing. I nodded and motioned for her to continue. "I did wrong, and not just with the Order. I betrayed. . . myself. My values. And it all ran together in that moment and I just—" She took a deep breath. "I don't know why I am telling you all this. I don't have a death wish, there is your answer."

My control was holding on by the thinnest thread imaginable. I wanted so badly to throw myself at her, cover those deliciously plump lips with my own and make her forget about every sentence she just uttered. I didn't want to take back what we did, I loved every moment of it. . . but to hear how bad it affected her, to know that she wanted to seek out death because of it. . .

It hurt, and *no one* hurts me.

"It's okay," I forced out. "I'll keep another one of your secrets."

My words were supposed to come out playful, but they came out strained and sounded not at all liked I hoped. I was tempted to tell her that Gil was waiting outside and the secrets remained between the *three* of us. . . but I dropped it.

"Where is Gillard?" she asked as if reading my mind and cocked her head to the side.

Damn it.

"Yes!" I heard Gil whisper from the hallway and amusement, mixed with a bit of bitterness, filled me.

I stood, digging in my pocket for my wallet.

"Get in here," I growled, raising my voice just for show.

The door opened and Gil strode in with the cockiest grin on his face. It annoyed me, but I was glad to finally see him enjoy himself, even if it was something as small as this. He stooped near my side with his hand out expectantly.

Grabbing whatever paper money I had in there, I shoved it into his palm.

"What was that about?" Silvia asked from the bed.

"A bet," I growled.

"To see who's name you would call first," he said with a smug smile.

My eyes shifted to Silvia's and a light blush coated her cheeks, no doubt remembering how she almost screamed my name in the heat of the moment as she came on my hand the other day. If I just hadn't covered her mouth, that handful of money would have been mine. . . but it dulled in comparison to the sight she had given me.

A sight you will never get again, a voice said in my mind. Instead I shook the thoughts away and gripped the back of Gil's neck, forcing his head to bow slightly.

"Gillard has something he wants to say," I said and sent a look to him. He cleared his throat and a small blush colored his ears.

"I'm sorry for what I said, Silvia," he said, his tone sincere. I pulled my hand away from his neck and gave his back a pat.

"It's uh okay—"

"It's not," Gil insisted, cutting Silvia off. "I know you don't have a choice on what the Order gives you. I know that you were only doing your job. And I really shouldn't have been so hard on you, especially after what Vance—"

"It's okay," Silvia said and climbed out of bed. "Really, let's just. . . not talk about it okay?"

Gil nodded and sent me a look, telling me it was my turn now.

"It's my fault anyway," I admitted. Silvia met me with a shocked expression. "I'm sorry, about everything. Vance saw it as a challenge and took advantage of my laziness. I am sorry, Silvia."

She shifted and cleared her throat before reaching for the weapons we stashed next to her nightstand.

"I still hate your kind," she grumbled.

A flare of excitement ran through me at the hint of playing our old game once more.

"Do you though?" I teased.

Her eyes widened and quickly she placed her weapons back in their straps.

"Maybe not as much as before," she admitted, still not looking at us. "But that was a given. It wasn't you two who hurt me in the first place, was it?"

Her eyes finally met mine and I saw right through her mask.

We may not have killed her family, or been the one to bite her against her will. . . but I had been hurting her, and I would do so again.

I didn't think I could stop myself, not after we have gone so far. Not after the taste and smell of her blood still lingered in my mouth and caused heat to pool in my belly. I would hurt her again, but I couldn't find the will in me to stop myself.

I heard Xin come down the hallway and quickly tried to mask the arousal speeding through me.

"Good to see you recovered," Xin said as she pushed through the door. "But that was a bit dramatic, no?"

I watched in envy as a smile spread across Silvia's face.

"Life would be boring without a bit of flavor every now and then," she answered.

I was going to do something stupid. I knew from the moment the idea popped into my head that I would somehow live to regret it. . . but I couldn't just stand around and do *nothing*.

I had tried to leave her alone the last few days, but it had been hard.

When we left Xin's compound I had been hopeful, but then that very same night I heard her muttering under her breath. I acted like I didn't hear it, but both Gillard and I knew that she was still really affected by what had happened.

And I didn't know how to fix it.

I wanted to make her forget what happened, but I also didn't want to force her into another situation she would regret. And as much as it killed me, I knew that I would have to wait for her to come to me this time around. That's when the idea popped into my mind.

When I was a kid, and still unable to protect myself from my father's abuse, I used to escape and run off into the forest. Not with the intention to actually run away, but just to get the prying eyes away from me. The compound was filled with people who watched my every move and I learned rather quickly that they were just spare eyes for my father, reporting on every little thing that I did.

So, I ran.

I learned the patterns, and began to see when I was alone and when I was being watched. And when I found that one time no one was looking, I would sneak out in the darkness of the shadows, listening intently for any footsteps that may have followed me, and when I knew the coast was clear, I snuck off toward the back of the compound. There lay an easy way to get over the walls, all I had to do was climb up a gnarled and twisted willow tree, and my freedom was at my fingertips.

The first night, I ran as fast as my small vampire legs could take me. As a child, I couldn't match the strength or stamina that the adults had, but I had learned to be fast as hell. I didn't stop running that night; I was intent on just leaving everything I knew behind. Forgetting about my clan, forgetting about my mother's corpse that had rotted in the basement, forgetting about what I was destined to do. . . and just *breathing*.

It was by accident that I found a meadow that overlooked one of the area's natural waterfalls. I had actually tried to find a road instead, but it was the happiest mistake I had ever made. By the time I made it there, I was panting and disgustingly sticky with my own sweat, but I didn't care because I *made it*. The moment I took in the rising sun over the rumbling waterfall was when I knew that this would be my spot.

It was pure, and untouched by my fathers clan. The loud rumbling of the waterfall drowned out everything else in the vicinity, including the thoughts that plagued my mind. Here I didn't have to think about the pain, it just simply vanished, and for the first time I was *truly* alone.

I promised myself that I would never show a living soul this place. That I would keep it all to myself in fear of what they would do to it, and in fear of the peace that they would take from me. . . But today was the day that I decided that it wasn't I who needed the peace of the waterfall any longer, it was Silvia.

"It's a surprise," I said for the fifth time as both Gillard and Silvia let out exasperated sighs. I gripped onto the steering wheel, nervous butterflies flew around in my stomach. "You will not be disappointed, I promise."

It had been a long time since we left the compound for anything other than business and I was itching to get out, but more importantly. . . I was itching to get Silvia back to her normal self. She hid it well. . . but she couldn't fool me.

"If we are going to a bar. . ." Silvia trailed off, shooting me a glare. She was sitting in the passenger seat and I longed to reach over and squeeze her thigh, but with our chaperone Gil in the back, I doubted he would let such an obvious display fly.

"Don't worry," I said and drove the car out of the

compound. As soon as the metal gates opened, my heart felt lighter. "It's much better than a bar."

I followed the road until I spotted a smaller trail-like dirt road that would barely fit the car we were driving and made a sharp left turn. Curses flew out of Silvia's mouth as her nails dug into the seat. Gillard lurched forward and held on to the back of my chair.

"You've lost your damn mind," Gillard hissed.

I couldn't help but laugh at them and speed down the narrow road. Silvia's heart was racing and it only pushed me to go faster, but alas the drive was too short for me to get any real joy out of it.

I slammed on the breaks just as we were coming close to the dead end, almost crashing us into the surrounded trees.

"I'm a human, remember?" Silvia just about screeched as I put the car into park. She pushed the door open and fell out of the car, scrambling to get away from me.

I peered in the rearview mirror to see Gillard propped up against the window, looking like his soul had already vacated his body.

"It wasn't that bad," I said in a light tone, excitement running through me as his eyes lit with anger.

Before he could complain I turned off the car and stepped out, narrowly missing the rock Silvia threw at my head. I straightened my clothes and sent her a smirk before continuing on my journey to the spot.

"Keir, where are we—"

"Hurry!" I called behind me. "It'll get cold for the puny human soon."

There was a light growl from Silvia, but I heard their footsteps behind me as I disappeared into the trees.

"Is she taking me out here to kill me?" Silvia asked under her breath.

I let out a small laugh and peered behind me to see Silvia and Gillard, far closer than they normally would have been and both staring at me with differing levels of fear and suspicion in their expressions.

"I wouldn't waste so much time trying to kill a hunter," I said and turned back to continue walking forward. I could hear the waterfall now. We would be there in a matter of minutes.

"Oh my," Gillard said in mock concern. "It's me you're going to kill, isn't it? I knew this day would come."

Silvia let out a light snort that made my heart soar. I enjoyed seeing them like this, they both were made from traumatic, soul-crushing events that were hard to come back from and needed someone who understood that level of pain, even if they refused to brush the topic themselves.

It was only seven more minutes until I broke through the barrier, the meadow showing itself to me. I hadn't been here in many months, but I was relieved to see that it was still in one piece and there were no unfamiliar scents detected, just clean, untainted air.

Usually by now, a wave of calmness would have fallen over me, but instead I was filled with nervousness. What would Silvia think of this? Would she think it was stupid? Would she hate it?

I had never shown anyone this before and now the reality of opening up like this to someone crashed into me all at once.

A small gasp rang out as Silvia stepped through the barrier of the meadow. I didn't dare to turn and look at her, I was afraid I couldn't handle the disappointment.

Gillard entered the meadow then, the only indication was the shuffle of his feet then a long pause.

"I didn't know this existed," he mumbled.

Silvia took another step forward, then another, then another until our arms nearly brushed across each other. I could feel the electric tension between us snap into place and all the worries I had about her hating it here drifted away with the sound of the waterfall.

I looked down at her and the world froze around me. Silvia's silvery eyes were wide and staring out at the waterfall below us. She took another hesitant step forward and her hands gripped at her shirt as she took in the sight before us. I had never seen someone display such awe as this. In a world such as ours, we were not given beautiful sights like this. There was nothing to be in awe about, nothing to look forward to, and nothing to love. . . but she showed all of it in those silver pools of hers.

The setting sun made her skin glow a beautiful hue that complimented her fiery hair. She had worn her hair down for the last few days, and I watched as, for the first time, she pushed it behind her ear, giving me a perfect view of her face as her eyes scanned the area.

This place now paled in comparison to the sight before me. I didn't care about the waterfall or the meadow, I only wanted to make sure that *this* sight would be burned into my memory forever. If this was the sight that I could see for the rest of eternity, I would have no qualms about ruling. I would rule for this, for her, and nothing else.

My father, the clan, the vampires that wanted to tear us down. . . no one could take this from me. Take *her* from me.

How had a measly hunter been able to achieve this? How did she become so important to me? When did she?

I didn't care about people, I didn't want to. There was no use, after all I had a clan to run soon. . . but she somehow wormed herself in here without me even noticing.

She turned to me, a small genuine smile resting on her face.

"This is a nice place," she said.

I waited for the sarcastic remark or insult. . . but there was none.

I turned my face away from her, feeling my cheeks heat unbearably. Running my hand over my face, I wasn't surprised to see Gillard glaring at me from the trees surrounding the perimeter of the meadow.

You're in trouble, his look said.

I fucking know, I wanted to tell him.

"Let's get back," he said, breaking the spell between us. "The human will get cold soon."

Silvia cleared her throat before turning and walking back the way we came. Gillard waited for her to pass him before sending me another look.

"We will have words when we get home," he said in a low tone and turned before I could respond.

I stood in my own silence, the waterfall behind me sounding far too noisy all of a sudden.

"*Fuck,*" I growled and walked after them.

We didn't wait until Silvia was asleep this time.

It didn't matter at this point, we couldn't make the situation much worse anyway. Gillard paced in front of the door, a glass of wine in his hand. The ache in my throat intensified as I watched him take a healthy gulp of his drink.

God I wish I could feed again.

And of course, my mind went straight to Silvia and the warmness that spread through me as her blood exploded across my tongue.

"This is wrong," he grumbled under his breath. "Raphael will have your head for this, Keir."

I sighed and ran my hand through my hair, tugging at the

strands a bit harder than usual. I knew that I was playing a dangerous game. . . One that may not be easy to come back from.

"There is nothing happening," I lied.

Gillard spun around, his eyes narrowed into slits and the grip on his glass tightening so tight I thought the glass would shatter.

"You *cannot* lie to me, Keir," he spat. "Lie to your father, lie to the clansmen, lie to the Order, but *never ever* to me, Keir. Not when I am the only thing keeping your ass safe at the moment."

I swallowed thickly, the guilt from his words settling on me.

"We are just fucking," I said then shifted. "Or at least I would like to be."

The glass shattered in his hands, sending the shards and the red liquid spilling all over my floor and carpet. I gritted my teeth, wanting to yell at him but knowing that I had no place to in the moment.

"You are *courting* her," he corrected for me. "This is not what you would do with the others. I *know* you, Keir. You took her to see the *fucking* sunset!"

"I took you too," I noted with a raised brow.

If looks could kill, my head would be on the floor with that broken glass by now.

I ran my hand over my face and let out a groan.

"I like this one, Gillard," I said, all the fight leaving me.

How much more could I lie? To myself? To her? It was becoming unbearable.

"The transfer of power is a month away, Keir," he said, his voice rising an octave.

"Then help me hide it!"

My own desperation and loss of control surprised me, and I

quickly tried to pull myself together, but Gillard saw all he needed to.

"Just. . ." He paused, letting out a heavy sigh. "Just tell me why. Make me understand and I will agree to help you hide it."

I dropped my gaze to the floor, unable to face him while I uttered the words.

"I don't know when it started," I said truthfully. "But I can't get her out of my head, and after seeing what that *bastard* did to her"—I took a deep breath to steady myself—"I just can't let that happen again. . . and I want to help. She is sad. *Was* sad."

Gillard took a deep breath and I heard him cross the room, but didn't dare look at him. What must he think of me now? Falling for the hunter even as she hurled insult after insult in our faces? He probably thought I was shirking my responsibilities, thinking that I was just trying everything and anything to get out of the transfer of power.

It was shame. . . I was ashamed of feeling something so weak and disgusting. I was no better than my mother and would probably end up like her, tied in the basement and starving while—

Gillard's hand gripped my shoulder, forcing my rapid fire thoughts to pause. I slowly looked up at him, surprised to see a small smile on his face.

"You're not a baby anymore," he said and lightly slapped my cheek, forcefully pulling me out of my shock.

"What do you—"

"Now you better be smart about this," he warned. "I can only help keep this in the dark for so long, and as soon as he finds out I can try to deflect, but I cannot let him know I was involved. Do you understand what I am saying?"

My throat felt tight as I nodded.

My father would spare me, maybe even Silvia because of her ties to the Order... but not him.

"Thank you," I whispered, my voice hoarse.

He nodded and let out a heavy sigh.

"Now, what's the plan?" he asked, his tone turning serious. "The sunset was a nice touch, but I assume you will need much more than that to get her to stop hating you."

I let out a small laugh and shook his hand off.

"I wait," I said and crossed my arms over my chest.

"Wait?" he echoed, his brows furrowing. "You don't *wait* for things, Keir."

I couldn't hide my smirk. *I don't wait for anything. . . not until now.*

"Now I do," I said.

He slowly looked back down to the mess of wine and glass that was currently seeping into my floor.

"I need another," he said with a heavy sigh.

Me too, buddy. Me too.

"Now get out," I ordered and began rolling my sleeves up.

He gave me a bewildered look.

"Did you just kick me out?" he asked with mock offense.

"Yes," I said and motioned toward the ground. "And clean that up, Silvia walks around barefoot half the time."

"Wait a minute—"

"I said I would wait," I interrupted him. "Didn't say that I wouldn't try to speed things up."

Gillard let out a sigh and fell to his knees, picking up each sharp before depositing it into the small trash can by my desk, grumbling under his breath the entire time.

"I can't believe you fucking lied to me—"

"Tick tock," I said and tried to hold in my laugh as he glared. "Her heart rate is slowing and I need to catch her before she falls asleep."

CHAPTER 19

SILVIA

Sleep still eluded me days after the event. And even if I could sleep, I found myself woken up by dreams of a vampire biting into me.

The worst part?

They weren't nightmares.

In my dreams I enjoyed being bitten by a vampire as much as I had enjoyed it in real life. In my dreams I imagined it was Keir again, biting me while she pulled orgasm after orgasm out of me. I would wake up panting and painfully horny.

I hoped to God Keir didn't smell anything, because if she did I would be mortified. I may have been able to come to somewhat of a truce with them, but I still couldn't believe I had given myself so freely to her.

I rubbed the bite on my neck, not liking how I could still feel Vance's fangs deep within me. The wounds may have scarred over, but sometimes pain would radiate from them, reminding me of how he bit me against my will and that the scars would now haunt me until the day I died.

Except. . . except the one that Keir had bitten over. That

was the one she bit into every night in my dreams, the same one that never hurt for a moment after she had healed it.

Groaning, I covered my head with the covers, trying to force myself to fall asleep. . . but I couldn't. Keir wouldn't leave my mind.

All I could think about was the way her face looked at the meadow today. She was expectant as she watched me and then there was a flash of something before she looked away. . . Why would she bring me there?

I had never known Keir to be sentimental, and her bringing us to this random meadow was something that I didn't expect from her, but it was beautiful nonetheless. I don't know how something so beautiful and peaceful was still untouched by man in this world.

The moment I stepped through those trees, the thoughts of the world fell away, and for the first time in months, I could think of something other than my debt and the death of my family. I felt weightless in that moment, and if Gillard had not pulled us away so early, I would have no doubt stayed there for hours if Keir allowed it.

She acted so human in the moment, I think that was what had startled me so much, and it was all too easy in that moment to pretend that she was just another human. Her title as heir to the world's most powerful vampire clan fell away, and all I saw was the person Keir *could have* been.

Keir would probably be just as entitled in human form. Always walking around with her head high, acting as if all the insults in the world couldn't hurt her. She would no doubt be someone with a successful business. I imagined she would make a killer business person, yet a less-than-tolerable boss.

We probably would have never met each other if she wasn't a vampire. . . but maybe if there were no vampires at all, my life would have turned out much different than it had.

Nonetheless, if she was human I probably would have fallen for her long ago.

She had a way with women, I could see it from the moment we met.

She was confident, she knew what she wanted. . . and God did she have the most kissable lips.

I would be intimidated by her. In a world where I wasn't a hunter, I probably wouldn't have the balls to talk to someone like her. She would be standoffish at first, but then when she noticed my interest that *fucking* smirk she always wore would no doubt be plastered on her face. She would be the first one to make the move, she would have to, I wouldn't have the courage—

"Silvia?"

Speak of the devil. I swallowed and pushed down all the ridiculous thoughts that plagued my mind.

"Yes?" I answered back hesitantly.

"Would you like to join me in my study for a drink?"

God yes.

"Sure," I replied and climbed out of bed.

I didn't bother getting dressed. Instead, I walked out in my silk pajamas that she had loved so much last time. The little daydream in my head left me feeling bold. Keir's face was priceless, and her eyes widened almost comically.

"Can your kind even get drunk?" I asked and led the way to her study.

"If the blood has enough alcohol content, yes," she said, her voice strained.

"Would you be able to eat food if it had blood mixed with it?" I opened the door, not missing the dark stain on the edge of her carpet. Instead of mentioning it I just walked over to the couch and made myself at home.

"I suppose," she mused, handing me an already-filled glass

of wine, another glass no doubt filled with blood occupying her other hand. "I just hate the texture."

"Classy tonight," I said and took a big gulp of my wine, liking the sweetness of it as it washed my nerves away.

Keir moved to sit on the same couch as me, though she made sure to keep ample space between us. I was grateful given the last few nights I had had increasingly embarrassing dreams about her, and I did not feel very confident in my ability to not fuck this up even more than I already had. I let my eyes roam down her relaxed form. She was in the band T-shirt and ripped jeans again. The clothes that made her look so human, that made her look too approachable.

"You haven't been sleeping well," she remarked, sipping from her blood-filled cup.

"No," I confirmed. "I have been having. . . dreams."

Heat rose up my neck and I had to look away from her.

"Nightmares?" she asked.

I tipped back my glass, finishing it faster than I anticipated. Keir stood to grab the bottle that was sitting on her desk, filling my cup before I even had to ask.

"Let's not get too drunk, like last time," she teased then paused. "Is it Vance?"

I swallowed thickly and debated exactly how much I wanted to tell her. I knew once the words came out, there was no taking this back. But was I okay with that?

I hadn't been okay with it. . . and to be honest, I still wasn't sure how I felt about what was happening between us. I wanted to hate her, hate the clan that murdered my parents. . . but I couldn't, not like before. Things were different now that I had seen it myself. Seen how human she could be. Felt how warm her hands felt, her lips felt.

"Vampire bites," I said and took a sip of the wine.

She let out a noise and sat back down on the couch.

"He was your first?" she asked.

"Obviously," I said, though there was no heat behind my words.

She let out a sigh and I peeked up at her, she was watching me intently.

"I'm sorry your first experience was like that," she said. Her gaze was hot and warmth flushed through me.

"My second experience was better," I said, the words coming out far more confident than I felt.

Her head tilted up slightly and her eyes became hooded. I squeezed my thighs together, feeling a warmth spread in my belly.

"I'm glad to hear that," she said, her voice turning husky. "My offer—"

"How would you keep it from them?" I rushed the words out before she could finish her sentence.

She leaned forward, closing just a bit of the space between us. Her eyes drifted down my form and I shivered, my nipples hardening in response. Her tongue darted out to lick her lips, and I couldn't help remembering how it felt when it circled my nipple.

"Any place that can be thoroughly cleaned can have your" —she paused, clearing her throat before continuing—"*our* scents wiped from it. Leaving no evidence."

I found myself leaning forward to try and bridge the gap between us, my eyes locked onto her lips. The same ones that had plagued my dreams and given me many restless nights since I first felt them against mine.

"They would hear," I whispered, shifting my gaze to her reddening eyes.

"We are far enough away from the other rooms that no one would know," she said, her eyes trailing my body once more. "Or I could force you to be quiet. You quite liked that last time."

I fucking *loved* it last time. It took everything I had not to close the gap between us.

"And if I wanted you now?" I asked, nervousness creeping up on me. "Would your offer still be open?"

In a flash the wine was pulled from my hand and Keir pushed my legs far enough open that she could kneel between them. Her hands trailed up my bare thighs, lighting small fires under my skin. I gripped her wrist as she slipped her hands under the hem of my slip.

"Do you want me, Little Hunter?" she teased, a smirk appearing on her face.

I swallowed thickly and leaned back against the chair, spreading my legs for her.

"I think you know the answer to that," I said in a cool tone that in no way reflected the turmoil inside of me now.

Her hands slipped under the straps of my underwear before one of her hands grasped my core without warning.

"Let me rephrase," she growled and leaned forward, her tongue reaching out to lick the bite on my neck. "Is this pussy wet for *me*?"

As if to restate her point, she slipped just two fingers into my underwear and teasingly ran them from my entrance to my clit. A small whimper forced its way out of my lips, and before I could back out, I wrapped my arms around her shoulders, bringing her closer to me.

I tried to bring my lips to hers but she pulled away, her free hand coming up to grip my chin and keep me from trying again.

"Answer the question," she said and circled my clit, sending shocks of pleasure throughout my body.

"Yes," I breathed and tried to capture her lips, but her grip held.

"Yes what?" she asked, her eyes dropping to my lips. I

glared at her and a smile spread across her face so wide that I saw her fangs. She circled my clit again, causing me to let out an embarrassingly loud moan. "Use your words, love."

I was positively dripping, no doubt making a mess of her couch and my underwear.

"My. . . *pussy* is wet for you," I growled.

"Good girl," she whispered and let out a small chuckle, but it soon died as I ran my thumb across her bloodstained lips. I should be disgusted, revolted by the person in front of me right now, but none of those thoughts entered my mind. All I could focus on was the pure need radiating through me after days of dreaming about those same lips on me.

"I hope this is not you trying to get me fired," I whispered. I pushed my thumb into her mouth and pulled her lips to the side, looking at those fangs that had made me lose my mind so easily. I brushed my thumb across her fang and she let out a low groan.

"They're. . . sensitive," she said around my thumb and lightly bit down, though not hard enough to break the skin. "I wouldn't offer to cover it up if I wanted you fired."

I pulled my hand away and trailed it down to her neck, her muscles jumping under my touch.

"And if I ask you to bite me again?" I whispered.

The air stilled and Keir turned stiff against me and pulled her hand out of my underwear.

"You are testing my control, *Silvia*," she said. My name flowed off her tongue with ease and heated my body.

"Maybe I want you to lose it," I said.

A growl ripped from her chest and her hands gripped at my thighs, sending shockwaves through me.

"If we are doing this," she said with a heavy voice. "We have to move. I was serious about us not getting caught. Even now with you dripping all over this couch, Gillard will for sure know what we were doing."

I swallowed thickly. There was no going back now.

"Where did you have in mind?" I asked.

A small devilish smile spread across her face, and in an instant, she lifted me so my legs were around her waist, and I had no choice but to once again circle my arms around her shoulders and pull her closer.

"The shower," she answered.

Shock ran through me but before I could open my mouth to speak, she moved at a pace so fast my vision blurred, and I didn't even realized we had left the space until the bright lights of the bathroom hit me. I expected her to put me down, but instead she continued walking and brought us straight into the shower. I barely caught the expansive bathroom before she reached around me and turned the shower on full blast.

A gasp was torn from my lips and I glared at her as the freezing cold water spilled over us. She leaned forward, blocking most of the water, causing it to run down her hair and soak the front of her shirt.

"Are you kidding me?" I asked, shivers racking my body.

She let out a light laugh and tilted her face so that our lips were just brushing. She pushed me against the cold tile, her hands trailing up my thighs.

"Are you sure?" she asked, her words coming out slow, hesitant even.

I paused. *Was I?*

This wasn't the first time we went this far, but the circumstances were far different now. Now I couldn't ignore what was happening between us. . . And now I had no excuse when it came to breaking my contract. Before we could play it off as small mistakes, but this was fully in my control, and after this, the only person I could blame was myself.

Keir had been honest about what she did and didn't want from day one. I, on the other hand, had been hiding behind poorly crafted lies and a hate that had no force behind it. But I was done hiding, I knew what I wanted.

"Yes," I whispered, and that was all the encouragement she needed.

Keir, with careful control, licked the length of my bottom lip, her hooded eyes watching me. I opened my mouth for her and she greedily began devouring me. Her kisses were hungry, and so hot I was sure they would brand me. Different than the hasty kisses she gave me the other times. This time she didn't rush and took her time exploring my mouth with her own.

A metallic taste exploded across my tongue, but instead of disgusting me I found my body heating more at the thought, and I arched into her, needing her more than ever.

When the water began to heat, she removed herself from my lips and trailed kisses down my throat. I let out a moan at the feeling of her tongue over a scarred bite. Her hand ran up my side before cupping my breast. I let out a gasp when her fingers came up and rolled my erect nipple.

I pulled at her soaked shirt, needed the offending fabric off her immediately. She chuckled against my neck and allowed me to remove it, then let my eyes trail over her exposed breasts. I bit my lip, feeling my now-swollen clit pulse with need. Trailing my hands over her nipples, a shaky moan left her lips and ignited a fire inside me. I was in control now, and her noise only fueled me. I smirked and rubbed the pad of my thumb over her nipple before pinching it lightly.

She let out a hiss and dove forward to cover my mouth with hers.

Keir did not remove my slip even as the water soaked right through it. Instead, she ripped my underwear off, much like she had the first night we were together. Her fingers were over my aching pussy in seconds. She trailed them lightly from my clit to my entrance and back, using just enough pressure to send shocks through me, but not enough to provide release. I whimpered and tried to grind against her hand, needing more friction than she was giving.

"Patience," she cooed.

Her fingers moved to apply more pressure to my clit and I threw my head back with a loud moan, not caring about the pain that went through my head when it made contact with the shower wall. She littered kisses down my neck while rubbing circles on my clit, pulling embarrassing sounds out of me. I tangled my hands through her hair and forced her mouth closer to my neck.

My hips bucked wildly against her, heat rushing through me. I was so close to orgasming, but just as I felt my body stiffen, she pulled her hands away.

"Please," I moaned as her fingers teased my folds.

Her mouth clamped on my neck, her fangs teasingly scraping against my skin. I tilted my head to the side, giving her access to my neck and praying that she would just finally bite down, right over Vance's bite and forever erasing him from that part of my body. . . but she just pulled away and left a small burning kiss in the area.

"On one condition," she said, running her two long fingers down my slit, teasing my entrance.

"Anything," I panted. "Please."

I would give anything for her to just fuck me against this shower wall. Better yet, bite me while she did it.

"Say my name," she ordered.

I paused and her fingers went back to my clit, pulling a whimper out of me. I was shaking by then, my body barely holding on after being teased so relentlessly.

"Say it," she growled, eliciting a burst of excitement through me. "Or I will leave you here in a panting, wet mess."

Swallowing thickly, I bit back my retort and complied.

"Keir," I said, my voice almost a whisper.

"Louder."

"Keir," I moaned as her fingers teased my entrance again.

"One more time."

"Keir!"

Her two long fingers slowly sank into me. Her thumb played with my overly stimulated clit as her fingers relentlessly pounded into me.

"Fuck," I moaned and arched into her, begging for her lips to touch my skin once more.

Her teeth found my ear and she bit down, sending small sticks of pain through me. The pain only added to the pleasure shooting through me, making me clamp down on her.

"Is this what you wanted?" she asked, scowling.

"No... faster," I moaned.

She laughed in my ear. She went even slower after I spoke.

"Did you think of me tonight?" she asked, almost stilling.

"Please, don't stop," I whined.

"Answer and you'll get rewarded," she promised.

She was enjoying this far too much.

"Yes, I did," I growled and was rewarded with her lightly massaging my G-spot. My breath caught and I let out a strangled moan.

"What did you imagine? Was it me fucking you like this?" she asked.

I swallowed, trying to form the sentence but with each stroke of her fingers, she chased it away.

"No," I choked out. She rewarded me with a thrust. "It was. . ." And another slower one, coaxing the words out. "It was meeting you again."

"Again?" she mused and continued with her lazy motions, clearly enjoying the struggle she was putting me through.

Another brush against my G-spot caused me to forget my thoughts.

"In a time, a place, where we could be together," I moaned.

Her thrusts became faster.

"Be careful of your next sentences. You are playing a dangerous game," she growled and nipped harshly at my neck.

"A place where you were human. A place where we could have a normal relationship." She paused, almost completely. Stilling. "A place where I could just be with you."

"Why are you doing this to me?" she moaned, her lips finding mine once more. She began pounding into me again at a frenzied pace. "Why do you give me hope?"

She was losing control. I could feel it as she shook against me. Her grip was harder than it should have been for a human, and I knew after this my pussy would be aching from how hard she was fucking me.

I *loved* it.

I couldn't answer her, I was lost in her fingers. I felt myself clench around her. My release was coming up faster than I had ever experienced.

I couldn't stop the words as I came. "Fuck, Keir."

Her assault didn't stop there, though. Her fingers kept pounding into me, and I felt myself start to shake.

"Why couldn't you just stay away for your own good?" She growled and bit down on my nipple through the slip. Water was running cold, but I barely noticed. Her motions were heating me up enough as it was.

"Say it again," she demanded.

"Keir."

"Again."

With each thrust she hit my G-spot, over and over.

"Keir."

She bit on my other nipple and I let out a small scream. My toes began to curl once more. She must have felt it because her thumb started to circle my clit.

"Keir... I can't," I panted.

"You can," she growled and covered my mouth with hers to swallow my screams.

I shuddered as I was hit hard with the next orgasm. Her fingers slowed but she didn't remove them. Instead, she kept them going, riding out my orgasm. She left kisses all over my face and slowly removed her fingers. Even with her holding me, I felt my legs shake violently.

She turned off the shower and I watched her face intently.

"If you keep giving me that face, I may think that you no longer hate me," she said, her eyes searching my face.

I don't really, I wanted to say. *I hated the idea of you. The idea of us.*

I couldn't find the words, so I just captured her lips again. She set me down slowly but when my feet finally hit the cold floor, my knees almost buckled, which caused me to grip on to her for support and break our kiss.

"Sorry," I murmured.

She helped me dry off in front of the mirror and gently rubbed the towel in my hair. I couldn't pull my eyes away from her as she methodically combed through my hair with her fingers, being careful to not pull at it too hard. There was a smile on her face but it was not her normal one, this one was soft. She was looking at me differently. It hurt.

I grabbed her wrist and slowly moved her in front of me, placing her between the counter and myself. I ran my hand over her bare chest and up her neck. Her nipples had already hardened and I longed to taste them.

"You are going to spoil me with these touches," she joked, but I didn't miss how her breath caught.

I leaned forward and planted kisses at the base of her throat.

Then lower.

Then lower.

I engulfed her nipple in my mouth. Her response was a small hiss and a hand tangled in my hair. I began swirling my tongue over the sensitive bud and ran the other between my thumb and forefinger. Her hand gripped the counter and she arched into my mouth. Her soft delicious moans filled the air.

My hands came down to her soaked pants and I began unbuttoning them. Her hands stopped mine.

"You don't have to," she said.

"You act like this is my first time with a woman," I said, giving her nipple a small bite. She growled and forced my lips to hers. She quickly lifted me up and placed me on the cold counter.

"Tonight is about you," she insisted.

Keir pulled me closer so I was almost fully off the counter. She slowly kissed her way down to my core.

"Take off the rest," she ordered, her voice vibrating against me.

I did as she asked and leaned back on my elbows. She smiled against my folds and gently lifted one leg over her shoulder. Her hands teasingly ran over my stomach as she gripped my arm and pushed it up to my breast. I watched intently as she began pinching my nipples.

"You look so perfect like this," she cooed.

Then, without warning, her mouth attacked my core.

Her eyes never left mine as her long fingers sank into me. Embarrassment flooded my system as she sucked on the bundle of nerves and I let out something akin to a scream, but she only continued. I closed my eyes and began rolling my nipples in my fingers, losing myself in the pleasure.

"Look at me," she demanded, stopping completely.

I forced my eyes open and was rewarded with her fingers thrusting deep inside me.

"Fuck, Keir," I moaned while she pounded into me. "*Please.*"

"Please what, love?" she asked and pulled my clit into her mouth with a long suck. Tears filled my eyes.

"Bite me," I forced out through my gasps.

She let out a low groan.

"Silvia," she warned. She trailed kisses from my clit to my inner thigh and watched my reaction as her teeth trailed the sensitive flesh.

"I want it, Keir," I said and tangled my hand in her hair, guiding her mouth closer. "Please."

In a flash, she opened her mouth wider and sank her teeth into me. I let out a pained sob, the same burning sensation spreading across my thigh. But slowly, with her fingers pounding into me and the slow spread of the vampire venom as she sucked on my wound, the pain mixed into pleasure.

"Oh, God," I moaned and arched against the counter, feeling heat rising in me. I was so *so* close. I couldn't stop the incoherent ramblings that spilled out of my mouth, and she began to suck on my clit again.

"Come for me, baby," she whispered against me.

My body went taut and white spots flashed before my eyes as I came violently on the counter. Her hands steadied me while her thumb rubbed circles on my clit, rolling me from one orgasm straight into the next.

She laughed at my reaction and left her position to pull me into her arms. I was surprised by the action, but by now my whole body was shaking and my head was pleasantly fuzzy from the vampire venom. Her hands ran through my wet hair as she tried not to pull too harshly.

"You know I am never going to let you go after this, right?" she asked, her voice heavy.

"I bet you say that to all your women," I mumbled against her chest.

She was so warm against me, and after so many sleepless nights, I wanted so badly to just curl up in bed with her right here and now.

"Maybe if I did, they would stay longer," she mused and lifted my chin up with her finger so she could stare deeply into my eyes. "So, I must ask now. . . Do you still hate me?"

My heart skipped when she spoke.

No, not really.

"Yes," I lied.

"Good. *Good*," she hissed and attacked my lips once more.

CHAPTER 20

KEIR

The Silvia I knew as a hunter, and the Silvia that she showed her fellow Order members were entirely different people. The Silvia I knew was reserved and hotheaded. But the Silvia who showed up to the Order and began chatting with various academy students was open, and her tone had a soft edge to it. Something I had never heard directed at me before. She listened to them and nodded, like what they were saying was the center of her world in that moment, totally forgetting about the vampire hot on her heels. The only indication that she still knew I was here was the glare she would send me every few minutes. She was warning me while simultaneously trying to keep up her image of the ruthless vampire hunter. To the outside, it looked like Silvia had finally tamed her little vampire, but between her and me, we knew who really tamed whom.

I ate up every minute of it greedily. I loved it. Loved the way she panicked when I told her I would be joining her today. Loved the way she fidgeted as she walked through the Order. It was gnawing at her insides, and I knew that it took all that she had to not explode on me. I had told her the reason I wanted to come today was to meet the captain, but in reality it was because I wanted to fuck her in some place other than a shower.

To no one's surprise, Gillard found out the morning after. He smelled her on the couch just like I knew he would. He gave me a hard look but didn't mention it. He kept his word, and I kept mine. I was grateful because after the moment we shared, I did not know if I could stay away from her. The way she moaned my name sounded like honey. I wanted to make her scream it, and I couldn't do that very well when I had to keep her a secret. It was infuriating and exciting all at the same time. I loved to see her squirm as she tried to hide her obvious arousal in public.

I had cornered her this morning before coming here, showering her with kisses, and left her panting against her bathroom sink. I didn't let her finish and I knew she was angry about it.

That was the point. I wanted her to sit there in her own wetness as she tried to act like an upstanding hunter. I wanted her to know that, no matter how she may fool those around her, she couldn't fool me.

Almost as if she had heard my thoughts, she glared at me as we rode the elevator up to the captain's office. I chuckled and followed her. Even in the vampire community, Captain Moore was somewhat of a mystery. Maybe that was why he was in the position he was in. I had heard of him from Gil, and others, but I had never met him in person.

Silvia led me down the hall before letting herself into his office without warning. I heard him let out a sigh, but his heart began pumping wildly as I ducked in behind her. With the mystery behind the man who practically ran the Order, I would have assumed that he was a scary being. He was rumored to rule over the many hunters in his organization by sheer intimidation alone. . . but seeing him now, I couldn't help but be disappointed. He was an older human with graying hair and sagging skin. He sat up straight at his desk, putting off an air of confidence, but I knew better. His heart and the smell of his sweat filled the space between us.

He was nothing to be scared of, and I wondered if any of the other clans had seen him, would they still follow the Order's rules?

I knew there was more to this organization than this single man. He was but the face for a much larger, darker group of people that ran the world with ironclad fists.

"What a surprise," he said, watching me as I followed Silvia into the room.

"Yes, I thought I would come and let you know how happy we have been with your hunter's service," I said, giving Silvia a sly grin.

Very satisfied indeed.

"She saved me from another attack," I said. "I thought you should know."

"I also ran low on supplies, so I needed to stock up. She begged me to come," Silvia grumbled, crossing her arms over her chest, causing her breasts to strain against the black material of her turtleneck.

I couldn't wait to have my mouth over them once more.

"I am glad to hear everything is going smoothly," he said, though with the downturn of his mouth, I knew he had reservations about our work. "Please, if you would like to discuss more, my office is open any time for you or your family."

I bristled slightly when he mentioned my family, but I gave him a smile anyway.

"I will leave you two to discuss. I will wait by the elevator," I said to Silvia and left the room.

It was surprisingly easy to hear even as far as the elevator. You would think with how often they worked with vampires that they would have better common sense.

"I heard you were stabbed," his gruff voice said.

I rolled my eyes at his crassness.

"Yes. Unfortunately the rebels got wind of me being a blood traitor and cornered me," she shot back.

I felt a sense of satisfaction rise in me. I loved her attitude.

"I am healed now," she tacked on to soften the blow.

"Good. Anything to report?" he asked.

"No, they are obeying the laws," she replied. "No mistreatment of humans that I have seen. Though I haven't been able to find their blood bags either."

The image of my father snapping the neck of his feeder forcibly pushed itself to the front of my mind. Father did a lot of illegal things that the Order wouldn't approve of. It was just Silvia didn't see it yet. She was too busy with me.

He gave a grunt. "Are you able to keep a handle on her?"

There was a pause. How much did Gil tell them about this job?

"Yes, you saw her. She's just excitable." My face twitched at her response.

"Glorified babysitting." He huffed. "Is there anything else I should be aware of?"

I could hear her shift, and there was a pause that filled the air.

Finally she answered, "No, nothing to report yet."

I didn't hear the captain respond, and Silvia left the office not a moment later. Her eyes were downcast as she walked toward me, her arousal still permeating the air around her.

Finally, I can have her to myself.

"Let's stop by your room for supplies," I said in a cheerful tone as she came to a stop in front of me.

A red blush tinted her cheeks, and I had trouble keeping my hands to myself as she led me back to the elevator. My mouth began to water as we stood side by side, her scent filling the small space. After feeding from her, I decided that I could never feed from another again.

Her blood was the sweetest I had tasted and so untainted by the poison of the modern-day world. I didn't know how I would live once the contract was up, but I knew for sure that I would try everything in my ability to keep her with me, even after the transfer of power.

The elevator dinged when we reached her floor, and we walked in silence to her room. The halls were quiet, though there was a hint of noise behind each door indicating that this area was filled with hunters.

I was strong, I had no doubt about that. But being surrounded by humans who kill people like me for a living, I guess you could say it unnerved me. I was waiting for them to pop out at any moment and attack.

"Is Cain in his room?" she whispered as she pulled me into her room. Her movements were quick, rushed, as if she was hiding me in here. It excited and endeared me all at once.

"The little witch?" I asked and took a deep breath. I could smell the slight reminders of burning nature, but I couldn't hear him.

"He's across the hall," she said.

I listened but I heard nothing from across the hall. The other rooms were a different story, but I decided not to mention it.

"Not that I can tell," I murmured.

She nodded and left me to my own devices as she

rummaged around for her supplies. I almost felt bad seeing how small her room was. It was barely a quarter of what she had at my house with only a small table, a bed, and a sad excuse for a kitchen. If she stuck around, I vowed that she would get a room ten times this size if she wanted it.

I walked around, letting my hand trail on the table she kept near the kitchen. I smiled as a thought appeared in my head.

"This will do nicely," I murmured, a thrill running through me. "Silvia, what is on this table?"

She hurried over to my side and searched the table for whatever I was pointing at. Her eyebrows were pulled together and her eyes were wide, panicked.

"What do you—"

Her words were cut off when I moved behind her, pushing her in between myself and the table. I ran my hands up her sides and she shuddered against me before pushing her back into me. I loved the way she reacted to my touches. She denied us for so long, but her body knew what it wanted and was ready for me.

"Bend over," I commanded. I heard her swallow but she obeyed. "Good girl."

I ran my hands across her back, pushing her shirt up slowly, feeling her smooth skin. I felt her shiver once more, and the scent of her arousal filled the air. She arched, pushing her ass into me.

"I always thought they had cameras in here," she said, her voice muffled by her position, but I heard her loud and clear.

I unhooked her bra but did not take it or her shirt off. I pulled them both up high enough so that her exposed breasts spilled over onto the table. She hissed as they made contact with the cold surface.

"I guess they are in for a show, hm?"

I grinned into her back and slipped my hands underneath her just enough so that I could pinch her nipples. She let out a soft moan and wiggled against my hold.

"Do you want it rough or sweet?" I asked, while pinching one of her nipples.

"Rough. We shouldn't waste time here," she said, her voice husky. The sound of it made my stomach heat. She spread her legs without me even having to ask.

I chuckled at her neediness.

"No one will come looking for us," I said, but I still obeyed her wishes.

I pulled down her pants, revealing her slick folds to me. She sucked in a sharp breath and arched even further, giving me a perfect view. I licked my lips at the sight of her, all exposed and ready for me. She must have been aching since we left this morning, and I'm sure if I left her like this, she would be dripping onto the floor in mere seconds.

I hit her cheeks with just enough force that her skin started to redden. She yet out a yelp but kept her legs spread for me.

"You have been waiting for this, haven't you?" I asked and let my two fingers massage her pussy.

She let out a louder moan and pressed herself against me. I pushed her back against the table, not allowing her to take control of this moment.

"Yes," she groaned and wiggled against my hold. She wanted more than I was giving her, and how could I resist someone as tempting as her?

Deciding not to waste a moment longer, I pushed two fingers into her, painfully slow, and was rewarded with a groan.

"Faster," she commanded breathlessly.

"I did say you would get it rough, huh?" I mused.

I couldn't be too rough with her, given that humans were far too fragile, but I would make sure she was taken care of.

I didn't expect her to answer. I used one hand to keep her down and pounded my two fingers into her, being careful not to hurt her with my strength but rough enough so that when we were done here, she would be left sore. I wanted her to have the reminder of me. Whenever she sat down or had a moment to rest, I wanted to be on her mind.

It was the least she could do after consuming mine so selfishly.

Silvia threw her head back and her loud moans began to fill the room. I pushed her shirt up as I fucked her from behind with my fingers, and I bent down to bite her back. My fangs ached and were begging to be buried in that beautiful flesh, but I held myself back. I wouldn't feed on her until she asked me to. She yelped at my actions, but I felt her walls tighten around me. I picked up the pace.

"Fuck, Keir," she moaned.

I pulled on her hair, forcing her head to tilt back. She hissed, but I covered what was exposed of her neck with my lips. I used this chance to fit a third finger inside her.

"Yesss," she moaned. "Bite me, please."

She brought her arms forward so she could pull at the collar of her turtleneck, exposing Vance's previous bite to me.

I left a kiss in the middle of the bite before I leaned forward and teased the scar with my fangs. The venom pooled in my mouth, and I began shaking as I tried to hold myself back from biting her.

"Are you sure?" I whispered against her heated skin.

"Yes," she groaned and tilted her head to the side.

With no more hesitation I bit down, her sweet blood filling my mouth and exploding across my tongue. I moaned as I swallowed down mouthful after mouthful of her delicious blood. My entire body was vibrating with pleasure as her blood washed through my system.

I could get lost in this feeling. The feeling of her blood combined with the way her pussy clenched my fingers. It was perfect, *she* was perfect. I had never felt myself fit so perfectly with anyone before, a human no less.

Anything after this would dull in comparison, I just knew it. No one's blood would be as sweet, and I would miss the that fiery look in her eyes as she fought me.

I knew she was close to falling over the edge. I felt my control slip just slightly and pounded my fingers into her harder than what I had wished. I was worried I had hurt her, but I felt her walls close in on me.

"That's it," I coaxed as I licked her wound. "Come, Silvia."

With another few pumps she was coming on my hand. I had to clamp my hand over her mouth to stop her loud screams. I could still hear her neighbors through the wall. They paused as our sounds reached them, and it wouldn't be good for Silvia if anyone were to interrupt us.

"Did I hurt you?" I asked as I slowly pumped out of her, trying to carefully ease her down off this high.

Silvia turned around in my arms. Her silver eyes were wide and her face was flushed. Her lips met mine, and I felt her pushing off the rest of her pants and taking off her top.

I smiled against her lips.

"I will need to teach you the definition of rough," she murmured against me.

I felt my own arousal skyrocket at her words.

"But that's for another time," she added on quickly. "Let me taste you."

Silvia pushed me toward the bed, which was close by. I let myself fall on top and allowed her hands to travel up into my shirt. They found my nipples easily, and I moaned when she pinched them just like I did hers. Her lips trailed fire down my throat, where she only stopped to remove my shirt.

In an instant her lips were back on my skin, and she easily took one of my nipples in her mouth. I let myself arch into the feeling and lay back against the soft bed. I unbuckled my pants and her hands replaced mine to pull them down. Her lips trailed down my stomach and she stopped at my mound to look up at me. Her eyes were absolutely feral, and her hair was like a thick mane begging to be pulled on.

I loved every moment of it. The blood that was still pouring from the wound was now smeared on me, making her look like a feral goddess. Her lips descended onto my aching pussy and my eyes fluttered closed against the feeling of her tongue attacking me.

"Fuck," I cursed as her thumb found my clit. I bucked against her as her tongue entered me.

I should have never doubted her experience with women. Her fingers and mouth switched, and she began sucking on my clit while she slowly pushed two of her fingers into me. I began losing myself in her motions, bucking my hips to meet her thrusts. She softly nibbled on my clit and I found my hand in her hair, pushing her into me.

I had to remind myself to be gentle with her. To keep myself in check even as she moaned against me and I felt my own climax rush. As she pushed me over the edge, her mouth did not stop until she cleaned up every ounce of wetness that had formed.

I sat up, completely out of breath. She looked up at me with twinkling eyes. I pulled her in for a kiss, enjoying the taste of myself on her tongue.

"Keir," my father's voice called.

Even from three floors away, his voice traveled through the quiet manor with ease, sending a chill up my spine. Father never called upon me unless I was in trouble, and immediately I tried to recollect how I fucked up this time.

It couldn't have been my relationship with Silvia... We had been meeting secretly for days now, and I always made sure we were out of hearing range. I started to clean up afterward due to Gil's nagging, so that couldn't be it either.

I was missing something.

My eyes shifted toward Gil's and I caught his hard expression. His glasses gleamed in the light and his mouth was set in a thin line. From the looks of it, he didn't know what the issue was either.

We were in the front foyer, just coming home from a short walk around the compound, giving Father the perfect time to intercept me. Fear threatened to overtake me, but I stayed planted, for myself and Silvia.

You will be in charge soon anyway... just need to hang in there.

"Rest early, Silvia," Gil said as we walked up the main staircase. The sun was just beginning to set so, realistically, it was too early for her to retire, but we both knew that this was not a conversation she would want to see.

Silvia remained blissfully unaware due to her stunted human hearing. A gift I should be grateful for at the moment.

"Sure, but don't think I won't awake if you try to sneak out again," she said, eyeing me suspiciously.

"We both know that I am far past that by now," I joked, but my panic rose when I heard my father's voice once more, this time harder. It was a warning.

"Gil and I have something to take care of," I said and hung my arm over Gil's form. He sent her a strained smile and pushed my arm away, what was supposed to look like a joking mood but came off more hostile than he intended.

He was just as nervous as I was.

"Okay. . ." she trailed and turned her back to us, walking in the direction of her room without looking back.

As soon as she rounded the corner, Gil and I both silently stalked toward Father's voice. We didn't need to talk about the gravity of the situation, we both understood by now what our roles were. But I so wished for someone to break the silence and put my frenzied mind out of its misery.

Father was in the feeding room, *again.* I could smell the blood even before we entered and had to mentally prepare myself for the sight that awaited me. I pushed open the door and walked in first, hoping to shield Gil from whatever it was we were about to see.

"I thought I would have to drag you in here," Father said as I entered. His hair was unusually messy and there was another dead human not a foot away from where he sat. She had obviously put up a fight, her own hair was a mess and her white feeding dress was ripped down the middle, exposing her. Her eyes were wide open, and there was a silent scream now forever frozen on her face. She was young, couldn't be a day over fourteen, if I had to guess.

I felt Gil shudder and Father's red eyes narrowed on him. I sidestepped so he would be locking eyes with me instead. This was my punishment to see, and I would be damned if he turned this on Gil.

His chest rose and I was sure he was going to yell at me for my insolence, but instead he slowly exhaled and sank into his chair.

My father was a warrior, you could see as much in the way he carried himself. In the way he commanded the room's attention. And in the way he treated vampires and humans alike.

But right now, and every time I saw him throw away feeders like garbage. . . all I saw was a weak man who was afraid that his power was being taken from him, and the only thing he could think to do was kill a weak human to prove that he still had *some* power.

"Came up as soon as I could shake the hunter off," I explained. "Have to stay on good terms with them if I will be in charge of this clan soon."

His eyes flashed and his upper lip curled, a growl threatening to explode from him. I knew it was a low blow, but he needed the reminder. No matter how much he intimidated me and pushed me around now, he had to remember that soon his throne would be *all* mine.

"What can I help you with?" I continued on, before he could open that disgusting mouth of his and say anything else.

His lips curled into a slimy smile.

"The Montres clan will be coming soon," he informed me. There was a look in his eyes that told me them coming was no coincidence.

As much as I liked to act like I shirked my responsibilities, there was one thing that I made sure I was caught up on: clan relationships. And for all the time that I had been preparing for this transfer of power, the Montres clan was not one that had ever stepped foot on our compound if it was not for an event where *all* local clan heads were invited.

We were not close, and to receive an invitation like this from a clan of our caliber was less likely than the entire vampire community dropping dead.

Another feeder walked in, dressed in the same white dress as the others. Her hollowed cheekbones and dull eyes told me she had been here a long time. She didn't even look at the dead body on the ground as she stretched herself over Father's lap, baring her neck to him.

"Your presence will, obviously, be required," he said as his hand gripped at the girl's waist. Vampire feeding was always intimate, which is why we had feeding rooms like this, and donors, but my father had always taken it a step further in front of me. I felt bile rise in my throat, and his tongue traced the girl's old scars.

"What is the topic of this meeting?" I asked.

"Blood," he said and sank his fangs into the girl's neck. A low groan escaped her lips and her hand gripped at the sides of my father's chair. He was being extra cruel to this one.

"'Cause you keep killing all the feeders?" The words came out before I could stop them.

He removed his fangs and sneered. Gil's hand pulled on the back of my shirt in warning. I had pushed him too hard tonight already, I knew that. But it didn't stop the bitterness rising in me.

I *hated* this man.

I didn't care if he was my blood father. To me he would be nothing more than a sperm donor and the one who gave me this kingdom. . . but even then I had no gratitude. I never wanted this power. All I wanted was to live a normal life, but instead I had to watch as he single-handedly destroyed the vampire world.

That knowledge and pure spite were the only things that pushed me forward.

"An act of kindness." He hummed, his eyes flitting over the dazed girl. "The Montres clan is running low."

There was no such act that would ever come from that man. He wanted them to owe us. I had no doubt in my mind that he had a hand in causing them to run low. He loved to back people into a corner. Make them rely solely on him. Just like the small feeder in his arms now, he would lull them into a false sense of security and strike when they were least expecting.

"Understood," I said and pushed Gil toward the door before he could kill the feeder on his lap.

"Also, bring the little hunter of course," he called as we left.

Fuck you.

Hunter Rules

rule 5 sec 1

There must be no sexual contact
between the Hunter and the
contractee.

CHAPTER 21

SILVIA

I didn't know how many times Keir had cornered me in my bathroom, but it was starting to become an annoying habit. Well. . . I wouldn't call it annoying for long.

Yes, she sometimes scared me with her presence.

Yes, she tended to get handsy. And of course she used the small private space to her advantage. . . but I couldn't say that I was totally put off by it.

Ever since our first night together, we had been inseparable. When Gillard left us to sleep, one of us would sneak into the other's room, and we'd end up not leaving for hours.

It had become a routine, one that I didn't know I needed until I untangled myself from Keir's arms. I lingered longer than I should, each time progressively spending more and more time with her.

And it was getting dangerous, for me and her.

"He said to behave," I snapped, reminding her of Gillard's words as her hands made their way up into my bra. Gillard knew way more than he let on and had taken to reminding me whenever he could. He never said it outright, but I could read between the lines.

She grinned against me and her lips found my neck, kissing the still-sore bite she left on me days before.

"But you look so delicious," she said. Her hand trailed down my stomach and caused me to inhale sharply. Her long fingers teased the hem of my underwear.

"Of course I would," I said with a huff.

She let me push her away without so much as a complaint. I turned to her, trying to steady myself on the counter behind me. I was already shaking from her attention, and if I didn't stop it now, I was sure to forget myself soon and I couldn't chance that today. Not when I was working *Raphael's* meeting today.

She crossed her arms and gave me a small pout.

"You are a vampire after all," I said. "You literally suck the life out of me for fun."

"Silvia," she chided, but she was in no way serious given the smile that played at her lips. My name on her mouth caused butterflies to soar in my stomach. "You practically beg me to bury my fangs in you."

I did, on more than one occasion, and while I loved every moment of it, shame never failed to fill me at the reminder of my perversions.

"Leave," I snapped. "Because now I need to shower your scent off."

"Can I watch?" she teased, her eyes shining once more.

"No," I muttered and crossed my arms over my chest. "We can meet tonight once it is less suspicious."

She huffed but agreed, then walked her way out of the bathroom.

"Don't miss me too much," she called out.

"I hate you," I murmured and faintly heard a laugh in the

hallway. Today was a special day. We had another job to complete. This time I had to be on my game because if Raphael had any indication that I was failing my job so spectacularly, I would no doubt be sent right back to the Order.

With that heavy thought weighing on my shoulders, I quickly got ready to shower where I scrubbed my skin, including my bites, until it was red. Her bites tingled as I scrubbed them and heat flashed through me. Unlike Vance's, they remained sensitive far after healing, and I didn't know if it was all in my head or she was just special.

I opted for the former.

This time, I wore my hair up, showing off just the top of the bites that marred my skin. No one would know they were Keir's. She had been careful and made sure to bite right where Vance had, so it looked like I was only bitten once. For a while I was ashamed of them, because of my known hate, but now I didn't care. Now I wore them openly.

Putting my hair down and hiding my neck was just another way I sank into myself, and it took me until now to realize that I was the one who had power here. I deserved to be here just as much as the vampires at my side, and the more I hid what had happened to me, the weaker I would look.

I tried to steel myself before I went out to see the other vampires. Anxiety gnawed at my stomach. The last time I had seen her father was when he was slapping the shit out of her, and I didn't know what to expect from him this time.

A part of me was scared.

Scared that he knew exactly what we were up to.

Scared that he would punish Keir.

At this point, the illusion of getting my debt paid had shattered. It was but a dream, and I refused to put so much faith in it until it was confirmed.

But that didn't mean Keir wouldn't get in trouble, and if he was so nonchalant about abusing his own child, what else was he willing to do to get his point across?

It was another five minutes of deep breathing before I ventured out to the hallway. Keir and Gillard were in a heavy conversation before both of their eyes snapped toward me. Gillard had his cool persona locked into place, but he gave me a forced smile as I met his eyes. Keir still had her shit-eating grin on her face, telling me she knew just how hard I had to scrub to get her scent off me.

I hate that stupid smile.

"Let's go," Gillard said and pushed me forward with a hand on my shoulder.

I didn't push his hand off this time. Instead, I allowed him to gently guide me throughout the manor. When we reached what I assumed to be the meeting room, he positioned me in a way that I would have full view of all the hallways connecting to this room.

"We don't expect anything to happen," he said and stood in front of me, but didn't remove his hands from my shoulders. "But as you know things can happen."

Has he ever tried to touch me this much?

It wasn't uncomfortable. It was friendly, but it was odd coming from Gillard. Even if his cool persona was just a front, he had rarely ever been this friendly with me.

His touch meant something, like he was trying to anchor me in the spot, willing me to stay. It felt like he was preparing me for what was to come, and it only made my earlier fears come alive under my skin.

"I understand," I said and leaned back against the wall, slipping out of his grasp.

I hugged my sword to my chest, making sure to have it ready if needed. Gillard nodded and motioned for Keir to follow. She gave me another smirk and left with a wave. I rolled my eyes at her.

Just as they entered the meeting room a figure dressed in a familiar Order uniform left the same room. I was met with hazel eyes and an emotionless mask that lifted a weight from my shoulder. Damon made his way toward me but instead of standing next to me, he leaned on the wall opposite to me. He was careful to position himself so he would not be leaning on his weapon, a bow and arrow. His hair was back to its messy, rolled-out-of-bed look, but his sharp eyes told me nothing got past him. He was probably even more alert than I was.

"Which clan are you with?" I asked, unsure that another clan would even want to hire a hunter.

"Montres," Damon responded.

He was never much of a talker in our academy days, so I wasn't surprised with his short response. I nodded and watched the door to the meeting room. There must have been a lot of vampires in that room to require two hunters.

It was risky.

"Your last incident was with a vampire?" he asked, breaking our silence. I was unsure where he'd heard that information from and worried that the shameful experience was now known to the entire Order.

"Yes," I confirmed but did not go into any detail.

"The captain almost threw a fit when he realized the rebels wanted you," he said, his expression giving no indication what he thought on the issue.

I raised my eyebrow at his response. "The captain didn't give a shit."

"But he did." Damon's eyes were hard on mine. "Was worried we would lose our best hunter. We can't take that hit, especially after a whole squad just went missing."

My back straightened and a cold fear was injected into my veins.

"*More* hunters have gone missing?" I asked.

As hunters we are supposed to be prepared for anything, including dying on missions. But never had we been prepared for squads and squads of hunters just disappearing off the face of this planet without so much as a trace. Many were pronounced dead after a few weeks, but that did nothing to bring closure to the people affected.

Nor did it explain why it was happening in waves.

Did the captain lie to me?

Damon nodded, his jaw clenched.

"I asked to be on the case, but I was refused," he said. "Captain said higher-ups are looking into it."

A foreboding feeling washed over me. Why was Damon refused? He was up in the charts with me. He was just as capable to investigate it as anyone else.

"We will talk about this later," I said in a low voice, all too aware of the prying ears of the vampires in the room over.

They didn't need to know how weak the Order was right now, and I didn't trust them for a second to keep this information to themselves.

Damon nodded, then when we both heard light footsteps. Our eyes sought out the sound. At the end of the hallway I spotted a human girl with long brown hair cascading down her back and eyes void of any emotion. She was wearing a long white gown that was stained with blood in some areas.

If I had not seen a feeder before, I would have assumed she was a ghost.

"State your business," I growled and turned toward her. The human girl didn't seem to be too much of a threat, but I didn't judge a book by its cover. Especially not when two clan heads are in a small room together.

"I am for feeding," she said and shifted slightly on her feet. Her eyes did not meet mine.

I knew her purpose, but I hadn't seen anyone in this manor use a feeder before.

"Are there other clans in the room, Damon?" I asked and walked toward the human.

"No, just the two." He paused. "They don't use feeders."

I stopped in front of her and began patting her down. The dress didn't cover much of anything and there was little to hide, but I would be damned if I let anything slip past me. I gripped her chin and forced her brown eyes to meet mine.

"You aren't going to do anything stupid, are you?" I asked, my voice low.

She swallowed thickly and flinched in my hold.

"Let the poor dear go," Raphael said from behind me. "She is for me."

Her panicked expression calmed and she let out a relieved sigh. I let go of her chin and stood back, watching as she walked toward Raphael's outstretched arms. I felt a sneer make its way to my face.

She was happy to go to him? Relieved? Did she not know that I could get her out of this if she just asked?

Just before she reached his arms, her head jerked to the side as a bullet flew through the window and buried itself in her head.

My blood ran cold.

"Get down!" I yelled and ran toward him.

Raphael ducked just before another bullet shot through the window and embedded itself into the wall where he was just standing.

"Sniper! Third building to your left!" Damon yelled. He was crouching by the window, his eyes barely peering over. "Get down, Silvia!"

I almost scoffed at him. They didn't want me, *obviously*. I had been in clear sight yet they chose to kill a feeder.

"Can your arrows reach him?" I asked, while covering Raphael's crouching body with my own. Even if I despised the man, I couldn't let him die here. I tried not to look at the dead girl whose blood was pooling on the floor even as the sticky liquid soaked the floor under my shoes.

"If I can break the window," Damon said and hit the glass window with the hilt of his dagger. It barely left a crack. "I will for sure get him, the fucker."

I let out a growl and ran into the meeting room, having to jump over the girl's dead body to do so. There were about six vampires in the room, including Gil and Keir who looked like they wanted to murder me. The others were gripping onto the table and shaking in fear. It was almost amusing to see vampires as high-ranking as these be scared, but I didn't let myself dwell on the thought.

"You'll be okay," I said and quickly sought out the only available chair in the room.

I hauled it out over my shoulders, feeling the bullets hit one of its legs and knocking it out of my grip. I had to dive forward as a bullet narrowly missed my face, grazing the skin on my cheek.

Looking at the dead human girl on the ground, I realized this may not be the same people who we were dealing with before. Their utter lack of regard for human life wasn't aligned with the values of the rebellion. I lifted the chair and threw it against the window that was already cracking due to the bullet holes.

"These are some quality fucking windows!" I shouted as the chair left the window cracked, yet not shattered, and bounced to the floor.

I dove again as another bullet came through an adjacent window. I quickly lifted the chair once more and this time, finally, the glass shattered. I crouched down and tried to peer over the broken window. Just like Damon had said, there was a sniper on one of the mansions not too far away from here. You could only tell because of the glare that bounced off their silver rebellion mask.

Damon ran over to the open window and stood up with his arrow fully drawn. He let go of the arrow, and in return, a bullet lodged itself into his shoulder. Damon's body was flung back against the wall, giving the sniper a clear view of his head.

I cursed and dove toward his foot, grabbing hold of his ankle. I was just able to yank his body fast enough that a bullet barely missed his head.

And now, the bullets came at us faster thanks to the open window.

"Silvia!" Keir yelled from the room.

My eyes met her father's. He was sitting against the wall underneath the windows. He gave me a sinister smile, like he was enjoying watching us struggle.

I grabbed the bow and arrows from Damon's hands. He reached to swat mine away, but I bared my teeth at him, and he flinched back and surrendered his weapons without anymore fight.

Crawling over to the window, I saw the sniper was making a run for it, sprinting across the building's roof. I took a deep breath and readied the bow, trying to follow the figure's silver mask.

I with a small prayer, I let the arrow go and watched in awe as it soared across the space and hit the target right in the arm, stopping the shooter entirely.

I looked toward Damon for an explanation. He winced before a small smile spread across his face. He had paled considerably and his chest heaved with each breath.

"The witches," he forced out through clenched teeth. "Helped craft it."

I looked toward Raphael. By now, there should have been vampires right around the corner, but none had shown themselves in the hallway yet.

It was weird. You would think that if a clan head was being attacked, his own personal guard would be by his side in seconds.

"I would suggest you call for your guards," I told Raphael, my voice low and my eyes narrowing in on him. "They can probably catch him before he escapes."

His eyes narrowed back at me. I knew what he was thinking.

How dare a human tell me what to do? his eyes seemed to say. *How dare a human as lowly as her insinuate my team cannot do their job?*

Keir and Gillard finally came back into the hallway now that the bullets had stopped, their presence interrupting the stare down I was having with Raphael. I broke it to meet their gaze, both of them were breathing heavily, their eyes wide with panic.

"Get a medic for Damon," I ordered. "If he dies here, the Order will have something to say about it."

It was a lie, but it got them moving. Gillard nodded and disappeared down the hallway, leaving Keir and I alone with a bleeding Damon and an angry Raphael

Keir looked like she wanted to say something but was interrupted by the rest of the vampires pushing out of the room. There were a few gasps from the crowd but besides that, no one dared move closer to Raphael.

I lowered myself to the ground next to Damon and pulled him onto my lap. He was losing blood, fast. The entirety of his black uniform was damp with it. He gritted his teeth at the pain of me moving him, but relaxed into my hold and turned his face into my stomach.

I ran my hand through his hair, trying to comfort him.

I had no clue when the medics would come, so I prepared for the worst case scenario: his death. He seemed to have the same idea, not caring about the crowd and pushing as close to me as possible.

"Thank you," he groaned, his hand still clamped on the bullet wound. "I think my contract with the Order will be up soon."

I swallowed thickly at his words. In the Order, the only way to end your contract was through death or repayment of the debt, so I knew all too well what his words meant.

"They were shooting to kill," I said, trying to change the subject. "You were lucky, when the medics get here they can heal you."

"I don't know about luck." He groaned as I pressed down on his wound to try and stop the blood loss. "It's you who's the lucky one. They *missed* you."

"They seem to have taken an interest in me," I murmured.

Damon let out a hacking cough that racked his entire body.

"I'm tired, Silv," he moaned.

"I know," I cooed and rubbed his back.

I heard the quick footsteps of a vampire fast approaching before they appeared by my side. It was a women, she gave me a tense smile before reaching out and shifting Damon to his side.

"Careful," I hissed as Damon's breath caught.

She didn't pay me any mind as she ripped Damon's shirt open, exposing his bloody, oozing wound. She brought out a vial of clear liquid from her white coat pocket and poured it on the wound. Blood slowly started to clot and a fine film of skin formed over the wound in less than thirty seconds.

It was vampire venom. I watched Damon's expression carefully, and finally when his eyes met mine, a red blush coated his face.

"I will take him from here," the medic said quickly, but her voice was soft.

I swallowed thickly and nodded, allowing her to lift Damon up as if he was nothing but a stuffed animal and run back down the hallway with him. I wanted to follow and make sure that he was okay, but was reminded of my current duties as I met the curious eyes of the vampires in front of me.

Gillard was next to Keir once more, his eyes falling to my lap where Damon's blood was now soaking into my uniform.

"Are you—"

"I'm fine," I said, cutting Keir off. I stood and met Raphael's gaze. His eyes still had that twinkle in them. "Glad to see the clan head is unharmed."

He leaned against the wall nonchalantly, as if there had not just been a shoot-out in his own home, and didn't even spare a second glance as another one of his staff picked up the dead feeder.

"Good work," Raphael said. "Though a pity to waste a feeder."

After an hour of questioning from Raphael's team, I found myself next to a bandaged-up Damon. His color had started to come back, and I was relieved to see that I didn't have to say goodbye to a fellow hunter.

The medical bay was far smaller than I expected for a manor this size. There were only four beds, evenly spaced, each with a bedside table that held a different type of flowers.

Damon's had pink snapdragons, a flower I had never seen in person before.

The smell of antiseptic and blood tickled my nose. I had yet to change out of my crusty blood-stained clothes, while Damon looked cozy in his white hospital gown. He was staring out the large windows next to him, his eyes locked on the building where the sniper had been hiding.

"Thank you," he murmured before turning to me. His eyes drilled into mine with an intensity that made me shift in my seat. "For staying with me."

I sent him a forced smile.

"Better than babysitting the vampire," I joked.

"No. I mean when I thought I was dying," he said. "I know the Hunters don't have a protocol for such things but..."

"I know," I said truthfully. "I would have done it for any one of us."

Being a hunter wasn't easy, and I would be damned if I allowed for a hunter to die alone. Many of us were alone in this world with only hunters to have our backs, so it was the least I could do.

"Thank you anyway," he said then looked back out the window. "I don't like this."

I sighed and leaned back in my uncomfortable plastic chair.

"Me neither," I mumbled. "This whole thing with the rebellion and hunters going missing. They were killing humans for God—"

"Come back with me," he interrupted, his eyes still trained on the outside.

"What?" I forced out, my mind still not catching up.

"It's dangerous," he said. "Come back to the Order. Give this job to someone who is more expendable. Our hunters are dying left and right. We need someone like you after that instead of wasting your skills here with some fucking—"

"Damon," the captain's voice called out.

We both jumped and turned around to see the captain walking into the medical bay. His forehead was shiny with sweat, his eyebrows were pulled together, and his mouth formed a deep frown.

"Why are you here?" The question spilled out of my mouth without even thinking.

The captain eyed me before stopping a good three feet away from me, then trained his eyes on Damon.

"I came to check up on you," he said. "It's not everyday that a rebellion attack happens." His eyes shifted down toward me again. "Though it has happened to you three times."

"I was just telling her she needs to come back—"

"Damon will stay here," the captain interrupted Damon again. His voice hard and the warning loud and clear.

"I don't need help," I spat.

Each time I had proven myself with the rebels so why on earth would he think that I needed help? It was an insult.

"Just to be safe," the captain said. "And it's not like Damon will be back in the field any time soon given his injury. I already informed Raphael. There will be no more fighting about this."

I gritted my teeth and tried to take a calming breath. I was seconds away from losing my shit.

"What about the missing hunters?" I growled at him. "Why did no one tell me? Why did you lie?"

The captain searched my face, before speaking.

"It's none of your business," he said, his normally composed mask cracking to show the anger underneath. "I won't warn you again to *stop* your insistent questions about it. Don't think that just because you are on a job now that I am not tallying up your punishments. The Enforcers will be waiting for you when you get back if *this* is how you insist on acting."

His bluntness never used to take me by surprise, but those words hurt. I didn't expect the Order to treat me special just because I was good at killing vampires, but if they really cared about the other hunters, it would be all hands on deck.

The threat of the punishment may have sent a bit of panic through me, but it didn't deter me. The fact that people, just like me, continued to go missing was far scarier than anything those bastards could do to me.

"You are not alarmed?" I asked. "*Your* hunters are going missing, and you don't think to send a team out there? Instead you have me here, babysitting an heir that has nothing better to do than drink and fuck."

My angry words stilled the room and no one spoke for a few moments afterward, letting me feel the full force of what I said.

Guilt weighed heavy in my belly when I thought of Keir and the way her father treated her. It was more than that, but I couldn't utter those words. I shouldn't.

Not if I wanted to keep this job and not if I wanted my debt paid off.

And what if it wasn't me just now who protected them from this attack? Would they have killed Keir and Gillard too?

It scared me to think about.

"The Order's business is just that," the captain growled, each word forced out of clenched teeth. "*The Order's* business, not some hunter who has proven skillful with a knife. The Order is not made of you and your friends, Silvia. You would do well to note that."

I swallowed thickly and nodded.

"Understood," I mumbled.

"The next time I see you will be at the debrief," he said. "Damon you have a week here. Report to me when you are done."

"Yes, sir," Damon said from behind me.

The captain's eyes flashed toward me once more before he spoke.

"Do *not* disappoint me, Silvia," he ordered. "Or you will be in the Order until the day you die."

CHAPTER 22

KEIR

J ust when I thought things couldn't get worse, I was hit
with yet another inconvenience. And this one was far
more annoying than the last.

I didn't know what Father was thinking when he
allowed *another* one of those Hunter bastards to invade our
compound. I had proven I could listen to his rules, as far as he
knew, so why was he continuing to shackle me down when I
had done nothing wrong?

That fucker had been here for *days*.

When Silvia told me the captain wanted Damon to stay
with us while he healed, I had originally thought it would be
one to two days tops, but he had been here for almost a
straight week.

No matter where Silvia was, Damon would most certainly
be right behind. So now, the time I spent with *my* hunter was
cut short. It had been almost a full week since she had allowed
me to touch her, and I was starting to get fed up.

Not to mention my throat was dry and my fangs were

aching from the lack of blood. I was worried that if I didn't get my blood soon, I may start to lose myself in the lust.

It hadn't happened since I was a child, and as a born vampire, I had better control than those who had been turned by vampire blood, but it took everything I had not to pull Silvia aside and sink my teeth into that buttery soft skin of hers.

If there wasn't so much on the line, I would have done it already.

I think that hunter was just placed here as a reminder. To make sure I didn't fuck up again. It was like the universe had sensed how obsessed I was with the little hunter and sent someone in to intervene.

But did they have to pick someone so annoying?

That hunter, *Damon*, knew how to piss me off.

When I first saw him, I didn't even bat an eyelash. He was boring, unmemorable, probably couldn't even hold a candle to the power Silvia had. . . But as he started getting comfortable I saw the real him, and he saw the real me.

It had taken mere hours for Damon to catch on to what was going on between Silvia and I, and after that, he made every moment unbearable. He would watch me with a smirk that would conveniently disappear when Silvia was looking, as if baiting me to call him out on it.

He would take his time getting comfortable next to Silvia, where his hand would brush across hers accidentally. Once was permissible, but every single time he sat down next to her?

Don't get me started on how his hands wandered when he reached over to the dagger she kept strapped onto her thigh.

I fucking saw it and it was doing exactly what he wanted it to.

The worst part?

Silvia was much more relaxed with him. She had gotten

used to my presence and had opened up somewhat, but it paled in comparison to how she leaned into his side, how she searched for him whenever we moved locations. It was almost as if she forgot her entire job here.

It angered me to be so blatantly ignored like that.

Why did this sad sack of a human, who couldn't even do his job right, get more of her attention? I was *fucking* her, for God's sake.

"We should spar." At the sound of Damon's voice, I tore my eyes from the paperwork in front of me to watch Silvia's reaction.

We were in my office where I was forced to go over weeks upon weeks of invoices and financial reports that I had pushed aside for a little extra time with the red-headed hunter. Gillard was sitting in the couch across from Silvia and Damon, also going over some of the paperwork. He was trying to lighten my load, but there was still so much more than the two of us could handle at the moment.

Silvia shifted on the couch, leaning away from Damon. Her red hair was up in a high ponytail, showing off just a sliver of skin above her turtleneck, right where the scars from my multiple bites showed.

Even through my annoyance, a prick of pride and a sick sense of pleasure grabbed ahold of me when I realized that no matter who caught her attention, I would always be permanently scarred on her body.

"You're injured," she said, not looking up from her book.

I couldn't help the smile that formed on my lips. Damon's eyes shifted toward mine, and I could sense his growing anger bubbling up inside him.

She doesn't care about you, my smile told him,

Then a smile of his own appeared on his face.

Watch this, it seemed to say.

"Then it will be easy for you," he said, goading her. His tone had changed to something lighter, more playful.

"It would be easy anyway," she responded, though I saw a flicker of interest pass across her face.

I was torn between wanting to see her finally kick his ass and forcing her to stay here so he couldn't put his dirty hands on her.

"It wouldn't be a fair fight," I murmured, deciding that seeing her beat that arrogance out of him would be the highlight of my week. "After all, Silvia is *the best*."

Silvia shot me a glare, though I didn't understand her anger. I was trying to help her. I even complimented her, which is not something I did for humans often.

"Come on," Damon whined. "The vampires have spoiled you. I wouldn't be surprised if you couldn't even keep up with me now."

Silvia's jaw twitched in response.

"Don't complain when you reopen your wound," she growled.

Damon let out a chuckle and pulled Silvia up from the couch, shooting me a look.

"Let's leave the heir to her work," he said. "Not like she would find much use out of two hunters fighting anyway."

Without allowing Silvia to respond, he pulled her out of the room, his hand on her wrist. The action angered me, and I suddenly regretted pushing her to spar with him.

Gillard shot me a questioning look.

"Should be fun," I said through gritted teeth and stood, pushing aside the mountain of papers I had to look over.

"You have to catch up on—-"

"Just a quick break," I interrupted him as I crossed the room, not wanting to let those two out of my sight.

With a groan Gillard got up and followed me outside.

And fun it was. Within the first ten minutes we had developed some sort of a crowd after people had heard the noise of the hunters. The indoor gym they were in had just enough space for them to spar, while Gillard and I had to stay outside. Luckily, this gym, and the surrounding ones, had glass windows along the far wall, giving us a perfect view of the two hunters.

The normally empty hallway filled with people as they heard the rumors spread that the hunter who had been protecting their next clan head was sparring with another.

There were murmurs of excitement filling the halls and people were already placing bets. I didn't blame them, or get angry; we didn't easily allow hunters into the compound, so any type of peek inside their world was a treat to the vampires here.

If you were a vampire who was contacted by the Order, it was a time for panic. They didn't have time to be curious or ask about the hunters' lives as they were too busy worrying about their own. So they never knew what a life as a hunter *really* entailed.

To vampires, hunters were a sign of fear and seen as vicious murderers, not the respected human savers they thought they were.

Silvia was already sweating bullets after she blocked hit after hit from Damon, who was also panting. They hadn't been at this long, but they didn't take their time with things. Right from the start they threw themselves at each other, viciously trying to take the other down.

Without a doubt, Damon's wound was a hindrance. He was sweating more than Silvia, and his chest rose and fell rapidly with every movement. Every hit she threw would be met with a block and in turn, she would dodge most of his punches. He was bigger than her, but she was by far faster.

Silvia had taken a few hits, and it took all that I had to stay rooted in my place and not tear the boy hunter limb from limb. The only thing giving me some sort of indication she was okay was the way her eyes were shining.

This was the Silvia I had longed to see.

The one who actually enjoyed what she was doing. The one who found joy and pleasure even after the years of pain she had experienced.

I knew her happiness was deep in there somewhere, though I didn't know what could pull it out of her. The sunset was a moment where I saw it, the other time was whenever she thought she was winning against me. I let her enjoy those moments.

But here I was witnessing a moment that brought her happiness, and it had absolutely nothing to do with me.

I didn't like it. Not one bit.

I wanted to be the one to pull this from her. *I* wanted to be the person she showed this to. What was it with me that didn't allow her to show this side of herself? I treated her well. Gave her orgasm after orgasm, and it still wasn't enough.

Damon was enjoying this despite the pain it may have caused him. He let out a throaty laugh as Silvia began circling him, her eyes running down his form as if trying to narrow in on the single weakness that could make her the winner of this battle

But as much as I hated to admit it, they were almost evenly matched. They had similar fighting style, no doubt taught to them during their training at the Order.

As if on cue, Silvia rushed toward Damon, but instead of punching him, she had to quickly dodge his well-timed punch.

I felt myself step forward when I saw how close it had gotten to her face, but it didn't take long for me to notice her smile. In an instant, she gripped his outstretched arm so he could not retract it. His eyes widened as her elbow snapped back and landed squarely on his chest. Damon was thrown off his feet and crashed against the wall of the gym. Silence settled around the spectators as they waited for him to recover.

The scent of blood pricked at my senses and caused my bloodlust to go haywire.

"I told you I would reopen your wound," Silvia chided and walked over to help him up.

Damon groaned and reached for her outstretched hand, but instead of letting her pull him up, he pulled her down to him. Damon changed their positions by rolling her to the ground and onto her back, then his hands wrapped around her slim neck.

I felt a growl make its way up my throat. She let out a small laugh, her eyes lighting up even more.

"Is that all?" he teased, his face getting dangerously close to hers.

Jealously raged inside me. I could tell he was enjoying this far more than what his facial expression let on.

Silvia's forehead collided with Damon's, causing him to jerk back in surprise. She used this chance to hook her arm around his neck and twist to change their positions. She wrapped her arms around his throat, putting him in a choke hold.

"Tap out," she commanded as he struggled against her. "You're lucky I didn't aim for your nose."

He didn't listen to her at first, just continued to buck wildly. On the ground, he tried to free himself from her grasp, but when he realized Silvia wasn't letting up, he slapped his palm against her leg three times. Silvia immediately let go and Damon sat up abruptly, coughing and spluttering.

Pride swelled in my chest. Of course she would win. I knew she would... even if there were a few times where she got hurt.

"I guess I was wrong to think you lagged on training." He let Silvia help him up this time, but winced when he rolled his shoulders.

"Let's get that checked," she offered and he nodded. Their eyes shifted over to us and it seems like they only just now realized they had a small audience.

Quickly the crowd dispersed, not wanting to get caught by the hunters. I kept my eyes trained on Silvia and Damon as they left the gym, both laughing lightly.

"That was shorter than I expected," I said, feeling my lips curl at the sight of her sweaty and panting figure. I needed to get her alone soon, and not just so I could feel her shudder under me again. I needed her blood now more than ever.

"A prolonged fight could kill humans. Y'all have more stamina than what we do," Damon said, walking toward us. His step faltered slightly and blood continued to leak from his wound.

"Let's hurry," Gillard said and went over to Damon's side. He surprised us all by wrapping an arm around the hunter's waist and helping him stand straight. The hunter's eyes flashed, but he allowed himself to be held.

"All right, show's over." I clapped and the remaining crowd scurried away with wide eyes.

After Gillard and his hunter passed me, I wrapped my own arm around Silvia, enjoying the way her cheeks flamed. "I would be more than happy to carry you to the healer as well."

"Don't you dare," she grumbled.

She kept my arm there for a second too long, almost like

she was basking in the touch and then shook me off to follow Gillard down the hall.

I was unaware that Damon was watching us until his piercing eyes caught mine.

I gave him a shit-eating grin.

I win, it said.

CHAPTER 23

SILVIA

Keir had to be purposefully pushing him. Whatever was keeping her from hiding our agreement had all but fizzled away after Damon and I sparred. Her jokes were cruder, her touches lingered longer, and her eyes darkened. She was not hiding anything around Damon.

She acted like she actually wanted to get caught, and it angered me. I had put so much on the line, and I thought for once we actually agreed on one thing. But it seemed I was wrong... *again*.

I should have known that when I entered into... whatever it was Keir and I were doing, that it would only be a matter of time before she lost interest in the secret keeping.

I had caught Gillard giving her a few glares, but he had yet to mentioned anything in front of Damon and me. It was him that scared me the most, however, if Damon got word back to the Order about what was really happening, the captain would pull me away from the job faster than I could punish Keir for her behavior.

And with it, my chance at getting rid of my debt would go up in smoke.

"Silvia, accompany me to my room," Damon demanded as we stood outside Keir's office.

The spar had ended a while ago and everything besides Keir's actions had gone well. When I caught his narrowed eyes, my heart began pounding in my chest.

How much has he seen? Has he caught on to what we are doing here?

I had been good about keeping up my previous attitudes toward the vampires, or at least I thought I had. And it's not like Damon was here to make sure nothing happened between me and the contract holder.

"Didn't know you swung that way, Silvia," Keir said, as I turned toward him.

"It doesn't matter," Gillard said, his voice hard.

Ice-cold panic filled my veins. Not only was Damon watching my expressions intently, but Gillard had caught on as well. His tone told me that he was very aware of what was happening, and he really only used that voice when he meant business.

I peered over my shoulder to catch Gillard's gaze, but it was locked onto Keir. His mask was back in place, but no one would have guessed that he was the same person who'd laughed with us over coffee. Now, he was the person who had first met me in the Order's base, the person doing Raphael's bidding.

"He's right," I said and sent Keir a harsh look. "I tolerate your comments, but it's not Damon's contract. He doesn't have to, so I would be careful with what you say."

I hope the message is clear enough.

Keir shrugged and let out a long sigh.

"No fun," she said with an overexaggerated pout.

As I turned back to Damon with a tense smile, I could feel

Keir's eyes burning holes in the back of my head, warning me that my comment wouldn't go unpunished.

His room was just a single door down from mine, meaning that we shared a wall. Another reason that Keir had been acting out recently.

She hadn't been able to sneak in the entire time that he had been here, and if her glares and angry comments toward Damon meant anything, it would be that she was enraged she wasn't getting her way.

Damon stayed silent as he walked to his door and only met my gaze when he opened it and gestured for me to enter.

I looked at him critically as he stood in front of me, not taking his invitation to enter. His jaw and neck were taut, muscles pulled tight. With a look toward his hands, I realized his fists were also clenched.

I haven't seen him like this before.

Even when the training got the best of us, or we were forced to take beatings from the higher-ups. . . he always took it with a straight face, sometimes even a smile. But I had *never* seen him angry.

"Even though they can probably still hear us in the room," he said. "I would like to talk to you about your contract."

Swallowing thickly I stepped in, ignoring the feeling of Keir's eyes still on me.

My whole body was telling me to run. Telling me to save myself and try to salvage whatever little bit of my contract I had left and try to push through, but I knew we had to have this talk.

"I talked to the others," he said as he shut the door behind him.

I stared into his room. It wasn't anything different from mine, though I caught some of his extra clothes and weapons scattered about. His bed remained unmade, and the chair to his small desk was pulled out as if he had been using it right before he left with us that morning.

He walked toward the desk and leaned against it, his arms crossing over his chest and his eyes meeting mine.

I felt uncomfortable under the intensity of his stare and shifted before clearing my throat.

"You'll have to be more specific," I said and mirrored his posture, crossing my arms over my chest and tilting my head so my gaze was no longer hidden behind my hair.

If he wanted to meet me head on, I would do the same to him. I had nothing to hide. . . that he knew about.

"Cain," he said, then his gaze shifted to his feet. "And the others who had a contract before yours with the heir."

I licked my lips, the idea of learning about the others who were with Keir before I was sounded too tempting.

"Why did you do that?" I asked instead of the question that was swirling around my mind.

"You're not curious?" he asked raising an eyebrow at me.

I turned to him and cocked my head.

"Of course I am," I said. "But the real question is, Why are you?"

Unease filled me at the thought of Damon going around and digging into Keir's old contracts. Not only was it highly confidential, but it was just plain weird. He had no reason to pry.

We were not close, never had been, there had to be more than he was letting on here.

Did he come on this contract knowing that he would run into me and prepare beforehand?

He shifted and let out a sigh.

"Cain asked me to look out for you," he admitted. "He heard I was coming to the compound and asked that I check in on you. But even before that, when I saw you with the heir at the last event, and then I heard you had been attacked—"

"Your point?" I growled not wanting to think of Vance's teeth in me.

"I was curious as to why *you* could tame the heir and not the others," he said finally. "I watched how she acted around you. She couldn't even take her damn eyes off you."

I averted my gaze, heat crawling up the back of my neck. Was it that obvious, even back then?

"I just didn't bend to her will," I said after a moment. "She said she came to respect me."

"That's exactly what she told the last girl," he said in a hard tone. "Right before she exposed what they were doing to her father and the Order. Keir *played* her, told her she was the best hunter she had ever met, and acted as if she would keep their relationship a secret so she wouldn't get in trouble. But she *lied*, Silvia."

Pain exploded in my chest, and I struggled to keep a calm expression, but my insides were raging with anger and hurt. I knew most of what Keir said was a lie. I knew she tried to play her cards just the right way so she could get what she wanted... but I wasn't that stupid, was I?

Wasn't this different?

Keir's words echoed through my mind.

I wouldn't offer to cover it up if I wanted to get you caught.

But what if that was also a lie?

"Why would she tell *you* that?" I asked, my eyes narrowing at him.

He stood up and took a step forward but I mirrored him and took a step back, not wanting him to come any closer. He held his hands up in surrender, showing me he wasn't a threat, but I didn't buy it.

"She's telling everyone who asks, Silvia," he said in a soft tone. "I just wanted to warn you."

My gut instinct was to yell at him. Try to convince him that there was nothing going on and ask him how he had the *balls* to assume otherwise. . . But instead I sighed and let a small smile fall to my face.

"I hate their kind," I explained. "Even if I did get a bit lonely on this contract, I wouldn't take a vampire to bed."

Damon cleared his throat, a small brush of pink coating his cheeks.

"That's not what Cain and I are worried about," he said quickly.

"So now it's Cain *and you*?" I asked.

What was Cain thinking?

He ran his hand through his hair and let out a heavy sigh.

"The last hunter said that she could be quiet forceful with her. . . humans," he explained. "Cain and I are not worried about what *you do*. We know you hate them. . ."

I nodded finally understanding.

"You're worried she's taking advantage of me," I finished for him.

"Or trying to manipulate you," he said. "Then will turn around and ruin this contract for you. Listen Silvia, he told me how crazy your debt is and I would hate to see her ruin that for you."

I rolled my shoulders and stood up straight. It would be a lie if I said I was thinking clearly all the time when it came to Keir, but I liked to think that my choices were my own here.

"I can handle myself," I said in a hard tone, indicating I was beyond done with this conversation.

He nodded quickly.

"I know you can, I just wanted to warn you," he said. "'Cause it's not just the heir you have to look out for. Do you know what the captain did to her when she admitted that there were many times she gave into Keir's acts?"

I shook my head. I really didn't want to hear about this.

I was already regretting my decision to sleep with her, what else could make this any worse?

"Her punishment was a week in the Dark Room with *three* broken fingers, Silvia," he said.

His words cut through me like knives. The air between us chilled. I shuddered as memories of the Dark Room filled me.

The Dark Room was a concrete room three floors underground The Order and was reserved for those who broke the most serious of rules. It was a place void of any light and sound, where you would get one stale meal a day consisting of moldy bread and half a cup of tap water. There was nothing to indicate how much time had passed, and there was nothing in that room besides you and the clothes on your back.

It was the punishment I had always feared the most. The Dark Room, no matter how short a time you spent in there, would haunt you for the rest of your life. It had to have been cursed by the witches or something because that place was enough to drive even the most sane hunters mad.

When I was in the Academy, I had a reputation for losing myself in battles, and when I almost killed another student, I had been thrown into the Room for two days. At the time I thought that was pure hell, but a week? With broken fingers?

"Three fingers?" I asked. "But there is only one clause in the contract that states no sexual—"

"Times," he interrupted. "Not clauses. They forced the times out of her."

My stomach twisted painfully and I cupped my hand over my mouth to stop myself from bending over and throwing up right in front of him.

Though I didn't know what was worse.

Thinking of the cruelty of the Order.

Or Keir's actions.

"I understand," I said, my voice muffled from my hand. I didn't dare remove it for fear of losing my lunch.

"If you need help—"

"I will let the Order know," I said in a curt tone and turned toward the door, unable to keep a straight expression any longer. "Thank you, Damon. Assure Cain that I am fine."

"Wait," he called as I took a step toward the door. "He also wanted me to ask. . . about the bites. He was worried Keir—"

"Tell him it's none of his business," I snapped.

I immediately regretted my tone and sent him a forced smile before hastily escaping toward the door.

"I'll be here!" he called as I exited and slammed his door behind me.

I didn't dare stop until I was safely in my room and had the door locked behind me.

With a heavy sigh, I leaned against the door, trying to catch my breath as I digested the information.

I jumped when the bed squeaked, realizing that Keir was waiting for me already. A small smirk was spread across her face, as if what Damon said wasn't an issue.

"He sure knows how to tell scary stories, doesn't he?"

"You shouldn't be in here," I muttered and cast my eyes down toward the dagger at my thigh. I made slow work of unhooking it and walking across the room to place it on my bedside table.

I didn't know how to face her after what Damon had told me. I almost wanted to tell her to leave and try to ignore her for as long as it took for me to digest what he said.

She wouldn't turn around and tell the Order what was happening, would she?

On one hand, I wanted to believe that she would keep her

word. That maybe I wasn't as much of a failure as I thought I was. But believing someone that had been through years of torture with me at the Order was easier than believing a childish vampire heir that had a tendency of lying.

I didn't know she'd moved from the bed until I felt her hands grasp my hips and pull me into her.

"Finally," Keir breathed and buried her head in the crook of my neck and shoulder, inhaling deeply. "I've waited for days to get a taste of you."

Her hands were quick to unwrap the sword's harness from my body and throw it to the ground.

"Is it true?" I asked. "I know you heard."

Her hands gripped at my hips so hard I felt a prick of pain, but it was almost numb compared to the emotion that tore up my insides.

"You know I didn't want *those* hunters coming in here and telling me what to do," she said. "I did what I had to get them away. You know that."

Her hands slipped into my shirt and I quickly gripped her wrists to stop her.

"They hurt her, Keir," I whispered. "Broke her fingers and threw her in a concrete box. Because of you."

A hand left my hip to grip my neck. My heart pounded in my chest and my breath caught.

"It takes two, Silvia," she growled and nipped at the exposed part of my throat. "You know this. I don't force myself on anyone. I don't need to. And whatever punishment she got, you should blame your precious captain."

I swallowed thickly and let out a shaky breath. It would be so much easier if I was still disgusted with her touch. Then I could push her away, like I should have. . . like the contract demanded, but I couldn't.

I loved the way she touched me. Loved the heat that

unfurled in my belly as her hands traveled my body. And I most certainly loved the way her fangs felt against my neck.

It was a disgusting, sickening type of need that she drew out of me, but I couldn't find a way to pull myself away from her.

"Are you lying to me?" I asked. "Like you lied to her?"

"I told you I wasn't," she growled. "What do I have to do to convince you I want to keep you?"

I let out a shaky breath as her teeth grazed my lobe.

"I have lied for you, to my father, to my best friend, to *your boss*," she growled. "And you believe *some hunter* over me?"

Her hand tilted my head to give her better access to my neck, her other hand slipping into my shirt and traveling across my belly.

"It's not safe to do this here," I snapped. "Stop it."

Her hand trailed inside my shirt, but instead of making its way up, it made its way behind and unclasped my bra.

Keir took the time to slowly draw patterns on my skin until her fingers brushed the underside of my breast. Then slowly, while giving me enough time to push her away, her fingers just lightly grazed my nipple. I shifted against her, grinding my backside into her.

I should push her away.

She could be lying to me and using this as a way to get me fired from this contract.

"I don't care," she murmured and bit the side of my neck, right over her previous bite. "You smell so good." Her wet tongue traced the bite. "Your arousal. Your blood. My scent mixed with yours." I felt the butterflies that had gathered in my stomach go straight to my core. "So *good*. Will you show me how good you can be tonight? I'm awfully hungry, Silvia."

A part of me fluttered when I heard her words. A part of me

desperately wanted her to praise me. But also a part of me was disgusted by how easily I was swayed.

As her delicate fingers played with my nipples, sending jolts of pleasure through me, the want to disobey her became smaller and smaller. I moaned against her, twisting my head so she had more access to my throat. It was a submissive act.

"It hurt to think you were setting me up." I groaned against her as the hand that wrapped around my throat made its way down and began unbuttoning my pants. "I was ready to leave here for good. Forgetting about the debt entirely."

Her hand cupped my pussy, pulling a groan from me. My body was vibrating with need after so long without feeling her against me.

"Oh?" she said, her voice had a playful edge to it. "Should I make it up to you then?"

She slowly started trailing her fingers up and down my already wet folds, but she was careful to keep her touches gentle. Her other hand continued to play with my nipple. I bucked my hips against her hand and she pinched my nipple in response. When I let out a strangled moan she applied more pressure to my clit, canceling out the small flash of pain.

It was easy to get lost in the waves of pleasure that were shooting through my body, but I needed more.

"Please," I moaned against her, gripping her wrist tightly. "I need you."

"If you sit pretty on the desk, I will make it up to you," she said in a husky tone and nipped at my neck.

Keir let go of me and removed her hand from my under-wear. I hurried over to the desk that was against the wall and faced it, waiting for her to push me down like she did at my small room in the Order. The absence of her fingers was driving me insane and even as my mind told me to stop this, I couldn't.

"Not like that," she said from behind me with a small chuckle.

Her voice came from behind but in an instant she lifted me and turned me around so I was sitting in place and facing her.

"Take off your clothes," she ordered.

I pulled off my top as she slowly undid my right shoe then my left. Keir made a show of slowly pulling down my pants, leaving my underwear on. She stepped back, her glowing red eyes taking in my almost-naked form. Instead of feeling self-conscious, I became heated under her stare.

She stepped forward, careful not to touch my overheated body. Her hands slowly wrapped around my underwear and pulled them off, exposing how wet I was for her. Once they were off, she threw them to the floor and spread my legs for a better view. Her fingers ran teasingly across my entrance. I had to lean back onto the cool wall to get a grip on my body.

"Please, don't tease me like that," I moaned as she circled my clit.

Her eyes snapped up to mine and she slowly entered me with two fingers, watching my face as they started to stretch me. I arched toward her as she pulled out and slowly pushed her fingers in once more.

"I wouldn't do that to you, Silvia," Keir growled, her control snapped and her hand began pounding into me, her thumb pushing against my clit with each thrust. "If I did that then I couldn't keep you, and I plan to keep this needy pussy as long as I may live."

"I won't be here forever," I gasped out as her fingers curled inside of me.

It was hard to keep my thighs from shaking as I felt myself tighten around her. Those damn fingers were causing all the words to exit from my mind. There were so many things I needed to say, but none of them made sense anymore.

"I don't give a fuck about contracts or the Order." Her motions became harder, causing the desk to bang against the wall. There was a slight panic alarm that went off in my head, but it started to cloud as I felt my climax build. "I'll make sure you're so fully obsessed with me by the end of this that you don't even dare think of anyone else. It's the least you could do after so thoroughly messing with my mind like this."

My body stiffened as white-hot pleasure burst through me, leaving black spots in my vision. Her fingers slowed as she rode out my climax, her heated gaze watching as I came apart because of her.

She had so much control over me, over my body, that it was sickening. I wasn't the same hunter that came in here wanting to cut off her head, and I had shown that even when faced with the knowledge of what she did to my fellow hunters, I still chose *her*.

"We are not finished," she growled and pulled me closer, this time causing me to lie flat on the desk. She hooked my shaking thigh over her shoulder and pushed the other aside. I gripped the sides of the desk, my fingernails digging into the wood as her fingers found my clit.

"Keir," I warned, giving her a weak glare.

Her lips twisted and she began to kiss my thigh, her tongue came out to trace the scar of her bite. I bucked my hips against her fingers, pleasure once again taking hold of me.

"Tell me," she coaxed. "Tell me you don't want this." Her fingers entered me and I cried out in response. "Tell me so when I see those eyes again, I can hear that instead of the sounds you are making right now."

She thrust against me.

"Say it."

"I can't," I croaked.

And I couldn't. It had taken her a mere two months to

completely turn everything I had ever thought about her kind on its head.

The pounding of her fingers quickened and I had to brace an arm against the wall so I wasn't thrown against it from her force.

"Don't tell me the little hunter has forgotten her hate," she teased, her eyes holding a small ounce of emotion that I couldn't decipher.

She added a third finger. Her teeth trailed against the skin of my thigh. I was almost worried that, with the pounding of the desk, she would break through the damn wall.

"I didn't—"

I tried to force the words out, but she started massaging my clit again, making me lose all coherent thought.

"Tell me how much you hate me then. If you don't, I will assume I have won this battle." Keir nipped harder at my thigh, clearing some of the fog that clouded my thoughts.

With her fingers pounding into me and the looks she was giving me, I couldn't decide if I hated her or not. I couldn't decipher if the heat I felt when staring at her was hate or want. I couldn't decipher if the squeezing in my chest was because of the hurt or something else entirely.

"I—"

She pounded harshly against me.

"Fucking hate you," I growled at her.

Her smirk faltered as I spoke but her movement quickened.

"You're such a *fucking liar*," she growled and without warning sank her teeth into the soft flesh of my thigh.

I may have been bitten a few times now, but the searing pain of her teeth tearing through my flesh still knocked the breath out of me and caused me to writhe under her. But just like all the other times, it was followed by a powerful pleasure that spread throughout my body as her venom spilled into my veins.

Even through the pain, the pleasure from Keir fucking me clouded my mind, and as the two feelings mixed I found myself cresting another orgasm. Keir knew how close I was because with a flick of her thumb against my clit, I was pushed so far over the edge that white clouded my vision.

She drank from me greedily, blood spilled from her lips and trailed down my leg. I let out a moan as the vampire venom infiltrated my mind. I was already in a haze because of the orgasm, but the venom only worsened it.

When she removed her teeth from my thigh, she took her time to lick the wounds, stealing every last drop of blood she could. When she looked up at me, a flash of heat went through me as I took in her crazed expression and bloodstained mouth.

I sat up, removing my leg from her shoulder, pulling her up with a hand tangled in her now-stained shirt. I needed her closer to me. Needed her lips on mine, but her hand on my throat stopped me.

"Open," she commanded.

I let my jaw drop open and waited as she forced the three fingers she had used to fuck me into my mouth. I could taste my release on them, and it was even more humiliating than the act of being so lost in her.

"You taste that?" she asked, her tone dangerous. "Lick it off."

Even through the humiliation that burned my face, I obeyed and cleaned my mess off her.

"You can't deny this, Silvia," she said and pulled her fingers out of my mouth. They now glistened with spit. "Your mouth may spew bullshit but your body cannot. You want me, no matter what that little hunter spouts."

"I hate you," I muttered, my eyes filling with tears.

In that moment I did have some hate for her. I didn't want to be seen like this. I didn't want to come face-to-face with my shameful acts. but here she was, rubbing it in my face.

Her hand tangled itself in my hair and forced my head back, baring my neck to her.

"Again," she growled against my neck, as she bit my skin.

"I hate you," I said louder, as I felt her fangs trail along my neck.

She groaned and in a flash her bloodstained mouth connected with mine and I worked fast to tear off her clothes.

CHAPTER 24

KEIR

L ast night was a mistake, and I knew it as soon as I left.

I let the jealousy and anger get the better of me and put Silvia in a situation I shouldn't have.

This morning, she wouldn't even look at me, and even after I dragged her along with us to our errand of the day, she remained perfectly stoic and didn't engage in conversation with me or Gillard.

The hunter had bid his goodbyes this morning, all while glaring daggers at me. He had no doubt heard what happened between us the night before and, in his mind, his worst fears were confirmed.

That was kind of the point last night. The whole reason why I fucked her against the desk. I knew he would hear. I wanted him to.

But it was a mistake, and now I was paying for it.

I wanted desperately to speak to her, but the outing today required both Gillard and me to be present, so I would have to wait until we got back to the compound.

Our car stopped in front of a run-down building that was

smack-dab in the middle of downtown Seattle. The outside brickwork was crumbling, and the building was tilted, making it look as though it would topple over any minute. That was the point though, to protect it from people like the Order who wanted to expose the not-so-legal vampire deals that lived below the surface.

To those who didn't know, they would see a decaying building, but to the those who did. . . they would see the entrance to one of the most powerful underground vampire organizations out there.

"This is where you have your meeting?" Silvia's voice cut through the silence. It was the first time she had spoken to me today and it caused my chest to twist.

"You'll understand soon," I said and stepped out of the car.

It was a gamble taking Silvia here, but I was serious about what I said last night.

I wanted her for as long as I could keep her, so showing her this side of my business was just a small introduction into what the rest of our existence together would be like.

I would have to trust that she wouldn't spill this to the Order.

The sun was hidden behind dark gray clouds, and a small chill filled the air. I looked over to our resident hunter, making sure that the Order uniform was enough for her.

"Here," Gillard said, stepping out of the car. He held a flannel in his hand and motioned for Silvia to take it.

I raised my eyebrow at him. That was a flannel that had been stuffed deep in my closet and had my scent packed into it.

Did he really steal the flannel just to give to her?

"You're a smart bastard," I complimented and reached for the flannel.

Silvia gave out a huff of annoyance but let me help her put on the oversized flannel that swallowed her form.

It wasn't really for the cold, but another way to mark her.

Hunters were not welcome, so anything to show that she was with my clan would only aid us in convincing those vampires not to attack her.

"Keep it on," I said in a low whisper. "For protection."

I pushed her into the decaying building while sending Gil a grateful smile. Most of the building was empty, save for two guards positioned near the stairs that led to the underground tunnels. They stood as tall as I did, one had a shaved head while the other had a full head of dark curly hair. They both had scars on their face, no doubt from the various turf wars they had engaged in.

Their gazes locked on Silvia and low growls sounded from their chests.

"What's with the hunter?" the one with a shaved head asked. His face was twisted in a scowl at the sight of Silvia.

I bared my teeth at him and growled. I heard vampires who resided below begin to scurry as they heard the news of a hunter in their safe space.

"Protection, of course," Gillard said from my side, flashing a small smile. "Tobias is expecting us."

They didn't pay any mind to him, too focused on the hunter in front of them.

"Let them pass," Tobias said, his voice echoing out from below us. It was loud enough for the vampires to hear, but it wouldn't reach Silvia's stunted human senses.

The vampires' faces paled at the order, and they both stepped aside, allowing us entrance into the underground.

I motioned for the others to follow me and led them down the concrete stairs. Silvia's hand brushed mine, and I looked back at her, but her eyes were downcast. I didn't know if it was because she was scared, or it was just an accident, but it made my heart soar.

Shaking my head free of thoughts of Silvia, I turned and continued down to the musky underground. The place was just as disgusting as it was when I visited years ago. The scent of dead bodies and blood were permanently etched into the foundation of this place, causing my stomach to twist uncomfortably. How people lived their lives down here was beyond me.

Tobias's scarred face and black eyes met us as soon as we turned the corner into the long underground hallway. His white curly hair was a mane around him, not too much unlike Silvia's. The only difference was his stopped at his chin. I heard her heart flutter and understood her reaction.

Tobias had a blank stare that was more similar to a ghoul than a vampire. Scars littered his face and only added to the otherworldly vibe he gave off.

In short, he was a child's worst nightmare.

"Long time, Tobias," I said, coming to a stop at the end off the stairs.

"Nice to see you, Keir," he said, his airy voice filling the silent hall. His soulless eyes narrowed in on Silvia. "What I would give to get such a talented hunter at my side. You sure are lucky, Keir."

Silvia's face was pleasantly dusted pink and her eyes darted to the floor.

I should compliment her more if that's the face she makes.

"She will guard the door," I explained and shifted so she was hidden behind me. Tobias may act like he had no idea what was going on, but that was just one of his many sides. He had been running this underground sector for years, and I had had many years to study him. I came back with one resounding conclusion:

He was smarter than he looked and I, for one, didn't want to get on his bad side.

In the legal world, soon, I would be the one with the most

power. . . but he had always had a choke hold on the underground and its dealings. Our reign as vampires simply could not exist without the work he had done behind the scenes.

"Understood," he said with a small smile and turned, walking down the narrow, dark hallways without a word.

I shot a look at Silvia and Gil, hoping my warning came across. Gil raised his brow at me, but I shook my head and motioned for them to follow me.

Tobias led us down the various tunnels in the underground until we stopped at his very own study. All the doors we had passed were closed, but I could hear the vampires behind them as they listened to us pass.

Everyone in the underground was here because they either couldn't live among the rest of society, or they just didn't want to. When I first found out that such a place existed, I was intrigued.

I would have given anything to get away from my father, but it was a lot less glamorous here than I had made it out to be.

As he opened the door, I was hit with a waft of stale blood and had to hold back my gag.

Why does he have to kill in his study?

"Stay here," I ordered Silvia and gripped her shoulders, pushing her back against the concrete walls.

I held our position for a moment, hoping that she would finally look me in the eyes, but she kept her gaze trained on my shirt. With a sigh, I left her outside and joined Gil and Tobias in the study.

The door shut behind us with a small click, and he motioned for us to sit at the chairs in front of his desk.

The room was dark and only lit with two lights on either side of us, one of which had a bulb out. There was a yellowing carpet beneath our feet, a surprisingly clean desk, and a few chairs, but there was nothing else in here. Nothing that told you the person you were meeting was the most powerful underground ruler we have had.

"I hope you have better insulation than the rest of the underground," I muttered, refusing to sit down. Even though the surfaces of his dark furniture and floors seemed clean, I felt as though there was a line of grime on everything.

"You shouldn't waste hope on such a stupid thing," he responded, cocking his head to the side. "Everyone who comes here knows that risk."

"We accept the risk," Gillard said, cutting me off from complaining. "We come to inquire about the Reiss murder."

He pulled out the same file that I had spent many nights reading through, staring at the soulless eyes of Silvia after her parents were brutally murdered.

I couldn't find anything, and I really didn't know where to start. Not to mention how odd it would look if it came out that the next clan head was digging around their hunter's past. I needed someone who I could trust to keep a low profile to work on this and, while I didn't trust Tobias as a vampire, he was a hell of a businessman.

Tobias accepted it with just the tips of his fingers and carefully turned the pages, as if it was covered in germs. An oxymoron if I ever saw one, seeing as he lived in utter filth.

"Your clan emblem is painted on the walls," he sang under his breath, almost as if he was excited about the prospect of my clan doing something so utterly stupid.

I gritted my teeth and tried to breath in through my nose. I wouldn't fight him, I couldn't. I just had to get over my annoyance, let him push my buttons, and get out of here before I fucked over this relationship.

"That's the problem," I growled. "No one in the clan would be that *stupid*."

His reddening eyes searched the page with obvious interest. I purposefully left out the picture of Silvia from the file, but from the way his lips slowly curled, and how his eyes narrowed, I knew that he had already come to the conclusion that it was her.

"The hunter is lucky to have the attention of someone like you," he murmured and closed the file. His gaze finally shifted to meet mine and a shiver ran up my spine.

This was the Tobias I didn't want to see. He changed from an airhead to a panther in an instant. He had seen something in that file that caught his interest, and while that was great for us, I was worried about what it meant for Silvia.

Tobias held out the file and without a word Gillard took it from him and hid it back in his jacket.

"We need your contacts to track down the killers," I said.

"Can I keep your hunter?" Tobias asked, his voice dangerously low.

Anger flashed through me and it took all I had to stay planted in my spot instead of lunging at the fucker and tearing his throat out.

"I will offer a blind eye to this place and its dealings," I said, glaring at him. "I will take over for my father soon. I was planning to crack down on the underground vampire clans in my domain, but if you are willing to help, I will turn a blind eye. *That's it.*"

"That's no fun." He gave me a mock pout and watched to see if I would crack.

But I wouldn't. Anything involving Silvia was nonnegotiable.

"Then don't take it," I said, walking toward the door. I was acting nonchalant but my mind was whirling.

What will I do if he doesn't take it? I have no one else to go to, no one I can trust. Xin may be an option but. . .

"Oh, I will take it," he said, his words stopping me in my tracks. *Thank God.* "But a word of advice. A warning, if you will."

"About the case?" I asked, not looking back at him. There was a smugness to his voice that grated on my nerves, he sounded far too comfortable for this conversation.

"About your father's dealings."

I glanced at him then, his eyes were still narrowed but there was something about his expression that put me on edge. It felt like the panther in him was circling me, waiting to strike.

"Go on," I forced through gritted teeth.

"Your father will not go out without a fight. He has something planned." He paused, the smirk widening. "Remember this for when you turn a blind eye. I am giving you this warning in good faith that you will remember it well."

I left the room without waiting another second, grabbing Silvia and forcing us down the hallway. She was smart enough not to say anything and just follow Gillard and I. The residents had yet to venture out of the concrete rooms, but I could feel the stirring. Tobias's words had put them on edge and they were curious to see what hunter I would give up so much for.

No one spoke until we passed the guards and loaded into the car. The seriousness of the situation weighing on our shoulders.

"He's dangerous," Silvia said quietly as we drove off.

"You have *no* idea."

Do you ever get that feeling in your stomach, one that's so heavy and twisted that you know in mere moments your life would go to shit?

That was the feeling I got as soon as I stepped inside the manor.

It hit me like a truck and froze me to my spot. I didn't want to move, or make a sound, for fear that if I did, the mirage in front of me would disappear. Time stood still and all I could think about was how much I wished I could have stayed in my happy bubble with Silvia and forgotten the rest of the world existed.

But life didn't work that way, it never did.

It never gave you the time of day or a moment's rest, and just when you thought things were going well, the universe made a point to show you just how wrong you were. And I knew soon I would see what it was trying to tell me.

I just wanted to spend a few more moments here. I didn't care that Silvia was upset with me, because I was afraid that this may be the last moment I could have with her.

The air of the manor was still, the only thing breaking the silence was Silvia's footsteps across the marble floor.

Father had a way with him. He was powerful, no doubt about that. . . but his darker side was the thing that people feared. It was the thing that made the normally buzzing manor fall silent.

I didn't know how he did it, but whenever he was angry there would be a cloud surrounding the compound, and once it was felt by any living creature that resided here, they made sure to run for the hills.

That was the thing I felt now.

I looked toward Gil and saw that he was just as frozen as I was. His face had paled considerably and his hands came to nervously tug at his hair.

This was different than the last time I was called to Father's feeding room. There was something brewing, something dangerous just beyond the horizon.

"Go up to my study and wait for us, Silvia," I said as I stepped toward her and let my hand lie on her shoulder. "Gil and I will be up in a moment."

She turned to me, her silver eyes still held the sadness that had fallen over her since the night before. I felt a wave of regret flow through me.

Will this be the last thing she remembers about me?

"If you take too long I'll turn in for the night," she said and shrugged my hand off her shoulder, a scowl marring her perfect lips.

"We won't be long," Gil said from my side.

Gil for the most part was a great actor, but he was positively terrible at hiding his fear. Silvia must have seen this. She eyed him warily before nodding and silently walking up the staircase alone. I waited until her form disappeared around the corner before I spoke to Gil.

"He hasn't called us," I said, though it was a last-ditch effort at trying to salvage whatever bit of freedom I could hold on to.

"He doesn't need to," Gil said and ran a hand through his hair, pulling the strands from the top of his head out of his loose ponytail.

"I suppose he doesn't," I echoed.

I listened for any type of rustling or call, but the house remained silent. I could still vaguely hear Silvia's heartbeat and the sound of her footsteps as they walked across the carpeted upstairs halls, but nothing else. Meaning Father was farther away, probably in his study.

There was a reason my study was on the opposite side of the house. I wanted to be as far away from him as possible, and if I couldn't hear him, then he couldn't hear me. It was the last ounce of freedom I was able to pry from his iron grip before I was forced to give up everything to rule this clan.

With a sigh, I motioned for Gil to follow me and walked the path to my father's office. As we got closer I could make out the small sounds of him drinking his blood. Surprisingly, he also had his guards still stationed outside his door. As we rounded the corner, the guards' eyes drifted toward me before they both turned their gaze straight ahead.

I walked between them and reached out to the doorknob, hesitating as a trickle of fear ran up my spine. I shouldn't be scared of the person I would be in charge of in mere weeks, but here I was, still cowering in front of him.

The last time I'd felt like this was when I was much younger and couldn't even hold my own.

"You're a disgrace," Father said, slamming his booted foot into my stomach.

He had been at this for thirty minutes now, and by this time I had stopped trying to get up. It was much safer just to lie down anyway. If he went on any further I'd faint, and the last thing I wanted was a broken nose from falling on the hard concrete floor.

Though it would be the best revenge if I showed up to tonight's event with a busted face and watched him squirm as I dodged question after question.

Today's fight had begun when I made an off-handed comment about the Order's newest contract they signed with all the vampire clan heads. It put a cap on how long they could rule and demanded that they somehow transfer their power to an heir or elected official.

It was far too human of a concept for Father, and many of the other vampires, to stomach.

"I don't want to rule," I said through my coughs. I wasn't able to brace myself and white-hot pain ripped through me as his next kick sent me flying across the room. I landed against the hard wall with a thud and felt a sharp pain make its way up my back.

"You have no choice," he spat and stalked over toward my

huddled form. "It's not like any of us wanted this in the first place. So suck it up and act like the heir you were born to be."

I pushed myself up and tried to run toward the door. Father was much too angry to deal with today and I was afraid that if I stayed for any longer, I may not wake up after I fainted next.

I was still slower than him and hadn't yet been able to hone my strength, so his hand easily shot out and yanked my hair before I got too far.

"Go knock up another woman, then." I groaned. He pulled my hair so hard my neck twisted at a painful angle and forced me to look into his glaring red eyes.

"You will be punished for your behavior," he vowed.

And I was. I was punished thoroughly for an entire month after that, making sure that I never forgot my place. I made it a point not to cross him since. I knew his threats were serious then, and the only reason he was keeping me alive was for his own gain.

Upon opening the door, the first thing I was met with was his glowing red eyes. He sat behind his large oak desk, sipping a goblet filled with blood. He surrounded himself with books. He had erected bookshelves on the sides of the room while leaving the wall behind him bare, save for the two large windows that looked over the entrance to the compound where he could see every person that entered or exited our gates. There were no chairs in his office besides his own, he didn't need them. After all it's not like he actually did business in here. There was a faint smell of drying blood somewhere on the carpet, telling me the blood in his cup had probably come from a freshly slit neck.

I stood near the entrance and bowed my head, a submissive act that boiled my blood on the inside, but I hoped it would make him less hard in whatever he was about to do. I had a million ideas going on in my mind about what this meeting could be about, but I didn't dare dwell on any one for fear it would come true.

Gil made a show of bowing to him, which my father waved off.

"I will not ask where your extracurriculars took you this afternoon," he said and stood before stepping from behind the desk and toward me. Each step reverberated around the room and just added another notch of panic to my ever-growing bank of volatile emotions that were swimming in my chest. "The Order called; they demand their hunter back."

He stopped a mere foot away from me, his expression hard and his jaw tight.

"Father—"

He slapped me so hard across the face my head whipped to the side and small white spots exploded across my vision. I didn't fight it or the sting that it left in my eyes. A slap was nothing compared to what he had done, or *could* do if I continued to anger him.

Though at least now I knew why he was so upset, and it was worse than anything I could have imagined.

"They say we have taken advantage of her," he spat. "Forced her to do things against her will."

He slapped the other side of my face, forcing my head to the side and right into Gil's line of sight. His lips were pushed into a straight line and his body was shaking.

I hated when Gil had to see this.

"You didn't react this way to the other hunters." I couldn't help the venom that seeped into my words. "If anything you thought it was humorous."

He grabbed the hair on top of my head and forced me to look him in the eyes. The pain of his slaps combined with the pain of his hair pulling made my eyes water.

"This was supposed to be our last hunter. The best hunter,"

he snapped. "The Order was our last resort because you continued to sully our name with your actions, and now the single most important hunter has been stolen out of our grasp."

"I don't need a hunter anymore," I growled. "Pay the contract fees and let her go. I have proven that I have changed my ways. The power transfer is in a few short weeks, I don't need a babysitter anymore."

Father's eyes flashed and I was worried for a moment he would hit me again, but instead he just let out an angry huff.

"If she was not here, my head would be on a stake because of those dirty rebels. So would yours," he said. "Now with the transfer of power closer than ever, we cannot take a chance on losing the only proficient hunter we have."

I swallowed thickly, remembering all the times Silvia had to jump in and save not only my clan but many others. I couldn't deny that, even though her main job was babysitting me, she had excelled in protecting us.

I couldn't respond to Father. I had no more reason to fight back. I had messed up, I knew that from the moment I finished with Silvia last night and heard Damon cursing in his room.

A simple act that came out of jealousy had single-handedly ruined everything that I had been trying to keep a secret.

"Does this mean we will have forfeit their services?" Gillard asked from my side. His voice was calmer than before, his shaking subsided. For once it seemed like he may have a viable plan hidden away in that thick skull of his.

"No." His hand tightened in my hair. "Thankfully, I was able stop them from doing anything too harsh. But I had to degrade myself to apologize to them. They seem to think that she may have wanted it. Which brings us to the next question and will determine our course of action."

His lips curled into a disgusting smile that made my skin

crawl. I wanted nothing more than to smack that smile off his face and pummel him into the ground.

"Did the little hunter beg for it?" he asked, his eyes lighting up.

It disgusted me to hear him speak like that. I didn't want him to think of Silvia in that way and sure as hell didn't want him daydreaming some sort of sick, twisted fantasy of her.

I didn't trust Damon for a single second, especially after it was now obvious it was him who had told the Order, but I couldn't get his words out of my mind.

Her punishment was a week in the Dark Room with three broken fingers, Silvia.

I didn't want the same punishment to fall on Silvia, and since this was supposedly their best hunter, would her punishment be worse? Gil and Father had made it clear that we would be extremely unhappy if they couldn't find a hunter that could do their job, and we were the biggest clan out there. With Silvia being the best of the best, I had a hard time believing that they would let her off with broken fingers and a week of starvation.

This is all my fault, I thought, my stomach turning to lead.

Everything from here on out would be a direct result of my words and actions toward Silvia and the Order. If I fucked this up...

"I forced her," I spat at him. "There was never a time where she willingly gave in and each time she would remind me of how much she hated our kind. I told her if she did not go along, we would not pay her debt."

He clicked his tongue, that sick smile of his twisting into a snarl.

"She will leave to go back to her precious Order tonight," he growled. "She will stay there to recuperate and probably be given the option to quit."

I almost hope she would.

"After she returns," he continued, his eyes narrowing. "You are to cease whatever you have been doing with her and ride out the contract until the transfer of power."

He let me go and made a show of pushing me so I would stumble out of his way. He let out a chuckle as I reached out to catch myself on the wall behind me.

"If you cannot complete this task, there will be a much bigger punishment waiting for you," he warned.

"I understand," I said but did not move, too frozen by my own thoughts.

I was relieved yet panicked all at the same time. I couldn't tell if I had made this better or worse for Silvia and just prayed that she knew what was good for her and quit.

"She is important to the Order, therefore she is important to us," my father reminded. "Be thankful that old sack of meat is easily manipulated."

I nodded, really listening to him. The only thing I could think of was how *fucking stupid* I was to think I could hide this and how close we were to utter destruction.

I didn't much care about what Father did to me, but the thought of Silvia being harmed by the Order or my father caused my whole body to panic.

I had told her that I wanted to keep her with me for as long as I lived, and it was true. I didn't want to think of a world without her in it, but what if that was the safest thing for her? What if the only way to guarantee that no harm came to her was to push her as far away from me as I could and hope for the best?

But Silvia... she wouldn't take things at face value.

She was smart and too damn nosy for her own good. I wouldn't put it past her to pry.

And as much as I wanted to keep up this ruse and try and be with her behind their backs. . . I couldn't risk it.

A pain ripped apart my chest when I realized what I would have to do.

Gillard's hands gripped my arms and he pulled my still-stunned form out of the room. Instead of taking me to my own room, he took me in the opposite way and out onto the grounds of the compound, far enough that we wouldn't be heard by any prying ears.

He was leading me to the garden on the far left of the property, the same one I had run through to escape when I was younger. Plants and beautiful flowers surrounded us, and he pulled me all the way to the back where we stood beneath a large oak tree that hid us from view.

I knew what he was thinking. We could devise a plan and work from there, but I didn't need to think of a plan. I already knew what we needed to do, and neither he nor Silvia would like it.

"I know that look, Keir," Gil grumbled under his breath. "Don't you dare try anything stupid."

"I have a plan," I said quickly. "But you will have to lie to her."

Gil let out an exasperated sigh and threw his hands up in the air, pushing me away from him.

"We should just tell her the truth," he said, his voice almost pleading. "If she knows, she can play along until you take over. Your father would be none the wiser and the Order would think it's a job well done—"

"And then what, Gil?" I asked, my voice harsh. Fury spread through me. "And then I steal her for myself? We wouldn't even get that far before both the Order and Father cut our heads off."

"I know it's more than just a simple crush, Keir. You *really* like her, and so do I. She at least deserves the truth about how you feel," he said, placing his hand on my shoulder. "Even if you cannot be together right now—"

I growled and gripped his shirt, pulling his face close to mine.

"She is a *human,* Gil," I hissed. "She'll die if we aren't careful, don't you understand? Father doesn't care about the Order. We should feel lucky he isn't trying to deal with this himself."

"She's a hunter, Keir," Gil retorted. "She can protect herself. If you really wanted to save her—"

"Like last time?" I said, cutting him off. His face dropped, and I immediately regretted my words as shame filled his expression.

"She deserves to know what is going on," Gillard said, his voice softer. "At the *bare* minimum she *deserves* to know, Keir. It's really a simple solution—"

"If Father thinks there is *anything* else between us, he will make this worse for *both of us,* do you understand Gil?" My voice finally lost its edge and my words came out choked. "He already knows Gil, they all do and I just can't—"

My words were cut off by a sob ripping through my chest. The tears that I had so carefully held back now began to fall.

Guilt and regret weighed on me so heavily they threatened to pull me to the ground with them. I knew this was a possibility, hell even at one point I wished this would happen, but now I couldn't even face what I had done.

"Please," I begged. "Just please help me with this. I need to make sure this works. I can't chance anything. Father—he—I haven't seen him that angry for years, Gil. It's serious. . . it's bad."

His expression dropped and was replaced with one of pity.

"Calm down, Keir. I'll help you," he said, his voice soft.

"Just reel yourself in. You aren't thinking clearly or making any sense."

I knew I wasn't. The thoughts zipping back and forth through my head alone were enough to make me dizzy, how could I even think to regurgitate them out for Gil to understand?

"Tell her I leaked it," I said. "Leave Father's part out of it."

"The captain will tell her what the real issue is," Gil pointed out.

"No he won't," I argued. "He will ask and then she will have to go along with it. But you know her Gil, she won't go along with it if she knows this was to save her. We have to force her to think that I was the person she thought I was all along."

"So your choice is to just make yourself the bad guy?" he said, his voice rising as he pushed me back. "Your plan is stupid, Keir."

"We will iron out the details when she leaves, but for now, keep it vague," I said. "The more she hates me again, the easier it will be to keep her safe."

I wiped the tears off my face and took a deep calming breath.

I prayed that she would take the bait.

It wouldn't work if she tried any of that savior bullshit she had been prone to whenever the rebels attacked us. For once I needed Silvia to actually hate me or else everything she had worked for would be for naught.

"Please, Gil," I begged again.

His eyes softened, then he let out a loud sigh.

"Fine," he breathed. "But please don't make me regret this."

CHAPTER 25
SILVIA

"What is this, some type of joke?" I asked while pushing myself off Keir's couch.

Whatever they were doing had ended pretty quickly, but it had to have been something bad because the moment Gillard opened the door to Keir's study, with her following behind him silently, he began spouting off nonsense about me taking a break and going back to the Order.

"No joke," Gillard said and pulled his glasses off to pinch the bridge of his nose. "Come with me, you are leaving tonight."

Tonight? Panic ran through me and alarms went off in my head. Why were they pushing me out so fast? I leaned to the side to try and catch Keir's gaze but her eyes were focused on the ground.

"Tonight?" I echoed. "Why so fast, what happened?"

There was a silence that spread across the room and Gillard shot a look back to Keir, but she ignored him.

"The Order asked for you back," she explained. Slowly she

looked at me and I couldn't help the shudder that ran through me when her dead eyes met mine.

What the fuck is happening?

"For what?" I asked and shifted on my feet.

The Order wouldn't pull me away from a contract for no reason, so that must mean something big happened. . .

"I'll tell you more on the way to the car," Gillard said with a sigh and stood up straight. He swept his arm out, motioning for me to follow him out of the door. "Please, Silvia. We don't have much time."

I wanted to stay and force it out of them. They both obviously knew way more than they let on and were just trying to bide their time. It angered me.

I had been with them for months and they couldn't simply tell me what had happened?

What if Cain or Jade was hurt?

What if so many hunters had gone missing that they were forced to call reinforcement?

Or maybe. . . Did they find out what Keir and I had been doing?

All of it was just too much to think about and with the anxiety of it all swirling around my mind, I had no choice but to follow him out of the room.

Keir's eyes watched me intently as I walked past her, but I didn't have a chance to question her as Gillard pushed me out into the hallway and guided me toward my room.

"I have taken the liberty to pack your things," he said by my side and motioned to the baggage that now stood outside my door. I hadn't seen it since the first day I had come here and seeing it here suddenly made this whole situation feel all too real.

"How long?" I asked, my voice shaking for reasons unknown to me.

I meant to pick it up but lost my grip when Gillard spoke.

"A week," he said from behind me.

I whipped my head around, his eyes already boring into me. He had kept his glasses off so now I had a perfect view of the mix of anger and pain that marred his face.

"Gil. . ."

"Hurry," he said and walked past me and down the hallway.

I shot one look back at Keir's closed door and followed behind him quickly.

Once we turned the corner, I felt him push me against the wall and cover my mouth with his hand. His eyes were wide, and I could feel the light shakes from his hand.

"Quiet," he whispered, his voice barely audible. "You've been caught."

My heart stopped and my body turned cold. I tried to focus on the rapid movements of his lips, trying to decipher what he was saying, but the sound of my own blood rushing through my veins drowned everything out.

I've been caught.

We *have been caught.*

Keir and I. . .

The image of my fingers being broken, and flashbacks of the Dark Room, flashed across my mind and a scream bubbled up in my throat.

I knew in my heart that my punishment would be ten times worse. The Enforcers. . . the ones in charge of punishing the Hunters. . . they were brutal and they absolutely hated every hunter in the Order. They had fun with torturing people and no doubt would make me regret ever going into the Order to begin with. Not to mention I was the last hope for this contract. . .

". . . she leaked it, Silvia," Gil said.

His words stunned even the rampant thoughts in my brain and brought everything to a grinding halt.

"What?" I asked behind his hand. "I'm sorry, start over."

He pulled back with a frown, loosening his grip on me.

"You were caught. The Order found out about you and Keir, and they demanded you back. We don't know to what extent they know, but they do. I wanted to warn you before you left," he said. "And. . ."

"Keir told them?" I asked, pain ripping apart my chest. "She told them that we. . ."

His hand quickly covered my mouth once more.

"Do not implicate yourself," he growled. "I am warning you because I have grown to care for you, Silvia, but now our time is up."

He pulled me off the wall and dragged me down the rest of the hallway, his grip on my wrist so tight I was beginning to lose feeling in my hand. I stumbled over my own two feet at the top of the stairs only to be saved by Gillard grabbing me by my arms and setting me safely down on the first step.

"I'm sorry, I—"

"Quiet," Gillard commanded. "Take a deep breath, and then we go."

His eyes burrowed into mine and his face was stone cold. I didn't realize I was shaking until his hands trailed down my arms and grabbed my hands in his.

"I'm scared," I whispered.

I had to be out of my mind if I was really telling this to a fucking vampires for God's sake. I flinched and waited for him to say something, but after a moment of silence, he just inhaled deeply and let it out. And then he did it again.

"Breathe," he demanded, though his voice had lost its edge.

I took a deep breath and exhaled it while gripping on to his hands.

"I will see you back here in a week," Gillard said. "Be smart, be careful, and please look out for yourself."

I nodded, speechless. There were no more words I could speak, nothing I could say would make this any better. If anything, me talking more would only make this situation worse for me.

The only thing that was left in my stunned mind was this:

I was a fucking dumbass to think that I could ever trust a vampire.

"It's a party," I muttered as I stepped into the captain's office.

He was standing in front of this desk and there were five hunters around him, two on each side and one hidden in the back, his eyes trained on me. They were all men and wore that standard Order uniform, but they also had on a nice shiny gold patch that sat right in the center of their chest.

I tried to keep my reactions to a minimum as they watched me walk in and throw my bag on the floor. Their eyes were trained on my every movement, and one even had a sadistic-looking smile plastered on his face.

I didn't know much about the ranking system of the Enforcers, but I knew that gold had to be one of the highest tiers.

When I had gotten in trouble and punished in the academy days, I only talked with silver patches. And while they were horrible people, they did not compare to the gold patches. My first encounter with a gold patch was the same one where they threw me in the Dark Room for the first time, so them being here meant that I was incredibly fucked.

Breathe, Gillard's voice traveled through my mind. *I will see you back here in a week.*

That's not looking very likely anymore, I through wryly.

"Silvia," the captain said, his tone grave. "It has come to our attention that Keir has been mistreating you."

I raised my chin and swallowed thickly.

"If that is what this is about," I said, hoping they couldn't hear the quiver in my voice. "Then why are there guards stationed at your side?" I paused and looked up and down the one that was smiling. "Ones with a tendency to maim."

The hunter let out a crazed chuckle and Captain shot him a look.

"Remove your weapons," the captain commanded.

I pulled my dagger out of its holster, but instead of throwing it aside, I flipped it in the air and caught it so the blade was facing behind me.

"Only if you tell me the real reason you brought me back," I growled.

Keir has been mistreating you. What the fuck did that mean?

"That silly vampire is rumored to fuck you against your will, babe." The chuckling hunter stepped forward and rubbed a hand over his buzzed hair. "We are here to check the bites, see if the stories match up."

Keir leaked our relationship. . . so why do they think it was nonconsensual?

If anything, agreeing to this would only help me, and I would probably get to keep my contract. But just looking at the gazes of the hunters at the captain's side told me that, even if I lied to them, I would not be exempt from punishment.

"I can show you the bites," I said and gripped the fabric of my turtleneck, pulling it down to show them the bites on my neck.

The hunter chuckled again.

"You don't think I was born yesterday, do you?" he asked

and took another step forward. "We aren't done here until we see *everything*."

My blood ran ice-cold, and I took a stunned step back. The captain wouldn't allow them to do this right here, right now. . . Would he?

The captain's eyes moved toward the left where he met the eyes of a tall hunter with messy black hair and matching black eyes who nodded, then turned to me.

He is the squad leader.

I rolled my head and stretched my neck before dropping down into a crouch. If they wanted a fight, I would oblige.

"I'm guessing that even if I confirm that Keir really did force me against my will"—*which she did not*—"you will still strip me of my dignity and force me to undress in front of all of you?"

"There is no room for dignity in the Order, Hunter," the one with black eyes said. "Chase."

The giggling man stepped forward pulling out his own weapons, two daggers, though much longer than mine.

I really hope none of these people are witches.

"Stand still for me, babe," Chase said with another chuckle and lunged forward. He might have overpowered me, but I was faster.

In an instant I threw my dagger at him. When he dodged I let out a crazed giggle of my own and lunged forward as well, pulling my sword out. I was able to slice the side of his torso faster than he could bring the daggers down on me, and he stumbled forward.

Turning quickly, I kicked the center of his back and he fell to the ground in a heap, grumbling and moaning. I looked back at the group to see the man who was next to Chase, the one with dark hair and piercing gray eyes, caught my dagger in midair, but not with his hands. He had a shield made out of purple, glowing magic that had my dagger embedded right in the middle of it.

Fucking witches.

"Don't fight this, Silvia," the captain commanded. "I don't want to hurt you any more than we have to."

I felt Chase behind me before I heard his weapons come down on me and was able to roll out of the way.

Just as I thought the coast was clear, a cold hand gripped the back of my neck while another forced the wrist that was holding my sword, twisting it painfully behind my back. I tried to keep grip of my sword, but the pain became too much, and I had to drop it. The sword fell to the ground with a loud clang, breaking the tense silence in the room.

The person behind me kicked the back of my knees and forced me to the ground. I groaned and tried to peer up at them, only catching dark black eyes and messy silver hair.

Another fucking witch.

Jade and Cain were nowhere near these people, and now I realized, neither was I.

Chase slowly stood up unsteadily and walked over to us while breathing heavy.

"Chin up, babe," he purred and brushed the tip of his dagger under my chin. "Don't want to hurt you."

He dragged the tip of the blade down my neck and pressed it even harder when he reached my turtleneck, slicing the fabric and, with it, a part of my neck.

I let out a pained hiss.

"Oops," he said with a chuckle and dragged it down my entire front before putting the dagger back into the holster on his thigh.

"Fuck you," I spat and squirmed against my captor's hold. The hands that were grabbing me started to burn in response.

"Stay still," the deep voice commanded from behind me.

Gritting my teeth I stayed still even as Chase bent down and ripped the rest of my shirt off with his bare hands.

"Oh would you look at that," he cooed when he caught sight of Keir's bite peeking out of my sports bra. "How many times did that vampire bite you?"

I growled at him and tried to lunge toward him, but the witch behind me tangled their hand in my hair and pulled my head back so I was forced to look at the ceiling.

"There are bites on top of bites," the witch behind me said in an uninterested tone, as if discussing the weather and not forcing me into this position and baring my naked torso to the world. "The heir probably thought she was being smart trying to hide the bites over ones that were already there. I theorize she wanted to keep Silvia for as long as possible."

Why would she try and hide it if she was just going to leak it anyway?

I don't know how they ended up deciding it was nonconsensual, but it was probably the only thing saving me right now.

It just... felt so *wrong.*

"You wouldn't have any other bites hiding anywhere else, would you?" Chase asked and leaned close enough that I could feel his breath waft across my chest.

His hand brushed the top of my leggings.

"I'm going to cut that microscopic dick of yours off and mail it to your mother," I threatened as a finger slipped under the waistband.

"That's enough," the captain said. "There are enough bites there to get an idea of what happened."

Chase pulled away with a pout and stood up to look back at his captain. Slowly the silver-haired witch behind me let me go, and I scrambled forward to stand.

I glared at the captain as I pulled off the rest of my ruined shirt. *This* was not the man that spent the holidays with us. The man in front of me was nothing more than a dog of the Order and it *sickened* me.

"My parents would be disgusted with you," I spat. "This is how you treat someone who has been assaulted by their contract holder?"

The words tasted sour and felt wrong in my mouth, but I was far too pissed to think about that. Like Gillard said, I needed to save myself.

"Why didn't you come to us?" the captain asked. "I was there, you could have told me."

The witch bent down to pick up my sword and handed it to me. I rolled my eyes and snapped the sword out of his dirty hands.

"Why would I when this is what you do to us?" I asked. "Plus if she was busy with me"—I swallowed the disgust down —"then she wouldn't be misbehaving."

There was a sound of distain from the leader. "Sounds like you liked it," he commented.

"Those words sound like they come from an entitled hunter who has little to zero debt to his name," I growled, then looked back to the captain. "I did what I had to in order to finish the contract."

The captain eyed me before sighing and waving off the hunters around him. There was a loud sigh from Chase as their leader motioned for them to leave the room.

The black-haired witch who had been holding my knife with magic gave it back to me with a forced smile as he passed. I grabbed it from him with a scowl and then turned my gaze to the only one who was silent during the whole exchange. He paused by me for just enough time for his brown eyes to turn just a bit red, then he passed me without a word.

Shock rattled me to my core.

Were my eyes playing tricks on me or was that a vampire in an Order uniform?

When the door shut the question launched itself from my mouth.

"Why the fuck is a vampire in the Order?" I asked, my voice far too loud.

"Worry about yourself," the captain shot back. "You should be grateful Damon told us what was happening or you would still be in that hellhole. How could you believe that I wouldn't pull you out of—"

Damon?" I echoed.

A pounding began behind my eyes, and suddenly, I was far too tired to deal with any of this.

Images of the hazed interaction between me and Keir in my room on the desk flashed across my mind. I should have been pissed. Furious that someone I trusted would go behind my back like that. . .

But instead, I felt a violent relief that Gillard and Keir were lying to me.

They were *fucking lying* to me. They had me believe that Keir had betrayed me, that she had gone back on everything she promised me.

Why? *Why?* Would they do that? How dare they?

"He and Cain were worried," he explained. "For good reason. Now you will stay here the next week and think about how you betrayed the Order. If you want to step out of this contract—"

"I don't," I forced out, my heart pounding in my chest. "I will never get a chance to pay off my debt like this ever again. This is a once-in-a-lifetime chance, and I will not give it up even if—"

"Even if I tell you that if you step out I will still forgive your debt in full?" he asked.

Holding in everything I wanted to spout at him, I walked toward my bag and hiked it over my shoulder.

"What's the catch?" I asked, looking toward the door.

There was no way he would just do that with nothing in return. I had learned that nothing here came for free, and even if it seemed like it, you could bet that there were a hundred different secret obligations you would have to pay forward after it.

That was how the Order worked.

They wrapped rotting garbage in a nice bow and told you to ignore the smell and shards of glass, hoping you wouldn't actually notice until it was too late.

"Join the Enforcers," he said. "Just for a year. There are things that are coming, Silvia. Bigger than—"

"Like the secret project you have my squad working on while you told me they wouldn't have to work at all?" I interrupted and turned toward him.

His jaw clenched and his face turned a bright red.

"Something bigger," he said. "You would be a part of—"

"I refuse," I said and walked toward the door, pausing as my still tingling hand gripped the knob. "I know shit when I smell it. Don't bother me until the contract is over. And even then the only thing you will get from me is a note from me in my empty dorm telling you to fuck off and forget I ever existed."

"Silvia—"

"You disappointed me," I said and pushed the door so hard it swung open violently, scaring the same enforcer group that had been standing outside of the room, no doubt listening in to our conversation.

The vampire met my eyes and he sent me a nod.

"So do I take it you are joining us?" Chase asked, a slimy smile spreading across his face.

"No," the vampire spoke. "She refused."

Chase frowned and the leader stepped forward.

"It would be a good opportunity for you," he said. "You are strong and we would teach you—"

I stepped close to him, grabbing the disgusting gold patch, and pulling him closer to me, our faces inches apart.

"Don't insult me," I growled and pushed him back toward his team, enjoying the way he stumbled over his own two feet. "Find me again and I will make good on my threat."

I turned and walked toward the elevator, Chase's voice calling after me.

"We'll see each other soon, babe!"

Like hell we will.

Hunter Rules

rule 2 sec 1

Contracts are legally binding.
To break a contract is to
break every value the Order
holds true.

CHAPTER 26

KEIR

"Please, Master, I swear I didn't—"

The human's pleas were cut off with a loud snap as my father's guards twisted her neck. The vampire didn't even flinch as the human died in his arms, the light escaping from her eyes, and threw her on the pile of dead humans in front of me.

I guessed it had been about a week that I had been chained in the basement and forced to watch as my father's lackeys killed human after human and threw them in front of me, but made sure that they were just out of reach so I was forced to smell the blood rushing through their veins as I starved.

My throat was so dry I could barely swallow and my fangs ached so bad I wanted to pull them right out of my head.

I prayed every night that my father would unchain me from this hell, but he never did. Instead, he let me bathe in my own guilt and hunger, forcing me to relive the past few months over and over again in my mind.

I fucked up, I knew that much before I was banished down

here. . . But seeing it in the lens of a hungry, blood-deprived state, I couldn't believe just *how* stupid I had been.

Not only had I believed that I would be able to banish my father from the kingdom he had forged with blood and violence for thousands of years, but I really thought after all of it that Silvia would want to stay by my side and rule with me. I thought that she would overlook my vampire status, and my people would overlook her hunter status. . . but I realized now that there was no way we could be together.

I do regret having Gillard lie to her, but there would be no other way for her to live in peace. . . and it was about to get ten times worse when she came back.

I had been through the conversation over and over again in my mind. It would hurt us both, but it was what had to be done. Silvia needed to believe that there was no way she could stick around because once she knew that I lied. . . I was worried that we would fall into our same habits.

And I was a sucker when it came to her.

I was ready to give her the world and burn anyone who even looked at her wrong, but I couldn't be that way. This conversation would be just as painful for me as it would be for her. We *both* needed to get a grip on ourselves, and I couldn't do it if she gave me that *goddamn* look that she did when she was miserable.

I would crack faster than the vampires that snapped the humans' necks in front of me.

"How much longer?" I growled. "The hunter should be coming back soon. Father sure would be pissed if I killed her due to hunger the day she came back."

The guard looked back to the other one who was standing against the door. He sighed in return.

"You know we have no choice—"

I lunged forward, pulling at the reinforced chains. The

metal groaned as it stretched and the metal on my wrist dug into my flesh and began burning me. It was coated with some type of magical shit from years ago when we still trusted witches, and it ate away at my skin. Luckily, or unluckily in my case, I was healing thanks to my vampire genes. But that just meant that it would keep eating away at my flesh, then healing, then eating away again.

"Get my father," I growled. "Do not forget who will be in charge of this clan in a few weeks."

I heard Father's shoes against the stone ground before I was even finished with my sentence. I wanted to watch the door and scream at him as he came in, but instead my eyes dropped to the piles of dead bodies that were in front of me. Some of them were old and already decaying, but the one on top caught my eyes as I realized the guard had been a bit too hard with her. Instead of just snapping her neck he had broken it completely, causing the bone to stick out and blood to flow down her neck.

Father stepped into the room, in his hands was a wild, flailing women with bright-red hair that rivaled Silvia's.

My heart dropped when I saw her and my hazed mind really thought for a moment that the person in his arms really was Silvia. I was ready to tear off these chains, even if it meant tearing my hands off with them.

I saw red before the girl let out a wail. The haze suddenly cleared when I realized it was not her in his arms.

He gave me a wicked smile before forcing the girl flush against him. Her wild green eyes searched the room frantically as she stood frozen again my father.

"She looks a lot like your hunter, doesn't she?" he asked and gripped her chin, forcing her to look me in the eyes.

The girl was scared and had tears running down her face, washing away some of the dirt that was smudged there.

She wasn't a normal feeder. She was dressed in regular human clothing and was far too upset to be here by choice.

I wanted to screw my eyes shut and look away as her wails got louder the harder Father gripped her chin, but I knew that if I did, Father's suspicions would be confirmed.

I let out a growl and he sent me a smile before he kissed the girl's cheek and sank his fangs into the side of her neck.

She screamed before going slack, her eyes hazing over as his venom made its way through her. When she let out a moan I had to avert my gaze, disgust filling me.

I didn't see when Father tore himself from her throat, but I heard it as well as the snap of her neck.

I knew what he was doing. He wanted to show me just how fragile the humans were. How fragile Silvia was. Why else would he go through the bother of finding a human that looked just like her?

He is fucking disgusting.

"I am thirsty, Father," I spat and turned back toward him. Blood stained his face and button-up, making him look just like the monster he really was. "If you knew what was good for this clan and our image you would let me out of here. We have played long enough."

His eyes flashed and I thought for sure that little quip would keep me in here for another week.

"You're a disgrace," my father said as he stepped toward the guard by the door and wiped his bloodstained hands on his clothing. "A disgusting excuse for an heir with a weakness for women and bending the rules. Time and time again I wondered why I did not just snap your neck after you came out of that vile woman's cunt. It would have saved me a lot of trouble."

I growled at him and tried to pull harder at the chain that connected me to the stone wall, but it was useless. I was too tired and the metal had been reinforced with magic. I wasn't getting out of this unless that bastard unlocked my restraints.

I hated how dependent I was on him. And I hated how I still *fucking* listened to him.

It was supposed to be only a matter of time before I took over, but Tobias's words floated through my blood-crazed mind. *Your father will not go out without a fight. He has something planned.*

It would be just like him, but the last few days sitting here while I starved gave me enough time to think of what I needed to do. I just needed to get out of here before I could start putting any type of plan in motion.

"Though," he added after a pause and turned toward me. "You either have a great deal of luck, or that hunter bitch is far too enamored with you to know what's best for her. She's on her way back. Lucky for us, she declined their offer to remove herself from the contract."

Silvia. . . Silvia is on her way back!

A part of me wanted to rejoice at the thought of being with her again, but that part was soon washed away under the crushing reality of our situation.

She should have stayed away. I gave her an out.

And if she came back now. . . would I even be able to keep myself in line enough to keep her safe? Father wasn't stupid, and her coming back to this job only proved that there was something bigger there than just a hunter and her contract.

. . . But how was he close enough for the captain to tell him what he offered her? That was who told him, right?

Unless. . . He couldn't have someone in the Order, could he?

I wouldn't put it past my father to have infiltrated the Order, but I thought they were better than that? And if someone really did infiltrate the Order. . . Silvia would be in danger.

"I didn't know you were close enough to the Order for them to tell you what they do with their own hunters," I growled and pushed myself to a standing position even as my legs shook and screamed at me to stop.

Father huffed and motioned for the guard closest to me to unlock me from my restraints. I waited patiently as he took a wrist in each hand and unlocked the cuffs.

"And you will be too," he said. "Once you take over."

As soon as the last restraint fell to the ground, I grabbed the vampire in front of me in a flash and sank my fangs deep into his neck.

Vampire blood was thick and left a film on my throat as it went down, but it was better than the decaying blood of the dead human bodies in front of me. The vampire groaned as my venom made its way through his body. Unlike with humans, our venom was less potent when in a vampire. It moved too slowly and could easily be fought off by their own vampire cells.

I pushed him away after I took enough blood to feel somewhat like myself again. He fell over the pile of dead bodies and lay there while he recuperated.

I walked slowly to Father, enjoying the disgusted look on his face far too much.

Keeping his gaze, I spit the excess vampire blood in my mouth directly on his pristine white shirt and pushed passed him, bumping his shoulder as I did so.

"Try that again," I warned. "And you will live the rest of your life in the dungeons while I destroy everything you have built."

Father let out a laugh that forced me to look back at him.

"That's what you want to do with your newfound power?" he asked and raised a brow at me, his eyes turning red. "You really think you can take me?"

I turned to face him, clenching my fists.

"Everything you have ever done to me since coming into my adulthood had been because I *allowed* it," I growled. "When we are done here you will never lay a hand on me or anyone in my clan ever again."

He let out another chuckle and shook his head.

"And that hunter of yours?" he asked. "Is she in your clan too? Curious as to why she would return to a place where the vampire she was supposed to protect treated her like a fuck toy. Am I missing something here?"

Steeling my face I turned on my heel.

"The hunter could die for all I care," I lied. "This is between me, you, and the clan. The Order is but a distraction keeping us from the real problem at hand."

Which is?" he asked.

I paused at the doorway.

"How on earth you would agree to giving up your clan when you so obviously plan to keep it," I answered, and without looking back to see his reaction, I walked out of the dungeon, dreading every step because each step meant that I was just *that* much closer to seeing the human who had wormed her way into my heart without permission.

CHAPTER 27
SILVIA

The days blurred together, every day the same thing over and over again.

Wake up.

Avoid my squad.

Work out in the academy training room until I felt like I was going to throw up.

Eat whatever I could scrounge up from the cafeteria after everyone had left.

And then hide in my room until the sun rose.

The only thing that brought me any bit of comfort was the feeling of my fist pounding into the punching bag. It brought a bit of pain every once in a while, my knuckles raw from the constant friction of the leather against my skin, and I ached more than the day after I woke up with Vance's bites littered over my body.

Sweat poured down my entire body, coating the Order-approved work-out gear. I could hear the whispers behind me as the academy students watched me work my ass off day after day.

They had seen me come here before, but this was far beyond my usual workout.

This time I had a bone to pick with the unstable emotions that plagued me during the night. They would crowd my small dorm, reminding me of how, just weeks before, Keir and I were in there doing the unspeakable. The me back then didn't fully understand the consequences of my actions, and she also didn't understand just how much of a liar Keir was really.

I didn't know what hurt more, Gillard telling me it was Keir who leaked us... or knowing that it was actually Damon who did it and Keir was forced to lie to her father and the Order to *save me*.

I had put everything together fairly quickly after I was left to digest the captain's words. Though I still couldn't understand why.

With a growl, I sent a kick to the punching bag and finally, after days of abusing it, the chains connected to the ceiling completely snapped and the bag flew across the room, plunging the space into a tense silence.

Why?

Why would she lie... on my behalf? Why would Gillard lie?

It all hurt, but that hurt quickly turned into anger.

I cried more than I'd like to admit, but it was easier to feel angry than it was to decipher why her actions had hurt me so much.

I almost wish it had been her that leaked... because then I could *actually* hate her.

"Ms. Reiss," a voice called from behind me.

I turned to find the enforcer squad leader watching me. His dark eyes seemed even darker under the fluorescents and there was a hint of a frown on his face. Behind him I spotted the vampire from last night. I was almost happy to realize that Chase wasn't in the room with them.

Looking past them I saw the academy students huddled toward the back of the training room, staring at the enforcers in fear.

I didn't blame them. They scared me as well and to get their attention was a death wish.

I took a deep breath, trying to calm the racing in my heart, and took a few steps toward them. I should have been embarrassed to be seen like this by them. My hair was a mess, I had huge dark circles from not sleeping, and I was as bare as they saw me in the captain's office.

"What can I help you with?" I asked, my voice coming out strained. I didn't realize how winded I was from the workout until I was snapped from my angry haze.

I eyed the vampire behind him critically. *What the fuck was the Order thinking?*

"I was put in charge of bringing you back to the compound," he said, looking at his hands, which I now saw held *my* bag. Then his eyes shifted back to mine. "And deliver a message."

I rolled my eyes.

"Ever the dramatic," I muttered and went to take the bag from his hands, but the vampire shot forward and grabbed my wrist.

On instinct I tried to pull my hand away, but he kept a tight grip on it. His eyes turned red and a low growl came from his chest.

"The message is for you." The leader's voice dropped so low it was almost inaudible. My gaze snapped to him as he leaned down. "Do you know what all enforcers have in common, Silvia?"

I gritted my teeth and tried to yank my hand from the vampire's grip, but again it was futile.

"That you don't have a concept of personal space?" I growled back.

The leader let out a huff, which was what I quickly realized was his version of a laugh.

"All our families were hunters," he said.

My eyes shifted to the vampire's and he nodded.

"Mine too," he said.

"And what does this have to do with—"

"Who were all also murdered," he finished.

A chill ran over me.

Shit.

"Hunters often get hurt or die in the line of duty," I said and finally the vampire let me go.

I gripped the bag and threw it over my shoulder.

I stood there, waiting for them to lead me out but they both just continued to stare at me.

"They were all in their homes," he said.

"Mine was in their car," the vampire said.

I didn't like the sound of this. My mind was whirling trying to piece everything together, but I couldn't.

"By vampires?" Was the only thing I would think of to ask.

The leader gave me one slow nod.

"Do you know how many enforcers there are here, Silvia?" the vampire asked.

I shook my head.

"Two hundred," the leader said. "In Seattle alone."

I blinked rapidly, the exhaustion of the workout sneaking up on me.

"Do you know how many enforcers have gone missing in the last few months?" the vampire asked.

"I don't like these games," I hissed.

"One hundred sixteen," the leader answered. "Accounting

for over 90 percent of the missing hunters who have been reported in the last year."

"Why are you telling me this?" I asked, my voice losing its edge.

Slowly I took a step back, looking at them in a different light. *Who are these people?*

"Why do you think?" he asked.

The vampire cleared his throat and the leader's head snapped over to the door. My gaze followed, and I saw just as the captain pushed through the door. His eyes searched the room before landing on us.

"It's time," he said loud enough for myself and everyone else in the training room.

I heard the academy students panicking, but I couldn't pull myself from the captain's gaze.

What on earth have I gotten myself into?

———

The vampire, who I later learned was named Jase, had come along with the leader to accompany me back to the manor. He didn't speak much, neither did the other, but he couldn't stop staring at me as we rode in the back of the limo Gillard had sent to get me.

"Has the heir ever told you that you smell delicious?" he asked as the manor came into view.

The leader, who I now knew as Isaac, let out a small huff.

"Don't make her uncomfortable," he ordered.

The vampire let out a small pout and looked out to the manor as we circled the large fountain. All that separated us from the vampires who waited for us outside were the doors to the car.

I wasn't surprised to see Gillard and Keir out there waiting, but I was sure as hell shocked to see her father with her as well. Keir looked like shit, her hair was messed up and her cheeks were hollowed. I couldn't imagine what he must have done to her in my absence.

"How long can a vampire live without blood?" I whispered.

"Two weeks," Isaac answered. "Though they should be ravenous far before that. They tend to go crazy and drink their own blood before they die of actual starvation."

I swallowed thickly.

"Why are you here with me?" I asked, and even as the car came to a stop, I refused to leave.

The vampire looked over to me, his once red eyes slowly returning back to brown.

"A message," he said, then looked back out the window. "From the captain to the king."

The driver left the car to open the door for us, forcing my hand.

I gripped the bag and climbed out of the car with the enforcers hot on my trail.

Luckily, I had been able to change and strap my weapons on, but I still felt uncomfortably bare in front of the vampires who awaited me. They knew what Keir and I had done, and I didn't know how to face them.

The walk was silent and I stopped a few feet away from the group, the enforcers right at my heels. I tried to meet Keir's gaze, but it was trained on Jase.

"The captain has a message," Isaac said, then looked down at me before continuing. "Tread carefully, or the next time, I will have your head cut off before you can even think of breaking a contract again."

My face flamed. This wasn't about me, was it?

"He knows what you're doing," Jase continued. "This is your warning. *Knock it off.*"

Keir stepped forward. "Who are you?" she growled.

Her voice sent excited shivers through me, and I cursed every God I knew, feeling disgusted that I still had such a reaction to her.

"I will be the one to tear your father's head off if he thinks of fucking the Order over," Jase answered.

I looked up toward Isaac to see him still staring at me.

"This isn't about you," he said and turned toward Keir. "I suggest you take your hunter inside now and let us have a chat with your father."

Your hunter.

Gillard took the initiative to step forward and grab my bag from me.

"This way, Miss Silvia," he said, a tense smile spreading across his face. "I have prepared your room for you."

I couldn't return the smile, but I followed him up the stairs, Keir following behind us closely. Just as I was being pushed through the door, I turned backward, catching the scowl on Isaac's face. Jase's face was twisted into a snarl and his eyes narrowed on to Raphael. . . who looked at me with so much fury that I thought I would drop dead right where I stood.

Keir shut the door behind us, cutting off my intense stare down with her father.

"Come, Silvia," Gillard said and pulled me toward the stairs. "We have a lot to catch up on. First off, we have two events coming up—"

I let him drone on until we reached the hallway that Keir and I were staying in. The image of it brought on an assault of emotions that I could no longer hold back.

Pulling on Gillard's arm, I turned him around and pushed him against the wall. My dagger was in my hands in a flash and I pushed it against his throat. I couldn't keep the fury locked inside me anymore.

"*You lied,*" I spat, the words spilling out with all the anger I had built up in the last week. "You *lied* to me after I *trusted* you. You made me believe that Keir was the one that—"

Keir's hand closing around my throat and yanking me back from Gillard stopped the words and breath from escaping my mouth. My dagger fell to the floor with a loud thud. She used her single hand to pull me against her, my back to her chest, and slowly she lifted me off the ground so just the tips of my boots brushed across the carpet.

"Keir," Gillard warned.

"He didn't lie," Keir said. "I would have told him if the Order hadn't caught on."

I struggled against her hold, clawing at her arm as I felt the world sway around me. I tried to grip for my sword but her other hand took my free arm and twisted it around my back.

"Put her down," Gillard hissed.

She obeyed but only so just my tiptoes were touching the floor, her hand still firmly planted on my neck.

"You need to get this into your *thick* skull, Silvia," she growled. "*I* am *exactly* the vampire you thought I was."

I looked toward Gillard, tears filling my eyes as I continued to struggle for breath.

Why? Why was she doing this? I thought she did this to save me?

"Let me go," I choked out.

"You got lucky the Order created that scenario, no doubt because of the nosy-ass hunter that stayed in the room next to you," she growled. "Did he tell your precious captain how much you begged for me?"

I tried to avert my gaze from Gillard, shame and embarrassment riddling my body, but Keir's hand kept my face toward him.

"Enough," Gillard growled and launched forward, pulling me out of Keir's arms.

I leaned against him, heavy coughs racking my body. I took gasp after gasp of fresh air and tried to steel myself, though I didn't know if I could. I was shaking violently, and all the hurt that I had so carefully buried came *right* back to the surface.

My stomach felt hollow and my mouth went sour. Although I had not eaten today, I still felt like I was going to throw up. I turned back to see Keir glaring down at me.

"You and all the Hunters are running my *fucking* life," she growled, each word cutting into me deeper than the last. "I can't wait 'til your sorry ass gets kicked out of here once your contract ends. You should be thankful I even pay you after the transfer of power. I have half a mind to pull the contract and tell the captain what *really* happened."

"You wouldn't," I gasped and turned, ready to lunge but Gillard caught me.

"I bet you just sat there and agreed to everything he said didn't you?" She egged me on. "How did it feel to lie to them knowing that you came on my hand less than twenty-four—"

Gillard let me slip enough so I could deliver a slap so hard to Keir's face that my palm stung afterward.

"I told them what they needed to hear," I growled. "But it's not like you would care. You are every bit as disgusting as I thought you were. You are just a fucking *child* that has had all the money in the world to soothe her needs, but even that couldn't buy your father's love now could—"

Gillard hand clasped around my mouth.

"Both of you shut *the fuck* up," he growled.

Keir stepped forward, her chest brushing across mine.

"Your parents are probably rolling in their grave right now wondering how their perfect daughter turned out to be such a vampire loving *whore* while they gave their lives to fight people like me." Keir's eyes shifted, almost as if she was going to back down but then she continued. "They are probably glad they got torn apart by vampires, 'cause then they wouldn't have to face a disgusting excuse for a hunter *like you*."

The silence was so potent after that I swore I could hear the sounds of my own heart breaking. The worst part?

Father and Mother would be horrified with me. Horrified after all my fights with them, that I still joined the Order. Disgusted that I would sell my body and my soul to the Order when they knew it would literally mean giving up anything I ever wanted in my life.

Because there was one thing they both wanted, even if they still pestered me about joining the Order.

They wanted me to be happy. They wanted me to be so utterly and blindly happy that even on a cloudy day I would look up and sigh as if the sun was shining on my face. They wanted me to chase my dreams and become the person *I* wanted to be, not the person *they* wanted me to be.

Gillard's hand fell from my face and I felt hot tears fall down my face.

"They would have loved you," I choked out.

. . . because at one point, I was happy.

So blindly happy that I couldn't see the complete monster in front of me. I took her as a saint, the only vampire I could stand after everything I went through.

And that was the single most damning thing I had done in my life up until this point.

I grabbed my bag out of Gillard's hand and stormed into my room, slamming the door behind me.

I wished so badly to go back.

CHAPTER 28

KEIR

Even though I knew I had to push Silvia away, I still felt as though I was too hard on her.

I knew mentioning her family was a low blow, but after the comment about my father...

It was all just so messed up.

Watching her come apart in front of me because of my words was heart-wrenching. For the first time, I saw what it really looked like for her to be hurt.

And I fucking hated it.

The way her eyes flooded with tears, the soft hurt gasp she let out, the way her heart skipped a beat in her chest... Why did this hurt so much?

I was supposed to be the heir to the most ruthless vampire clan there was and here I was losing myself over some stupid hunter. A human no less!

Their normal life expectancy was normally a blip in my memory, but these three months seemed to drag on forever and ever.

Last night in particular was the longest night I had to suffer through.

I was thinking of bringing in a blood bag tonight and fucking her until dawn, just to solidify the fact that I *really was* the awful vampire that I had told her I was. . . but I couldn't bring myself to do it.

Not after I heard her soft sniffles.

She spent most of the night crying, but it was so soft I almost didn't realize what was happening.

It hurt my heart to realize that *I* was the one doing this. *I* was the one tearing apart her life.

I only hoped that she would come out stronger than before, because if not. . . I couldn't stand myself.

Nor could I control myself around her. The only thing keeping her safe, and us apart, would be her total hatred of me.

The sun had risen only moments ago and I found myself sitting at my cold desk, looking over the brutal murders of Silvia's family.

I couldn't count the nights that I sat here pouring over gruesome images of her family's torn limbs. I had memorized the entire layout of the house, every drop of blood that vampires spilled, and even the expressions of her family members.

They were terrified and in pain. The notes from the coroner's office had told me they all died from loss of blood.

Meaning that they were awake for the entire time the attack had happened and, based on how the blood had pooled around the bodies. . . sat there for however long it took them to bleed out.

Probably moaning and crying out for help.

. . . but no one heard anything.

That was the strangest thing.

Silvia's family lived in a quiet, unassuming neighborhood

full of humans. The closest vampire territory was twelve miles away. A vampire could run that length in record time. . . but it also meant that there should have been some trail.

But there wasn't any.

And how did the neighbors not hear the commotion?

These were certified, top-tier hunters. Not only should they have been able to defend themselves, but just the act of them fighting off the vampires should have made some noise.

"Gillard," I called, hearing the footsteps of my best friend racing up the hall.

I wanted to stop him before he got to Silvia, allow her a bit more time to sleep in. Not moments later my door opened, his head popping through the opening.

He too looked like he hadn't slept much. Dark purple was smudged across his under eyes, and he looked paler than I had seen him since we had accepted him from that abusive clan he was in.

"Should I be worried that you stopped me from awakening our hunter?" he asked, a small scowl on his face.

"I know you are angry." I sighed and leaned back in my chair.

I was angry too. I hated every moment of this fucking nightmare I had put myself in.

But it would all be worth it in the end. At least I hoped.

"Angry?" He scoffed. "I am *livid*, Keir!"

"Gil," I warned. "Keep your voice—"

"You can't say shit like that!" he continued. "I watched you ruin the best relationship of your life in less than three seconds! She was the only person—"

"Gil," I growled and stood up, bringing my fists down onto the table. "We were not together, there was no relationship. And you know nothing about what is good—"

Gillard let out a loud laugh.

361

"I don't know what's good for you?" he asked. "That's what you are about to say right?"

"Gil—"

"I have watched you grow up for *two hundred* years, Keir," he growled. "And I have yet to see anyone pull you in as fast as she did. You are risking *everything* you have for this hunter, and you can't even admit that you like her!"

"Enough!" I growled and slammed my fist down. The wooden desk was far too fragile for my strength and my fist broke through the table.

I heard Silvia shift in the next room and paused to meet Gillard's gaze.

"I'm sorry," Gillard whispered. "I just... care for her."

"I know." I breathed. "*I know.* The transfer of power is coming soon and after that..."

"Do you really think he will let it go?" Gillard asked. "Tobias hasn't been known to lie to us yet."

No he hadn't. As seedy and disgusting as he seemed, he had proven to be one of the most loyal people I had worked with in the underground.

That's why I trusted him as much as I did to look into Silvia's case. I trusted that he would not only find the killers, but also keep my name as far away from it as possible.

"I don't know," I admitted. "I have a plan though, if he doesn't."

I heard Gillard swallow, his face dropping.

He didn't have to ask to know what I was planning.

If Father didn't step down it only meant one thing, treason. And in our clan, treason was met with the old-fashioned sword to the throat.

Silvia finally let out a soft groan before I heard her get out of bed.

I took a deep breath, centering myself for what was to come.

I imagined her puffy eyes and scratchy throat. I imagined the hateful looks that she would give me. I needed to think of it now, prepare myself... because if I didn't, I knew for certain that seeing her like that would tear a hole so deep in my chest that I wouldn't be able to handle myself.

"Will you continue to treat Miss Silvia the same as last night?" Gillard asked softly before turning to the door.

"Yes," I said in a firm tone, then added, "But you can be there for her if you want... as a friend."

I shouldn't have been jealous. If anything Gillard would be helping me, because with him at her side maybe she wouldn't look so fucking miserable.

But a part of me wanted to be the one to make her happy, not Gillard. *I* wanted to be the one she ran to. The one she clung to as her heart was breaking.

"As a friend," Gillard said under his breath, almost as if he didn't think it was possible. "That would be... nice."

I nodded and fixed my clothing before closing the file and stowing it away in my drawer.

"Let's go get her," I said and followed him outside of the room.

Dread weighed on me, heavier and heavier with each step. I didn't want to see Silvia, yet it was the only thing I could think about since she had slammed the door in my face last night.

Gillard stepped forward and knocked on her door. I could hear Silvia inside startle before calling out to us.

"In a minute," she yelled and I heard her scurry across the room. The fabric of her uniform clothing broke the silence and I stood a step back, realizing that I was much too close because in just a few seconds—

The door opened and Silvia appeared in the doorway, looking far worse than I could have imagined.

She was in her normal uniform and her hair was tied up, showcasing the bites that got us into this mess in the first place. Terror ran through me as I felt my fangs pulse. Even though I had had my fill of blood, I wanted nothing more than to sink my teeth into her sweet flesh once more. I wanted so badly to feel her writhe under me as my venom course through her body.

But her face. . . yes, her eyes were puffy and red. . . but there was an air about her. When her eyes met mine they only stayed for a few second before they shifted to Gillard.

Fury and hurt welled up in me.

Why is she acting like she doesn't care?

I should have been happy to see this, but inside I didn't like it. I didn't want her to act like we were nothing. I wanted her to be just as in pain as I was. . . I mean she sounded like she was wounded last night, but was it over now?

Was I nothing but a casual get-together that you could cry out in one night and then be over with forever?

"We have something planned today, right?" she asked Gillard. "I think I remember you mentioning it last night."

Her voice was strong, unaffected, though I heard the small bit of huskiness hidden in there.

But that could have been from the sleep.

"Yes," Gillard said, then cleared his throat. "We have people coming over to discuss the transfer of power."

"Negotiations," I cut in, wanting her attention on me.

But to my dismay, she just nodded and shut the door behind her.

"Do we have time for coffee?" she asked.

"We are running behind schedule," Gillard said with a

small smile. "Though I already ordered ahead and it should be waiting for us down there."

The smile she gave Gillard made my chest clench.

"How thoughtful."

"You will stand here," Gillard said. He placed his hands on Silvia's shoulder, then moved her into a space where she would have a view of the room and the hallways which led to it. She didn't push his hands away this time, which sent a fresh wave of jealousy through me. "Once we leave, you will follow. The meeting will start in twenty minutes. Stay here until then."

"I understand," she said and stood straight up with a hand on her sword.

Hours had past since we first got coffee, and now was the time to get some actual work done. Voices filled the hallway, only muffled by the double doors that separated us from the largest conference room we had.

Gillard smiled at her and removed his hands. He let her go to meet the guests, and I followed without a glance at Silvia.

"Seems you took my words to heart," I said just outside the double doors. I could hear various vampires on the other side. Fixing the collar of my shirt, I made sure that I was presentable.

This was my first big task that I would have to undertake before I took my position, and it was by far the most important. This meeting would tell us who would stay with the clan, and who we would need to cut. I had met with clans over the last year to discuss what they wanted, but this was the *formal* event. After this everything would be written down and signed. We would be bound to our contracts so everything that happened here was far more important that any other meeting we had held thus far.

Meetings like this happened every year and I had seen my fair share of fights break out and blood spilled, but this one would be worse. They were here to see if I was fit to even rule, which made this all the more nerve-racking.

I knew that I was fit. I wanted to do right by the kingdom and finally banish the monster who had been taking advantage of our positions and power, to give back to the people who suffered the most.

. . . but what if *they* didn't see that? What if they wanted the monster?

"We just have her for such a short time, so we might as well make the most of it," he said with a sad smile.

I nodded, and without another word, I opened the doors. In front of me was the biggest conference room we had, and right in the middle was a long, dark wooden table that sat some of the most powerful clan heads in our region.

Some even came from a few states over, though there were some notable ones missing. I took note of it all and held my chin up high, stepping in like I owned the place. . . because I *fucking* did.

Xin was present as well as the Kazimir's clan head. Though there were many more than I expected present, and they all turned to stare at me as I entered. And of course, my father watched me like a hawk as I entered. He was standing near the back of the room, blood in hand. A few of the older clan heads surrounded him, chatting with him like he was an old friend. . . but little did they know, Father didn't have friends.

Father was the type of man who preyed on people and used them until he had sucked them dry. There was no such thing as a *friend* in his mind. Either you were useful, or you weren't, and that was that.

"Keir, good to see you," Ian said. He stood and bowed to me. I returned the bow. "I apologize for my son's actions last time and hope that they have not strained our future relationship."

Ian was nowhere near the scum Vance was, but even just a mention of what that sorry sack did to Silvia made anger flash through me. I had to push down my feelings and push out the image of Vance's disgusting hands on her.

"Yes, it was unfortunate, but I have never had issue with you, Ian," I said and gave him a small smile. "If issues like that do not occur again, you can rest assured knowing that our alliance will stay strong."

Visible relief washed over his face. Before he could respond Xin came over to greet me with a smile. Her hair cascaded down her back like a dark curtain. She rarely ever put it down, stating that it was just too much of a burden, but it made her look so much more regal when she did. It paired well with the blood-red dress she was wearing and made her skin stand out so it almost looked like she was glowing.

This was the queen she needed to show to the rest of the clan heads. Something I would have to do as well soon.

"Keir, looking good as always," she said, side-eyeing Ian. Ian shifted uncomfortably before muttering an excuse and leaving us.

"Play nice," I reminded with a smile.

She clicked her tongue before dropping her voice down to a whisper.

"I wanted to check on your hunter," she said. "Is she well?"

I swallowed thickly. This was not the time to be discussing this. Not in a room full of possible enemies that were ready to cut off my head at any sign of weakness.

"She is fine now, my lady," Gillard said for me. *Ever the*

fucking savior. I didn't deserve him. "She is guarding outside, but I ask that you leave her to her duties."

Xin gave me a suspicious look.

"I thought we liked the human," she said.

I looked around the room for Father. He was chatting with Ian now, a fake smile plastered on his face. As if he felt my stare, his gaze flitted toward mine and his mouth pressed into a thin line.

It was a warning.

I don't know what those hunters had told my father last night, I could only catch bits and pieces of it before I was so focused on Silvia and her pain that I could barely breathe, but whatever it was. . . it had pissed him off.

When I caught his scowl as I took Silvia into the house, my entire body froze. I had made my father angry many times, but never *like that.*

"She is just a hunter," I said. "No need to bother with her."

Xin gave me a look that told me she wanted to fight my words, but again Gillard jumped in to save me from total doom.

"Xin, is there anything we should discuss about the power transfer?" he asked, his hand lingered on my back.

I took comfort in the gesture, knowing that I wasn't alone in this.

"No, I am quiet comfortable. Though I would like you to visit me more with that little hunter," she said. "I quite like her."

Xin was trying to test me. She knew that as soon as the words left her mouth I would want to refuse that she ever see Silvia again.

"You can have her when her contract is up," I said, keeping my voice steady.

Xin didn't reply. She only hummed softly and bid us

goodbye before going off to speak to the other clan heads, leaving me shaky and nervous that Father had heard too much.

I looked toward Father and felt a wave of relief fill me as I realized he was in a deep conversation with another clan head. He was speaking loud enough to drown out whatever had just transpired between me and Xin.

I didn't even feel Gillard leave my side before there was a glass of blood forced into my hands.

"Your eyes are red," he whispered.

I nodded stiffly and downed the glass, enjoying the explosion of sweetness on my tongue. The blood, while not as delicious as Silvia's, would help quench my thirst for the time being. The days of starvation were really sneaking up on me, and if I wasn't careful I would slip up and possibly hurt Silvia.

But maybe that was what Father was hoping for.

Watching him now, I couldn't see what Tobias was talking about. He had been chatting as he normally would, and I had yet to hear him or any one else around here mutter.

"Victor isn't here," Gillard said so low I almost didn't hear it.

Victor. Even just the thought of his name held so much hatred and disgust that I had a hard time keeping my grimace off my face.

Victor belonged to a clan the eastern side of the United States. A clan so vile and disgusting they made even some our cruelest clan members pale in comparison.

They had no care for rules and would go after each and every human that was available for them. They didn't care about blood laws or the contracts that bound them to us and the Order. They just continued to live in their bubble, barely restrained by me and the other clans heads.

And it just so happened to be the clan that Gillard came from.

When I first met Gillard, he was merely a quarter of the man he was now and looked like they had been starving him for nearly a decade.

They had a thing against what they labeled "weak" vampires. They would prey on them and their born children until they sought out asylum in another clan or just dropped dead.

We were lucky to have saved Gillard in time.

But knowing the type of people this clan held, I wasn't surprised that he didn't come. They didn't care about others or the formalities of the world they were brought into. If anything, they actively went against everything because they wanted to show everyone that there was no way to control them.

The only issue was that with a clan as prominent as his. . . it would mean that we would have to go to him. We couldn't risk him thinking that just because there was a power transfer, that he would be let off the hook.

Father didn't care about what he had been doing and only "stepped in" when the other clan heads pressured him to do so. And even the act of "intervening" was just Father taking a trip to Victor's clan compound where they sat and ran through body after body of unwilling humans, laughing and getting high off their screams as their fangs sank into them.

I had seen it once, when I was barely an adult vampire, and was disgusted by what I saw.

It was all a horrifying ruse that made me sick to my stomach.

It reminds me why I have to take this position. Because people like him. . . and my father were here running the world and trading our humans like blood bags that could be thrown away at any second.

"We can discuss it later," I mumbled and took a gulp of my blood.

Father's eyes met mine before he cleared his throat and all the clan heads paused in what they were doing.

"Shall we get the negotiations started?" he asked, a sly smile spreading across his face.

There were a few claps and cheers, but most of the clan heads turned to me, as if waiting for me to give them permission to start the negotiations.

Pride flittered inside of me and I stood tall, locking eyes with every single one of them.

"Let's begin," I announced.

At my command people started sitting and I met my father's narrowed eyes with a grin.

That's right, old man, I thought. *I am in charge now.*

CHAPTER 29

SILVIA

I t had been more than two hours since the meeting had started, and my feet were beginning to ache from standing in one position for too long.

I couldn't hear anything they were saying behind the closed doors, but the tension was so palpable that it filled the entire hallway. I it played at my senses and made the air heavy. I caught a small glimpse of the inside of the conference room, my heart dropping when I saw just how many people were packed into that tiny room.

I locked eyes with Keir's father immediately and shuddered at the intensity of his scowl.

Whatever the enforcers said to him last night left a bad impression on him, and if I were any smarter. . . I may have feared for my life. But I knew the contract protected me. . . even if Keir was adamant she didn't want to.

I didn't want to think about the vampire that kept me up bawling my eyes out last night, but it was hard when we were so close. Her words were burned into my mind, and I couldn't think about just how right she was when she said how disgusted my parents would have been if they were still alive. . . But if they were alive I would have never been in this situation to begin with.

I would have never been recruited by the Order and shackled with so much debt that I would be with the Order for as long as I lived. I would have never had to take this contract to get rid of the weight of my debt. And I would have never met the only vampire who had made me lose all my rationality and dignity.

A lot of things would have been better if my parents were alive, but we couldn't change that, now could we?

And Jane. . .

Thinking about her was the worst. Maybe that was why Keir didn't bring her into this. . . but I shouldn't give her such credit. She probably just forgot, but it didn't stop my mind from flashing to her cold, dead body.

I shouldn't have even entered her room. As soon as I saw my parents and the state of the house, I should have run out and called the Order. . . but I *had* to know. I had to check if the sister who I had looked up to my entire life was okay. All I could think about was seeing her, saving her. I had *some* hope that she was still alive as I pushed through the house. . . but I was mistaken.

Our relationship may have been strained as we grew up, but after we came into adulthood things smoothed over, and I ended up going to her for anything and everything that was happening in my life. She was my safeguard, the one person who wouldn't judge me no matter what the situation was. Sure, she had some snarky replies and sarcastic remarks. But they were all lighthearted, and when push came to shove, she would always be there for me, rubbing my back and braiding my hair as I cried in her arms.

I remember when I came crawling to her about my girl

troubles. Nat had been a hot topic of conversation for a while, while she was still human. Jane was excited that I could find someone as easygoing as her and hoped that she could talk some sense into my normally stubborn side, though we both knew she was far too soft to stand a chance.

I couldn't help but think of what she would have thought of Keir.

Pain exploded in my chest, but not because of Keir's words.

Because this is the first time in a long time that I had wanted to share something with my sister, and I just realized that I couldn't. Not now, not ever.

Knowing me, I would have called Jane up right after the first day, if I was still a hunter that is, and talked her ear off about how rude and inappropriate Keir was. She would have laughed and told me that I had met my match and she was excited to see someone, *anyone*, else taking up my time.

Go rant to your new girlfriend, she'd probably say.

I swallowed down the feelings of guilt and pain that suddenly washed through me.

Jane was the best big sister I could have asked for.

She was probably sick and tired of me annoying her so much after so many years of being unable to take care of myself, but still she always picked up on the second ring when I called.

That was why I rushed over in the first place.

And then I called her again when I was outside of the house, dread crashing my entire world.

I had been anxious back then and the worst flashed through my mind, but I didn't know that for the first time the crazed throughs swirling around my mind would be right.

I took a deep breath and shifted on my feet, grabbing my sword in hand. I needed something, *anything*, to steady me, and my previous fixation proved to be unavailable at the moment as she did God knows what in the room behind me. Her entire personality changed as the door opened.

I tried not to look, really. I tried to act like the hunter I was supposed to be. Aloof and unbothered. . . but I had to sneak a peak after I felt the holes she had been burrowing into my head finally disappear.

And to say I was shocked was an understatement.

The Keir that I had once known did not have any chance against the Keir that stood in front of that room.

That Keir stood tall, with an easy smirk on her face and a relaxed posture that told everyone in the room that she knew they were here for *her* and nothing else. In mere seconds, she consumed the space so thoroughly I found it hard to breathe.

Her power. . . I remembered so distinctly her aura filling the room when we first met. It was terrifying, and I hadn't really felt it since, until now.

Whatever was going on in that room had to be some serious stuff, and I couldn't imagine what a room full of vampires, probably important ones by the looks of it, could be discussing if it wasn't violence and blood.

After all. . . what else did they even care about?

I shifted as the doors opened without warning.

I turned and watched as the vampires spilled out. Xin first gave me a wide grin as she passed. She looked as though she wanted to stop and talk to me, but she was quickly pushed out of the way by Gillard who came to stand by me and see off each of the vampires, bowing at them and saying goodbye as they passed.

There were many more powerful vampires filing out of that room than I had seen during my entire time at the Order and I could feel their stares. It made me extremely uncomfortable and my skin heated in shame as I bowed my head slightly as they passed.

I shouldn't be bowing to these vampires, but I would be damned if I made any more problems for Keir and Gillard.

"Silvia Reiss, is it?" a voice said from above me, shiny black shoes and pressed black slacks filled my view. I had heard that voice once before, as I was pressed into Keir coming down off a vampire venom high.

Forcing the grimace down, I looked up to see a slightly older copy of Vance in front of me. His dark-brown hair was pulled into a high ponytail, his eyes were red, and his strong jaw and features left no question in my mind who he was.

"The resemblance is uncanny," I said, a smile pulling at my lips.

I wanted to hate the man as much as I hated his son. Even now, fury burned in the pit of my stomach when I thought of his son's teeth in my neck. If I wasn't so preoccupied by the job that I had now, Vance would have heard from me a long time ago, though the circumstance would be different then and I wouldn't leave without a souvenir.

"I see I don't have to explain too much," he said jokingly, though his smile dropped quickly. "You look better than when I saw you last."

It's a lie, I probably look even worse now with how last night went.

"I would hope so," I said and rolled my shoulders. His eyes snapped to the small bit of skin not hidden by my turtleneck, the scars his son left now on display to the world. "Last time I let my guard down around a vampire."

His head bowed.

"I wanted to apologize for my son, Silvia," he said, his voice full of remorse.

It seems real, but it wasn't him who did it.

I could feel Gillard's eyes on me as well as all the vampires who passed us.

"It was not you who bit me, was it?" I asked, though feeling the heavy tone it left in the air around us, I realized that probably wasn't the best thing to stay.

Swallowing my hesitation, I reached out and gripped his hand. His jumped, his eyes flashing to mine. I shook his hand and sent him a smile.

"Let's start over shall we?" I asked. "I don't want to make any assumptions about you—*or your clan*—because of what happened."

A hesitant smile spread across his face and he shook my hand back.

"I would like that," he said. "It is nice to meet you, Miss Reiss. I am Ian, the head of the Kazimir clan. My clan door will be open to you for as long as you may live. Please take it to heart, you have found an ally in me. There is not many a time where we find a hunter with the dedication and strength you have shown."

I wanted to die right there on the spot. If only he knew what a whirlwind of events happened because I went into that room with Vance.

"It's nice to meet you too, Ian," I said. "I appreciate and accept your offer. Though please don't feel offended if I literally never set foot in your compound ever again."

He let out a booming laugh, dissipating the tension that filled the air. The vampires who had chosen to linger quickly dispersed, leaving just the three of us in the hall.

"You're an interesting human, Miss Reiss," he said.

"Silvia," I corrected. "Just Silvia."

I pulled my hand from his and motioned for him to join the others.

"Please don't let us keep you, Ian," Gillard said. "I am sure after the negotiations you have quiet a lot to attend to back home."

Ian nodded, a light smile spreading across his face.

"That I do, Gil," he said. "And thank you both. Until next time."

With a bow he quickly left us and I turned to Gillard, who was looking at me strangely.

"What?" I hissed in a low voice.

He just shook his head and fixed his eyes back to the doors. Keir and her father appeared in the doorway, walking side by side. There was a obvious divide between them, though Keir's mask was still firmly in place, a smile resting on her face.

"We were missing some key players," she noted, then turned to her father. "Any reason why Victor didn't show?"

Her father walked toward me and stopped mere inches away. Panic seized my throat and I was frozen in my spot. I wished that I had the courage to talk back to this man like I did before I came here. I wanted to yell at him, take this chance to lunge forward and slit his throat. . . But all the rage shriveled up and died inside of me as I felt the heat off his skin and his eyes looked me up and down disgustingly.

"You will accompany my daughter to another clan on the East Coast," he said, a smirk pulling at his lips. "It will be the last event you have to go to as her hunter and then the transfer of power is just about done."

Keir stepped forward and I wanted so badly to meet her eyes, but I kept my eyes locked on her father.

"Good," I said, though I couldn't hide the slight tremor in my voice. "The faster we can get this over with the faster my contract will be completed, and I can get out of here for good."

He reached forward, grabbing a strand of hair from my ponytail. He brought the strand to his nose and inhaled my scent deeply. My stomach twisted.

I am going to puke.

"Victor's clan is less hospitable to humans than we are," he said in a low voice. "You will need to keep your wits about you. The last thing I need is a visit from those hunters again worrying that we *damaged* their property." His eyes flashed and he tugged on my hair far harder than he should have before throwing it to the side like it was a piece of garbage.

I gritted my teeth, but couldn't stop the words from spilling out of my mouth.

"I am *not* the Order's property," I growled.

Raphael's chest puffed and he was about to say something, but Gillard's hand gripped my shoulder and pulled me back, causing me to stumble into him.

"Go pack your things," Gillard said quickly. "We will come get you when we are ready."

Sensing that he saved me from Raphael's wrath, I nodded quickly, bowed toward the vampires, and turned back down the hallway. I speed walked to my room, praying that Raphael wouldn't trail after me and make me regret ever setting foot inside this house. Because if his eyes said anything, it was that that he was itching for a chance to treat me just like he did his daughter all those nights ago.

CHAPTER 30

KEIR

I knew that Silvia could handle herself.

She hadn't been named the top hunter for no reason, if she was anything less than competent. . . But that didn't make me feel better about taking her along with me.

Gillard couldn't come for obvious reasons, he was a traitor there and if they couldn't even treat their own clanspeople well, you could bet that the traitors would get even worse punishment. The last I had heard of Victor's punishment to traitors was a few years ago. They hung the vampires from the biggest building they owned by hooks embedded into their arms and left them out there for two weeks while they starved to death. It became national news when it got out that when the Order had asked them to take the bodies down, they refused.

Victor of course didn't care that there was a standoff between him and the biggest hunters in his area. He also didn't care when he killed all but one and sent him back to the Order covered in his fellow hunters' blood. They were needlessly cruel and I was scared to bring another human into their midst. I looked toward Silvia as she slept in the seat in front of me. She was curled as tight as she could get into the seat, and her exhausted face was finally relaxed. Her hair was a mess around her head, her ponytail becoming loose after the hours she had slept, and her deep breaths filled the cabin.

We took a small private plane that had enough room for about four vampires, but held just the two of us, a pilot, and a small flight crew. It was safest this way, but it didn't make the situation between us any easier.

We had taken off almost five hours ago and she fell asleep as soon as the airplane was in the air. There were so many things I wanted to ask her. So many things I wanted to tell her that were just begging to be released.

Has she flown before? It looked like she had.

Does she know who Victor is? Though from her reaction I assumed the Order didn't keep them up to date on the clans that were not in their area.

Is this her first time going to New York?

And most of all. . . *Is she okay?*

It had been terrifying to see her snap at my father like she had in the hallway. I wanted to intervene, tear her from him and stand in between them. The image of the redhead's neck being bitten into by my father flashed through my mind and I knew that if I had even made so much as a move in her direction, Father would act on all his threats.

It took me until that moment to realize that he didn't really care about the Order's contract at all, even though he had been very adamant about getting her back and punishing me for losing her so spectacularly. . . He seemed awfully relaxed about a broken contract. Even went so far as egging her on, knowing that Silvia with her fiery temper, couldn't miss a chance to snap at him.

It was suspicious, so I decided to implement my plans

sooner than I had hoped. As we flew through the sky, Gillard was no doubt working hard on the ground trying to get things ready, and today had played a huge part in how successful this plan was going to be.

Between the two of us, we identified seven large clan heads, including Xin and Ian, that we planned to call on if there was an outright war with my father and me. We watched them closely as we went through negotiations, and it was quite obvious who was still loyal to my father. . . and all it took was one perfectly poised question from Xin.

"There are many clans suffering with blood supply at the moment. The smaller they are the more of a disadvantage they are at, given the majority of the fresh supplies are going to bigger clans," she said through the loud clambering of the men around her. *"What do we plan to do to make sure every clan at this table can get access to a blood supply without stepping outside the Order's blood contracts?"*

Now *that* question had caused an uproar, and even though there was an Order spy right outside of our door, there was an outcry to cut all the contracts with the Order once and for all.

The clan heads who voiced their opposition to the Order were out immediately. It was known that Father hated the Order, which was why it was so surprising for him to call on them for a hunter in the first place.

Xin and Ian had both vocally stated they wanted to keep the alliance between vampires and the Order, stating that as bad as the supply was, it would be even worse if the Order wasn't there to keep bloodthirsty, selfish vampires in their place.

Those who agreed but stayed silent were put on a "maybe" list for Gillard to look into later. . . And I just hoped that he could rally enough support in the next few days, before I came back to Seattle, to secure my position.

Silvia let out a loud groan as she felt the plane dip. We would be landing soon and I was grateful that she slept on the plane. Given her sleeping patterns at the house, I was sure that sleep could sustain her for at least another eight to ten hours, though we would have to see.

The last thing I wanted her to do was fall asleep in Victor's compound and be unable to protect herself.

She sat up straight, rolling her neck and checking that no one took her weapons from her.

"Should I be worried?" she asked.

My heart skipped a beat and I was forced to look outside as we descended through the clouds. This was the first time she had spoken to me since our fight.

"Yes," I replied truthfully. "I cannot protect you here."

She let out a bitter laugh causing me to look back at her. She pulled her long hair out of her ponytail to run her hands through it.

I wanted to badly to replace her hands with mine, feel those soft red locks through my fingers once more.

"You never protected me anyway," she spat.

I wanted to fight her. Tell her that the last few days I had tried my hardest for Father to believe that I had nothing to do with her. I was trying *so hard* to protect her from my father, from the Order... but I couldn't.

"Victor is dangerous, Silvia," I warned. "And so are his clanspeople. You cannot wander alone, hell you probably can't even sleep while you're there. Humans are weak and I do not want your blood on my hands."

Her face dropped as my words hit her and she looked outside the window.

"Prepare for landing," the captain announced.

Silvia was quiet the rest of the time it took us to land. As soon as the plane slowed, I wasted no time getting out of my seat and putting on the coat I brought with me. As she started to unbuckled her seat belt I leaned forward, placing both of my hands on the sides of her chair. She jumped back, flattening herself against the back of her chair, trying to get as far away from me as she could.

Her heart pounded in her chest and the sweet scent of her blood rushing to her cheeks filled the space between us, making my mouth water and my fangs ache.

"I am serious, Silvia," I growled. "Watch yourself here."

I stood up and left the cabin without waiting for her to respond, I didn't need to. It wasn't a conversation, it was an order. She, as *my* hunter, needed to obey because I was serious when I said that this place could very well be her downfall if she were to lose focus.

She ran after me as I walked toward the door. The captain's crew had already opened the door, and the cold New York air hit me in the face.

Stepping outside the plane, I could see the cityscape in the distance, but we were as far from the city as we could get, landing at one of Victor's private airports. It was small, and reserved just for the private jets of the other vampire clans, but it was another show of just how rich and powerful his clan was.

Father had his own landing strip a few miles away from the compound, but it was nothing like the small airport that Victor had build for himself. Father at least knew that it was a waste of resources, but Victor didn't much care.

My eyes traveled across the dark tarmac, the sun almost completely set, and only a few feet away from us stood Victor who was currently leaning against his limo. His pink lips stretched into a smirk, his normally blue eyes already blood red, and his black hair fell messily around his face.

He was one of the youngest turned vampires I had ever

met, which made his power all the more troubling. I refused to bring the topic up in front of Victor, but Gillard had told me the rumors that circulated the compound. Apparently he was the sex slave of the previous clan head. One that was so favored by him, he couldn't help but turn him into a vampire at the ripe age of seventeen, forcing him to stay in a teenager's body for the rest of his life.

It only took two years as a vampire, cuddling up to his new master and gaining his trust, for him to turn around and brutally murder him. But he didn't stop there. There were many rumors of what he did to the body, ranging from cutting it up and squeezing his blood into the cups of his closet confidants, to skinning him and having him stuffed. . . I didn't know what part was true, but I knew for a fact that he got his revenge.

I think we all just wished it stopped there, but instead he took over and killed anyone who fought him until people were too scared of him to even say no.

And that was how he became the most ruthless vampire in the United States, just shy of my father's legacy. Though my father had made an effort to tone it down as he got older, it would seem Victor only got worse.

"Keir," Victor said in a pleasant voice as I descended the steps to meet him.

Silvia's steps echoed behind me, her heart even louder than the planes engine.

"Victor," I cooed with a smile. "Sad to see you couldn't make the negotiations today."

He smiled and stepped forward, slipping his arm through mine. I tried not to grimace at the contact as his eyes playfully watched for my reaction.

"That's why you brought them to me," he sang, then turned to look behind us. "Is this the hunter I heard about?"

Silvia met his eyes and I saw her hand cover the handle of her dagger immediately, her body becoming rigid.

"Yes," I said with a sigh. "She will be gone soon though. Contract is almost up."

Victor turned to me with a pout, which combined with his youthful face made him look more childlike than ever.

"That's not very fun," he said and removed his arm from mine as the driver came to open the door to the limo for him. "I wanted to play with her."

I gritted my teeth but followed him into the limo.

"The contracts are strict," I said then let a fake smirk fall to my face. "I tried for a while, but her and the Order are quite serious. Even pulled her away for a bit."

Silvia slid into the backseat next to me, her face unfeeling, though I could feel the tension rising in her body.

"Yes," Victor said with a hum, looking Silvia's body up and down. "Your father said something like that."

Alarm bells went off in my head.

Why were he and my father talking?

"I didn't know he was reporting to you," I said, the harsh tone in my voice unmistakable.

Victor sent me a smile, then threw his head back and let out a loud laugh.

"Don't be so jealous, Keir," he teased. "Not my fault your father and I just agree on things more."

Like throwing away human lives?

I sent Silvia a look, though she was too busy glaring at Victor for the rest of the ride to his compound.

"Scent her," Victor commanded as we came to a stop at the room that was reserved for Silvia's stay.

It had been years since I came into his compound, and I wasn't surprised to see that nothing had changed since. The previous clan head had a thing for dark Victorian decoration and made sure that his insanely huge mansion, located almost thirty miles away from New York City and smack-dab in the middle of the densest forest the state could manage, was the most outrageous thing you ever laid your eyes on.

Everything from the paint on the outside to the wallpaper on the inside was in a strict color scheme consisting of black, dark red, and gold. They had stuck to their theme religiously, and I wasn't even surprised to see that, when Silvia opened her door, the entire room was painted a dark blood red accented with small gold designs on the walls.

It was too nice a room for a human.

I looked toward him and raised my brow, daring him to try to order me again. He held his hands up in the air and a small smile spread across his face.

"I'm just saying," he said with a chuckle. "Don't want my clan members getting the wrong idea."

I looked back toward Silvia as she threw her bag on the bed and gave me a questioning look.

"She will be coming to the negotiations," I said. "So there is no need."

Victor let out another small chuckle, though this time I didn't understand what was so funny. Scenting her was not in my plan and I knew that if my mouth went anywhere near her throat, I couldn't hold myself back from drinking from her.

"She most definitely will not," he said from my side, his tone sharp. I looked toward him, his face still held that playful look, but his eyes were narrowed.

"She's my hunter for the time being and where I goes, so does she," I growled.

Victor shook his head and turned to walk down the hall.

387

"The Order's *dog* is not allowed out of that room until you two leave," he said and turned toward me as he reached the end of the hallway. "Now scent her, or I can guarantee you someone will sneak in while you are off with me and take what you refuse to."

I couldn't stop the growl that exploded out of my chest.

How dare he?

Victor may have been powerful, but this was no way to treat the next clan head. He was treating me as if I was still my father's daughter and not the person who had a say in what our future clans looked like together. Victor was cocky because he knew that the only thing keeping his clan from being the number one in the country was his own bloodlust.

And that smile he gave me told me he knew he was winning this battle.

"Fine," I spat and stormed into the room, slamming the door behind me.

Silvia, who was in the act of pulling out her nightclothes, jumped at the suddenness of my movements.

"Keir? What are you—"

"Take your shirt off," I growled and stalked toward her.

Immediately she dropped the slip in her hands and covered her chest, backing into one of the bed's four pillars.

"No," she growled. "We aren't doing this."

When I reached her, I grabbed ahold of her shoulders and made quick work of ripping off the shirt. She gasped and sent a fist toward me, but I caught it with ease and used the momentum to pull her to me.

"I need to scent you," I said, my voice coming out huskier than I intended.

I pulled at the band in her hair, sending it cascading around her form. I didn't need to undo her hair in order to scent her, but I *really* wanted to feel it again and couldn't help myself.

"No you don't," she growled and used her hand to push me away.

I couldn't help but notice that this entire time she hadn't grabbed for her weapon and it made my heart soar.

"I do," I insisted and ran my hand through her soft hair before grabbing a handful of it and pulling, forcing her to bare her neck to me.

I tried not to let my eyes wander and focus on the bites on her neck, the same place I planned to mark her. My fangs ached and the fire in my throat felt unbearable as I closed in on her neck.

She let out a gasp as my lips brushed across my bites and her hand grabbed my shirt. She had traded fighting for pulling me closer. I let go of her hand and wrapped my arm around her waist, holding her to me while I ran my tongue up the length of her throat.

"Don't let this go to your head," I whispered in her ear before nipping at her lobe.

"Fuck you," she growled.

I wish.

I wanted nothing more than to ravish her right here, right now, but I knew that Victor had to be waiting for me and could probably hear us now, so I had to be careful with my words.

I pulled her head back and tilted it to the other side, licking the scars my bites had left. Her gasp was the only warning I had before the scent of her arousal flooded the room. My grip on her tightened and I closed my eyes, freezing against her.

Selfishly, I inhaled deeply, enjoying the scent of the blood rushing up to her face and the scent of her wetness. I stayed frozen around her for far longer than I would like to admit, trying to rein in my self-control when all I could think, feel, and hear was *her*.

I didn't realize how deeply she had invaded my entire being until this moment. I could remember even moan, every word, the way she felt against me, the way she reacted when I kissed her, the sound of her laugh, the way her blood tasted as it exploded over my taste buds. All of it was circling around me, making it almost impossible to tear her from me.

But slowly, I did. With my head screaming at me the entire time, I unraveled myself from her and removed my hand from her hair, only to stare down at her angry panting form.

"Don't *ever* do that again," she warned. "I have had enough of you."

The hurt was a mere pinprick in the haze of lust and anger that was rising inside me.

"Do *not* leave this room, Silvia," I growled. "I mean it, and do not shower my scent off."

I watched as her anger built up inside her, eager to watch her explode. . . but I couldn't let myself, because I knew as soon as the fiery hunter came back, I would lose myself.

I turned and ran out of the room and down the hall to where Victor was waiting for me with a smirk.

"That hunter sure is responsive, isn't she?" he asked.

"I need blood," I hissed and walked past him.

He let out a loud laugh.

"Down the hall to the right!" he yelled after me. "Wait for me and I will bring you a special cup!"

Hunter Rules

rule 6 sec 1

Every hunter is assigned a
number. This number is <u>you</u>.
This number will be the key to
everything at the Order. Do
not write this number down and
<u>do not</u> share it, even with
your fellow Hunters. Breaking
this rule will subject you to
<u>immediate dismissal.</u>

CHAPTER 31

KEIR

T he next time Victor came in, he had a tray in his hands with two all-gold cups on top. I could smell the fresh blood from my seat at the head of the long dining table.

My mouth watered.

He walked toward me, his footsteps echoing in the empty room. There was a certain extravagance to this clan that could only be shown by a completely empty dining room decked out as if it was a room for kings. As vampires, we didn't need a place like this.

We didn't have meals, we had blood.

We didn't get surrounded by people to drink, as it was far too intimate much of the time.

It just showed how much the previous clan head, and Victor, had put into looking the part of a human king. Or maybe...

"Does this place remind you of your human meal times?" I asked as I took the golden cup from his tray.

He smiled at me and placed the tray on the table before

sliding into the seat next to me. He leaned forward on his elbows and grabbed his own cup, taking a sip before answering.

"I had a dream as a young boy," he said as he pulled his cup away. Blood stained his lips and teeth. "I wanted to be like the kings in the stories my mom read. Originally, Hector didn't have this dining room, then he turned me and I begged him to build it."

Hector, I mused. So that was the old clan head. I'm surprised he even remembered it after so many years.

"I dreamed of sitting at the head," he continued, motioning to me before leaning back in his chair. "And ruling over my subjects. I wanted their love and adoration but as I grew"—his voice dropped to a whisper—"I realized fear was much more powerful than any love could be."

I took a sip of my blood, trying not to moan as it coated my throat.

"Good, isn't it?" he asked and took gulp of his own.

"Very," I said and took one more sip before putting it on the table.

It was just enough to wipe Silvia's scent from my mind for the time being and allow me to focus on the conversation at hand.

"So," I said and leaned back, crossing my arms over my chest. "What does your clan want to negotiate before the transfer of power?"

He hummed and put the cup down. He trailed his fingertip around the rim, not caring about the blood staining his skin.

"Don't you mean, what I need?" he asked, his eyes locked onto the blood-filled cup.

I let out a small huff causing his eyes to flash toward me. His brows pushed together and his lips pressed into a thin line. He didn't like my response.

"Your *clan* is better off than even mine in some aspects," I said and leaned forward. "Pray tell, what else could you need?"

"Blood," he answered firmly. "Just like everyone else, we need blood, and the Order has been stingy with it."

His fingertips stopped trailing the top and instead gripped the stem so hard it bent in his hand, causing some of the blood to fall to the table.

"Your restrictions probably come because of your actions," I noted. "If you just listen to your contract—"

"I am *tired* of the humans telling me what to do!" He growled and stood, causing his chair to fall to the ground with a loud clang. The cup in his hand was thrown across the room and sent blood splattering across the table.

"Victor," I said with a sigh.

"Don't"—he slammed his fist against the table—"treat me like a child, Keir."

Swallowing my retort, I sat up straight and looked him head on. Even though he was just as old as me, if not older, he was still very much a child. He had been through too much, turned too soon. In a normal circumstance I would have felt bad for him, but through the years he had lost my respect after he put not only the lives of his clan in danger but the humans in New York as well.

"Sit," I said in a softer tone and motioned to the seat. "Tell me how I can help and I will try my best."

He paused for a moment, breathing heavily, then slowly sat back down.

"We have. . . an idea," he said his eyes shifting to mine.

"We?" I echoed.

He nodded. "Your father, myself, and a few other clans heads," he answered.

My throat constricted.

"My father will be stepping down," I reminded him.

A smirk flashed across his face.

"That's why you are here, isn't it?" he asked.

It took everything I had to stay seated in my chair. I knew that *bastard* wouldn't have gone without a fight.

"What is it?" I asked.

He sat back, all the anger from earlier dissipating.

"We need to expand the range," he said. "For *fresh* blood."

"What's wrong with the blood bank?" I asked.

He just shrugged.

"Nothing really, just tastes horrible," he said. "And there really isn't enough."

He's lying, I know he is. The Order had done their calculations, and while sometimes we find ourselves running out of the donated blood, we have made due with feeders. Which from the taste of the blood he handed me, I knew he must have had them too.

"And, how do you plan to get more?" I asked, not quite getting it.

He clapped his hands and a servant burst through the door carrying a stack of papers.

"That's where you come in, Keir," he said, and the servant put the papers in front of me.

Hesitantly, I flipped a few pages to see the contract all clans signed with the Order and there were various parts where the lines were crossed out and new lines were handwritten in. All thoughts left me when I started reading their demands.

Initiate a curfew, those walking outside after it are fair game to the clan.

Double the supply from the prisons.

Mandatory blood donations for all ages.

Orphans.

"You will deliver this to the Order," he said and waved the

servant off. "And then demand that this be put in place *before* your transfer."

I shook my head.

What the actual fuck is this?

"You aren't serious," I said, looking back up at him. He was smiling. "I will not even entertain—"

"Yes you will," he said, cutting me off. "You *will* go to the Order, hand this to the man in charge, and demand our rights."

"Go to your own Order office," I hissed and pushed the papers back to him.

Victor clicked his tongue. "We can't," he said. "Must come from HQ."

I growled and clenched my hands into fists, pushing them against my thighs. "Orphans?" I asked.

He smiled. "Delicious aren't they?" he asked and reached over to take my cup. "The ages of five to seven are the sweetest, I have found. After that, give them a few more years then we can create our own farm—"

I stood up abruptly and covered my mouth with my hand, my stomach lurched and my mouth dried.

A child? He bled a child for this?

Oh God, are they—are they feeding on the children?

"What?" he asked in mock surprise. "Not sweet enough for you? Maybe a newborn, I have those handy if you would like—"

I couldn't stop my retching as I pushed away from the table. I stumbled to the door, ready to get Silvia from this hellhole and leave, but his voice stopped me.

"You'll ask for it," he said. "And you will use your hunter as the bargaining chip."

No.No.No.No.No. NO!

He can't—?

I gripped onto my shirt, trying to calm myself, but all I

could think about was how I had left Silvia in the room alone while I was here with this psycho.

"I would never—"

"Or I will," he threatened.

I turned back to him to see that his innocent mask had fallen and in its place was the most evil grin I had seen on a vampire.

"I have my men outside her door right now," he explained and stood. "If you run, they will get her faster than you can and then, do you know what else I am planning to do?"

I didn't answer as he came closer. I didn't want to know.

"Well," he said in a playful tone. "Not *me*. But you know, same deal."

I gritted my teeth.

"I don't want to play this game with you," I growled.

"No game," he said and came to a halt in front of me. "Though I do wish you would have brought Gillard, it would have been so much more *fun*."

Fuck.

This really can't be happening right now.

"Why?" I asked, my voice hollow.

He smiled and took a step back.

"It was always the plan, Keir," he said. "You really think your father would have stepped down without a fight? And no offense, but I would hate to have to work with you to get this done. You're too *soft*."

Red flashed before my eyes and before I could stop myself I lunged at Victor, sending us both to the floor. Gripping his shirt, I forced his face closer to mine, snarling.

"Don't fuck with me, Victor," I growled. "Orphans? Mass murder? You are *losing it*."

He let out a laugh and threw his head back, his eyes trailing the ceiling above us.

"Think of it as a trade," he said. "I don't even *need* the life of your hunter for this, I just need to borrow her. . . unless." His eyes trailed back to mine. "Unless you have grown an attachment to her?"

Fear laced my veins.

If I admitted to the attraction, would he be more inclined to let her go?

Even as the thought traveled through my mind, I knew he wouldn't. If it had already gone this far, Father and him had no reason to back down now.

This had been planned all along, they wanted me here so they could tear Silvia and me apart. They wanted to see me freak out and run after her so I would be easier to manipulate. They knew that inside I would be furious, and I would lash out at them.

. . . but what they didn't know was that I wasn't willing to let them win.

They thought with a little bit of push, that I would be bending to their will, lost to my own fear and panic. But they were *wrong*. With each passing moment, I used this time to center myself.

This would hurt. I knew it would. . . but I also knew that if I could keep an eye on Silvia, *act* like I was one of them. . . that I could help her.

I stood and pulled him up with me.

"I have not," I said and fixed his shirt. His smile dropped, obviously not happy that I wasn't an angry mess in front of him. "I am just not aligned with brutalizing humans the way you and Father want to."

Victor shrugged.

"You'll come around," he said and placed his hand on my shoulder. "Now, when you take the hunter back to the compound, your father will have made arrangements for her. We will send word to the Order that we have one of theirs and if they do not negotiate the terms. Well...they can use their imagination."

I swallowed thickly and focused on taking calm breaths.

"How does Father plan to convince them?" I asked, taking a step away from him. "You know they won't give in easily, even if we have someone from their organization."

I shoved my hands in my pockets, unable to stop them from shaking. Victor's smile appeared once more, cursing whatever little hope I had.

"You'll see," he said and walked past me toward the doors. "Though I would suggest you go have fun with her while you can, she won't be much fun when she realizes what will happen to her."

I couldn't even turn to look at him.

"Why did you have me scent her?" I asked.

He let out a laugh, forcing me to turn to him. He was leaning against the doorframe now, two large vampires stood on either side of him, both of them eyeing me with caution.

"It was funny," he admitted with a sly smile, then nudged the guard next to him. "And these imbeciles needed to make sure they killed the right human, if it came to that." He let out an exaggerated sigh. "We have taken it on ourselves to pilot our farming plan. There are just far too many humans in this place. Wouldn't want to *accidentally* kill the wrong human now would we?"

Gritting my teeth I walked toward him.

"Get the plane ready," I ordered. "We are leaving."

Victor pouted.

"You don't want more time with your hunter?" he asked. "I can even give you a room in the dungeon if you're worried she'd fight you."

All the blood that I drank was threatening to come up my throat.

"We are *leaving*," I growled and pushed past him.

"I'll have a servant come get you when it's ready," he called after me as I sped down the hallway.

When I opened Silvia's door, I was surprised to see her still in her Order uniform and perched on the bed.

With one inhale I could tell that, for once, she listened to me and didn't wash off my scent. As I walked closer, I realized that she was leaning against one of the bed's four posts and her eyes were closed.

She was sleeping.

I kneeled in front of her, looking at her relaxed face as she slept.

I may have misunderstood how tired she really is.

It was better that she was asleep. I didn't know what to say to her.

I wanted to tell her, but I didn't know how to tell her that I was going to hand her over to my father and use her as leverage against the Order, fighting to change rules that I myself didn't even believe in.

I am so stupid.

I really underestimated what my father was capable of, and while I was panicking about him figuring out that I liked the hunter more than I should have, he was plotting to destroy the order of our society as we knew it.

It just proved how immature I still was.

If this was what the head of our clans had been plotting, whatever flimsy plan that had worked its way into my mind had been mere child's play in comparison. . . And now I had no idea what to do.

I was angry, scared, sad. . . but I couldn't change anything.

If I ran with her right now, not only would we not make it far, but Father was at home with Gillard. There was no doubt in my mind he would leverage him to force me to do his bidding.

I let out a pained moan and leaned forward to rest my head in Silvia's lap. I could hear her heart beat faster as she came to and the hitch in her breath as she realized I was back, and touching her.

I expected her to push me off, yell at me for my earlier indiscretion. . . but instead she just threaded her hands through my hair.

"Are you. . ." she paused as I wrapped my arms around her waist. "Okay?"

I shook my head. All the words I wanted to say to her piled into my throat, all of them trying to rush out in that moment, but none of them were strong enough. I couldn't even bring myself to warn her, in fear that this—*our last*—moment together would be full of anger and panic.

"Did something happen?" she asked.

I shook my head again.

"Just let me—" I couldn't finish and choked on my own words.

Her hand came to rub my back, a soothing gesture that made me melt into her. I wanted to see more of this side from Silvia, but that would be taken from me soon and it hurt my heart.

"It's okay," she said then let out a small huff. "Or at least I *hope* it will be."

It won't, I wanted to tell her. *It's going to get worse, and you will really start to hate me.*

"Do you really hate me?" I asked. "Right now, I mean. In this very moment."

She stilled, her hand stopping its motions.

Please say yes, I begged. *Please, please say yes.* Please, *give me the strength I need to complete this mission.*

"I don't think I ever did, Keir," she said softly. "You may be annoying as hell, listen to no one but yourself, you can be selfish and unbearable. . . but I have never *hated* you. I guess. . . even in some moments. . . you could say I may have liked you."

No. Fuck.

Every ounce of self-control I had snapped and I found myself lunging forward, capturing her lips with mine. She was startled by my sudden movement, but quickly her arms wrapped around my shoulders. Her lips parted for me, allowing my tongue to slip through and massage hers.

She moaned into me as my hands gripped her hips and pulled her close before pushing us both into the bed behind her.

"You shouldn't have said that," I growled against her and trailed my lips down to her neck.

The urge to bite her was stronger than ever as she quickly pulled her shirt over her head and gave me access to her throat. I peppered kisses down her bare neck, fangs pulsating as the scent of her blood overwhelmed me.

"It's okay," she whispered huskily. "You can take it."

I growled at her while undoing her bra.

"Just us," I said against her skin. "No venom." I kissed her collarbone. "No alcohol." I placed a light kiss on her nipple while watching her reaction. Her eyes were hooded as she watched me. She arched her back, and I took the hint to take her nipple into my mouth and start sucking.

She writhed against me, her hands flying to her leggings,

but she was too slow. As soon as her panties and leggings had been pulled to her midthighs, I cupped her folds.

She threw her head back and tried to widen her legs as far as her leggings would allow. She was magnificent like this. I loved watching how she reacted to my touches. How her breath came out in pants as I teased her. The way she gasped when I entered her. The way she pulled me closer to her as if lying on top of her, and being inside her, was still too far away.

I craved every moment of this so strongly that I knew for as long as I may live, I could not—*would not*—be able to choose anyone else.

This *hunter,* the one with the fiery soul and cold eyes, was the one who had changed everything for me.

"I'm sorry," I whispered as I leaned forward and placed a kiss on her lips.

I curled my fingers inside of her and delicious moan fell out of her mouth. I used my thumb to circle her clit and she attacked my lips with her own, groaning into my mouth.

"I'm sorry," I repeated and pounded my fingers into her.

I should stop. I should run far away from her, maybe then I could make up for what was about to happen. . . but I couldn't.

I couldn't bring myself to leave her because I knew, as soon as we separated, there would be no getting back to this point. I would try my hardest to make sure that she comes out of this alive, but even that I couldn't promise.

"Keir," she moaned and ran her nails across my back before trying to grip at my shirt and pull it over my head.

This may be the last time she says my name like that, I realized.

I didn't want to say goodbye to this. I knew before, in order to keep her protected, I had to distance myself from her. . . but that wasn't goodbye.

This felt like a goodbye. . . It was a goodbye.

Guilt washed over me and my vision clouded. I sped up my

motions, stopping her from trying to undress me and trying to wash away my own horrible thoughts.

"Say it again," I commanded with a hard thrust. "Say my name."

I bit her lip when she didn't listen, but not hard enough to draw blood. I was already losing myself in her, blood would only complicate it.

"*Keir*," she groaned again.

Satisfied I untangled myself from her and pulled my fingers out so I could pull down the rest of her pants. She whined but I made quick work of tearing off her leggings and positioning myself between her legs.

I gave her wet slit one long lick before latching onto her clit and sucking. Her back bowed and her hands gripped onto the blanket so hard her knuckles turned white. Sliding two fingers into her, I resumed my motions, her moans filling the room.

At this point, I didn't care if Victor heard us. I deserved this much. *We* deserved our moment.

I felt her clench around my fingers and her pants came out heavier now. She came with a shout, her body freezing and her hand coming to pull at my hair as I continued to suck on her swollen clit.

"*Fuck. . . fuck*," she moaned and sat up abruptly. I let her pull me up and capture my lips with hers.

When she pulled away, I couldn't help but stare at her. Taking in every last detail before it was snatched away from me.

Her silver eyes were alight, her red hair was a mess around her head, and her skin was delicately flushed.

"We are leaving," I whispered against her. "Get dressed."

I was about to climb off the bed when her grip stopped me.

"Thank you," she whispered.

My brows furrowed, she had no reason to thank me.

"For saying sorry," she said. "I may not forgive you, but I appreciate the sentiment."

I swallowed thickly.

Please, please, please don't ever forgive me. I won't deserve it.

"Let's go," I choked out, each letter feeling as though it was carved into my skin.

CHAPTER 32
SILVIA

Sometimes I wished life had a little warning it gave you before it wanted to fuck you over.

Nothing crazy, maybe just a gut feeling or a ringing in my ears, but I didn't get that.

Not when I walked in on my entire family's mutilated corpses, and not when I was brought into a room to face Raphael and some random vampire guards with Keir at my side.

It had been a long plane ride back and forth from New York, where we barely even stayed a full day, and not only did I not get to talk with Keir about what the fuck was going on, but I was dead on my feet.

It took all my concentration to keep Raphael's glare as he stood up from his chair and motioned the guards over to us. We were in a study, not too unlike Keir's, with books ringing the walls and a single desk in the back of the room. There were no chairs, though I doubted the vampire needed them.

The guards, decked in an all-black uniform that rivaled the Order-appointed clothes I was wearing, beelined toward us. I gripped the hilt of my dagger and stepped to the side, shielding Keir.

I may have been angry with her for all the shit she had pulled, but there was no way I would stand by and watch as her father assaulted her again.

But they didn't go to her. . . They came to my side, their hands gripping my arms hard enough to make me cry out, and forced me to my knees.

"What the *fuck* do you think you are doing?" I growled and tried to pull my arms from them, but they were too strong.

I tried to look back at Keir, but one of the guards gripped my chin and forced me to look forward.

Raphael walked around the desk with a sinister smile spreading across his face. His movements were calculated, slow, like he was stalking his prey.

"Getting a hunter the Order *actually* cares about was no easy task," he said and continued to walk toward me until he was a mere foot from me. The guard forced me to meet his eyes, his grip was so hard pain shot through my face.

"What is the meaning of this?" I growled, though it came out mumbled due to the guard's hold.

"I wasn't sure you were as high-valued and proficient at your job as they said you were," he continued, ignoring me. "That was, until they demanded you back. *That* was when I knew we had the right person for the job."

Keir was silent behind me. I tried to free my head out of the guard's grasp once more, but that apparently made them mad and the other guard tugged on my ponytail. Pain seared my scalp and I couldn't stop the whine that escaped my lips.

"They wouldn't take kindly to their hunter being harmed," Keir said from behind me. Her tone was flat, unfeeling.

It hurt. . . though I was glad she was stepping in.

Where the hell is Gillard?

"Don't be stupid, *Keir,*" her father spat at her. His red eyes bore into me, and a feeling of dread weighed on me. "You know they need a little incentive. After all, they should know that we don't make empty threats."

"What's the plan?" Keir asked.

My stomach turned to lead and my heart, as broken as it had been since her words the other night, crumbled.

No, my mind screamed. *This can't be happening.*

"I have some questions about the Order before we give them the contract," he said, his eyes shifting behind me. "The easier she gives them, the easier this will be for her."

I struggled against the hold and let out a growl.

Why is she just standing there?

"The Order will come after you," I growled.

Raphael's eyes shifted toward mine again and he lowered himself so we were face-to-face.

"That's the point, *dear,*" he said. I flinched when his hand came to brush my cheek. His touch disgusted me. "I put a lot of effort into making the Order think you were needed here, if they didn't come I would be offended."

"What do you mean?" I asked.

Raphael shook his head and let out a light chuckle.

"Do you really think we can't protect ourselves against those rebel humans?" he asked. "They aren't advanced enough to even get up to our compound, let alone infiltrate it."

The world stilled around me. But the rebels did infiltrate the compound, multiple times. I had stopped them with my bare hands. . . What the fuck does he mean they didn't infiltrate the compound?

"I fought them—"

"You fought who *I* wanted you to fight," he said. "I needed the Order to believe I needed you, and I think it worked out pretty well myself. Now we have the best thing we could have gotten, and hopefully something that will pull the Order out of their hiding place."

"I thought this was for the contract—"

"I will bring you up to speed later," Raphael said in a firm tone, cutting Keir off. "Bring her to her new room."

I didn't stand a chance as they dragged me out of the room. I kicked and screamed and cursed at Keir, but nothing could save me.

No one wanted to.

"I'm going to kill you, you sorry *bitch*—"

My yells were cut off by a the guard's hand clasping around my throat. His red eyes bore into me and his mouth was twisted into a snarl.

He squeezed until the sides of my vision went blurry before allowing me to breathe. I took in deep gulps of air while glaring at him.

"Just cut to the chase," he growled. "We could go all day, and night. Unlike you *pathetic humans*—"

I spit in his face and laughed as he jumped back.

I pulled at the chains that were binding me to the metal chair they had me on. Shortly after I was dragged out of the room, they forced me into a cell in the basement with only a single metal chair in the middle. It looked like some fucked-up medical room, minus the sterile equipment.

Instead the two vampire guards took turns trying to wear me down through torture techniques that paled in comparison to the Enforcers'. A little hitting there, choking, some knife wounds, nothing that I hadn't dealt with before.

"That's cute," I said, leaning forward, testing out the chains again. I peered over the guard's side to my audience.

The cell I was in and the dungeon hallway were lit with only a few dimming bulbs, but I could see distinct pairs of red eyes staring back at me. Raphael and Keir had been here for the entire time, but Gillard was new.

At first I was ashamed that he had to see me like this, but then I realized that *all* of them had probably conspired against me from the beginning to make this happen.

It became clear after Raphael's words that they only brought me here to get back at the Order. This entire time, running through hunter after hunter until they got someone like me. But for *some* reason, they thought that I knew more about the Order than just your average hunter.

"I know *nothing*," I growled. "Just because I slit your kinds' throats well doesn't mean the Order trusts me."

"Again," Raphael commanded.

I jerked against the chains as they descended on me.

"You probably get off on this don't you?" I growled and kicked my legs out toward the guard, but it was no use. "Sick *freak.*"

"Shut up," the guard growled and this time they took ahold of my hand and squeezed it so hard the cracking of my bones filled the room.

The other guard grabbed my throat as I screamed in pain, cutting it off.

I let out a loud groan but still managed to pull a smile to my face.

"She's fucking crazy," the one choking me said to the other, his hand loosening.

I brought my head forward, connecting it with his nose. He jerked back, his hand flying up to his face and curses streaming from his mouth.

"Give her some blood," Raphael said from beyond the cage.

I looked toward the guard still by my side as he brought his wrist up to his mouth.

No, no, no, no!

I flailed around, trying to break from the chains. A single hand pushed down on my shoulder, pinning me to the chair, but I turned my head, hoping that I could still save myself.

The other vampire guard had recovered and was by my side in a flash. He put one hand on my forehead and the other in my chin. While pushing my head painfully into the metal, his hand forced my mouth open.

My feral scream was cut off by the guard forcing his bleeding wrist into my mouth.

As little as I knew about vampires, there was one thing everyone on this planet knew like the back of their hand.

Vampire venom could be used for healing, and sex, but their blood was cursed. They told us, don't ever, *ever* drink blood from a vampire. Because if you do, it will start the process of turning you into one of them. The entire ritual for turning a human into a soulless monster required a huge amount of vampire blood to be ingested while the vampire had to drain you of most of yours.

Or they could just kill you.

Either way, as long as your heart stopped you would become one of them.

The humane way, if there even was one, was to drink your blood so that when the vampire blood entered your system, it would slowly take over your entire being. It hurt, to put it simply. Becoming a changed vampire was said to be the most excruciating thing on this planet.

But you know what was worse?

Leaving the blood in the system with no way for it to do what it so desperately wanted to.

It would attack your blood system trying to find a way to

turn you, but it would be torturous and it would last as long as it took to kill you. Based on the looks Raphael was giving me from beyond my cage, they had no plan to kill me anytime soon.

The blood was thick as it fell into my mouth, it had a strong metallic taste to it and coated my tongue. I couldn't help the gag as the vampire forced me to drink. I tried desperately not to swallow, but when the guard with the bleeding wrist plugged my nose, I had no choice.

I drank gulp after gulp of his rotten blood, praying that for once life would give me a break. Hoping that the pain wouldn't be too bad and no one here would get carried away and kill me.

I didn't want to think of what would happen if they made me into a vampire. I couldn't bring that thought into existence because it scared me so deeply.

"Father," Keir said from beyond the cell. "That is too far."

The guard above me shifted his eyes to his companion and looked to the group behind them, asking for permission to continue.

Tears rolled down my face and I felt a burning in my throat that just become more and more intense as the moments passed.

"Enough," Raphael hissed.

The guards pulled away from me, and I took in deep gulps of air, but with each breath it felt like glass was embedded in my lungs. The pain started as a burning sensation running through my body and then slowly, starting from my fingers and toes, I felt the ache.

I at first compared it to a muscle cramp, but then it got worse as it spread throughout my body. The fire combined with the venom, feeling like it was literally eating at my skin, became too much for me to bear.

I slammed my jaw shut and turned my head away from the

vampires' eyes. I was crying, though I squeezed my eyes shut in hopes of keeping all the screams of pain inside of me. They had gotten what they wanted. In this state, they far outweighed the Enforcers, and I regretted provoking them.

The Order may have been cruel, but never this cruel. They wouldn't resort to vampire blood as a form of torture. Even *they* had boundaries.

Everything fell apart when the guard's fingertips brushed against my leggings. His touch was as light as a feather, almost unnoticeable. . . if the whole area hadn't been on fire.

I bit my lip so hard my own blood filled my mouth.

I couldn't stop the sobs now. They flowed freely along with all the words I had been trying so desperately to hold back.

"Please. *Please, please,*" I begged. "Please *stop it. Stop, stop, stop.* I don't know—I *can't tell you anything!*"

The guard to my right trailed his hand along my arm and I jolted in my chains, but that was an even worse move because the chains at my wrists and ankles pulled pained screams from me.

"It hurts," I moaned and tried to meet the eyes of Keir behind the guards. "*Please, please, I'm sorry, I—I'll be goo—*"

The slap from the guard came out of nowhere and caused my head to jerk to the left. Pain flashed through me so strong I was sure I'd pass out. . . or at least I hoped I would.

But I heard every moment of the vampires' laughs as I screamed.

The next time I blinked, Raphael was standing in front of me, his hand running through my hair and gripping it so hard I felt like my entire scalp was about to be ripped off.

"The Order has files on every single hunter and mission," he said in a low and slow voice, like he was talking to a child. "I need you to tell me if you recognize any of these numbers, you got it?"

I couldn't even say no at this point, I was too far gone. Too lost in my pain as the blood attacked my entire body. I felt myself nod.

He began listing off numbers that were in the form of Order missions, sometimes he would throw in a hunter's ID number, but while I recognized where the numbers came from, I had no memory of those people or the files. . . until one.

". . .seven three three three five six zero," he paused when he saw the flash of recognition in my eyes, a sinister smile pulling to his face.

"Tell me what that belongs to," he commanded, his hand stroking my cheek and causing me to cry out as the pain exploded under my skin.

What that belongs to. . . so he didn't even know it was a who. Whoever had given Raphael these numbers had forgotten to mention how mission numbers and hunter numbers differ. Which was a good and bad thing for me. . . good because I could lie my way out of this. . .

Bad because I knew that number.

"Look, Silv!" Jane yelled and pointed toward the larger monitor that showcased the newest hunter rankings.

She bolted forward, ignoring Mother's yells. I tried to follow her, but Father had a tight grasp on my hands. I looked up toward him and pouted.

A smile spread across his face and he hoisted me up into his arms to place a kiss on my cheek. I groaned as I felt his dark stubble brush across my cheek.

"Ew, Daddy!" I said, though I was laughing. "Stop it!"

He laughed, his silver eyes flashing. Father was tired, bags under his eyes, yet he promised us that he would take us to the Order to see the rankings refresh. Mother talked about her change in the rankings, and it was Jane who insisted we go.

Almost felt bad for Father, seeing how tired he was, but the excitement of the rankings outweighed everything else.

"Do you remember Mommy's number?" he asked and stepped toward the monitor.

I nodded and turned to look at the monitor, pointing to the very first number that now lit up the screen.

7333560.

I remembered it so easily because the repeating numbers, and I had seen it time and time again on the papers she brought home and on her equipment. It was stamped on almost everything.

"Mommy!" Jane yelled excitedly. "You are at the top."

Mother stepped toward her, her bright-red hair standing out against the all-white interior of the Order. Her green eyes were lit with excitement.

"I am," she confirmed, her soft voice carrying toward me. Her eyes shifted to me, a smile spreading across her face. "What do you think, Silv? Think you can beat Mommy some day?"

The monitor that had been placed in the front hallway of the Order had since moved to a more secure location farther inside the building, as we began the contracts with the vampire clans. Our numbers were also removed from all weapons and material they gave us, only to be used for rankings and documentation.

Our numbers could never be used with our names and whether that was to dehumanize us or keep our identities unknown remained a mystery to me.

"My very first mission," I lied through gritted teeth.

His brows furrowed and his grip on my hair tightened.

"Which was?" he asked.

I leaned forward my voice dropping to a whisper.

"I snuck into a compound," I gasped. "It was late, maybe few years ago while I was still in training."

Raphael motioned for the guard to come closer, and I saw

him take out a pen and paper to jot down notes. Pain racked my body and I groaned out.

"The vampire was in their study," I said. "They heard me but stayed still for me anyway. They didn't even flinch when I pulled out my sword. They knew what was coming to them."

"Get on with it," he growled. "Why were they important? What was the assignment? Kill them?"

I leaned forward and dropped my voice to whisper.

"The assignment. . ." I trailed and Raphael's eyes lit up. "Was to *fuck* your mom. And she was *quite* interested in my sword if you know what I—"

Pain exploded on the entirety of my left half as Raphael slammed me back into the metal chair.

"Don't you understand your situation?" he growled, his spittle flying everywhere.

He was mad, more furious than I had ever seen him before, but it was worth it.

"It's you who doesn't understand *your situation*," I growled back. "Get the Order on the phone and make your demands or kill me. You are wasting our time."

With a huff Raphael threw me aside and stormed out of the cell.

"Continue until she tells me what that number means, don't let her sleep and keep feeding her blood until she vomits," he ordered.

"Fuck you!" I growled as the guards descended on me once more.

CHAPTER 33

KEIR

My hands shook as I exited my father's vehicle and stood in front of the Order's Seattle home office.

I never realized how big and overpowering the sleek building was until I looked at it now. Maybe it was just because I didn't know if I would make it out of there this time. For all I knew, it could be my very last time in this building.

The all-black building climbed toward the sky with windows so dark it seemed to suck in all the light that surrounded it. It could be seen for miles, and there was no mistaking it, or the hunters that surrounded the perimeter, all dressed in their appointed Order uniforms. Many of them even more nervous than I was.

They eyed me warily, a few reaching for the weapons they had on their backs.

The folder that was not even a pound weighed more than a thousand in my hands. It burned my skin with the disgusting lies it told. *We* didn't want these terms. *We* wanted to work with the Order in peace.

We wanted Silvia—

Before, I didn't fear the Order and, truth be told, I wasn't scared *of* them even now. . . I was scared that they couldn't help me.

Scared that they may agree to these disgusting terms.

Scared that they *may not* agree to these terms.

Silvia's, Gillard's, and my own life now rested in the palms of their hands.

Walking into the Order, I swiftly made my way up to the captain's office, desperately trying to not let the memories of Silvia and me here come crawling back. I couldn't bear to think of her for any moment longer than I already had or I risked breaking down.

Father had made me stand there next to him as they did unspeakable things to her. I had to watch as she screamed in pain and cursed at us.

I knew I deserved the curses, I would take them readily. . . but I couldn't stand the sight of them hurting her.

She reminded me too much of my mother in that moment. When I was still young, I didn't know what the world held for me, so when Father chained Mother in the basement and let her slowly go insane. . . I lost a part of myself that day.

And now I had to experience it over again. Though this time was worse because when I was younger, I was too weak to save her. I was a child. . . But now I had the power to save her. Now it was just my own cowardice and fear that stopped me.

Never in my life had I wanted to kill my father more than in that moment. I wanted to inflict the same pain on him that he was doing to Silvia and make him beg for her forgiveness. Though I knew no begging could ever be enough for what he —*we*—did.

Gillard was not much better off than I was. While I was able to hide him behind me most of the time, he still heard and saw glimpses of what was happening to her. He had been silently crying as I left, watching the guards as they pumped her with vampire blood that made her skin so sensitive even a brush of air could make it feel like her skin was falling off.

Shuddering, I called the elevator and waited. Impatience and panic played at my senses, as I thought about how I was here while Silvia was no doubt being tortured in my fucking base—

"You smell," a voice called from behind me.

I didn't have to turn to know it was the vampire that had brought Silvia back to my compound.

I tried to keep my breathing and my expression neutral even as I turned to face him.

His blood-red eyes stared into me, and I knew without even asking that he could smell everything that had been happening to Silvia in my father's dungeon.

"Coming up?" I asked, the elevator dinging faintly behind me.

He cocked his head, but followed me into the elevator anyway.

The short ride took longer than ever before as I felt his eyes burrowing into my entire being.

"Something is wrong," he noted. "With Silvia. I smell her on you."

Swallowing thickly, I nodded. There was no use in hiding it. Soon, the whole Order would know.

"What is it?" he asked. "Is she why you are here?"

"In a way," I said and shifted my gaze back to his as the doors opened. "Though I would much rather wait until we reach the captain's office to discuss—"

The doors tried to close but a human with dark hair and dark eyes gripped the opening, causing them to bounce back.

The other hunter who had brought Silvia back home, I noted.

He was glaring at me and stepped into the elevator without a word.

The vampire pressed the button to close the doors and then the button for the floor level above us.

"I don't have time—"

My words were cut off as the vampire pressed the emergency hold button and stopped the elevator completely. The human next to me reached up to the ceiling of the metal box and, pushing lightly, revealed a small hideaway. He grabbed the camera that was in there and forcefully pulled it out before throwing it to the ground and stomping on it.

I was at a loss for words.

Am I going to die?

"Tell us, vampire heir," the human said and leaned back against the metal wall. "Then we will tell you what to tell the captain."

I raised my brow at him, the grip on the folder in my hand tightening.

"Excuse me?" I asked with a scoff. "Who are you to tell me—"

"I'm Jase," the vampire said from my side. I eyed him suspiciously. Even though his position was relaxed, with his hand to his side, I didn't trust him for a bit. "That is Isaac." He jerked his chin toward the human.

"We have Silvia's interest at heart," Isaac said. "I run the Enforcers, or at least a squad of them. So tell me, what happened?"

His tone lowered and he shifted, obviously not happy with my questioning of him.

"This is a conversation for the captain," I growled. "And if you really had Silvia's *interests* at heart then you would let me do what I need to."

"What if I tell you the captain wouldn't do anything even if you told him Silvia was in trouble?" he asked.

I froze, my blood turning to ice.

"What makes you think I am here for that?" I asked.

Isaac shook his head and let out a huff.

"What else would you be here for?" he said. "Plus, we have been keeping tabs on you since we left her with you, and she hasn't been seen around the compound for days. It's obvious something is wrong."

"Why are you—"

"Back to the point, Keir," the vampire ordered, his tone cool.

He's starting to annoy me.

"The *captain* will do his job. Not some low-level hunters. Besides he asked for her back," I said. "Made a big deal about it, even offered for her to drop the contract. He would help no matt—"

"Who told you he offered that?" the vampire asked.

I glared at him.

"My father knew," I admitted.

Jase's gaze snapped to Isaac who nodded. Some sort of understanding passed between them that eluded me entirely. My brain was already fried from everything that had happened in the past few days and I barely had enough energy to make it to this damned place, let alone have a secret meeting with two random hunters.

"The Order. . ." Isaac trailed. "Has a reputation to uphold, Keir. One to the public, and one to the hunters that join us."

"So?" I asked, getting annoyed. "Look if you *really* cared for Silvia you would let me—"

"What do you know about the missing hunters, Keir?" Jase asked, cutting me off again.

421

Growling I stepped forward and grabbed his shirt, pulling him to me.

"I am *done* playing your games," I hissed. "Let me off this damn elevator or I will kill both of you before you even have time to blink."

Isaac let out a heavy sigh and reached around it to press the emergency hold button once more.

"The Order," he said. "Once they feel as though a hunter has become too much trouble, will dispose of them in a way that slips under the radar. Something to save face and continue to keep us in a good light, internally and externally."

I paused and let the vampire go. My mind was whirling.

"Are you saying my father and the—"

"No," Jase interrupted. "The captain despises your father, but he knows about his plan. He knew about it from the beginning."

The world stopped around me, and even as I heard the ding of the elevator, I couldn't move. The captain knew Father was going to use Silvia?

He *knew* that all of this was a sham to get the strongest hunter so they could blackmail the Order and he just. . . *let him?*

I stepped out of the elevator, pushing all the emotions down so far inside me I could taste their bitterness.

"Tell him about what you came to do," Isaac said from behind me. "Mention Silvia if you want to, but don't mention you told us."

I looked back at them just as the doors were closing, there was a smile on his face. One so cruel and sinister that it chilled me to the bone.

What is he planning?

"You know we cannot agree to this shit." The captain hissed and threw the papers down on his desk, scattering them everywhere.

I didn't even try to dive forward and catch the ones that fell.

I was standing up facing his desk, faintly aware of the hunters who were waiting for me outside of his room. I didn't know if he called for backup or what, but from the heartbeats I could tell that there were three people waiting outside for me.

When I inhaled deeply, I could just catch a whiff of burning trees. . . and magnolias?

The captain stood, his eyes traveling my form as if sizing me up. Did he really expect me to fight for these rules?

He was wearing a button-up with a white vest over it today, looking much more spiffy than I had seen him in the last few visits. I doubt that when he put on that outfit today, that *this* was the news he expected he would be getting. . . I didn't believe those hunters. Not a single bit.

I had seen my fair share of hunters and they all had a tendency to think they were the key to this entire universe. That they were the ones keeping this world safe from all the vampires that tried to break their rules.

Their words didn't help the panic I was already feeling, but I would be damned if their little speech stopped me from getting Silvia out of that hellhole.

She deserves as much.

"All I want," I said and swallowed thickly. "Is your help with Silvia."

He raised an eyebrow.

"Why do you need *help* with my hunter?" he asked.

"If you refuse, they want me to use her as blackmail."

He scoffed and tugged on his vest.

"You didn't seriously think that would work?" he asked.

My body stiffened. "Excuse me?"

He shook his head and walked around his desk to stand right by my side. His heartbeat was no more erratic than it had been when I knocked on his door a few moments ago.

"Coming in here, acting like you didn't just sexually assault that same—"

"She's being tortured!" I yelled, the anger and pain that I had been hiding away finally boiling up to the surface. "They are mutilating her, starving her, filling her with *vampire* blood. She is going to—"

"Die?" he asked, cutting me off. He raised a brow at me, a smirk slowly spreading across his face.

"You think this is a joke?" I asked and took a step back. My own shock overtaking every ounce of self-control that I had.

I gripped onto his vest and pulled him to me as growls erupted out of my chest.

"I think that Silvia can protect herself," he said. "And that it's laughable that you think I would believe this."

"It's *true*," I hissed.

"And even if she *couldn't* protect herself"—his eyes narrowed into slits—"I have *never* changed a contract because of blackmail, and I don't plan to anytime soon."

I pushed him away from me in disgust. He hit the table, a loud screech filling the room. The hunters outside shifted.

"I *need* you to help me *save* her," I said, my voice sounding utterly pathetic as I begged for this old man's help. "I can work with you on a plan. Something, *anything!*"

He let out a sigh and ran his hand through his hair.

"Then you what?" he asked. "Turn on me and kill both myself and my best hunter?"

My fists clenched at my sides. I imagined myself lunging forward and taking a bite out of his neck.

I imagined making his death slow and painful, so he could just feel a fraction of what Silvia was feeling right in this moment.

How could he be so dense?

The Order likes to save face, they had said. . .

"You're either ashamed of her, or you *want* her to die," I said. "That's the only reason you don't want to save her."

The smile on his face grew.

"I know my hunters better than you, Keir," he said, then his smile dropped completely. Without breaking our stare down, he reached behind him and pushed the rest of his papers off his desk. "Now take your shit and get out. If I do hear that your clan has actually killed one of my hunters. . ." He paused taking a single step forward. "Then I will have your entire clan's heads on wooden sticks."

Disgust filled my entire being.

"*Fuck you,*" I growled, then turned on my heels.

I swung the door open, not caring that in my haste I tore it off its hinges. Growling aloud, I stepped out of the room and glared at the hunters who were waiting for me outside the room.

It was a group of three men, the human in front and the witches behind him. The human had a buzzcut and stared at me with an amused smile while the witches didn't seem to even care about me.

Ignoring them I turned back to the elevator. As I walked down the hallway, I heard them enter the room I had just left.

"Where are Isaac and Jase?" the captain barked.

"Out," replied one of them. By his amused tone, I guessed it was the smiling one.

"Let me follow her, I would love to give—"

"Shut *up!*" the captain interrupted. "Wait until she leaves."

On cue, the elevator dinged. I had the urge to stay here until they thought I was gone just to spy, but decided to leave.

If Silvia can't count on her own Order. . . then I will have to figure something else out.

She needs me and I swear that this time, I won't let her down.

CHAPTER 34
SILVIA

I lost track of how long I had been in this hellhole at somewhere around eighteen to twenty days.

I had tried to base it on the sun, but when I had seen my food tray for the day and scurried over to devour the stale bread, I found it to be harder than usual. That was my first clue that I had been sleeping for too long.

The second was a guard, who when it was time to take me in for "questioning" complained about not being able to *play* for over two days. His words sickened me.

After I had been too weak to torture, they had decided that the human should be transferred to a longer-term confinement. The cell they had chosen, while not as terrifying as the torture room, hadn't been much better. It was a cell that was even smaller than the Dark Room the Order had thrown me in. It allowed me enough space to walk around, though they had taken out anything useful from it.

There was no bed.

No running water.

A bucket for human excrement.

And that *was it*.

Food time was once a day and many times, I only got a piece of bread and a quarter glass of water. It was enough to keep a human body alive, but just barely. I was sleeping longer, more often, and at times I couldn't even stand.

But I forced myself to. No matter how hard my legs shook or how much pain I was in. . . I forced myself to stand because I *would not* allow these vampires to take more away from me than they already had. I needed to be strong for when I would finally be able to escape, though I no longer had hope that I would be able to do it.

At first, I had been thinking of a plan to run. I had walked through every possible scenario of escape I could think of. Sometimes I would think of a plan that got me so excited that I was tempted to try and break out right that second. . . but my weakening body quickly showed me that there was no way that I would be getting out of here by myself.

I had once thought that the Dark Room was the worst possible punishment I had ever received. But the Dark Room would have been a vacation compared to the hell Raphael was putting me through.

At least in the Dark Room all of the torture, besides the starvation, came from my own mind. But here, I had to watch as the vampires taunted me from just beyond the cell's metal bars. They would stand out there before they took me to the interrogation room and watch as I panicked.

I tried *so* hard to fight them. To spit at them, to kick them, to berate them and curse them. . . but inside I was terrified each and every time.

They still tried to prod me for information, especially about my mother's number. They had many other numbers that they tried now and then, but when I stopped reacting, they tried to make a game out of it. They would yell the numbers at me when I was least expecting, trying to get me to slip up and spill information.

Their favorite was when I was about to sleep. They would lie in wait, hiding from view, and attempt to scare it out of me. Maybe they had been hoping that, by that time, I would be too delirious to even think about disobeying them.

Another was when I was so in pain from the vampire blood in my veins that I was on the verge of blacking out. They would make fun of my cries as I begged them to stop and entice me with treats in the form of breaks and vampire venom if I would just tell them what the numbers meant.

Right after, they carved my skin up only to heal it with vampire venom and do it again.

And again.

And again.

But I never caved. At first, I had stayed strong because of my obligations and loyalty to the Order. I may have hated what they had done to me, but there were thousands of other hunters' lives at stake if I spilled any information. I couldn't live with myself if I found out that people like Jade, Cain, Damon, and all the other academy students got hurt because of something I said.

And then, after a while. . . it wasn't enough to just wish for their protection. I was in here dying because of these people and they have *still* yet to come save me. They must have known by now, right?

Right?

Then, as I stared at the rotting ceiling of my cell, as my entire body ached and the life was fading from me. . . I didn't even think of all those hunters. I didn't care about a single one of them.

The only people I could think of in that moment, were my family.

Mother and Father were probably rolling in their graves, overcome with anger and worry about their only living child being tortured.

Jane on the other hand... She would be upset with me.

Sometimes, when I was lying there, I would hear her voice. She would be yelling at me. Telling me to get up. Telling me to fight. She would push me to find out who killed them. Push me find out how the fuck Raphael got my mother's number out of everyone else's.

It was the only thing that kept me going.

Because Jane would have gone out fighting. She wouldn't have rested until she got revenge on every single person that was involved in the death of our family. And right now, the only clue I had to solving this thing was that Raphael had my mother's number.

My mother had made the top of the list a few times, and while her and my father were known as "the best" hunters in the Order during their time, I knew it was only because of their work *together*.

So why was he just asking about my mother?

If there was something about her that he wanted to know... maybe a mission, or something, my father would have also been involved. But he never mentioned his number or any other one that I recognized.

I was starting to go crazy in this space. Every day I woke up with Jane's voice whispering in my ear. She would tell me that they were coming for me soon. That all I needed was to hold out a little bit longer.

Every day I hoped for the Order to come and save me. I imagined the hunters dressed in their all-black garb running down the hallway and tearing down the door to my cell...

But after the date of my check-in *and* the transfer of power passed... I began to lose hope.

Tonight, I think it was night, was the first time Keir had visited me in days.

I heard her shoes against the concrete as she walked down the hallway. I thought it was the guard at first, but their steps had always been quicker, harder. Keir's were lighter and they had a sort of air about them that just screamed royalty.

It was obvious she didn't belong in this dungeon.

I peered up from my place, seated in the corner, to see her red eyes shining through the darkness. I could just make out a hint of her frown as the dim light near the outside of the metal bars lit up her face.

It hurt to look at her. Hurt to see the face that I had given up everything for. The person I once trusted more than I ever should have trusted any single person on this planet.

She *ruined* everything. Even if the Order would save me, there was no way in hell they would have taken me back. I was a *disgrace*. I had not only breached the contract, but I had let myself get captured. And for what?

I had nothing to show for myself. I had failed the *easiest* mission that was out there! It didn't matter that Raphael was using this to get information from me, I should have been able to smell this from a mile away.

The job was too good to be true, and now that I had time to think about it, how had I been so stupid as to not see it?

My whole debt. They bargained my *entire* debt like it was nothing! That alone should have swayed me. I knew it felt wrong. I should have listened to my gut. I should have listened to Damon.

And then the fucking playboy of an heir? I should have known.

I let out a laugh.

"Miss me?" I asked and shakily tried to stand, but my knees buckled, and I was forced to the ground.

Pathetic, I growled at myself.

"I convinced Father to let me take you out for a bit," she said. "To shower, get some real food. But only for thirty minutes at most."

I forced another laugh out. It caused my throat to ache.

"*You* convinced him?" I echoed. "Aren't you like a queen or something? *He's* supposed to listen to *you*."

I pushed myself off the ground, using the wall as support. I didn't want to admit to her how good a shower would feel right now. The dirt, blood, and my own tears had dried and stuck to me like a film. I knew I must smell disgusting, but I had gotten used to the putrid smell after a while.

"He needs something in return," she said, ignoring my question. "Some information, anything. Just something to let him know that you are cooperating. If you can promise him that you will tell him what he needs to know then you—"

"How many more times do I have to tell you creatures no!" I yelled and took a step forward.

Pain shot up my leg. The vampire venom, while the effects sometimes faded, felt like it had a permanent home in my system. Every time they would feed me blood until I puked, and it would enter my blood stream, hell-bent on destroying everything in the process... but it *never* went anywhere.

It just stayed inside my body, trying its hardest to prepare me for my death and then the inevitable transition into a vampire.

It was the only reason I hadn't killed myself yet.

I still had my sports bra and panties on. I am sure if I wanted to I could either use that, or even the Order uniform I still had on, to find *some* way to set myself free.

But I couldn't do it.

The only thing worse than this hellhole was knowing that only a cursed life remained for me.

At one point, I really believed vampires were no different than us. I believed that they had thoughts and feelings and they actually *cared* about things. But I was wrong. Just like I always was.

They were monsters, every single one of them. They only cared about blood and how to secure more of it. I knew from the start that I couldn't trust Keir, yet I let her play me like she did every other hunter.

Keir's eyes shifted downward before she spoke again.

"Gillard wanted me to tell you he's sorry," she whispered. "He wanted to come see you, but Father—"

"Don't bore me with that shit," I growled. "Get the fuck out of here, I have had enough of you."

"Silvia," she said. Her pained voice shot through me. "I'm sorr—"

"That's funny," I said with a bitter laugh and took another step forward. "You said that while you were *fucking* me the last time."

"Silvia, I—"

"But then you locked me in a cage," I interrupted. "Fed me blood. Tore my skin. *Degraded* me. Sorry doesn't *cut* it, Keir. I *know* you are full of bullshit!"

She stumbled back.

"I tried," she said pitifully. "I swear I tried my best to—"

"To what, hm?" I asked. My hands coming to clutch my ratted shirt. "If you *really* tried, your father's head would be at my feet."

"You don't underst—"

"Leave!"

The power in my words made her flinch and her red eyes locked onto mine. My stomach twisted and I barely had enough time to lurch forward as I vomited blood all over the floor.

I didn't hear Keir's steps as she fled, but when I pulled myself up and looked over to the entrance with teary eyes. . . she wasn't there.

Sometimes I would dream about Keir.

Dream about what we had together. Though it felt stupid at times, given that it was nothing serious. I had done this before, messed around with girls. . . but something about this time was different.

I didn't hate her then, and she saw right through me. After being alone for so many years, I had gotten used to the wall that was constantly erected between even me and my teammates. I didn't let anyone in, didn't care to explain myself when I did wrong, and didn't care about others in general.

Cain and Jade were an exception, though it hurt to think of them. Even they had no idea what was going on inside me.

But Keir seemed to know everything, even when I didn't want her to. She knew just how to push me, just what words to say to make me rethink everything I had done in my life, and I couldn't get her face out of my mind.

Tonight, I dreamed about lying in her bed.

I dreamed of her waking me in the middle of the night, but not just for sex. Because she had missed me. She had been working all day and only got a bit of time at two in the morning to come wake me up and remind me that she was still there.

My mind made up a little story of what *could have* been after she had taken over. What *could have* been if she kept her promise of keeping me. In my dream, I didn't think about why I was with her, even after all the awful things she had said and done. I didn't think about how she had lied and hurt me or how my real body was wasting away.

Because it didn't matter. All that mattered was that she was *there*.

But I couldn't stay long in that dream, even my sleep-deprived mind heard the footsteps of a vampire fast approaching.

My eyes shot open and I pushed myself up from my position on the ground to see someone fiddling with keys.

Gillard.

His glasses shone in the darkness, the dim light lighting up his face just enough for me to see the panic-stricken look on his face.

"We are getting you out of here, Silvia," he whispered from the darkness and finally unlocked the cell door.

He made his way over to me faster than I could blink, his hands wrapping around me and holding me to him.

"Sorry," he whispered as he picked me up. "This will hurt for a bit."

I didn't have the energy to fight him, and no words came out over the sound of my own beating heart. I didn't want to be happy that Gillard was here. I didn't want to be excited at the chance of freedom, *or whatever this was.*

...but I was.

I was *ecstatic*. Finally, I was leaving this place. Finally I was going to see the outside world. Finally, I was going back to the Order.

I leaned into Gillard's arms, fresh tears leaking from my face. My weak hands gripped his shirt as he ran out of the dungeon.

"Don't speak, okay?" he asked softly. "I will get you out of here, but you just need to be quiet."

I nodded and buried my head in his chest.

I should have been ashamed of myself for cuddling into a vampire like this, but I couldn't help myself. The warmth radiating off him was the first I had felt in weeks. His scent, which I had never thought twice about before, invaded my senses and sent a calming wave over me.

Even though his grip on me hurt, I clung to him. This was the first nonviolent touch I had received and I wanted—*needed*—more of it.

I could feel him running through the house, his steps jostling me, but I refused to look. Refused to let the excitement I was feeling diminish. I was worried that if I even took so much as a glance at the almost-forgotten world around me that it would rip me from this dream.

I hope to God I'm not dreaming, I thought as I felt a burst of cool air wash across my skin.

"Just a few more feet," Gillard whispered.

Finally, I turned my head to get a peek of where we were going, only to see that we were in the back garden. Trees and brush filled with colorful flowers surrounded us. The stark contrast of colors made the surrounding environment almost look fake. Inhaling deeply, I greedily took in the fresh air and sweet scent of flowers.

I will never forget this moment, I vowed.

He carried me through the garden, weaving in and out of trees. Their branches cut at my skin, threatening to pull a scream from my throat, but I swallowed it.

Just a little longer.

As we came to the back wall, Gillard began pacing, looking for something unknown to me. When we came across a giant willow tree that was nestled into the back corner of the expansive garden, he let out a sigh of relief.

As we got closer I saw a glint in the darkness and then,

right over the stone wall that separated this compound from the outside, a pair of blood-red eyes.

I tensed in Gillard's hold, but he held on tight.

"No," I whispered and tried to free myself. I thrashed in Gillard's hold, tried to push him away from me, but I was still too weak.

This isn't what I thought.

It's another lie.

Why is he doing this?

"Shh," Gillard hissed and crouched down before looking back the way we came, back at the mansion behind us. "It's your friend. The *hunter.*"

The hunter?

I turned to look back up at the vampire perched on the wall, we were close enough now that I could just make out the golden patch sewed onto his Order uniform.

"Jase," I breathed. My eyes stung and my throat closed when I realized what was happening.

The Order. . . The Order has come! They've come for me! I am getting out of here!

Relief burst inside me, and I almost couldn't contain the crazed giggle that was bubbling up my throat. I tried to scramble out of Gillard's hold and reach toward Jase, but he held on.

"Easy," he whispered. "I will hoist you over."

I nodded and held onto Gillard as he stood. He walked over to the willow tree, grabbing a few of the stray branches to pull himself up the wall. Jase's outstretched hand filled my view and I reached for him. When his hand clasped around my wrist and he pulled me to him, I quite literally melted against him.

In that moment, I didn't care that he was a vampire or an enforcer. All I cared about was that I was *finally* home.

This was the place I belong. *Here* with my fellow hunters.

How could I have ever thought different?

I was so adamant about paying off my debt and fleeing, yet here they were. Saving me.

"Are you sure you will stay?" Jase asked Gillard.

I looked back down at Gillard, there was a small, sad smile on his face.

"If I don't," he said. "I am not sure what will become of Keir. With her father still in power... it doesn't look good."

Keir's father never gave up his clan?

My mind flashed to the pained look she gave me when she visited my cell. That whole time... her father had still been in charge? *Is that why she couldn't help me?*

Jase nodded and then his eyes trailed to the house.

"Is she with him now?" he asked.

Gillard response was a slow nod. The air stilled around us and a slight wind chilled my skin.

What are we waiting for?

I looked back down toward Gillard and couldn't help but wonder what exactly had happened to him and Keir while I was down in the dungeon. If the transfer of power didn't work... were they still at the mercy of her father? It had to have been bad if Jase had offered to let *Gillard* of all people come back with us.

"Are you sure?" I found myself whispering. "Are you sure you won't leave?"

Gillard frowned.

"I'll see you again, Silvia," he vowed before he jumped back to the ground, landing in the soft grass with a small thump.

Raphael... he was going to hurt them when he found out I had escaped. Just like he had to me, if not worse. It was obvious that he hated his daughter, and if she wasn't needed now for the transfer of power or to keep me here... What would happen to her? What would happen to Gillard?

"Wait," I said and twisted in Jase's hold.

Gillard's eyes flashed to me and suddenly, there was light.

A light so bright that it blinded me shot directly in my eyes. Jase's grip on me tightened and with a curse I felt us fall back.

That was when I heard it. The sound of bullets and arrows flying through the air. I could hear them whoosh past us and embed into the trees of the forest behind us.

One hit Jase, I knew that from the splatter of blood that sprayed across my face.

I tried to catch a glimpse of Gillard as my eyes adjusted to the light, but couldn't as the entire view of the house and the garden faded.

That was when I felt the pain.

Though, funny enough, at the time I didn't know it was from an arrow lodging itself in my head. All I knew was that I hurt, *badly*. Much worse than what those guards had done to me while I was a captive.

It was like all the vampire blood in my body had awakened to make this my most painful injury yet. So painful that even as the world ceased to exist around me, the pain followed me into the darkness.

The last thing that I knew was Jase calling my name and the feeling of hands on me.

CHAPTER 35
KEIR

Death makes you do terrible things.

Though I couldn't help but think that my father had everything coming to him.

The night that we had planned to get Silvia out of the dungeon was a night I would remember for the rest of my existence. While Gillard worked to sneak her out, I had a plan to overthrow my father. This plan had taken some time to put together, and each day that passed was another that Silvia was stuck down in the basement, dying, while I lived with the monster who tortured her.

My hands were tied in a lot of ways. I couldn't leave the house unless Father knew about it. I had played the part of evil vampire well enough that he had believed me when I told him that Silvia meant nothing to me. . . but he wasn't stupid enough to believe that I would let him stay in power.

I had tried desperately to convince him that I thought him taking over was great. That I never wanted this position in the first place. . . But he had seen right through it, and so I was forced to be inside at all times.

I had tried to figure out a way to get word to the other clan heads, the ones Gillard had identified before I left for Victor's house, but it was too risky. It wasn't just my life at stake anymore. Gillard and Silvia were both in trouble if Father got even a whiff of my plan. . . they would pay for it.

Now that it was clear that the Order wouldn't help us. . . there was no need to keep Silvia. At least for the contract portion of Father's plan. On top of that, Silvia was so stubborn that she refused to give my father any information about the Order.

If she had given just a *little* bit of information, she would have been free of that cell, but still, she refused.

Even though she had made it clear to Father that she would not be giving any more information to him about the Order, he didn't show any sign of ending this.

That was. . . until the torture sessions got further and further apart. It wasn't noticeable at first, maybe a day or two, but then once it started to pass three days, then four. . . I knew it was bad news.

He had been waiting for the vampire blood to leave her system.

So it wasn't so much that he still thought Silvia was useful. . . it was that he didn't want to chance turning her into a vampire. *That* was what stirred me to put this plan into action, because I was sure if I waited another day, I would see first-hand how cruel my father could be as he snapped the neck of my little hunter.

But I couldn't do anything by myself, especially when I did not have the power or title to do so. Father still controlled all the guards, and if he wanted to, he could gather all the clan heads here and have them watch as he tried me for treason.

The original plan had been set for the date of the transfer of power. . . but that took an unexpected turn.

The ceremony had been set for weeks prior. Invitations had been sent, people were to gather. It was supposed to be a moment of celebration, a proud moment in our clan's history. My people would bow before me and pledge their alliance and no more would Father terrorize us.

But on the day of, with my mind echoing with Silvia's screams. . . I walked out to an empty courtyard.

Chairs and a stage had been set up, but there was not a soul in sight.

That's when I knew that no matter what, I would have to play it low-key. I couldn't rampage. I couldn't let Father know how horrified I was. I couldn't let him see through me. . . so I planned and did what I could to ensure I could get Silvia out of here alive.

Even if it meant risking my own life in the process.

I would do it for her. It was what I owed her.

So that's how I ended up storming down the empty hallway to my father's room with two vampire guards behind me and the witches from the Order at my side. The vampires were hard to gather in secret, but I had at least ten who were willing to help me. Two stayed behind me while the others ensured the coast was clear for Gillard to escape with Silvia.

It hadn't taken long for me to realize that Isaac had been telling the truth about the Order, so he was the first one I tried to get in contact with. Little did I know, he and his team were already on standby and were just waiting for the right opportunity to break in and save her.

When I asked him why he had gone to such lengths to save a hunter he didn't even really know, he just looked at me, his dark eyes burrowing into my skull and said, "We have unfinished business, and I refuse to let a vampire as vile as your father take my team member from me."

Team member. Even though they had never worked

together and he was actively going behind the Order's back to break her out... he still thought of her as a teammate. It stirred something, a kind of bitter storm, to rage inside me.

I wanted to be the person to say that. *I* wanted to be the one to save Silvia... But it didn't matter anymore.

As long as she could get out of here safely, I would live through everything else.

If everything went well, Gillard should be making his way down to the dungeon right now.

I sent a look to the two witches by my side, pausing at the door to my father's study. Ash, the witch with dark-silver hair and black eyes was to my right. His thin lips were pursed into a tight line and his breathing was heavy. He was a witch who could warp space and would be what we needed in case we needed to exit... Though his power had some limits, so I prayed that he remembered the way to the front door.

Knox was to my left. He was almost the opposite of his brother but was just as reserved. His pitch black hair stood up every which way and his light-gray eyes watched our surroundings like a hawk. He had a thing for wards and, if worse came to worst... he could protect at least one of us.

I had spoken to them only a few times through the wall that protected our property from the forest beyond, but I made sure to drill them as hard as I could.

I may have been backed into a corner, but I would make sure that the people I surrounded myself with would aid me in this venture, not hinder me, because in this case... hindering me could lead to my death.

My father shifted in his study. He knew I was out here. The stench of the witches should have been powerful enough to call to him. I heard the creak of plastic before something snapped inside. I assumed it was my father's pen.

Maybe the surprise of the vampires behind me was what really pushed him over the edge.

The witches nodded and without hesitation I pushed the door in and ran into the room. Father bolted up, a growl escaping from his chest. His eyes were wild and he looked as though he was ready to pounce.

The dark room was lit with only the moonlight that shone through the windows behind him, causing his blood-red eyes to cut through the darkness. The light filtered in from the hallway behind us and gave me just a glimpse at Father's snarling, furious face.

"What are you doing, Keir? Why are there witches with you?" he asked, his hands clenching into fists. His breathing came out heavy now and his face flushed.

"It's obvious," I said and waved the vampires forward.

Their feet against the marble barely made a sound as they walked closer, but with each step my father took one back, until his back was flush against the wall.

"You will regret this," he threatened.

The vampires stalked over to him, and when they were close enough, they both lunged forward to grab his arms. My father howled like he had been burned and flung his arms around wildly. Father jerked out of their holds and kicked one of them, sending them flying. The other growled and tried to latch on to him, but Father was quicker and used his strength to punch the vampire so hard his face caved in.

Knox stepped in front of me, his shimmering magic filled the air. His brother stepped closer, and I felt warm wisps of his magic brush across my side and send jolts of electricity through me. Father paused his assault on the corpses and turned to glare at us.

I knew now why he hated witches. Father hated anything

more powerful than he was and now he came face-to-face with his own worst nightmare.

Sensing he was being backed into a corner, he stood straight and his eyes locked onto mine.

"If you take me now," he said. "You won't be able to stop the guards."

I raised a brow at him.

"Stop it, Father," I said. "You have lost. Now surrender like a good vampire before I make them tear your head off."

A smile spread across his face.

"Then your hunter is as good as dead," he said.

We should have been fine with the number of guards we had. All the others were off resting, or just on duty. This should have been a foolproof plan. As long as Father was distracted, Silvia could make a break for it. My entire body froze and I listened carefully as the earpiece in the witches' ear came to life.

"We're surrounded," Isaac said. "Gillard just dropped off Silvia but we should prepare—"

The line was cut off by gunshots. They were close.

"Isaac?" Ash asked. When there was no answer his eyes shot to me then he turned to his brother, panic evident on their face.

"Chase?" Knox asked.

There was silence from both earpieces.

I turned to glare at my father, only to see a slow smile was spreading across his face.

"What have you done?" I asked.

Father shrugged and pushed his hands into his pocket. "Nothing that I didn't already tell you I would," he said and stalked forward. "As soon as I refused to let you ruin *my* kingdom, you should have known how this would turn out."

"It's not your *kingdom*, Father," I spat and waved the

witches forward even as dread threatened to tear me apart. "It's *my clan.*"

Knox waved his arms in the air. Bright lights pushed out of his palms and began swirling around my father. Father growled and screeched as the magical lights grew tighter and tighter. My father had nowhere to escape as the lights around him turned to ropes and forced his arms to his sides. He let out a pained howl and the smell of burning flesh filled the air.

"Nice touch," I muttered.

Father fell to the ground, panting. His mouth was twisted into a snarl, and even as the magical ropes burned him, he continued to struggle.

"You can stop now," I said and knelt down so I was face-to-face with him. He averted his gaze, but I reached out to grab his chin and force him to look at me.

"You're a disgrace," he spat. "I gave you *one job,* to get the contracts approved and you—"

"Already talked to the other clan heads," I lied. "They know what you were doing now, and all of them fully support me killing you to take my rightful position."

They hadn't known, well, some of them had. The ones Gillard got to before Father's plans came to fruition. It was a mighty army.

Me, Ian, and Xin. These were the only people at my side now, but it didn't matter. I was going to do this whether or not I had the backing.

His face paled, and for the first time, it seemed like I had actually succeeded in scaring my father.

Who knew all it took were some witches?

"You wouldn't," he whispered.

I shrugged.

"They support me and even offered to be here to assist," I said.

"And no one will do any dealings with Victor from now on. Every single one of your supporters will be outcast and forced to starve... And if they ever so happen to prey on unwilling humans..."

"The Order will deal with them," the witch said from behind me. They walked toward me and grabbed at Father's bindings with their bare hands, forcing him to a standing position.

I stood as well.

I shouldn't have enjoyed the way my father's face blanched. Or how he began to panic. Or how he begged for his life.

I should have felt disgusted, ashamed to see the man I once saw as all-powerful was nothing more than a shaking mess, but I couldn't help the sense of power that exploded in my chest. I was the sole person in charge of his life, and that feeling alone was addicting.

It made me realize how easily my father had fallen into the darkness. He could have been an honest vampire at the start. He could have wanted to truly make a difference and protect the people in his clan, but he too had been tempted by the power that he held.

Though I swore to myself that no matter how much I wanted to give in to temptation. No matter how much I wanted to slaughter the man in front of me. . . I would be better.

For my clan. For Gillard. For Sil—

"She's dead," Chase's voice called from the witch's earpiece. "Arrow to the head. They were lying in wait, though we got most of them now."

I never knew two words could bring one being so much pain. It exploded in me all at once, chasing away every bit of power I just thought I had. Those *two words* felt like they had violently pushed me off the edge of the abyss and straight into the never-ending darkness that awaited me.

I couldn't breathe. I couldn't feel. The world froze around me and there was not a single thought that entered my mind other than Silvia.

I was too late.

I didn't want to believe it, I couldn't. The girl who I had worked so hard to free from this hell, she had been so close to leaving and yet... she died?

The same girl who stood up for me when my father beat me? The same girl who saw through all of my bullshit? The same girl who had single-handedly made me enjoy this life again?

She couldn't be—*No.*

No, *no.*

"You did this," I growled to my father.

My hand shot out and gripped his throat. His eyes widened and he struggled in my grip, but the magic kept him bound so tightly, he had nowhere to go. I was going to pay him back slowly for everything he had done to Silvia, and I wouldn't stop until I felt like he had experienced everything that she had and more.

"Keir, I—"

"She's coming!" Jase yelled through the earpiece.

"Who's coming?" the witch asked.

"Silvia!" Isaac yelled. If I strained my hearing, I could just faintly make out the sound of feet hitting the soft ground outside my father's window.

Then I heard the screams.

"Blood," I breathed, my grip on my father loosening. "She still had blood in her system."

Before I could even rejoice that the girl I had fallen for lived, the windows to my father's study shattered. The only thing I could see as the vampire ran past was a flash of fiery-red hair.

I had let myself dream of this moment once. The moment that Silvia would be a vampire. It was a silly thought, one that I knew would never come true given her hate of our kind.

But I *did* hope that she would change her mind so that I wouldn't have to think about how fragile and short-lived humans were. I would be able to enjoy my time with her knowing that it would never end. I would be able to live with her in the way I wanted, love her in the way I wanted.

Forever. She would be mine forever.

But I didn't think about how the change would be for her. How she would react when the vampire blood finally killed off every living cell in her body and she was forced to become a monster.

Silvia was by my side in seconds, her hand coming out to grasp my arm. Her snarling face was covered in her own blood and her eyes were bright red. There was a wound in the middle of her forehead that was slowly closing due to her newfound vampire abilities.

Arrow to the head.

I knew as a newborn vampire Silvia would be. . . less than agreeable. The bloodlust would be unbearable and all her emotions, the hate, the fear, the anger, would be heightened. I had seen enough changes to know that becoming a turned vampire was not an easy process, even after death.

Her body was not her own. Her mind was not her own. She would run purely on instinct and anything in her path would be seen as a threat. Including me.

Her own personal hell.

"Silvia," I said softly and placed my hand over hers. "I got him. You don't need to worry. Let's get you some blood—"

"I should kill you," she choked out, her voice husky as if she had been screaming. She glared at me with all the hate she had in her body.

I remembered seeing her in the dungeon not long ago and feeling a sort of guilt—or maybe even disappointment—that the girl with so much hate, so much power, had all but deteriorated before my eyes.

But *this* Silvia, she was deadly.

Even covered in blood and with her death wound still present on her forehead, she was magnificent. She was beautiful and strong as a human, but as a vampire, she would be unstoppable.

"But then I couldn't tell you how sorry I am," I whispered. "Or make it up to you."

Her eyes flashed and I worried that those were my last words, but instead she turned and threw my father across the room, ripping him out of my hands.

"Silvia," the witch protested. "Let me deal with—"

"Fuck off," she growled and walked over to my father, who was cowering at the sight of her.

"Listen," he begged. "I didn't think—"

But he couldn't finish his sentence because Silvia had already grabbed the nearest object to her, which happened to be Father's letter opener that had been thrown to the floor during the commotion, and drove it right into his face.

He screamed in pain, but Silvia was unbothered and simply pulled it out before stabbing it into him again.

And again.

And again.

And again.

"We should stop her," the witch whispered by my side.

I shook my head.

"Let her," I said. "She deserves this much."

"But the *rules*—"

"It's fine," I said.

The vampire, Jase, was the first to appear in the doorway, his face coated with blood and his chest heaving up and down. His wild, red eyes took in what Silvia was doing to my father, then passed to me.

"The transfer of power—"

"Let's not," I interrupted. "Let's *not* do this right now."

"This is *not* in the plan," he growled and crossed the room at a speed that was even too fast for my senses to catch. "Silvia."

His hand gripped her wrist and forced her to a standing position. My father's blood stained her hands and face.

As sick as it was. . . I found myself quiet enamored by her blood-covered self.

Silvia snarled at him and tried to jerk her arm out of his grasp, but he held on too tight. When she let out a pained moan, I crossed the space between us and gripped Jase's wrist as hard as I could without breaking it.

His gaze flashed to mine and then down to his wrist.

"Don't you *dare* touch her," I said.

Silvia's snort startled me.

"Now you're worried about that?" she asked with a laugh. "Predictable."

Isaac appeared in the doorway then, his heart pounding and his face slick with sweat. I had been too consumed by Silvia to hear his footsteps and cursed myself because as soon as Silvia met his eyes, she tensed.

I may have been angry with Jase for hurting Silvia, but in that moment I met his eyes and knew that, for just this time, I would have to work with him. His other hand reached out to pin her bloodied arm to her body and I released his arm so that I could force Silvia to look me in the eyes.

Turning her head was as hard as trying to break stone, but when she realized we had her trapped she began to freak.

"Silvia," I said in a calm voice as she tried to twist out of our hold.

She was strong, but she didn't have a lot of strength before the transition, so she was weaker than a newly changed vampire should be.

Isaac stood up straight, his eyes fell over the scene and a long sigh escaped his lips. He was putting together quickly what had happened and what it meant for Silvia's future.

"*Fucking hell,*" he groaned.

My father was still lying on the ground, his breath coming out in uneven pants. He couldn't even make a sound after Silvia had so thoroughly destroyed his face. And then, as Silvia struggled in our hold, her red eyes narrowing at me and curses flying out of her mouth. . . his heart stopped.

The silence was deafening and before I could stop myself, I fell to my knees in front of her. She stilled then. Even through her bloodlust haze, she realized that something was happening.

I could hear the vampire guards running up the hallway, they would be in the room with us in a matter of seconds.

"I'm sorry," I whispered to Silvia.

"Don't!" Isaac yelled from the hallway. "Ash! Knox! Stop her!"

But they were too late.

I shifted so that I would have enough room to kneel and touch my forehead to the ground, my hands faced upwards, to show Silvia that I meant no harm. It was an uncomfortable position, but that was how it was supposed to be.

When you surrendered yourself to your clan head, you need not be comfortable. Your entire body and soul should be showcased to the one who took a vow to protect you, and the only thing that should be going through your mind was a prayer that your newest leader wouldn't cut off your head while you were vulnerable.

But that was not what was swirling around my head.

What was in my mind was a different kind of fear.

Silvia would hate this more than anything I ever did before. There would be no going back from this. A part of me was relieved that the burden I had been carrying for most of my life would no longer be my own. It was the coward inside me, she was happy.

Happy that I didn't have to deal with the burden.

Happy that Silvia would be forced by my side forever.

Happy that now… now I could be *me*.

I heard Gillard jump through the window before the vampires descended on us. The crackling of glass under his shoes was barely audible above the shouts of the hunters around me. But he didn't let them stop him.

Like the perfect vampire he was, he simply crossed the room, stood behind me, and copied my position.

"What are you doing?" Silvia asked.

There was a hush that fell over the room as the vampire guard reached us. There were about ten pairs of footsteps, and when they caught sight of their fallen king and kneeling heir, they rushed inside to kneel behind me.

"On behalf of Carpe Noctem," I said, my voice muffled by the bloodstained carpet. " I, Keir, heir apparent, accept you, Silvia, as clan head."

There was a stirring behind me, none of the others wanted to speak first.

"Keir," Silvia said, her voice losing its anger. "What the fu—"

"I, Gillard, advisor to the clan head, accept you, Silvia, as clan head," Gil interrupted her, and against everything I was taught, I lifted my head to look at Silvia.

A mix of shock and panic was displayed on her face. She shook her head and opened her lips, but no sound came out.

The vampires behind us slowly, one by one started to announce their status and accept Silvia as the new clan head. She took a step back but was unable to go any farther due to my father's corpse at her feet.

"No," she breathed.

I sat back on my heels as grabbed her hand. Jase didn't even fight me as I pulled her closer to me.

"Repeat after me," I said softly.

She shook her head and tried to pull her hands from mine, but I held on tightly.

"No,no,no,no," she whispered and looked toward the others to help her, but no one moved. It was in our hands now. The Order had no standing here.

"I, Silvia," I said slowly. "Promise to rule over this clan with—"

"No!" she yelled and ripped her hands from mine. I reached forward to grasp her hand, but my hand clasped around empty air.

She backed away, falling over my father's body. Then she scrambled up, just narrowly missed Jase's hands, and backed toward the wall. Her red eyes were filling with tears.

"Silvia," Gil whispered from behind me. "Please, Silvia. Just listen to Keir and we can get you some blood—"

"I don't want this!" she yelled and clawed at her wild red hair. "I don't want any of this! I just want to go home! Please, please don't make me. Please—"

"Silvia," I said and stood. Moving as carefully as I would if I was trying to capture a wild animal. "Let me help you."

She pushed herself into the wall, a few books falling loose. She jumped as they hit the ground.

"Don't come closer!" she warned, her arm flying out, motioning for me to back away.

I took another step and regretted it as soon as her eyes flashed toward the open window.

"Silvia, *don't*," I warned.

She let out a shaky breath and every muscle in her body tensed as she tried to lunge for the window.

Jase was the first to get to her, his hands circling around her ankle.

Then Knox's magic started to swirl around her, but she clawed at the floor like a madwomen and kicked Jase right in the face.

I lunged toward her, but she was too fast.

My fingertips just grazed the material of her shirt before she dove toward the window.

Her head snapped back to me as she perched on the windowsill, the scent of her blood filled the room as the glass from the broken window cut into her skin.

"If you have any decency," she said in a thick voice. "Don't come looking for me."

And with that, she was gone.

"Go after her," I commanded to the vampire guards.

Even though I wasn't their true clan head, they followed my order as if I were. All of them jumped up and body after body raced past me and followed Silvia through the window.

I turned to Isaac, noticing Chase right behind him. His signature smirk was wiped clean off his face.

"If you do not—"

"Shut it, Keir," Isaac growled and motioned for his team to follow him. "We will get the *clan head*."

He cursed and spat on the ground before disappearing

down the hallway. The witches lingered for a moment but left when I waved them away.

Gil who had still been kneeling, slowly got up and walked to my side. His eyes were trained on the window behind me.

"I hope she doesn't kill too many humans," he whispered. "She would never forgive us."

I swallowed thickly and held my head high.

"We're in trouble, Gil," I said and turned to the window. If I strained, I could hear the commotion of the guards fighting with Silvia.

We are more than in trouble. We are completely fucked.

KEIR'S AND SILVIA'S STORY ISN'T OVER YET...

PREORDER LOST CLAUSE NOW!

WANT EXCLUSIVE CONTENT?

Join my Patreon and you will get access to all stories BEFORE they are published.

If you join now you will get free stories and deleted chapters!

There is also a tier for NSFW art that is exclusive for my Patreon members

Check it out here or go to https://www.patreon.com/ellemaebooks

IF YOU LIKED THIS, PLEASE REVIEW!

Reviews really help indie authors get their books out there so, please make sure to share your thoughts!

ACKNOWLEDGMENTS

Contract Bound has been one of my favorite pieces to write. I fell in love with Silvia and Keir and can't wait to see what is in store for them and the rest of the gang. Thank you to everyone who gave me a chance and has been here through my growth as a writer. I still have a long way to go but I am happy that I have all you here supporting me along the way.

About the Author

Elle is a native Californian who has lived in Los Angeles for most of her life. From the very start, she has been in love with all things fantasy and reading. As soon as Elle found out that writing books could be a career, she picked up a pen and paper. While the first ones were about scorned love and missed opportunities of lunchtime love, she has grown to love the fantasy genre and looks forward to making a difference in the world with her stories.

Loved this book? Please leave a review!

For more behind the scene content, check out my Patreon!

twitter.com/mae_books
instagram.com/ellemaebooks
goodreads.com/ellemae
patreon.com/ellemaebooks
tiktok.com/@ellemaebooks

Lightning Source UK Ltd.
Milton Keynes UK
UKHW020639210922
409198UK00009B/974